Taken at the Flood

Taken at the Flood

THE HUMAN DRAMA AS SEEN BY
MODERN AMERICAN NOVELISTS

Collected and Arranged by

ANN WATKINS

Harper & Brothers Publishers

NEW YORK AND LONDON

Contents

v

CONTENTS vii

Night School
    from THE EDUCATION OF HYMAN KAPLAN,
    by Leonard Q. Ross   308

The Family of the Victim
    from MONDAY NIGHT, by Kay Boyle   313

The Trespasser
    from THREE BAGS FULL, by Roger Burlingame   327

The Handbag
    from THE LOST WEEKEND, by Charles Jackson   333

Awakening
    from BARREN GROUND, by Ellen Glasgow   339

Sidewalk Café
    from DODSWORTH, by Sinclair Lewis   351

The Bootlegger
    from KIT BRANDON, by Sherwood Anderson   358

The Arrest of Helianos
    from APARTMENT IN ATHENS, by Glenway Wescott   367

Introduction

THERE are certain passages forever memorable which stand out from the novels one has read. Occasionally a single passage will keep an entire book warm and alive. Why? Has some special skill gone into its writing? Is it the emotional impact that is unforgettable? Or has there been an echo of some personal thought or desire? From my long and constant preoccupation with these questions came the first concept of this book. I realized that if the answers could be found, a collection of passages which had the power of survival might be made.

The rereading of passages which had won a permanent place in my own memory, and the reading of others suggested by those in whose sensitiveness and wisdom I believed, led to the setting of a few simple standards. First, it was obvious that a passage must stand alone and be complete in sense. It also must be an emotional unit without loose ends. The emotion should be universal in the sense that it has associations with common experience. (There is usually something nostalgic in enduring passages.) Most important, it must have movement. This does not necessarily mean physical action. In the choice from Thomas Wolfe's *The Web and the Rock*, for instance, the entire scene takes place within the boy's mind, yet there is violent conflict and definite emotional progress from one point to another.

Having determined on these bases of selection, it was necessary to fix boundaries in time. The period of my choice comprised the quarter century which began in 1920. I limited the collection to the work of American citizens. I imposed no final restrictions on the character of the novels from which I would choose. Their scenes need not be American. Even their people need not be Americans. The novels could be historical or contemporary. This gave the widest possible range for variety of subject and technique.

Within this broad frame, a pattern presently emerged. Its stem, or backbone, was fully evident running through the era selected. It was a truly new era. Following the First World War, the best American art was no longer concerned with dreams, fantasy, or that synthetic remaking of the world "nearer to the heart's desire" sometimes called romance. Instead, writers were eager to write about the world and human life as it stood before them, with conflicts revealed even when they were ugly. As the era advanced, this became what American readers wanted to read. The stem of the design, then, was truth and from the rich body of literature before me I realized that it would be possible to build a structure of passages which would reflect virtually the whole of life.

The pattern was kaleidoscopic. There were scenes of war, catastrophe and storm. There were intervals of human life in violent contest with nature in mountain, prairie, forest and on the sea. In the historical novels there was the fight with the wilderness which was the origin of our unique democracy. There were the "seven ages of man," from birth to burial. There was love thwarted and love fulfilled. There were poverty and luxury, ugliness and loveliness, hate and compassion, fear and security. In almost every life aspect there seemed to be several pieces from which to choose. My job, then, was to try to select enough and only enough of each to give the same symmetry to the design as that which existed in the scheme of life itself.

In the progress of selection, pitfalls of course appeared. In the best fiction of the period certain phases predominated. Many writers, for instance, had focused with such success on the adolescent mind that there was danger of loss of balance if too many of these excellent passages were included. The preoccupation with war was inevitable and if the purpose of this collection had been merely to point the trend of the era, more of it would have found a place. But my concept was broader than this. I wanted to reach the whole range of thinking. So while I included certain selections from the dominant themes, I by-passed others to search for authors who had brilliantly revealed some important glimpse of life obscured by the trend.

The question arose as it always will: what is a novel? E. M. Forster in the introduction to his *Aspects of the Novel*, anticipated the demand for a definition by falling back on Abel Chevalley who said that a novel was "a fiction in prose of a certain extent." Forster limited that extent to fifty thousand words, adding: "If this seems to you unphilosophic will you think of an alternative definition which will include *The Pilgrim's Progress, Marius the Epicurean, The Adventures of a Younger Son, The Magic Flute, The Journal of the Plague, Zuleika Dobson, Rasselas, Ulysses* and *Green Mansions*, or else will you give reasons for their exclusion?" But his elastic formula is obviously the one accepted by American publishers and public and, while a few of the most celebrated "novels" of my period, in my judgment, come perilously near being collections of sketches or stories, it would be presumptuous to judge them by my own indefinable concept of what the ideal novel should be.

My first criterion is selecting the novels was reality. I avoided plot syntheses in which the characters were dimmed or flattened. Events become real only when the human response to them is shown in full dimension. In the best fiction the characters create the story. It is hardly necessary to say that plots to which the characters must be fitted do not exist in realistic novels. Such stories were discarded even if they contained passages which met other standards.

In every case I have tried to be fair to the novel's intent. I have been tempted to include certain digressive passages which stood alone, but have discarded them if they were outside the sweep of the novel's motive. Such a passage in its context may be an integral part of the whole, whereas by itself it may betray the author.

Finally came the question of arrangement. It is said that the great artist never focuses long or intensely enough on a scene to let the reader forget that there is a world outside. If he writes in one chapter of a man in a death house, he makes the reader aware, in the next, that outside the prison walls there is normality and freedom. Otherwise the confinement has neither drama nor meaning. Likewise ugliness can exist only when there is beauty with which to compare it. Without contrast life would not be endurable. So I have arranged these passages with the consciousness that normal life continually swings from pain to pleasure, from anger to sympathy, from conflict to harmony. Thus I hope that the reader of this volume will see, in movement as well as in substance, a clear reflection of that picture of life in its entirety which these American authors, have, in concert, produced.

I am greatly indebted to the authors whose works from which I have selected passages for their permission to reprint them in the anthology.

ANN WATKINS

West Redding, Conn.
April 1946

Acknowledgments

GRATEFUL acknowledgment is made to the following authors and publishers for the material included in this volume:

D. Appleton-Century Company, Inc. for MISS LULU BETT by Zona Gale, and STATE FAIR by Phil Stong.

John Dos Passos for THREE SOLDIERS, published by George H. Doran Company.

Doubleday & Company, Inc. for BARREN GROUND by Ellen Glasgow.

Farrar & Rinehart, Inc. for ACTION AT AQUILA by Hervey Allen, DELILAH by Marcus Goodrich, and FEBRUARY HILL by Victoria Lincoln.

Edna Ferber for CIMARRON, published by Doubleday, Doran & Company.

Harcourt, Brace & Company for MONDAY NIGHT by Kay Boyle, THREE BAGS FULL by Roger Burlingame, THE DEEPENING STREAM by Dorothy Canfield, DODSWORTH by Sinclair Lewis, and THE EDUCATION OF HYMAN KAPLAN by Leonard Q. Ross.

Harper & Brothers for LAMB IN HIS BOSOM by Caroline Miller, A TREE GROWS IN BROOKLYN by Betty Smith, APARTMENT IN ATHENS by Glenway Wescott, and THE WEB AND THE ROCK by Thomas Wolfe.

Houghton Mifflin Company for THE HEART IS A LONELY HUNTER by Carson McCullers.

Charles Jackson for THE LOST WEEKEND, published by Rinehart & Company.

Alfred A. Knopf, Inc. for A WALK IN THE SUN by Harry Brown, LIFE WITH FATHER by Clarence Day, A BELL FOR ADANO by John Hersey, and THE TREES by Conrad Richter.

J. B. Lippincott Company for THEIR EYES WERE WATCHING GOD by Zora Neale Hurston.

Little, Brown & Company for SO LITTLE TIME by John P. Marquand.

Liveright Publishing Company for THE ENORMOUS ROOM by E. E. Cummings, and AN AMERICAN TRAGEDY by Theodore Dreiser.

David Lloyd for THE GOOD EARTH by Pearl Buck, published by The John Day Company.

Random House, Inc. for SANCTUARY by William Faulkner, and STORM by George Stewart.

Reynal & Hitchcock, Inc. for LIGHTSHIP by Archie Binns and STRANGE FRUIT by Lillian Smith.

Evelyn Scott for THE WAVE.

Charles Scribner's Sons for KIT BRANDON by Sherwood Anderson, THE GREAT GATSBY by F. Scott Fitzgerald, FOR WHOM THE BELL TOLLS by Ernest Hemingway, and THE YEARLING by Marjorie Kinnan Rawlings.

The Viking Press, Inc. for HOLD AUTUMN IN YOUR HAND by George Sessions Perry, and THE GRAPES OF WRATH by John Steinbeck.

Taken at the Flood

John Andrews Goes to Paris

From *THREE SOLDIERS*

By John Dos Passos

Three Soldiers was written after the Armistice of 1918 by a soldier. In stripping war of all heroics and lamenting its corrosive effect on man's spirit, it jarred a reading public accustomed to the glory and gallantry of battle. Its influence was wide, and its theme is still powerful and insistent.

The novel's three chief characters are Fuselli, who studied the angles, Chrisfield, who dreamed of killing a particular officer, and John Andrews, the musician. Of the three, Andrews is the most tragic. With an artist's sensibility, he feels keenly not only the violence but the suffocation of war, and welcomes the wound which brings him a temporary release. In the arid weeks after the Armistice, his frustration mounts to a fury. The war is over, men are going back to their homes, their work, and he is still trapped. En route from the hospital to his company, he meets Henslowe, the deserter, and sees Paris for the first time. Back with his division, he sees his chance for freedom when he learns that the Army is sending selected men to French universities to study. He knows that at whatever cost, he must be one of them. At the end of the chosen passage, his joy is the crowing exultation of one who, after weeks of despair and humiliation, has by some unbelievable accident triumphed over the system.

ANDREWS left the station reluctantly, shivering in the raw grey mist under which the houses of the village street and the rows of motor trucks and the few figures of French soldiers swathed in long formless coats, showed as vague dark blurs in the confused dawnlight. His body felt flushed and sticky from a night spent huddled in the warm fetid air

1

of an overcrowded compartment. He yawned and stretched himself and stood irresolutely in the middle of the street with his pack biting into his shoulders. Out of sight, behind the dark mass, in which a few ruddy lights glowed, of the station buildings, the engine whistled and the train clanked off into the distance. Andrews listened to its faint reverberation through the mist with a sick feeling of despair. It was the train that had brought him from Paris back to his division.

As he stood shivering in the grey mist he remembered the curious despairing reluctance he used to suffer when he went back to boarding school after a holiday. How he used to go from the station to the school by the longest road possible, taking frantic account of every moment of liberty left him. Today his feet had the same leaden reluctance as when they used to all but refuse to take him up the long sandy hill to the school.

He wandered aimlessly for a while about the silent village hoping to find a café where he could sit for a few minutes to take a last look at himself before plunging again into the grovelling promiscuity of the army. Not a light showed. All the shutters of the shabby little brick and plaster houses were closed. With dull springless steps he walked down the road they had pointed out to him from the R.T.O.

Overhead the sky was brightening giving the mist that clung to the earth in every direction ruddy billowing outlines. The frozen road gave out a faint hard resonance under his footsteps. Occasionally the silhouette of a tree by the roadside loomed up in the mist ahead, its uppermost branches clear and ruddy with sunlight.

Andrews was telling himself that the war was over, and that in a few months he would be free in any case. What did a few months more or less matter? But the sane thoughts were swept recklessly away in the blind panic that was like a stampede of wild steers within him. There was no arguing. His spirit was contorted with revolt so that his flesh twitched and dark splotches danced before his eyes. He wondered vaguely whether he had gone mad. Enormous plans kept rising up out of the tumult of his mind and dissolving suddenly like smoke in a high wind. He would run away and if they caught him, kill himself. He would start a mutiny in his company, he would lash all these men to frenzy by his words, so that they too should refuse to form into Guns, so that they should laugh when the officers got red in the face shouting orders at them, so that the whole division should march off over the frosty hills, without arms, without flags, calling all the men of all the armies to join them, to march on singing, to laugh the nightmare out of their blood. Would not some lightning flash of vision sear people's consciousness into life again? What was the good of stopping the war if the armies continued?

But that was just rhetoric. His mind was flooding itself with rhetoric that it might keep its sanity. His mind was squeezing out rhetoric like a sponge that he might not see dry madness face to face.

And all the while his hard footsteps along the frozen road beat in his ears bringing him nearer to the village where the division was quartered. He was climbing a long hill. The mist thinned about him and became brilliant with sunlight. Then he was walking in the full sun over the crest of a hill with pale blue sky above his head. Behind him and before him were mist-filled valleys and beyond other ranges of long hills, with reddish-violet patches of woodland, glowing faintly in the sunlight. In the valley at his feet he could see, in the shadow of the hill he stood on, a church tower and a few roofs rising out of the mist, as out of water.

Among the houses bugles were blowing mess-call.

The jauntiness of the brassy notes ringing up through the silence was agony to him. How long the day would be. He looked at his watch. It was seven thirty. How did they come to be having mess so late?

The mist seemed doubly cold and dark when he was buried in it again after his moment of sunlight. The sweat was chilled on his face and streaks of cold went through his clothes, soaked from the effort of carrying the pack. In the village street Andrews met a man he did not know and asked him where the office was. The man, who was chewing something, pointed silently to a house with green shutters on the opposite side of the street.

At a desk sat Chrisfield smoking a cigarette. When he jumped up Andrews noticed that he had a corporal's two stripes on his arm.

"Hello, Andy."

They shook hands warmly.

"A' you all right now, ole boy?"

"Sure, I'm fine," said Andrews. A sudden constraint fell upon them.

"That's good," said Chrisfield.

"You're a corporal now. Congratulations."

"Um hum. Made me more'n a month ago."

They were silent. Chrisfield sat down in his chair again.

"What sort of a town is this?"

"It's a hell-hole, this dump is, a hell-hole."

"That's nice."

"Goin' to move soon, tell me . . . Army o' Occupation. But Ah hadn't ought to have told you that. . . . Don't tell any of the fellers."

"Where's the outfit quartered?"

"Ye won't know it; we've got fifteen new men. No account all of 'em. Second draft men."

"Civilians in the town?"

"You bet. . . . Come with me, Andy, an' Ah'll tell 'em to give you

some grub at the cookshack. No . . . wait a minute an' you'll miss the
hike. . . . Hikes every day since the goddam armistice. They sent out a
general order telling 'em to double up on the drill."

They heard a voice shouting orders outside and the narrow street filled
up suddenly with a sound of boots beating the ground in unison. Andrews kept his back to the window. Something in his legs seemed to be
tramping in time with the other legs.

"There they go," said Chrisfield. "Loot's with 'em today. . . . Want
some grub? If it ain't been punk since the armistice."

The "Y" hut was empty and dark; through the grimy windowpanes
could be seen fields and a leaden sky full of heavy ocherous light, in
which the leafless trees and the fields full of stubble were different shades
of dead, greyish brown. Andrews sat at the piano without playing. He
was thinking how once he had thought to express all the cramped boredom of this life; the thwarted limbs regimented together, lashed into
straight lines, the monotony of servitude. Unconsciously as he thought
of it, the fingers of one hand sought a chord, which jangled in the badly
tuned piano. "God, how silly!" he muttered aloud, pulling his hands
away. Suddenly he began to play snatches of things he knew, distorting
them, willfully mutilating the rhythms, mixing into them snatches of
ragtime. The piano jangled under his hands, filling the empty hut with
clamor. He stopped suddenly, letting his fingers slide from bass to treble,
and began to play in earnest.

There was a cough behind him that had an artificial, discreet ring to it.
He went on playing without turning round. Then a voice said:

"Beautiful, beautiful."

Andrews turned to find himself staring into a face of vaguely triangu-
lar shape with a wide forehead and prominent eyelids over protruding
brown eyes. The man wore a Y.M.C.A. uniform which was very tight for
him, so that there were creases running from each button across the front
of his tunic.

"Oh, do go on playing. It's years since I heard any Debussy."

"It wasn't Debussy."

"Oh, wasn't it? Anyway it was just lovely. Do go on. I'll just stand
here and listen."

Andrews went on playing for a moment, made a mistake, started over,
made the same mistake, banged on the keys with his fist and turned
round again.

"I can't play," he said peevishly.

"Oh, you can, my boy, you can. . . . Where did you learn? I would
give a million dollars to play like that, if I had it."

Andrews glared at him silently.

"You are one of the men just back from hospital, I presume."

"Yes, worse luck."

"Oh, I don't blame you. These French towns are the dullest places; though I just love France, don't you?" The "Y" man had a faintly whining voice.

"Anywhere's dull in the army."

"Look, we must get to know each other real well. My name's Spencer Sheffield . . . Spencer B. Sheffield. . . . And between you and me there's not a soul in the division you can talk to. It's dreadful not to have intellectual people about one. I suppose you're from New York."

Andrews nodded.

"Um hum, so am I. You've probably read some of my things in *Vain Endeavor*. . . . What, you've never read *Vain Endeavor*? I guess you didn't go round with the intellectual set. . . . Musical people often don't. . . . Of course I don't mean the Village. All anarchists and society women there. . . ."

"I've never gone round with any set, and I never. . . ."

"Never mind, we'll fix that when we all get back to New York. And now you just sit down at that piano and play me Debussy's 'Arabesque.' . . . I know you love it just as much as I do. But first what's your name?"

"Andrews."

"Folks come from Virginia?"

"Yes." Andrews got to his feet.

"Then you're related to the Penneltons."

"I may be related to the Kaiser for all I know."

"The Penneltons . . . that's it. You see my mother was a Miss Spencer from Spencer Falls, Virginia, and her mother was a Miss Pennelton, so you and I are cousins. Now isn't that a coincidence?"

"Distant cousins. But I must go back to the barracks."

"Come in and see me any time," Spencer B. Sheffield shouted after him. "You know where; back of the shack. And knock twice so I'll know it's you."

Outside the house where he was quartered Andrews met the new top sergeant, a lean man with spectacles and a little mustache of the color and texture of a scrubbing brush.

"Here's a letter for you," the top sergeant said. "Better look at the new K.P. list I've just posted."

The letter was from Henslowe. Andrews read it with a smile of pleasure in the faint afternoon light, remembering Henslowe's constant drawling talk about distant places he had never been to, and the man who had eaten glass, and the day and a half in Paris.

"Andy," the letter began, "I've got the dope at last. Courses begin in

Paris February fifteenth. Apply at once to your C.O. to study somethin'
at University of Paris. Any amount of lies will go. Apply all pull possible
via sergeants, lieutenants and their mistresses and laundresses. Yours,
Henslowe."

His heart thumping, Andrews ran after the sergeant, passing, in his
excitement, a lieutenant without saluting him.

"Look here," snarled the lieutenant.

Andrews saluted, and stood stiffly at attention.

"Why didn't you salute me?"

"I was in a hurry, sir, and didn't see you. I was going on very urgent
company business, sir."

"Remember that just because the armistice is signed you needn't
think you're out of the army; at ease."

Andrews saluted. The lieutenant saluted, turned swiftly on his heel
and walked away.

Andrews caught up to the sergeant.

"Sergeant Coffin. Can I speak to you a minute?"

"I'm in a hell of a hurry."

"Have you heard anything about this army students' corps to send
men to universities here in France? Something the Y.M.C.A.'s getting
up."

"Can't be for enlisted men. No I ain't heard a word about it. D'you
want to go to school again?"

"If I get a chance. To finish my course."

"College man, are ye? So am I. Well, I'll let you know if I get any
general order about it. Can't do anything without getting a general
order about it. Looks to me like it's all bushwa."

"I guess you're right."

The street was grey dark. Stung by a sense of impotence, surging with
despairing rebelliousness, Andrews hurried back towards the buildings
where the company was quartered. He would be late for mess. The grey
street was deserted. From a window here and there ruddy light streamed
out to make a glowing oblong on the wall of a house opposite.

"Goddam it, if you don't believe me, you go ask the lootenant. . . .
Look here, Toby, didn't our outfit see hotter work than any goddam
engineers'?"

Toby had just stepped into the Café, a tall man with a brown bulldog
face and a scar on his left cheek. He spoke rarely and solemnly with a
Maine coast Yankee twang.

"I reckon so," was all he said. He sat down on the bench beside the
other man who went on bitterly:

"I guess you would reckon so. . . . Hell, man, you ditch diggers ain't
in it."

"Ditch diggers!" The engineer banged his fist down on the table. His lean pickled face was a furious red. "I guess we don't dig half so many ditches as the infantry does . . . an' when we've dug 'em we don't crawl into 'em an' stay there like goddam cottontailed jackrabbits."

"You guys don't git near enough to the front. . . ."

"Like goddam cottontailed jackrabbits," shouted the pickle-faced engineer again, roaring with laughter. "Ain't that so?" He looked round the room for approval. The benches at the two long tables were filled with infantry men who looked at him angrily. Noticing suddenly that he had no support, he moderated his voice.

"The infantry's damn necessary, I'll admit that; but where'd you fellers be without us guys to string the barbed wire for you?"

"There warn't no barbed wire strung in the Oregon forest where we was, boy. What d'ye want barbed wire when you're advancin' for?"

"Look here . . . I'll bet you a bottle of cognac my company had more losses than yourn did."

"Tek him up, Joe," said Toby, suddenly showing an interest in the conversation.

"All right, it's a go."

"We had fifteen killed and twenty wounded," announced the engineer triumphantly.

"How badly wounded?"

"What's that to you? Hand over the cognac?"

"Like hell. We had fifteen killed and twenty wounded too, didn't we, Toby?"

"I reckon you're right," said Toby.

"Ain't I right?" asked the other man, addressing the company generally.

"Sure, goddam right," muttered voices.

"Well, I guess it's all off, then," said the engineer.

"No, it ain't," said Toby, "reckon up yer wounded. The feller who's got the worst wounded gets the cognac. Ain't that fair?"

"Sure."

"We've had seven fellers sent home already," said the engineer.

"We've had eight. Ain't we?"

"Sure," growled everybody in the room.

"How bad was they?"

"Two of 'em was blind," said Toby.

"Hell," said the engineer, jumping to his feet as if taking a trick at poker. "We had a guy who was sent home without arms nor legs, and three fellers got t.b. from bein' gassed."

John Andrews had been sitting in a corner of the room. He got up. Something had made him think of the man he had known in the hospital who had said that was the life to make a feller feel fit. Getting

up at three o'clock in the morning, you jumped out of bed just like a
cat. . . . He remembered how the olive-drab trousers had dangled
empty from the man's chair.

"That's nothing; one of our sergeants had to have a new nose grafted
on. . . ."

The village street was dark and deeply rutted with mud. Andrews
wandered up and down aimlessly. There was only one other café. That
would be just like this one. He couldn't go back to the desolate barn
where he slept. It would be too early to go to sleep. A cold wind blew
down the street and the sky was full of vague movement of dark clouds.
The partly-frozen mud clotted about his feet as he walked along; he
could feel the water penetrating his shoes. Opposite the Y.M.C.A. hut
at the end of the street he stopped. After a moment's indecision he gave
a little laugh, and walked round to the back where the door of the "Y"
man's room was.

He knocked twice, half hoping there would be no reply. Sheffield's
whining high-pitched voice said: "Who is it?"

"Andrews."

"Come right in. . . . You're just the man I wanted to see." Andrews
stood with his hand on the knob.

"Do sit down and make yourself right at home."

Spencer Sheffield was sitting at a little desk in a room with walls of
unplaned boards and one small window. Behind the desk were piles of
cracker boxes and cardboard cases of cigarettes and in the midst of them
a little opening, like that of a railway ticket office, in the wall through
which the "Y" man sold his commodities to the long lines of men who
would stand for hours waiting meekly in the room beyond.

Andrews was looking round for a chair.

"Oh, I just forgot. I'm sitting in the only chair," said Spencer Sheffield, laughing, twisting his small mouth into a shape like a camel's
mouth and rolling about his large protruding eyes.

"Oh, that's all right. What I wanted to ask you was: do you know
anything about . . . ?"

"Look, do come with me to my room," interrupted Sheffield. "I've
got such a nice sitting-room with an open fire, just next to Lieutenant
Bleezer. . . . An' there we'll talk . . . about everything. I'm just dying
to talk to somebody about the things of the spirit."

"Do you know anything about a scheme for sending enlisted men to
French universities? Men who have not finished their courses."

"Oh, wouldn't that be just fine. I tell you, boy, there's nothing like
the U. S. government to think of things like that."

"But have you heard anything about it?"

"No; but I surely shall. . . . D'you mind switching the light off? . . .

That's it. Now just follow me. Oh, I do need a rest. I've been working dreadfully hard since that Knights of Columbus man came down here. Isn't it hateful the way they try to run down the 'Y'? . . . Now we can have a nice long talk. You must tell me all about yourself."

"But don't you really know anything about that university scheme? They say it begins February fifteenth," Andrews said in a low voice.

"I'll ask Lieutenant Bleezer if he knows anything about it," said Sheffield soothingly, throwing an arm around Andrews's shoulder and pushing him in the door ahead of him.

They went through a dark hall to a little room where a fire burned brilliantly in the hearth, lighting up with tongues of red and yellow a square black walnut table and two heavy armchairs with leather backs and bottoms that shone like lacquer.

"This is wonderful," said Andrews involuntarily.

"Romantic I call it. Makes you think of Dickens, doesn't it, and Locksley Hall."

"Yes," said Andrews vaguely.

"Have you been in France long?" asked Andrews settling himself in one of the chairs and looking into the dancing flames of the log fire. "Will you smoke?" He handed Sheffield a crumpled cigarette.

"No, thanks, I only smoke special kinds. I have a weak heart. That's why I was rejected from the army. . . . Oh, but I think it was superb of you to join as a private. It was my dream to do that, to be one of the nameless marching throng."

"I think it was damn foolish, not to say criminal," said Andrews sullenly, still staring into the fire.

"You can't mean that. Or do you mean that you think you had abilities which would have been worth more to your country in another position? . . . I have many friends who felt that."

"No . . . I don't think it's right of a man to go back on himself. . . . I don't think butchering people ever does any good. . . . I have acted as if I did think it did good . . . out of carelessness or cowardice, one or the other; that I think bad."

"You mustn't talk that way," said Sheffield hurriedly. "So you are a musician, are you?" He asked the question with a jaunty confidential air.

"I used to play the piano a little, if that's what you mean," said Andrews.

"Music has never been the art I had most interest in. But many things have moved me intensely . . . Debussy and those beautiful little things of Nevin's. You must know them. . . . Poetry has been more my field. When I was young, younger than you are, quite a lad. . . . Oh, if we could only stay young; I am thirty-two."

"I don't see that youth by itself is worth much. It's the most superb medium there is, though, for other things," said Andrews. "Well, I must go," he said. "If you do hear anything about that university scheme, you will let me know, won't you?"

"Indeed I shall, dear boy, indeed I shall."

They shook hands in jerky dramatic fashion and Andrews stumbled down the dark hall to the door. When he stood out in the raw night air again he drew a deep breath. By the light that streamed out from a window he looked at his watch. There was time to go to the regimental sergeant-major's office before tattoo.

At the opposite end of the village street from the Y.M.C.A. hut was a cube-shaped house set a little apart from the rest in the middle of a broad lawn which the constant crossing and recrossing of a staff of cars and trains of motor trucks had turned into a muddy morass in which the wheel tracks crisscrossed in every direction. A narrow board walk led from the main road to the door. In the middle of this walk Andrews met a captain and automatically got off into the mud and saluted.

The regimental office was a large room that had once been decorated by wan and ill-drawn mural paintings in the manner of Puvis de Chavannes, but the walls had been so chipped and soiled by five years of military occupation that they were barely recognisable. Only a few bits of bare flesh and floating drapery showed here and there above the maps and notices that were tacked on the walls. At the end of the room a group of nymphs in Nile green and pastel blue could be seen emerging from under a French War Loan poster. The ceiling was adorned with an oval of flowers and little plaster cupids in low relief which had also suffered and in places showed the laths. The office was nearly empty. The littered desks and silent typewriters gave a strange air of desolation to the gutted drawing-room. Andrews walked boldly to the furthest desk, where a little red card leaning against the typewriter said "Regimental Sergeant-Major."

Behind the desk, crouched over a heap of typewritten reports, sat a little man with scanty sandy hair, who screwed up his eyes and smiled when Andrews approached the desk.

"Well, did you fix it up for me?" he asked.

"Fix what?" said Andrews.

"Oh, I thought you were someone else." The smile left the regimental sergeant-major's thin lips. "What do you want?"

"Why, Regimental Sergeant-Major, can you tell me anything about a scheme to send enlisted men to colleges over here? Can you tell me who to apply to?"

"According to what general orders? And who told you to come and see me about it, anyway?"

"Have you heard anything about it?"

"No, nothing definite. I'm busy now anyway. Ask one of your own non-coms to find out about it." He crouched once more over the papers.

Andrews was walking towards the door, flushing with annoyance, when he saw that the man at the desk by the window was jerking his head in a peculiar manner, first in the direction of the regimental sergeant-major and then towards the door. Andrews smiled at him and nodded. Outside the door, where an orderly sat on a short bench reading a torn *Saturday Evening Post*, Andrews waited. The hall was part of what must have been a ballroom, for it had a much-scarred hardwood floor and big spaces of bare plaster framed by gilt- and lavender-colored mouldings, which had probably held tapestries. The partition of unplaned boards that formed other offices cut off the major part of a highly decorated ceiling where cupids with crimson-daubed bottoms swam in all attitudes in a sea of pink- and blue- and lavender-colored clouds, wreathing themselves coyly in heavy garlands of waxy hothouse flowers, while cornucopias spilling out squashy fruits gave Andrews a feeling of distinct insecurity as he looked up from below.

"Say are you a Kappa Mu?"

Andrews looked down suddenly and saw in front of him the man who had signalled to him in the regimental sergeant-major's office.

"Are you a Kappa Mu?" he asked again.

"No, not that I know of," stammered Andrews puzzled.

"What school did you go to?"

"Harvard."

"Harvard . . . Guess we haven't got a chapter there. . . . I'm from North Western. Anyway you want to go to school in France here if you can. So do I."

"Don't you want to come and have a drink?"

The man frowned, pulled his overseas cap down over his forehead, where the hair grew very low, and looked about him mysteriously.

"Yes," he said.

They splashed together down the muddy village street.

"We've got thirteen minutes before tattoo. . . . My name's Walters, what's yours?" He spoke in a low voice in short staccato phrases.

"Andrews."

"Andrews, you've got to keep this dark. If everybody finds out about it we're through. It's a shame you're not a Kappa Mu, but college men have got to stick together, that's the way I look at it."

"Oh, I'll keep it dark enough," said Andrews.

"It's too good to be true. The general order isn't out yet, but I've seen a preliminary circular. What school d'you want to go to?"

"Sorbonne, Paris."

"That's the stuff. D'you know the back room at Baboon's?"

Walters turned suddenly to the left up an alley, and broke through a hole in a hawthorne hedge.

"A guy's got to keep his eyes and ears open if he wants to get anywhere in this army," he said.

As they ducked in the back door of a cottage, Andrews caught a glimpse of the billowy line of a tile roof against the lighter darkness of the sky. They sat down on a bench built into a chimney where a few sticks made a splutter of flames.

"Monsieur désire?" A red-faced girl with a baby in her arms came up to them.

"That's Babette; Baboon I call her," said Walters with a laugh.

"Chocolat," said Walters.

"That'll suit me all right. It's my treat, remember."

"I'm not forgetting it. Now let's get to business. What you do is this. You write an application. I'll make that out for you on the typewriter tomorrow and you meet me here at eight tomorrow night and I'll give it to you. . . . You sign it at once and hand it in to your sergeant. See?

"This'll just be a preliminary application; when the order's out you'll have to make another."

The woman, this time without the baby, appeared out of the darkness of the room with a candle and two cracked bowls from which steam rose, faint primrose-color in the candlelight.

Walters drank his bowl down at a gulp, grunted and went on talking.

"Give me a cigarette, will you? . . . You'll have to make it out darn soon too, because once the order's out every son of a gun in the division'll be making out to be a college man. How did you get your tip?"

"From a fellow in Paris."

"You've been to Paris, have you," said Walters admiringly. "Is it the way they say it is? Gee, these French are immoral. Look at this woman here. She'll sleep with a feller soon as not. Got a baby too!"

"But who do the applications go in to?"

"To the colonel, or whoever he appoints to handle it. You a Catholic?"

"No."

"Neither am I. That's the hell of it. The regimental sergeant-major is."

"Well?"

"I guess you haven't noticed the way things run up at divisional headquarters. It's a regular cathedral. Isn't a mason in it. . . . But I must beat it . . . Better pretend you don't know me if you meet me on the street; see?"

"All right."

Walters hurried out of the door. Andrews sat alone looking at the flutter of little flames about the pile of sticks on the hearth, while he sipped chocolate from the warm bowl held between the palms of both hands.

He remembered a speech out of some very bad romantic play he had heard when he was very small.

"About your head I fling . . . the Cross of Ro-me."

He started to laugh, sliding back and forth on the smooth bench which had been polished by the breeches of generations warming their feet at the fire. The red-faced woman stood with her hands on her hips looking at him in astonishment, while he laughed and laughed.

"Mais quelle gaîté, quelle gaîté," she kept saying.

The straw under him rustled faintly with every sleepy movement Andrews made in his blankets. In a minute the bugle was going to blow and he was going to jump out of his blankets, throw on his clothes and fall into line for roll call in the black mud of the village street. It couldn't be that only a month had gone by since he had got back from the hospital. No, he had spent a lifetime in this village being dragged out of his warm blankets every morning by the bugle, shivering as he stood in line for roll call, shuffling in a line that moved slowly past the cookshack, shuffling along in another line to throw what was left of his food into garbage cans, to wash his mess kit in the greasy water a hundred other men had washed their mess kits in; lining up to drill, to march on along muddy roads, splattered by the endless trains of motor trucks; lining up twice more for mess, and at last being forced by another bugle into his blankets again to sleep heavily while a smell hung in his nostrils of sweating woolen clothing and breathed-out air and dusty blankets. In a minute the bugle was going to blow, to snatch him out of even these miserable thoughts, and throw him into an automaton under other men's orders. Childish spiteful desires surged into his mind. If the bugler would only die. He could picture him, a little man with a broad face and putty-colored cheeks, a small rusty mustache and bow-legs lying like a calf on a marble slab in a butcher's shop on top of his blankets. What nonsense! There were other buglers. He wondered how many buglers there were in the army. He could picture them all, in dirty little villages, in stone barracks, in towns, in great camps that served the country for miles with rows of black warehouses and narrow barrack buildings standing with their feet a little apart; giving their little brass bugles a preliminary tap before putting out their cheeks and blowing in them and stealing a million and a half (or was it two million or three million) lives, and throwing the warm sentient bodies into coarse automatons who must be kept busy, lest they grow restive, till killing time began again.

The bugle blew. With the last jaunty notes, a stir went through the barn.

Corporal Chrisfield stood on the ladder that led up from the yard, his head on a level with the floor shouting:

"Shake it up, fellers! If a guy's late to roll call, it's K.P. for a week."

As Andrews, while buttoning his tunic, passed him on the ladder, he whispered:

"Tell me we're going to see service again, Andy. . . . Army o' Occupation."

While he stood stiffly at attention waiting to answer when the sergeant called his name, Andrews' mind was whirling in crazy circles of anxiety. What if they should leave before the General Order came on the University plan? The application would certainly be lost in the confusion of moving the Division, and he would be condemned to keep up this life for more dreary weeks and months. Would any years of work and happiness in some future existence make up for the humiliating agony of this servitude?

"Dismissed!"

He ran up the ladder to fetch his mess kit and in a few minutes was in line again in the rutted village street where the grey houses were just forming outlines as light crept slowly into the leaden sky, while a faint odor of bacon and coffee came to him, making him eager for food, eager to drown his thoughts in the heaviness of swiftly-eaten greasy food and in the warmth of watery coffee gulped down out of a tin-curved cup. He was telling himself desperately that he must do something—that he must make an effort to save himself, that he must fight against the deadening routine that numbed him.

Later, while he was sweeping the rough board floor of the company's quarters, the theme came to him which had come to him long ago, in a former incarnation it seemed, when he was smearing windows with soap from a gritty sponge along the endless side of the barracks in the training camp. Time and time again in the past year he had thought of it, and dreamed of weaving it into a fabric of sound which would express the trudging monotony of days bowed under the yoke. "Under the Yoke"; that would be a title for it. He imagined the sharp tap of the conductor's baton, the silence of a crowded hall, the first notes rasping bitterly upon the tense ears of men and women. But as he tried to concentrate his mind on the music, other things intruded upon it, blurred it. He kept feeling the rhythm of the Queen of Sheba slipping from the shoulders of her gaudily caparisoned elephant, advancing towards him through the torchlight, putting her hand, fantastic with rings and long gilded fingernails, upon his shoulders so that ripples of delight, at all the voluptuous images of his desire, went through his whole body, making it quiver like a flame with yearning for unimaginable things. It all muddled into fantastic gibberish—into sounds of horns and trombones and double basses blown off key while a piccolo shrilled the first bars of "The Star Spangled Banner."

He had stopped sweeping and looked about him dazedly. He was alone. Outside, he heard a sharp voice call "Attenshun!" He ran down the ladder and fell in at the end of the line under the angry glare of the lieutenant's small eyes, which were placed very close together on either side of a lean nose, black and hard, like the eyes of a crab.

The company marched off through the mud to the drill field.

After retreat Andrews knocked at the door at the back of the Y.M.C.A., but as there was no reply, he strode off with a long, determined stride to Sheffield's room.

In the moment that elapsed between his knock and an answer, he could feel his heart thumping. A little sweat broke out on his temples.

"Why, what's the matter, boy? You look all wrought up," said Sheffield, holding the door half open, and blocking, with his lean form, entrance to the room.

"May I come in? I want to talk to you," said Andrews.

"Oh, I suppose it'll be all right. . . . You see I have an officer with me. . . ." then there was a flutter in Sheffield's voice. "Oh, do come in"; he went on, with sudden enthusiasm. "Lieutenant Bleezer is fond of music too . . . Lieutenant, this is the boy I was telling you about. We must get him to play for us. If he had the opportunities, I am sure he'd be a famous musician."

Lieutenant Bleezer was a dark youth with a hooked nose and pince-nez. His tunic was unbuttoned and he held a cigar in his hand. He smiled in an evident attempt to put this enlisted man at his ease.

"Yes, I am very fond of music, modern music," he said, leaning against the mantelpiece. "Are you a musician by profession?"

"Not exactly . . . nearly." Andrews thrust his hands into the bottoms of his trouser pockets and looked from one to the other with a certain defiance.

"I suppose you've played in some orchestra? How is it you are not in the regimental band?"

"No, except the Pierian."

"The Pierian? Were you at Harvard?"

Andrews nodded.

"So was I."

"Isn't that a coincidence?" said Sheffield. "I'm so glad I just insisted on your coming in."

"What year were you?" asked Lieutenant Bleezer, with a faint change of tone, drawing a finger along his scant black moustache.

"Fifteen."

"I haven't graduated yet," said the lieutenant with a laugh. "What I wanted to ask you, Mr. Sheffield. . . ."

"Oh, my boy; my boy, you know you've known me long enough to call me Spence," broke in Sheffield.

"I want to know," went on Andrews speaking slowly, "can you help me to get put on the list to be sent to the University of Paris? . . . . I know that a list has been made out, although the General Order has not come yet. I am disliked by most of the non-coms and I don't see how I can get on without somebody's help . . . I simply can't go this life any longer." Andrews closed his lips firmly and looked at the ground, his face flushing.

"Well, a man of your attainments certainly ought to go," said Lieutenant Bleezer, with a faint tremor of hesitation in his voice. "I'm going to Oxford myself."

"Trust me, my boy," said Sheffield. "I'll fix it up for you, I promise. Let's shake hands on it." He seized Andrews's hand and pressed it warmly in a moist palm. "If it's within human power, within human power," he added.

"Well, I must go," said Lieutenant Bleezer, suddenly striding to the door. "I promised the Marquise I'd drop in. Good-bye . . . Take a cigar, won't you?" He held out three cigars in the direction of Andrews.

"No, thank you."

"Oh, don't you think the old aristocracy of France is just too wonderful? Lieutenant Bleezer goes almost every evening to call on the Marquise de Rompemouville. He says she is just too spirituelle for words . . . He often meets the Commanding Officer there."

Andrews had dropped into a chair and sat with his face buried in his hands, looking through his fingers at the fire, where a few white fingers of flame were clutching intermittently at a grey beech log. His mind was searching desperately for expedients.

He got to his feet and shouted shrilly:

"I can't go this life any more, do you hear that? No possible future is worth all this. If I can get to Paris, all right. If not, I'll desert and damn the consequences."

"But I've already promised I'll do all I can. . . ."

"Well, do it now," interrupted Andrews brutally.

"All right, I'll go and see the colonel and tell him what a great musician you are."

"Let's go together, now."

"But that'ld look queer, dear boy."

"I don't give a damn, come along . . . You can talk to him. You seem to be thick with all the officers."

"You must wait till I tidy up," said Sheffield.

"All right."

Andrews strode up and down in the mud in front of the house, snapping his fingers with impatience, until Sheffield came out, then they walked off in silence.

"Now wait outside a minute," whispered Sheffield when they came to the white house with bare grapevines over the front, where the colonel lived.

After a wait, Andrews found himself at the door of a brilliantly-lighted drawing room. There was a dense smell of cigar smoke. The colonel, an elderly man with a benevolent beard, stood before him with a coffee cup in his hand. Andrews saluted punctiliously.

"They tell me you are quite a pianist . . . Sorry I didn't know it before," said the colonel in a kindly tone. "You want to go to Paris to study under this new scheme?"

"Yes, sir."

"What a shame I didn't know before. The list of the men going is all made out. . . . Of course perhaps at the last minute . . . if somebody else doesn't go . . . your name can go in."

The colonel smiled graciously and turned back into the room.

"Thank you, Colonel," said Andrews, saluting.

Without a word to Sheffield, he strode off down the dark village street towards his quarters.

Andrews stood on the broad village street, where the mud was nearly dry, and a wind streaked with warmth ruffled the few puddles; he was looking into the window of the café to see if there was anyone he knew inside from whom he could borrow money for a drink. It was two months since he had had any pay, and his pockets were empty. The sun had just set on a premature spring afternoon, flooding the sky and the grey houses and the tumultuous tiled roofs with warm violet light. The faint premonition of the stirring of life in the cold earth, that came to Andrews with every breath he drew of the sparkling wind, stung his dull boredom to fury. It was the first of March, he was telling himself over and over again. The fifteenth of February, he had expected to be in Paris, free, or half-free; at least able to work. It was the first of March and here he was still helpless, still tied to the monotonous wheel of routine, incapable of any real effort, spending his spare time wandering like a lost dog up and down this muddy street, from the Y.M.C.A. hut at one end of the village to the church and the fountain in the middle, and to the Divisional Headquarters at the other end, then back again, looking

listlessly into windows, staring in people's faces without seeing them.
He had given up all hope of being sent to Paris. He had given up thinking about it or about anything; the same dull irritation of despair droned
constantly in his head, grinding round and round like a broken phono-
graph record.

After looking a long while in the window of the café of the Braves
Alliés, he walked a little down the street and stood in the same position
staring into the Repos du Poilu, where a large sign "American spoken"
blocked up half the window. Two officers passed. His hand snapped up
to the salute automatically, like a mechanical signal. It was nearly dark.
After a while he began to feel serious coolness in the wind, shivered
and started to wander aimlessly down the street.

He recognised Walters coming towards him and was going to pass
him without speaking when Walters bumped into him, muttered in his
ear "Come to Baboon's," and hurried off with his swift business-like
stride. Andrews stood irresolutely for a while with his head bent, then
went with unresilient steps up the alley, through the hole in the hedge
and into Babette's kitchen. There was no fire. He stared morosely at the
grey ashes until he heard Walters's voice beside him:

"I've got you all fixed up."

"What do you mean?"

"Mean . . . are you asleep, Andrews? They've cut a name off the
school list, that's all. Now if you shake a leg and somebody doesn't get
in ahead of you, you'll be in Paris before you know it."

"That's damn decent of you to come and tell me."

"Here's your application," said Walters, drawing a paper out of his
pocket. "Take it to the colonel; get him to O.K. it and then rush it up to
the sergeant-major's office yourself. They are making out travel orders
now. So long."

Walters had vanished. Andrews was alone again, staring at the grey
ashes. Suddenly he jumped to his feet and hurried off towards headquarters. In the anteroom to the colonel's office he waited a long while,
looking at his boots that were thickly coated with mud. "Those boots
will make a bad impression; those boots will make a bad impression," a
voice was saying over and over again inside of him. A lieutenant was also
waiting to see the colonel, a young man with pink cheeks and a milky-
white forehead, who held his hat in one hand with a pair of khaki-
colored kid gloves, and kept passing a hand over his light well-brushed
hair. Andrews felt dirty and ill-smelling in his badly-fitting uniform. The
sight of this perfect young man in his whipcord breeches, with his
manicured nails and immaculately polished puttees exasperated him. He
would have liked to fight him, to prove that he was the better man, to
outwit him, to make him forget his rank and his important air. . . . The

lieutenant had gone in to see the colonel. Andrews found himself reading a chart of some sort tacked up on the wall. There were names and dates and figures, but he could not make out what it was about.

"All right! Go ahead," whispered the orderly to him; and he was standing with his cap in his hand before the colonel who was looking at him severely, fingering the papers he had on the desk with a heavily veined hand.

Andrews saluted. The colonel made an impatient gesture.

"May I speak to you, Colonel, about the school scheme?"

"I suppose you've got permission from somebody to come to me."

"No, sir." Andrews's mind was struggling to find something to say.

"Well, you'd better go and get it."

"But, Colonel, there isn't time; the travel orders are being made out at this minute. I've heard that there's been a name crossed out on the list."

"Too late."

"But, Colonel, you don't know how important it is. I am a musician by trade; if I can't get into practice again before being demobilized, I shan't be able to get a job . . . I have a mother and an old aunt dependent on me. My family has seen better days, you see, sir. It's only by being high up in my profession that I can earn enough to give them what they are accustomed to. And a man in your position in the world, Colonel, must know what even a few months of study in Paris mean to a pianist."

The colonel smiled.

"Let's see your application," he said.

Andrews handed it to him with a trembling hand. The colonel made a few marks on one corner with a pencil.

"Now if you can get that to the sergeant-major in time to have your name included in the orders, well and good."

Andrews saluted, and hurried out. A sudden feeling of nausea had come over him. He was hardly able to control a mad desire to tear the paper up. "God, Lord, Lord, Lord, Lord," he muttered to himself. Still he ran all the way to the square, isolated building where the regimental office was.

He stopped panting in front of the desk that bore the little red card, Regimental Sergeant-Major. The regimental sergeant-major looked up at him enquiringly.

"Here's an application for School at the Sorbonne, Sergeant. Colonel Wilkins told me to run up to you with it, said he was very anxious to have it go in at once."

"Too late," said the regimental sergeant-major.

"But the colonel said it had to go in."

"Can't help it. . . . Too late," said the regimental sergeant-major.

Andrews felt the room and the men in their olive-drab shirt sleeves at the typewriters and the three nymphs creeping from behind the French War Loan poster whirl round in his head. Suddenly he heard a voice behind him:

"Is the name Andrews, John, Sarge?"

"How the hell should I know?" said the regimental sergeant-major.

"Because I've got it in the orders already. . . . I don't know how it got in." The voice was Walters's voice, staccato and business-like.

"Well, then, why d'you want to bother me about it? Give me that paper." The regimental sergeant-major jerked the paper out of Andrews's hand and looked at it savagely.

"All right, you leave tomorrow. A copy of the orders'll go to your company in the morning," growled the regimental sergeant-major.

Andrews looked hard at Walters as he went out, but got no glance in return. When he stood in the air again, disgust surged up within him, bitterer than before. The fury of his humiliation made tears start in his eyes. He walked away from the village down the main road, splashing carelessly through the puddles, slipping in the wet clay of the ditches. Something within him, like the voice of a wounded man swearing, was whining in his head long strings of filthy names. After walking a long while he stopped suddenly with his fists clenched. It was completely dark, the sky was faintly marbled by a moon behind the clouds. On both sides of the road rose the tall grey skeletons of poplars. When the sound of his footsteps stopped, he heard a faint lisp of running water. Standing still in the middle of the road, he felt his feelings gradually relax. He said aloud in a low voice several times: "You are a damn fool, John Andrews," and started walking slowly and thoughtfully back to the village.

Andrews felt an arm put round his shoulder.

"Ah've been to hell an' gone lookin' for you, Andy," said Chrisfield's voice in his ear, jerking him out of the reverie he walked in. He could feel in his face Chrisfield's breath, heavy with cognac.

"I'm going to Paris tomorrow, Chris," said Andrews.

"Ah know it, boy. Ah know it. That's why I was that right smart to talk to you. . . . You doan want to go to Paris. . . . Why doan ye come up to Germany with us? Tell me they live like kings up there."

"All right," said Andrews, "let's go to the back room at Babette's."

Chrisfield hung on his shoulder, walking unsteadily beside him. At the hole in the hedge Chrisfield stumbled and nearly pulled them both down. They laughed, and still laughing staggered into the dark kitchen, where they found the red-faced woman with her baby sitting beside the fire with no other light than the flicker of the rare flames that shot up from a little mass of wood embers. The baby started crying shrilly when the two soldiers stamped in. The woman got up and, talking automatically to the baby all the while, went off to get a light and wine.

Andrews looked at Chrisfield's face by the firelight. His cheeks had lost the faint childish roundness they had had when Andrews had first talked to him, sweeping up cigarette butts off the walk in front of the barracks at the training camp.

"Ah tell you, boy, you ought to come with us to Germany . . . nauthin' but whores in Paris."

"The trouble is, Chris, that I don't want to live like a king, or a sergeant or a major-general . . . I want to live like John Andrews."

"What yer goin' to do in Paris, Andy?"

"Study music."

"Ah guess some day Ah'll go into a movie show an' when they turn on the lights, who'll Ah see but ma ole frien' Andy raggin' the scales on the pyaner."

"Something like that. . . . How d'you like being a corporal, Chris?"

"O, Ah doan know." Chrisfield spat on the floor between his feet. "It's funny, ain't it? You an' me was right smart friends onct. . . . Guess it's bein' a non-com."

Andrews did not answer.

Chrisfield sat silent with his eyes on the fire.

"Well, Ah got him . . . Gawd, it was easy," he said suddenly.

"What do you mean?"

"Ah got him, that's all."

"You mean . . . ?"

Chrisfield nodded.

"Um-hum, in the Oregon forest," he said.

Andrews said nothing. He felt suddenly very tired. He thought of men he had seen in attitudes of death.

"Ah wouldn't ha' thought it had been so easy," said Chrisfield.

The woman came through the door at the end of the kitchen with a candle in her hand. Chrisfield stopped speaking suddenly.

"Tomorrow I'm going to Paris," cried Andrews boisterously. "It's the end of soldiering for me."

"Ah bet it'll be some sport in Germany, Andy . . . Sarge says we'll be goin' up to Coab . . . what's its name?"

"Coblenz."

Chrisfield poured a glass of wine out and drank it off, smacking his lips after it and wiping his mouth on the back of his hand.

"D'ye remember, Andy, we was both of us brushin' cigarette butts at that bloody trainin' camp when we first met up with each other?"

"Considerable water has run under the bridge since then."

"Ah reckon we won't meet up again, mos' likely."

"Hell, why not?"

They were silent again, staring at the fading embers of the fire. In the dim edge of the candlelight the woman stood with her hands on her hips, looking at them fixedly.

"Reckon a feller wouldn't know what do with himself if he did get out of the army . . . now, would he, Andy?"

"So long, Chris. I'm beating it," said Andrews in a harsh voice, jumping to his feet.

"So long, Andy, ole man. . . . Ah'll pay for the drinks." Chrisfield was beckoning with his hand to the red-faced woman, who advanced slowly through the candlelight.

"Thanks, Chris."

Andrews strode away from the door. A cold, needle-like rain was falling. He pulled up his coat collar and ran down the muddy village street towards his quarters.

In the opposite corner of the compartment Andrews could see Walters hunched up in an attitude of sleep, with his cap pulled down far over his eyes. His mouth was open, and his head wagged with the jolting of the train. The shade over the light plunged the compartment in dark-blue obscurity, which made the night sky outside the window and the shapes of trees and houses, evolving and pirouetting as they glided by, seem very near. Andrews felt no desire to sleep; he had sat a long time leaning his head against the frame of the window, looking out at the fleeing shadows and the occasional little red-green lights that darted by and the glow of the stations that flared for a moment and were lost in dark silhouettes of unlighted houses and skeleton trees and black hill-sides. He was thinking how all the epochs in his life seemed to have been marked out by railway rides at night. The jolting rumble of the wheels made the blood go faster through his veins; made him feel acutely the clattering of the train along the gleaming rails, spurning fields and trees and houses, piling up miles and miles between the past and future. The gusts of cold night air when he opened the window and the faint whiffs of steam and coal gas that tingled in his nostrils excited him like a smile on a strange face seen for a moment in a crowded street. He did not think of what he had left behind. He was straining his eyes eagerly through the darkness towards the vivid life he was going to live. Boredom and abasement were over. He was free to work and hear music and make friends. He drew deep breaths; warm waves of vigor seemed flowing constantly from his lungs and throat to his finger tips and down through his body and the muscles of his legs. He looked at his watch: "One." In six hours he would be in Paris. For six hours he would sit there looking out at the fleeting shadows of the countryside, feeling in his blood the eager throb of the train, rejoicing in every mile the train carried him away from things past.

Walters still slept, half slipping off the seat, with his mouth open and his overcoat bundled round his head. Andrews looked out of the window, feeling in his nostrils the tingle of steam and coal gas. A phrase out of the "Iliad" came to his head: "Ambrosial night, Night ambrosial unending." But better than sitting round a camp fire drinking wine and water and listening to the boastful yarns of long-haired Achaeans, was this hustling through the countryside away from the monotonous whine of past unhappiness, towards joyousness and life.

Andrews began to think of the men he had left behind. They were asleep at this time of the night, in barns and barracks, or else standing on guard with cold damp feet, and cold hands which the icy rifle barrel burned when they tended it. He might go far away out of sound of the tramp of marching, away from the smell of overcrowded barracks where men slept in rows like cattle, but he would still be one of them. He would not see an officer pass him without an unconscious movement of servility, he would not hear a bugle without feeling sick with hatred. If he could only express these thwarted lives, the miserable dullness of industrialized slaughter, it might have been almost worth while—for him; for the others, it would never be worth while. "But you're talking as if you were out of the woods; you're a soldier still, John Andrews." The words formed themselves in his mind as vividly as if he had spoken them. He smiled bitterly and settled himself again to watch silhouettes of trees and hedges and houses and hillsides fleeing against the dark sky.

When he awoke the sky was grey. The train was moving slowly, clattering loudly over switches, through a town of wet slate roofs that rose in fantastic patterns of shadow above the blue mist. Walters was smoking a cigarette.

"God! These French trains are rotten," he said when he noticed that Andrews was awake. "The most inefficient country I ever was in anyway."

"Inefficiency be damned," broke in Andrews, jumping up and stretching himself. He opened the window. "The heating's too damned efficient. . . . I think we're near Paris."

The cold air, with a flavor of mist in it, poured into the stuffy compartment. Every breath was joy. Andrews felt a crazy buoyancy bubbling up in him. The rumbling clatter of the train wheels sang in his ears. He threw himself on his back on the dusty blue seat and kicked his heels in the air like a colt.

"Liven up, for God's sake, man," he shouted. "We're getting near Paris."

"We are lucky bastards," said Walters, grinning with the cigarette hanging out of the corner of his mouth. "I'm going to see if I can find the rest of the gang."

Andrews, alone in the compartment, found himself singing at the top of his lungs.

As the day brightened the mist lifted off the flat linden-green fields intersected by rows of leafless poplars. Salmon-colored houses with blue roofs wore already a faintly citified air. They passed brick-kilns and clay-quarries, with reddish puddles of water in the bottom of them; crossed a jade-green river where a long file of canal boats with bright paint on their prows moved slowly. The engine whistled shrilly. They clattered through a small freight yard, and rows of suburban houses began to form, at first chaotically in broad patches of garden-land, and then in orderly ranks with streets between and shops at the corners. A dark-grey dripping wall rose up suddenly and blotted out the view. The train slowed down and went through several stations crowded with people on their way to work,—ordinary people in varied clothes with only here and there a blue or khaki uniform. Then there was more dark-grey wall, and the obscurity of wide bridges under which dusty oil lamps burned orange and red, making a gleam on the wet wall above them, and where the wheels clanged loudly. More freight yards and the train pulled slowly past other trains full of faces and silhouettes of people, to stop with a jerk in a station. And Andrews was standing on the grey cement platform, sniffing smells of lumber and merchandise and steam. His ungainly pack and blanket-roll he carried on his shoulder like a cross. He had left his rifle and cartridge belt carefully tucked out of sight under the seat.

Walters and five other men straggled along the platform towards him, carrying or dragging their packs.

There was a look of apprehension on Walters's face.

"Well, what do we do now?" he said.

"Do!" cried Andrews, and he burst out laughing.

Father Hires a Cook

From LIFE WITH FATHER

By Clarence Day

This little book places a milestone. Already it is a historical story. Telling of family life in Victorian New York, its contrast with the present is perhaps more extreme than a story of the seventeenth century. Yet the endurance of its humor is proved by the enthusiastic laughter with which a play based upon it is still received—not merely by elderly nostalgists but by the newest generation.

O NE late afternoon when Father came up from downtown, he found his home much upset. Our cook had walked out and left us. I was a child of four, George was two, and there was a new baby besides. Mother was ill. She hadn't been able to leave us to go to an agency. And as she was no hand at cooking herself, the outlook for dinner was poor.

This state of affairs was unprecedented in all Father's experience. In his father's home, they never changed their servants suddenly; they seldom changed them at all; and as his mother was a past mistress of cooking, he had always been doubly protected. Since his marriage, he had had to live a much bumpier life. But this was the worst yet.

He asked Mother, who was lying in bed, what she was going to do about it. There were no telephones then, and she couldn't do anything at all, at the moment; but she said she would try to go to an agency in the morning and see what she could find. "In the morning? Good God!" Father said. "Where is the place, anyhow?" And he clapped on his hat and strode out again, over toward Sixth Avenue.

As I heard the story years afterward, it was late when he got there, and he bounded up the front stoop two or three steps at a time, and went quickly into the little office, where the gaslights were burning. He had never been in such a place before, and to his surprise it was empty, except for a severe-looking woman who sat at a desk at one side. "Where do you keep 'em?" he urgently demanded, his mind on the question of dinner.

She looked at him, got out her pen, and opened a large book deliberately. "I will take your name and address," she informed him, "and then, if you please, you may give me the details as to what kind of person you require and when you would wish her to call."

But Father had no time, he told her, for any damned fol-de-rol. "Where do you keep 'em?" he said again. She was standing in the way of his dinner. I can imagine how his face must have reddened and how his eyes must have blazed at her. "I am asking you where you keep them!" he roared.

"Why, the girls are in there," the lady explained, to calm him, "but clients are not allowed in that room. If you will tell me the kind of position you wish me to fill for you, I will have one come out."

Before she'd half finished, Father had thrown open the door and gone in. There sat a crowd of the girls, young and old, sickly and brawny, of all shapes and sizes; some ugly, some pretty and trim and stylish, some awkward; nurses, ladies' maids, waitresses, washerwomen, and cooks.

The manager was by now at Father's elbow, trying to make him get out, and insisting that he tell her the position he wished her to fill. But Father was swiftly glancing around at the crowd, and he paid no attention. He noticed a little woman in the corner, with honest gray eyes, who sat there, shrewd-looking and quiet. He pointed his cane over at her and said, "I'll take that one."

The manager was flustered, but still she kept trying to enforce her authority. She protested she didn't yet know the position. . . .

"Cook," Father said, "cook."

"But Margaret doesn't wish to be a cook, she wants—"

"You can cook, can't you?" Father demanded.

Margaret's plain little face was still pink with excitement and pleasure at being chosen above all that roomful by such a masterful gentleman. Father had probably smiled at her, too, for they liked each other at once. Well, she said, she had cooked for one family.

"Of course she can cook," Father said.

He said afterward, when describing the incident, "I knew at once she could cook."

The manager didn't like this at all. The discipline of the office was spoiled. "If you are going to take her anyhow," she said acidly, "what day would you wish her to come, and will you please give me your name?"

"Yes, yes," Father said, without giving it. "Come on, Margaret." And he planked down the fee and walked out.

Margaret followed him through the door and trotted over to our home at his heels. He sent her down to the kitchen immediately, while he went upstairs to dress.

"I don't know why you make such a fuss about engaging new servants. It's simple enough," he said comfortably to Mother that evening, after Margaret's first dinner.

It was the first of a long series, for she stayed with us twenty-six years.

In the summers, when we went to the country, our usual plan was to hire a temporary cook to go with us, so that Margaret could stay in town. We hated to leave her, but the idea was that somebody must stay to take care of the house. There were no electric burglar alarms in those days, and few special watchmen. Little Margaret made a pretty small watchman, for she was no size at all, but she had an indomitable spirit. So we'd leave her on guard while we went up to our summer home in Harrison with a substitute cook.

But this didn't work well. No matter how few the substitute's faults were, Father had no patience with them. One summer, I remember, there was a nice woman, Delia, who got on well with Mother because she was so obliging and pleasant, but who didn't suit Father at all. "I don't give a damn how obliging she is," he kept saying. "If she won't oblige me by cooking something fit to eat, she can go."

This didn't sound unreasonable, but Delia cooked well enough for the rest of us, and Mother hated to risk getting someone else who'd be temperamental. Our dining-room consequently became a battleground morning and night. At breakfast, Father would put down his coffee cup in disgust and roar: "Slops! Damn it, slops! Does she call this confounded mess coffee? Isn't there a damned soul in Westchester County who knows how to make coffee but me? I swear to God I can't even imagine how she concocts such atrocities. I come down to this room hungry every morning and she tries to fill me with slops! Take it away, I tell you!" he would bellow to the waitress. "Take this accursed mess away!" And while she and Delia were frantically hurrying to make a fresh pot, he would savagely devour his omelet and bacon, and declare that his breakfast was ruined.

The longer Delia stayed with us, the more alarmed Father became. He ate heartily, as Mother kept pointing out to him, but he said he didn't feel nourished. He said it was no use to argue about it; he felt all gone inside. One night after he had had a four-course dinner, he fretfully got up from the table, went into the library with his cigar, and moaned that he was starved. His moans were, as always, full-throated, and they came from the heart. Every now and then, when his miserable condition seemed to strike him afresh, he laid down his book and shouted "Starved! Starved!" in a grief-stricken roar.

When Mother went in the library to quiet him, he told her he'd be damned if he'd stand it. "I refuse to be sent to my grave, do you hear me, by that infernal bog-trotting imbecile you keep in my kitchen."

"Now Clare, a Japanese is coming tomorrow, I told you. This is Delia's last night. I do hope you'll like Tobo. He won't know our ways right at the start, of course, but he is a very good cook."

Father was appeased for the moment by the dismissal of Delia. But the next night, when he found that the first dish was too Oriental, he said in an annoyed tone to Mother, "Will you kindly explain to your man Tobo that I am not a coolie?" And after eating the rest of his dinner, he pushed his plate away and went up to his bedroom, declaring vehemently that he was poisoned. He undressed, lay down on his sofa, and filled the air with deep groans.

From time to time he stopped and dozed a little, or listened to what he could hear of our talk. His feeling was that we shouldn't be talking at all. We ought to be sitting with bowed heads in silence until he recovered. "Poisoned!" he suddenly boomed, to remind us. "Oh, God! I am poisoned!"

At this point, Mother, who was down in the library, laughed. Father heard her. He jumped up from his sofa and marched from his bedroom indignantly into the hall. "I am a sick man!" he thundered robustly. "And nobody in this house gives a damn!"

Mother hurried upstairs to see what he wanted. He insisted on her rubbing his back. Sick or well, that always soothed him, and he would have liked her to do it for hours. He loved to close his eyes, with someone's hand moving quietly on him, while a feeling of comfort flowed into his thoughts and his nerves.

Mother didn't think much of rubbing, however. She didn't like it herself. When anyone rubbed her, she stiffened and resisted at once. Consequently she had no idea of the right way to do it. When she had to rub Father, she always got tired of it in a very few minutes.

She gave him some hasty little rubs and digs as well as she could, but just as he was beginning to relax, she said, "There now, Clare, that's enough." Father was so disappointed by this that it reminded him that he was poisoned, and the only cure he could think of was the dismissal of Tobo.

The next day old Margaret was sent for to come at once to the country, and the house in town was locked up and left to take care of itself.

She came in a hack from the Harrison station. She was an odd sight. Her face looked familiar in her little black bonnet, tied under her chin, but she seemed strangely swollen and bulky; she stuck out in queer places; and as she crowded through the back door, she bruised me with her hard, bony hip. Only it wasn't her hip, it turned out; it was her favorite saucepan, which was tied to her waist under her skirt. Several large spoons, a dipper, a skillet, and two pair of shoes were made fast under it elsewhere. In her arms she had some bundles wrapped in newspapers, which Mother thought at first held her clothes, but when Margaret opened them we found they contained cheeses, melons, fresh coffee, a leg of lamb, some sweet potatoes, and other provisions. Margaret had no faith at all in being able to buy any supplies in the country. She had brought as complete a larder to Harrison as though we were at the North Pole.

"But didn't you bring any clothes with you, Margaret? Not even an apron?" asked Mother.

Little Margaret pursed her lips closely together and didn't answer at first. Then, as Mother stood waiting, she said unwillingly, "I have me other clothes on me."

She had wanted to have her hands free, it seemed, to bring us something good to eat. So under her street dress she was wearing two other dresses on that hot summer day, a collection of stiffly starched petticoats, three aprons, two nightgowns, and pretty much all the rest of her wardrobe.

As she was climbing upstairs to unpeel and unpack herself, Father saw her. "Is that you, Margaret?" he called, suddenly feeling much better. "Thank God!"

Old Margaret was just the kind of cook that we wanted. Lots of cooks can do rich dishes well. Margaret couldn't. But she cooked simple, everyday dishes in a way that made our mouths water. Her apple pies were the most satisfying pies I've ever tasted. Her warmed-up potatoes were so delicious I could have made my whole dinner of them.

Yet even Margaret sometimes miscalculated. A large, royal-looking steak would be set before Father, which, upon being cut into, would turn out to be too underdone. Father's face would darken with disappointment. If the earth had begun to wobble and reel in its orbit he could scarcely have been more disapproving. He would raise his foot, under the table, and stamp slowly and heavily three times on the rug. Thud; thud; thud.

At this solemn signal, we would hear Margaret leave the kitchen below us and come clumping step by step up the stairs to the dining-room door.

"Margaret, look at that steak."

Margaret would step nearer and peer with a shocked look at the platter. "The Lord bless us and save us," she would say to herself in a low voice. She would then seize the platter and make off with it, to better it the best way she could, and Father would gloomily wait and eat a few vegetables and pour out a fresh glass of claret.

Father and Margaret were united by the intense interest they both took in cooking. Each understood the other instinctively. They had a complete fellow-feeling. Mother's great interest was in babies—she had never been taught how to cook. All she wanted was to keep Father pleased somehow; and if it was too difficult she didn't always care about even that.

At table it was Father who carved the fowl, or sliced the roast lamb or beef. I liked to watch him whet the knife and go at it. He had such a fine, easy hand. To a hungry boy, he seemed over-deliberate and exact in his strokes, yet in a moment or two he had done. And usually the cooking had been as superb as the carving. Sometimes it was so perfect that Father's face would crinkle with pleasure, and with a wink at us he'd summon Margaret with his usual three measured thumps. She would appear, clutching her skirts with both hands, and looking worried. "What's wanting?" she'd ask.

"Margaret," Father would tell her affectionately, "that fricasseed chicken is good."

Margaret would turn her wrinkled face aside, and look down, and push the flat of her hand out toward Father. It was the same gesture she used when she said "Get along with you" to flatterers. She couldn't say that to Father, but she would beam at him, and turn and go out, and stump back down the dark little stairs without ever a word.

Every once in a while, when the household bills were getting too high, a platter with three tiny French chops on it would be placed before Father, and a larger dish full of cold corned beef or Irish stew before Mother. At this sight we boys would stop talking and become round-eyed and still.

Father would look over at Mother's dish to see if it seemed appetizing, for he often said there was nothing better than one of Margaret's stews. The stew usually seemed possible enough to him, yet not quite what he wanted. He would then ask Mother if she'd have a chop.

Mother always said, "No."

"They look nice and juicy," Father would urge her, but she would say again she didn't want any, and turn her eyes away from the platter.

Father would then look around at the rest of us doubtfully. He had four sons, all with appetites. He would clear his throat as though getting ready to offer a chop to each boy in turn; but he usually compromised by saying, "Will anyone else have a chop?"

"No, Clare," Mother would quickly and impatiently reply, "they're for you. The rest of us are going to have stew tonight." And she'd smile brightly but a little watchfully around at us boys, to be sure that we were making no fuss about it, while she hurried to get the thing settled.

We boys would then earnestly watch Father while he ate the three chops.

Not that we didn't like Margaret's stew, which was the best in the world, but we regarded dinner as a special occasion, and we often had stew for lunch.

If some of us had taken up Father's offer, and left him with only one chop or none, I suppose that he would have asked Mother, "Where are the rest of the chops?" and been very cross about it when she told him there weren't any more. But his offer of them to us was sincere, though it cost him a struggle. He wanted plenty of food bought for everyone. His instincts were generous. Only, it made him cross if he suffered for those generous instincts.

Long after Margaret died, Father was speaking one night of how good her things always had tasted.

"I wish she could hear you," said Mother. She smiled tenderly at the thought of that gallant and dear little figure. "If anybody ever was sure of going to Heaven," she added, "I know it was Margaret."

This struck Father as a recommendation of the place. He took a sip of cognac and said casually, "I'll look her up when I get there. I'll have her take care of me."

Mother started to say something but checked herself.

"What's the matter?" he asked.

"Well, Clare dear," said Mother, "Margaret must be in some special part of Heaven, she was so good. You'd be very fortunate, Clare, to get to the same part as Margaret."

"Hah!" Father said, suddenly scowling. "I'll make a devil of a row if I don't."

The Party

From THE GREAT GATSBY

By F. Scott Fitzgerald

At the point in the novel where this scene occurs, the background of Gatsby is wholly unknown. Jordan Baker learns some of it in the hour she is with him while the party goes on outside, but it becomes known to the reader only as the design of the story unfolds through the book. But the whole essence of the scene which so triumphantly captures the mood of an era is in this mystery which surrounds its central character. In that upheaval when social strata were confused, when prohibition brought criminals to season the upper crust and men and women of all groups clung to the momentary security of fancied wealth, Gatsby was accepted by all without inquiry. To his drifting, cynical guests he is merely the fabulous host; in the orgy of waste and splendor he supplies, most of them ask no questions or even bother to meet him. The real story of his life, uncovered by Carraway, the "I" of the story, is an interplay of love, innocence and international gangsterism.

THERE was music from my neighbor's house through the summer nights. In his blue gardens men and girls came and went like moths among the whisperings and the champagne and the stars. At high tide in the afternoon I watched his guests diving from the tower of his raft, or taking the sun on the hot sand of his beach while his two motor-boats slit the waters of the Sound, drawing aquaplanes over cataracts of foam. On week-ends his Rolls-Royce became an omnibus, bearing parties to and from the city between nine in the morning and long past midnight, while his station wagon scampered like a brisk yellow bug to meet all trains. And on Mondays eight servants, including an extra gardener, toiled all day with mops and scrubbing-brushes and hammers and garden-shears, repairing the ravages of the night before.

Every Friday five crates of oranges and lemons arrived from a fruiterer in New York—every Monday these same oranges and lemons left his back door in a pyramid of pulpless halves. There was a machine in the kitchen which could extract the juice of two hundred oranges in half an hour if a little button was pressed two hundred times by a butler's thumb.

At least once a fortnight a corps of caterers came down with several hundred feet of canvas and enough colored lights to make a Christmas tree of Gatsby's enormous garden. On buffet tables, garnished with glistening hors-d'œuvre, spiced baked hams crowded against salads of harlequin designs and pastry pigs and turkeys bewitched to a dark gold. In the main hall a bar with a real brass rail was set up, and stocked with gins and liquors and with cordials so long forgotten that most of his female guests were too young to know one from another.

By seven o'clock the orchestra has arrived, no thin five-piece affair, but a whole pitful of oboes and trombones and saxophones and viols and cornets and piccolos, and low and high drums. The last swimmers have come in from the beach now and are dressing up-stairs; the cars from New York are parked five deep in the drive, and already the halls and salons and verandas are gaudy with primary colors, and hair bobbed in strange new ways, and shawls beyond the dreams of Castile. The bar is in full swing, and floating rounds of cocktails permeate the garden outside, until the air is alive with chatter and laughter, and casual innuendo and introductions forgotten on the spot, and enthusiastic meetings between women who never knew each other's names.

The lights grow brighter as the earth lurches away from the sun, and now the orchestra is playing yellow cocktail music, and the opera of voices pitches a key higher. Laughter is easier minute by minute, spilled with prodigality, tipped out at a cheerful word. The groups change more swiftly, swell with new arrivals, dissolve and form in the same breath; already there are wanderers, confident girls who weave here and there among the stouter and more stable, become for a sharp, joyous moment the centre of a group, and then, excited with triumph, glide on through the sea-change of faces and voices and color under the constantly changing light.

Suddenly one of these gypsies, in trembling opal, seizes a cocktail out of the air, dumps it down for courage and, moving her hands like Frisco, dances out alone on the canvas platform. A momentary hush; the orchestra leader varies his rhythm obligingly for her, and there is a burst of chatter as the erroneous news goes around that she is Gilda Gray's understudy from the Follies. The party has begun.

I believe that on the first night I went to Gatsby's house I was one of the few guests who had actually been invited. People were not invited—they went there. They got into automobiles which bore them out to Long Island, and somehow they ended up at Gatsby's door. Once there they were introduced by somebody who knew Gatsby, and after that they conducted themselves according to the rules of behavior associated with an amusement park. Sometimes they came and went without having met Gatsby at all, came for the party with a simplicity of heart that was its own ticket of admission.

I had been actually invited. A chauffeur in a uniform of robin's-egg blue crossed my lawn early that Saturday morning with a surprisingly formal note from his employer: the honor would be entirely Gatsby's, it said, if I would attend his "little party" that night. He had seen me several times, and had intended to call on me long before, but a peculiar combination of circumstances had prevented it—signed Jay Gatsby, in a majestic hand.

Dressed up in white flannels I went over to his lawn a little after seven, and wandered around rather ill at ease among swirls and eddies of people I didn't know—though here and there was a face I had noticed on the commuting train. I was immediately struck by the number of young Englishmen dotted about; all well dressed, all looking a little hungry, and all talking in low, earnest voices to solid and prosperous Americans. I was sure that they were selling something: bonds or insurance or automobiles. They were at least agonizingly aware of the easy money in the vicinity and convinced that it was theirs for a few words in the right key.

As soon as I arrived I made an attempt to find my host, but the two or three people of whom I asked his whereabouts stared at me in such an amazed way, and denied so vehemently any knowledge of his movements, that I slunk off in the direction of the cocktail table—the only place in the garden where a single man could linger without looking purposeless and alone.

I was on my way to get roaring drunk from sheer embarrassment when Jordan Baker came out of the house and stood at the head of the marble steps, leaning a little backward and looking with contemptuous interest down into the garden.

Welcome or not, I found it necessary to attach myself to some one before I should begin to address cordial remarks to the passers-by.

"Hello!" I roared, advancing toward her. My voice seemed unnaturally loud across the garden.

"I thought you might be here," she responded absently as I came up. "I remembered you lived next door to—"

She held my hand impersonally, as a promise that she'd take care of me in a minute, and gave ear to two girls in twin yellow dresses, who stopped at the foot of the steps.

"Hello!" they cried together. "Sorry you didn't win."

That was for the golf tournament. She had lost in the finals the week before.

"You don't know who we are," said one of the girls in yellow, "but we met you here about a month ago."

"You've dyed your hair since then," remarked Jordan, and I started, but the girls had moved casually on and her remark was addressed to the premature moon, produced like the supper, no doubt, out of a caterer's basket. With Jordan's slender golden arm resting in mine, we descended the steps and sauntered about the garden. A tray of cocktails floated at us through the twilight, and we sat down at a table with the two girls in yellow and three men, each one introduced to us as Mr. Mumble.

"Do you come to these parties often?" inquired Jordan of the girl beside her.

"The last one was the one I met you at," answered the girl, in an alert confident voice. She turned to her companion: "Wasn't it for you, Lucille?"

It was for Lucille, too.

"I like to come," Lucille said. "I never care what I do, so I always have a good time. When I was here last I tore my gown on a chair, and he asked me my name and address—inside of a week I got a package from Croirier's with a new evening gown in it."

"Did you keep it?" asked Jordan.

"Sure I did. I was going to wear it to-night, but it was too big in the bust and had to be altered. It was gas blue with lavender beads. Two hundred and sixty-five dollars."

"There's something funny about a fellow that'll do a thing like that," said the other girl eagerly. "He doesn't want any trouble with *anybody*."

"Who doesn't?" I inquired.

"Gatsby. Somebody told me—"

The two girls and Jordan leaned together confidentially.

"Somebody told me they thought he killed a man once."

A thrill passed over all of us. The three Mr. Mumbles bent forward and listened eagerly.

"I don't think it's so much *that*," argued Lucille sceptically; "it's more that he was a German spy during the war."

One of the men nodded in confirmation.

"I heard that from a man who knew all about him, grew up with him in Germany," he assured us positively.

"Oh, no," said the first girl, "it couldn't be that, because he was in the American army during the war." As our credulity switched back to her she leaned forward with enthusiasm. "You look at him sometimes when he thinks nobody's looking at him. I'll bet he killed a man."

She narrowed her eyes and shivered. Lucille shivered. We all turned

and looked around for Gatsby. It was testimony to the romantic speculation he inspired that there were whispers about him from those who
had found little that it was necessary to whisper about in this world.

The first supper—there would be another one after midnight—was
now being served, and Jordan invited me to join her own party, who
were spread around a table on the other side of the garden. There were
three married couples and Jordan's escort, a persistent undergraduate
given to violent innuendo, and obviously under the impression that
sooner or later Jordan was going to yield him up her person to a greater
or lesser degree. Instead of rambling this party had preserved a dignified
homogeneity, and assumed to itself the function of representing the
staid nobility of the country-side—East Egg condescending to West
Egg, and carefully on guard against its spectroscopic gayety.

"Let's get out," whispered Jordan, after a somehow wasteful and in-
appropriate half-hour; "this is much too polite for me."

We got up, and she explained that we were going to find the host: I
had never met him, she said, and it was making me uneasy. The undergraduate nodded in a cynical, melancholy way.

The bar, where we glanced first, was crowded, but Gatsby was not
there. She couldn't find him from the top of the steps, and he wasn't
on the veranda. On a chance we tried an important-looking door, and
walked into a high Gothic library, panelled with carved English oak, and
probably transported complete from some ruin overseas.

A stout, middle-aged man, with enormous owl-eyed spectacles, was
sitting somewhat drunk on the edge of a great table, staring with unsteady concentration at the shelves of books. As we entered he wheeled
excitedly around and examined Jordan from head to foot.

"What do you think?" he demanded impetuously.

"About what?"

He waved his hand toward the book-shelves.

"About that. As a matter of fact you needn't bother to ascertain. I
ascertained. They're real."

"The books?"

He nodded.

"Absolutely real—have pages and everything. I thought they'd be a
nice durable cardboard. Matter of fact, they're absolutely real. Pages and
— Here! Lemme show you."

Taking our scepticism for granted, he rushed to the bookcases and
returned with Volume One of the "Stoddard Lectures."

"See!" he cried triumphantly. "It's a bona-fide piece of printed matter.
It fooled me. This fella's a regular Belasco. It's a triumph. What
thoroughness! What realism! Knew when to stop, too—didn't cut the
pages. But what do you want? What do you expect?"

He snatched the book from me and replaced it hastily on its shelf, muttering that if one brick was removed the whole library was liable to collapse.

"Who brought you?" he demanded. "Or did you just come? I was brought. Most people were brought."

Jordan looked at him alertly, cheerfully, without answering.

"I was brought by a woman named Roosevelt," he continued. "Mrs. Claud Roosevelt. Do you know her? I met her somewhere last night. I've been drunk for about a week now, and I thought it might sober me up to sit in a library."

"Has it?"

"A little bit, I think. I can't tell yet. I've only been here an hour. Did I tell you about the books? They're real. They're—"

"You told us."

We shook hands with him gravely and went back outdoors.

There was dancing now on the canvas in the garden; old men pushing young girls backward in eternal graceless circles, superior couples holding each other tortuously, fashionably, and keeping in the corners— and a great number of single girls dancing individualistically or relieving the orchestra for a moment of the burden of the banjo or the traps. By midnight the hilarity had increased. A celebrated tenor had sung in Italian, and a notorious contralto had sung in jazz, and between the numbers people were doing "stunts" all over the garden, while happy, vacuous bursts of laughter rose toward the summer sky. A pair of stage twins, who turned out to be the girls in yellow, did a baby act in costume, and champagne was served in glasses bigger than finger-bowls. The moon had risen higher, and floating in the Sound was a triangle of silver scales, trembling a little to the stiff, tinny drip of the banjoes on the lawn.

I was still with Jordan Baker. We were sitting at a table with a man of about my age and a rowdy little girl, who gave way upon the slightest provocation to uncontrollable laughter. I was enjoying myself now. I had taken two finger-bowls of champagne, and the scene had changed before my eyes into something significant, elemental, and profound.

At a lull in the entertainment the man looked at me and smiled.

"Your face is familiar," he said, politely. "Weren't you in the First Division during the war?"

"Why, yes. I was in the Twenty-eighth Infantry."

"I was in the Sixteenth until June nineteen-eighteen. I knew I'd seen you somewhere before."

We talked for a moment about some wet, gray little villages in France. Evidently he lived in this vicinity, for he told me that he had just bought a hydroplane, and was going to try it out in the morning.

"Want to go with me, old sport? Just near the shore along the Sound."

"What time?"

"Any time that suits you best."

It was on the tip of my tongue to ask his name when Jordan looked around and smiled.

"Having a gay time now?" she inquired.

"Much better." I turned again to my new acquaintance. "This is an unusual party for me. I haven't even seen the host. I live over there—" I waved my hand at the invisible hedge in the distance, "and this man Gatsby sent over his chauffeur with an invitation."

For a moment he looked at me as if he failed to understand.

"I'm Gatsby," he said suddenly.

"What!" I exclaimed. "Oh, I beg your pardon."

"I thought you knew, old sport. I'm afraid I'm not a very good host."

He smiled understandingly—much more than understandingly. It was one of those rare smiles with a quality of eternal reassurance in it, that you may come across four or five times in life. It faced—or seemed to face—the whole eternal world for an instant, and then concentrated on you with an irresistible prejudice in your favor. It understood you just so far as you wanted to be understood, believed in you as you would like to believe in yourself, and assured you that it had precisely the impression of you that, at your best, you hoped to convey. Precisely at that point it vanished—and I was looking at an elegant young rough-neck, a year or two over thirty, whose elaborate formality of speech just missed being absurd. Some time before he introduced himself I'd got a strong impression that he was picking his words with care.

Almost at the moment when Mr. Gatsby identified himself a butler hurried toward him with the information that Chicago was calling him on the wire. He excused himself with a small bow that included each of us in turn.

"If you want anything just ask for it, old sport," he urged me. "Excuse me. I will rejoin you later."

When he was gone I turned immediately to Jordan—constrained to assure her of my surprise. I had expected that Mr. Gatsby would be a florid and corpulent person in his middle years.

"Who is he?" I demanded. "Do you know?"

"He's just a man named Gatsby."

"Where is he from, I mean? And what does he do?"

"Now you're started on the subject," she answered with a wan smile. "Well, he told me once he was an Oxford man."

A dim background started to take shape behind him, but at her next remark it faded away.

"However, I don't believe it."

"Why not?"

"I don't know," she insisted, "I just don't think he went there."
Something in her tone reminded me of the other girl's "I think he
killed a man," and had the effect of stimulating my curiosity. I would
have accepted without question the information that Gatsby sprang
from the swamps of Louisiana or from the lower East Side of New York.
That was comprehensible. But young men didn't—at least in my provincial inexperience I believed they didn't—drift coolly out of nowhere
and buy a palace on Long Island Sound.

"Anyhow, he gives large parties," said Jordan, changing the subject
with an urban distaste for the concrete. "And I like large parties. They're
so intimate. At small parties there isn't any privacy."

There was the boom of a bass drum, and the voice of the orchestra
leader rang out suddenly above the chatter of the garden.

"Ladies and gentlemen," he cried. "At the request of Mr. Gatsby we
are going to play for you Mr. Vladmir Tostoff's latest work, which
attracted so much attention at Carnegie Hall last May. If you read the
papers you know there was a big sensation." He smiled with jovial con-
descension, and added: "Some sensation!" Whereupon everybody
laughed.

"The piece is known," he concluded lustily, "as 'Vladmir Tostoff's
Jazz History of the World.'"

The nature of Mr. Tostoff's composition eluded me, because just as
it began my eyes fell on Gatsby, standing alone on the marble steps and
looking from one group to another with approving eyes. His tanned skin
was drawn attractively tight on his face and his short hair looked as
though it were trimmed every day. I could see nothing sinister about
him. I wondered if the fact that he was not drinking helped to set him
off from his guests, for it seemed to me that he grew more correct as the
fraternal hilarity increased. When the "Jazz History of the World" was
over, girls were putting their heads on men's shoulders in a puppyish,
convivial way, girls were swooning backward playfully into men's arms,
even into groups, knowing that some one would arrest their falls—but
no one swooned backward on Gatsby, and no French bob touched
Gatsby's shoulder, and no singing quartets were formed for Gatsby's
head for one link.

"I beg your pardon."

Gatsby's butler was suddenly standing beside us.

"Miss Baker?" he inquired. "I beg your pardon, but Mr. Gatsby would
like to speak to you alone."

"With me?" she exclaimed in surprise.

"Yes, madame."

She got up slowly, raising her eyebrows at me in astonishment, and
followed the butler toward the house. I noticed that she wore her

evening-dress, all her dresses, like sports clothes—there was a jauntiness about her movements as if she had first learned to walk upon golf courses on clean, crisp mornings.

I was alone and it was almost two. For some time confused and intriguing sounds had issued from a long, many-windowed room which overhung the terrace. Eluding Jordan's undergraduate, who was now engaged in an obstetrical conversation with two chorus girls, and who implored me to join him, I went inside.

The large room was full of people. One of the girls in yellow was playing the piano, and beside her stood a tall, red-haired young lady from a famous chorus, engaged in song. She had drunk a quantity of champagne, and during the course of her song she had decided, ineptly, that everything was very, very sad—she was not only singing, she was weeping too. Whenever there was a pause in the song she filled it with gasping, broken sobs, and then took up the lyric again in a quavering soprano. The tears coursed down her cheeks—not freely, however, for when they came into contact with her heavily beaded eyelashes they assumed an inky color, and pursued the rest of their way in slow black rivulets. A humorous suggestion was made that she sing the notes on her face, whereupon she threw up her hands, sank into a chair, and went off into a deep vinous sleep.

"She had a fight with a man who says he's her husband," explained a girl at my elbow.

I looked around. Most of the remaining women were now having fights with men said to be their husbands. Even Jordan's party, the quartet from East Egg, were rent asunder by dissension. One of the men was talking with curious intensity to a young actress, and his wife, after attempting to laugh at the situation in a dignified and indifferent way, broke down entirely and resorted to flank attacks—at intervals she appeared suddenly at his side like an angry diamond, and hissed: "You promised!" into his ear.

The reluctance to go home was not confined to wayward men. The hall was at present occupied by two deplorably sober men and their highly indignant wives. The wives were sympathizing with each other in slightly raised voices.

"Whenever he sees I'm having a good time he wants to go home."

"Never heard anything so selfish in my life."

"We're always the first ones to leave."

"So are we."

"Well, we're almost the last to-night," said one of the men sheepishly. "The orchestra left half an hour ago."

In spite of the wives' agreement that such malevolence was beyond credibility, the dispute ended in a short struggle, and both wives were lifted, kicking, into the night.

As I waited for my hat in the hall the door of the library opened and Jordan Baker and Gatsby came out together. He was saying some last word to her, but the eagerness in his manner tightened abruptly into formality as several people approached him to say good-by.

Jordan's party were calling impatiently to her from the porch, but she lingered for a moment to shake hands.

"I've just heard the most amazing thing," she whispered. "How long were we in there?"

"Why, about an hour."

"It was . . . simply amazing," she repeated abstractedly. "But I swore I wouldn't tell it and here I am tantalizing you." She yawned gracefully in my face. "Please come and see me. . . . Phone book. . . . Under the name of Mrs. Sigourney Howard. . . . My aunt. . . ." She was hurrying off as she talked—her brown hand waved a jaunty salute as she melted into her party at the door.

Rather ashamed that on my first appearance I had stayed so late, I joined the last of Gatsby's guests, who were clustered around him. I wanted to explain that I'd hunted for him early in the evening and to apologize for not having known him in the garden.

"Don't mention it," he enjoined me eagerly. "Don't give it another thought, old sport." The familiar expression held no more familiarity than the hand which reassuringly brushed my shoulder. "And don't forget we're going up in the hydroplane to-morrow morning, at nine o'clock."

Then the butler, behind his shoulder:

"Philadelphia wants you on the 'phone, sir."

"All right, in a minute. Tell them I'll be right there. . . . Good night."

"Good night."

"Good night." He smiled—and suddenly there seemed to be a pleasant significance in having been among the last to go, as if he had desired it all the time. "Good night, old sport. . . . Good night."

But as I walked down the steps I saw that the evening was not quite over. Fifty feet from the door a dozen headlights illuminated a bizarre and tumultuous scene. In the ditch beside the road, right side up, but violently shorn of one wheel, rested a new coupé which had left Gatsby's drive not two minutes before. The sharp jut of a wall accounted for the detachment of the wheel, which was now getting considerable attention from half a dozen curious chauffeurs. However, as they had left their cars blocking the road, a harsh, discordant din from those in

the rear had been audible for some time, and added to the already
violent confusion of the scene.

A man in a long duster had dismounted from the wreck and now
stood in the middle of the road, looking from the car to the tire and
from the tire to the observers in a pleasant, puzzled way.

"See!" he explained. "It went in the ditch."

The fact was infinitely astonishing to him, and I recognized first the
unusual quality of wonder, and then the man—it was the late patron
of Gatsby's library.

"How'd it happen?"

He shrugged his shoulders.

"I know nothing whatever about mechanics," he said decisively.

"But how did it happen? Did you run into the wall?"

"Don't ask me," said Owl Eyes, washing his hands of the whole
matter. "I know very little about driving—next to nothing. It happened,
and that's all I know."

"Well, if you're a poor driver you oughtn't to try driving at night."

"But I wasn't even trying," he explained indignantly, "I wasn't even
trying."

An awed hush fell upon the bystanders.

"Do you want to commit suicide?"

"You're lucky it was just a wheel! A bad driver and not even *trying!*"

"You don't understand," explained the criminal. "I wasn't driving.
There's another man in the car."

The shock that followed this declaration found voice in a sustained
"Ah-h-h!" as the door of the coupé swung slowly open. The crowd—it
was now a crowd—stepped back involuntarily, and when the door had
opened wide there was a ghostly pause. Then, very gradually, part by
part, a pale, dangling individual stepped out of the wreck, pawing ten-
tatively at the ground with a large uncertain dancing shoe.

Blinded by the glare of the headlights and confused by the incessant
groaning of the horns, the apparition stood swaying for a moment before
he perceived the man in the duster.

"Wha's matter?" he inquired calmly. "Did we run outa gas?"

"Look!"

Half a dozen fingers pointed at the amputated wheel—he stared at it
for a moment, and then looked upward as though he suspected that it
had dropped from the sky.

"It came off," some one explained.

He nodded.

"At first I din' notice we'd stopped."

A pause. Then, taking a long breath and straightening his shoulders,
he remarked in a determined voice:

"Wonder'ff tell me where there's a gas'line station?"

At least a dozen men, some of them a little better off than he was, explained to him that wheel and car were no longer joined by any physical bond.

"Back out," he suggested after a moment. "Put her in reverse."

"But the *wheel's* off!"

He hesitated.

"No harm in trying," he said.

The caterwauling horns had reached a crescendo and I turned away and cut across the lawn toward home. I glanced back once. A wafer of a moon was shining over Gatsby's house, making the night fine as before, and surviving the laughter and the sound of his still glowing garden. A sudden emptiness seemed to flow now from the windows and the great doors, endowing with complete isolation the figure of the host, who stood on the porch, his hand up in a formal gesture of farewell.

Minna's Homecoming

From FEBRUARY HILL

By Victoria Lincoln

February Hill *is the story of a family whose cycles of prosperity have depended on the adventures of its women. Grandma lives on the tinseled memories of other days of which her "cracked bronze slippers" are a relic. Minna keeps the family going by her sporadic liaisons, while her husband Vergil moves between alcoholic intervals and the study of dead languages. There are three daughters and a son. Dottie, the oldest and least equipped for the family profession, has found her way out of the atmosphere she loathes in deciding to marry René La Forrest, a respectable young man. Jenny, a pretty girl of fifteen, has been interrupted in a promising career of shoplifting by her admiration of a boy who gave her a ride in his car and shamed her by his superiority to her family's way of life. Joel is only barely aware of the stigma on his family and Amy is far too young to recognize it.*

In the chosen passage Minna has just returned from a week end with "a gentleman" bearing presents for all the family. For two of the group they come too late; Joel wishes desperately he had had his watch earlier, when a man he admired asked him the time, and Dottie is in a mood of "refusing to be bought." In this scene hidden, hostile forces within the family meet and the separate doubts of the growing minds cast first shadows on the family life.

IN THE late afternoon darkness Minna stamped up the woodpath through the trees. She had taken a taxi up the hill. She had presents for everyone. There was a light burning in the kitchen window. The rocking shadow of Grandma was silhouetted against the shade.

44

"My," she said to herself, mounting the step, turning the doorknob, "my, it's nice to be home."

She stepped into the kitchen.

"Hello," she said. "Hello! How you been?"

She stood in the doorway, radiant, flushed with the cold, the white fox around her neck, the white gloves pressed together, surveying her family.

"My," she said aloud, "my, it's nice to be home."

Grandma in the rocking chair, Amy on her knee, Joel behind the stove with a book, Jenny and Dottie laying the table, the bedroom door open and Vergil beyond it, his spare back hunched over the littered work table, all shoulder-blades and defiance—she saw them all before they could move, hugged them to her heart all together, her family and her home. Texas? To hell with Texas.

"I brought you all presents," she said. Her voice was warm and triumphant.

Amy sprang from Grandma's lap and ran to her.

"Ma! Ma! What'd you bring me? Ma. Mutt got in a fight with a dog and licked him. Oh, Ma!"

Black eyes looked at black eyes. They laughed, the same big, careless, affectionate laughter.

Grandma shouted over Amy's strong little voice.

"Have a nice party, Minna? My, what a lovely neckpiece. Puts me in mind of that boa you used to have a long time back."

Minna kissed her mother.

"Well, Ma," she said. "Well. You make out all right while I was gone?"

Grandma smiled, stretched out her little feet in the cracked bronze slippers and settled her auburn curls.

"Fine. Sure, dearie, we made out fine."

"That's right," said Minna, nodding. But she was a little disappointed. "Dottie? Jenny?"

Jenny ran up to her.

"Ma, you look so nice."

Dottie stood on the opposite side of the table, her heavy hands hanging down at her sides.

"Hello, Ma."

Joel came up to her diffidently.

"Well, Joel, what you been up to?"

My, he looked like Vergil. She kissed him, squeezed him hard. Funny little feller.

"Gil, here I am, Gil. Home and no bones broken."

She went into the bedroom.

"Leave Ma be a minute, Amy darling."

On an impulse she closed the door before she crossed to him.

"Well, then, Gil."

She put her arm around him. His shoulder-blades stuck out like wooden fans under the shiny gray cloth. She kissed his flaccid cheek.

"Glad to see me?"

He held up one lean hand, imploring a moment's silence, underlined two words on the page before him, and wrote, with meticulous care, several Greek letters in the margin of the page, closed his book and sighed. She waited for him. It was part of a familiar game.

"So you've come home, Minna."

"Sure, Gil. Same as always. How you been?"

The bright, hot Texas sun. Florida water. He certainly knew how to make a party go.

"You look sort of peaked, Gil. Been hitting it up?"

He looked away.

"I've had a slight cold."

She smiled broadly.

"Sure. Ma take care of you all right?"

She hoped that he would complain that the children had bothered him, that Grandma had neglected him. He'd certainly been sick enough yesterday, by the looks. She wanted very badly to feel that they all needed her and Vergil most of all.

"Missed me some, Gil?"

He regarded the table leg intensely. He ran his tongue over his dry lips.

"I've been very busy," he replied.

She unclasped the fur, drew off the gloves, laid them on the shelf behind the curtain. He had not commented on them. Neither had he commented upon the card case and the feather boa, long ago.

She stood before the long mirror and looked at herself.

"Well, anyway," she said, "I'm home."

Her voice sounded older, rather tired.

"Guess I'll go out and see what the girls got for supper," she said slowly.

She opened the door again. The kitchen was warmer than the bedroom.

"Set down, Minna," said Grandma. "Supper ain't ready yet. Set down and have a cup a coffee."

She sat down heavily on a straight-backed kitchen chair. She looked at them one by one. Amy came to her, climbed upon her lap, talking high and shrill. Grandma rocked, her green earrings swung, and the rose nodded on her shoulder as she began an intermittent commentary.

Jenny brought the coffee and she drank it, leaning sidewise to avoid Amy's darting little head. She did not hear their voices or her own answers. She hardly knew when Amy took the empty cup from her hand and sank to the floor beside her to salvage the residue of coffee-soaked sugar with a greedy finger and a lapping tongue. She sat and looked at them.

"Feeling sort of tired, Minna?"

"Yes. Sort of."

Dottie was slamming covers on the stove, thumping the sugar bowl down on the table. Her mask was as meek as milk, but her pale eyes met Minna's with unwonted light. Dottie was thinking, Mrs. René La Forrest. That'll learn 'em. Work myself to death all day and come home and slave all night, and her coming in with beautiful new furs and all. Wicked old woman. They'll see.

Minna watched the pale, malevolent eyes. Poor Dottie, she thought, the only homely one in the family. Always been yeller like that since she was a baby.

She turned her face toward Jenny, her dearest. My, she was pretty. That lovely red hair. And her eyes. Bright blue when she was a baby and then they began to change, till they got to that funny smoky hazel that wasn't blue or brown—that lovely midway color babies' eyes get. And every morning she'd think, bet you this morning they'll be brown; but they never were. They always stayed like that. So thin, too, sort of wild looking. She didn't need nobody, really. Didn't need a ma like some girls, off by herself all day the way she was.

"You been out in the country," she said to Jenny. "Your nose is all windburned. And you got some more freckles. You go with her, Joel?"

Joel put down his book and stood up.

"No," he said. "She went out before we was awake."

He looked at Jenny. Minna knew that look. She had known it before Joel was born. She wished that she had not asked the question.

"You are a bunch, I must say," she exclaimed brightly. "You ain't even asked to see your presents."

"Presents!" screamed Amy. "Presents! Presents!"

She dragged the suitcase to her mother's feet.

"Open it, Ma. Presents! I was fit to bust a gut waiting for you."

"Amy, you talk so tough. Amy, why didn't you hurry me up?"

The black eyes regarded her with canine softness under the black mop of hair. The snub nose screwed itself into wrinkles, the square mouth smiled shyly.

"I dunno," said Amy.

Minna kissed her.

Didn't want me to think it was just presents she cared about. Wanted me to know she was glad her Ma was home, same as I used to be when I was a kid.

Minna was grateful to Amy. She kissed her once more.

"Ain't you the funny little kid," she said. She opened the suitcase. "You ain't got nothing in here, Amy," she said, teasing her.

"Where is it? Ma, where is it?"

"Look outside the door."

There was a big bandbox on the snowy porch. Amy dragged it in.

"Yours is the best, Amy."

"Then," said Amy, "I'm going to wait and see the others first."

She sat down on the floor. Jenny and Joel came closer. Grandma got out of her chair. Her mad old eyes were sparkling and she was flushed under the spots of rouge. Grandma loved presents.

She hugged them to her soiled green waist: a five-pound box of chocolates, copies of *True Romances*, *True Story*, *Screen World*, and a tall bottle of Black Narcissus perfume. Grandma went back to her chair and tore open the box of candy.

"Ma, you'll spoil your supper."

"We may all be dead before supper. Have some, everybody? Amy, here's a little pink candy posy for you."

Minna sat down on the floor. She gave a little gasp at the last inch.

"Jees, my corsets is getting tight. Old and fat."

She fumbled through her clothes, peach, orchid, nile green. Got a stain on the flowered chiffon. And they always said gin didn't spot.

"Here, Joel, here's yours."

It was a watch on a leather strap with a square nickel case, plain and nice. She watched him nervously.

"Do you like it, Joel?"

He put it on.

"Is the strap too long?"

"No. It's just right in the last hole."

He thought, If I'd of had it then, I could of told him the time. I'd of said—I'd of said. . . .

The exact words escaped him, but he could feel the conversation— just right, light, keen, intimate. He stood in the tangle of tall weeds at the snowy roadside and the skater balanced before him on the dark ice, laughing, admiring.

"Like it, Joel?"

He started and looked annoyed. He blinked around the warm, bright kitchen.

"Thank you, Ma."

"Anything else you rather have?"

"No. No, only the next thing I want some skates."

"Skates! Well, whatever—"

She checked herself. Something in his pointed face and his drooping eyes excluded her. She turned to the girls.

"You two get them just alike," she said. "Stockings."

She reached up and laid the boxes on the table. She pulled a long box out from the bottom and laid it on the top. A nice, dark purple necktie. She looked at it hesitantly.

"I'll wear 'em tomorrow," thought Jenny. "Maybe she'll buy me some spike heel slippers. You almost can't swipe a shoe to fit."

She threw her arms about her mother.

"Oh, Ma, you're so sweet."

Light beige. She might swipe a scarf to go with them, tan with green on it. Only—only suppose he was to find out? Suppose Berkley was to find out how she swiped things? Suppose he was to find out all about her, about the stockings, even, and how her Ma got them.

She turned to Dottie.

"You ain't opened yours yet."

"You can keep them," said Dottie.

Everyone looked at her.

"Why, Dottie," said Minna, helplessly. "Why, Dottie, don't you like them?"

"I said, 'You can keep them,'" repeated Dottie. There were reddish purple patches on her face and neck, and her voice was hoarse. No one had noticed her for some time, and in that interval she had been working herself into the first really satisfactory rage of her life. She could do it now. She had some place to go when she got out.

"Do you think I'd touch your dirty things?" she went on, warming to the subject. "Do you think we don't know where they come from?"

Amy glared at her.

"I hate you, Dot," said Amy. "I'd bite you, too, only you'd taste too rotten."

Dottie ignored her.

"But I won't have to stand it any more," said Dottie. "I'm going to marry a good clean boy who knows a good girl when he sees one. He knows all about you too. He's a Catholic, and I'm going to turn."

She paused to savor the effect of this last bombshell. It was her big moment.

"Oh, Dottie," said Minna, inanely, "you'd never."

"Wouldn't I just," said Dottie. "You'll see. And here's what I think of your dirty presents."

She poked a lid from the stove and thrust the box down upon the hot coals. A smell of acrid smoke filled the kitchen.

Minna sat still on the floor, staring with big, stupefied eyes.

"And if you want to know what you are," Dottie pursued, her voice
shaking but a little lowered, for she had begun to be frightened at her
own temerity, "you're just a—"

"Wouldn't say that if I was you, Dottie," remarked Grandma. She
took another piece of candy. "I'm sure you're too nice to go saying dirty
words."

Dottie closed her mouth, slowly. She looked bewildered. Somehow
she had been cheated of her sensation. She dropped the lid lifter with
a clatter and walked out of the room.

"Poor old Dottie," said Minna.

Grandma smiled.

"I never set eye on the old lady," she observed, "but I'd swear to God
that Dottie's the living spit of her Grandma Harris."

She raised a deliberate little hand and settled her curls.

"About that Canuck," said Joel, curiously. "Do you suppose he's all
Dottie cracks him up to be?"

Grandma gave a push to the rockers.

"Cows far away have long horns," she observed cryptically.

"She might bring him home for us to see, if he's so special," said Joel.

"Oh, I don't know," answered Minna, gently.

She had put the long box at the bottom of the suitcase again. She
glanced toward the bedroom door. It was closed. Maybe it would be
better to wait awhile before she gave it to him. She could wait until
she'd been downtown some day next week. Lookit, Gil, she'd say, I got
you a necktie at Steigers'. They was having a sale.

"Now," said Amy, "I'll look at my present."

"My friend, Mr. Jennings, picked it out himself," Minna said. "It was
the most expensive present in the store, Amy. I told him I had a little
girl looked like me. He wanted to hear all about you."

She watched the child eagerly, saw her break the strings and take it
out. It was a bewildering object. It looked like a head of cabbage. When
you wound it up the leaves unfolded one by one and a white rabbit with
pink electric lights for eyes came out, and a music box played "Too
Much Mustard." Then, pop! The lights went out, and it was a head of
cabbage again.

Everyone was enchanted. Jenny clapped her thin hands, and Joel
crouched upon his haunches, chuckling.

"My," said Grandma, "that Mr. Jennings must be a lovely friend."

"Jees," said Amy, "I never. Jees."

None of them gave Dottie a second thought.

Wang Lung's Marriage Day

From THE GOOD EARTH

By Pearl Buck

This passage was chosen not for its unquestionable fidelity to the rural scene in China but because it reveals the elemental lure of the land for all farmers everywhere. Wang Lung's primitive motives in his youth, the later impact of riches upon a heart dedicated to the soil, his struggles with pride and shame, the appeal of the city to the broadened consciousness of his children, the play of sex and guile in the growing family breed emotions which are universal and can never be dominated by an alien scene.

The selected passage is from the first chapter of the novel where the power and goodness of the earth are felt as in, perhaps, no other novel of the era.

IT WAS Wang Lung's marriage day. At first, opening his eyes in the blackness of the curtains about his bed, he could not think why the dawn seemed different from any other. The house was still except for the faint, gasping cough of his old father, whose room was opposite to his own across the middle room. Every morning the old man's cough was the first sound to be heard. Wang Lung usually lay listening to it and moved only when he heard it approaching nearer and when he heard the door of his father's room squeak upon its wooden hinges.

But this morning he did not wait. He sprang up and pushed aside the curtains of his bed. It was a dark, ruddy dawn, and through a small square hole of a window, where the tattered paper fluttered, a glimpse of bronze sky gleamed. He went to the hole and tore the paper away.

"It is spring and I do not need this," he muttered.

51

He was ashamed to say aloud that he wished the house to look neat on this day. The hole was barely large enough to admit his hand and he thrust it out to feel of the air. A small soft wind blew gently from the east, a wind mild and murmurous and full of rain. It was a good omen. The fields needed rain for fruition. There would be no rain this day, but within a few days, if this wind continued, there would be water. It was good. Yesterday he had said to his father that if this brazen, glittering sunshine continued, the wheat could not fill in the ear. Now it was as if Heaven had chosen this day to wish him well. Earth would bear fruit.

He hurried out into the middle room, drawing on his blue outer trousers as he went, and knotting about the fullness at his waist his girdle of blue cotton cloth. He left his upper body bare until he had heated water to bathe himself. He went into the shed which was the kitchen, leaning against the house, and out of its dusk an ox twisted its head from behind the corner next the door and lowed at him deeply. The kitchen was made of earthen bricks as the house was, great squares of earth dug from their own fields, and thatched with straw from their own wheat. Out of their own earth had his grandfather in his youth fashioned also the oven, baked and black with many years of meal preparing. On top of this earthen structure stood a deep, round, iron cauldron.

This cauldron he filled partly full of water, dipping it with a half gourd from an earthen jar that stood near, but he dipped cautiously, for water was precious. Then, after a hesitation, he suddenly lifted the jar and emptied all the water into the cauldron. This day he would bathe his whole body. Not since he was a child upon his mother's knee had anyone looked upon his body. Today one would, and he would have it clean.

He went around the oven to the rear, and selecting a handful of the dry grass and stalks standing in the corner of the kitchen, he arranged it delicately in the mouth of the oven, making the most of every leaf. Then from an old flint and iron he caught a flame and thrust it into the straw and there was a blaze.

This was the last morning he would have to light the fire. He had lit it every morning since his mother died six years before. He had lit the fire, boiled water, and poured the water into a bowl and taken it into the room where his father sat upon his bed, coughing and fumbling for his shoes upon the floor. Every morning for these six years the old man had waited for his son to bring in hot water to ease him of his morning coughing. Now father and son could rest. There was a woman coming to the house. Never again would Wang Lung have to rise summer and winter at dawn to light the fire. He could lie in his bed and wait, and he also would have a bowl of water brought to him, and if the earth were fruitful there would be tea leaves in the water. Once in some years it was so.

And if the woman wearied, there would be her children to light the fire, the many children she would bear to Wang Lung. Wang Lung stopped, struck by the thought of children running in and out of their three rooms. Three rooms had always seemed much to them, a house half empty since his mother died. They were always having to resist relatives who were more crowded—his uncle, with his endless brood of children, coaxing,

"Now, how can two lone men need so much room? Cannot father and son sleep together? The warmth of the young one's body will comfort the old one's cough."

But the father always replied, "I am saving my bed for my grandson. He will warm my bones in my age."

Now the grandsons were coming, grandsons upon grandsons! They would have to put beds along the walls and in the middle room. The house would be full of beds. The blaze in the oven died down while Wang Lung thought of all the beds there would be in the half empty house, and the water began to chill in the cauldron. The shadowy figure of the old man appeared in the doorway, holding his unbuttoned garments about him. He was coughing and spitting and he gasped,

"How is it that there is not water yet to heat my lungs?"

Wang Lung stared and recalled himself and was ashamed.

"This fuel is damp," he muttered from behind the stove. "The damp wind—"

The old man continued to cough perseveringly and would not cease until the water boiled. Wang Lung dipped some into a bowl, and then, after a moment, he opened a glazed jar that stood upon a ledge of the stove and took from it a dozen or so of the curled dried leaves and sprinkled them upon the surface of the water. The old man's eyes opened greedily and immediately he began to complain.

"Why are you wasteful? Tea is like eating silver."

"It is the day," replied Wang Lung with a short laugh. "Eat and be comforted."

The old man grasped the bowl in his shriveled, knotty fingers, muttering, uttering little grunts. He watched the leaves uncurl and spread upon the surface of the water, unable to bear drinking the precious stuff.

"It will be cold," said Wang Lung.

"True—true—" said the old man in alarm, and he began to take great gulps of the hot tea. He passed into an animal satisfaction, like a child fixed upon its feeding. But he was not too forgetful to see Wang Lung dipping the water recklessly from the cauldron into a deep wooden tub. He lifted his head and stared at his son.

"Now there is water enough to bring a crop to fruit," he said suddenly.

Wang Lung continued to dip the water to the last drop. He did not answer.

"Now then!" cried his father loudly.

"I have not washed my body all at once since the New Year," said Wang Lung in a low voice.

He was ashamed to say to his father that he wished his body to be clean for a woman to see. He hurried out, carrying the tub to his own room. The door was hung loosely upon a warped wooden frame and it did not shut closely, and the old man tottered into the middle room and put his mouth to the opening and bawled,

"It will be ill if we start the woman like this—tea in the morning water and all this washing!"

"It is only one day," shouted Wang Lung. And then he added, "I will throw the water on the earth when I am finished and it is not all waste."

The old man was silent at this, and Wang Lung unfastened his girdle and stepped out of his clothing. In the light that streamed in a square block from the hole he wrung a small towel from the steaming water and he scrubbed his dark slender body vigorously. Warm though he had thought the air, when his flesh was wet he was cold, and he moved quickly, passing the towel in and out of the water until from his whole body there went up a delicate cloud of steam. Then he went to a box that had been his mother's and drew from it a fresh suit of blue cotton cloth. He might be a little cold this day without the wadding of the winter garments, but he suddenly could not bear to put them on against his clean flesh. The covering of them was torn and filthy and the wadding stuck out of the holes, grey and sodden. He did not want this woman to see him for the first time with the wadding sticking out of his clothes. Later she would have to wash and mend, but not the first day. He drew over the blue cotton coat and trousers a long robe made of the same material—his one long robe, which he wore on feast days only, ten days or so in the year, all told. Then with swift fingers he unplaited the long braid of hair that hung down his back, and taking a wooden comb from the drawer of the small, unsteady table, he began to comb out his hair.

His father drew near again and put his mouth to the crack of the door. "Am I to have nothing to eat this day?" he complained. "At my age the bones are water in the morning until food is given them."

"I am coming," said Wang Lung, braiding his hair quickly and smoothly and weaving into the strands a tasseled, black silk cord.

Then after a moment he removed his long gown and wound his braid about his head and went out, carrying the tub of water. He had quite forgotten the breakfast. He would stir a little water into corn meal and give it to his father. For himself he could not eat. He staggered with the tub to the threshold and poured the water upon the earth nearest the door, and as he did so he remembered he had used all the water in the cauldron for his bathing and he would have to start the fire again. A wave of anger passed over him at his father.

"That old head thinks of nothing except his eating and his drinking," he muttered into the mouth of the oven; but aloud he said nothing. It was the last morning he would have to prepare food for the old man. He put a very little water into the cauldron, drawing it in a bucket from the well near the door, and it boiled quickly and he stirred meal together and took it to the old man.

"We will have rice this night, my father," he said. "Meanwhile, here is corn."

"There is only a little rice left in the basket," said the old man, seating himself at the table in the middle room and stirring with his chopsticks the thick yellow gruel.

"We will eat a little less then at the spring festival," said Wang Lung. But the old man did not hear. He was supping loudly at his bowl.

Wang Lung went into his own room then, and drew about him again the long blue robe and let down the braid of his hair. He passed his hand over his shaven brow and over his cheeks. Perhaps he had better be newly shaven? It was scarcely sunrise yet. He could pass through the Street of the Barbers and be shaved before he went to the house where the woman waited for him. If he had the money he would do it.

He took from his girdle a small greasy pouch of grey cloth and counted the money in it. There were six silver dollars and a double handful of copper coins. He had not yet told his father he had asked friends to sup that night. He had asked his male cousin, the young son of his uncle, and his uncle for his father's sake, and three neighboring farmers who lived in the village with him. He had planned to bring back from the town that morning pork, a small pond fish, and a handful of chestnuts. He might even buy a few of the bamboo sprouts from the south and a little beef to stew with the cabbage he had raised in his own garden. But this only if there were any money left after the bean oil and the soybean sauce had been bought. If he shaved his head he could not, perhaps, buy the beef. Well, he would shave his head, he decided suddenly.

He left the old man without speech and went out into the early morning. In spite of the dark red dawn the sun was mounting the horizon clouds and sparkled upon the dew on the rising wheat and barley. The farmer in Wang Lung was diverted for an instant and he stooped to examine the budding heads. They were empty as yet and waiting for the rain. He smelled the air and looked anxiously at the sky. Rain was there, dark in the clouds, heavy upon the wind. He would buy a stick of incense and place it in the little temple to the Earth God. On a day like this he would do it.

He wound his way in among the fields upon the narrow path. In the near distance the grey city wall arose. Within that gate in the wall through which he would pass stood the great house where the woman had been a slave girl since her childhood, the House of Hwang. There were those who said, "It is better to live alone than to marry a woman who has been slave in a great house." But when he had said to his father, "Am I never to have a woman?" his father replied, "With weddings costing as they do in these evil days and every woman wanting gold rings and silk clothes before she will take a man, there remain only slaves to be had for the poor."

His father had stirred himself, then, and gone to the House of Hwang and asked if there were a slave to spare.

"Not a slave too young, and above all, not a pretty one," he had said.

Wang Lung had suffered that she must not be pretty. It would be something to have a pretty wife that other men would congratulate him upon having. His father, seeing his mutinous face, had cried out at him,

"And what will we do with a pretty woman? We must have a woman who will tend the house and bear children as she works in the fields, and will a pretty woman do these things? She will be forever thinking about clothes to go with her face! No, not a pretty woman in our house. We are farmers. Moreover, who has heard of a pretty slave who was virgin in a wealthy house? All the young lords have had their fill of her. It is better to be first with an ugly woman than the hundredth with a beauty. Do you imagine a pretty woman will think your farmer's hands as pleasing as the soft hands of a rich man's son, and your sun-black face as beautiful as the golden skin of the others who have had her for their pleasure?"

Wang Lung knew his father spoke well. Nevertheless, he had to struggle with his flesh before he could answer. And then he said violently,

"At least, I will not have a woman who is pock-marked, or who has a split upper lip."

"We will have to see what is to be had," his father replied.

Well, the woman was not pock-marked nor had she a split upper lip. This much he knew, but nothing more. He and his father had bought two silver rings, washed with gold, and silver earrings, and these his father had taken to the woman's owner in acknowledgment of betrothal. Beyond this, he knew nothing of the woman who was to be his, except that on this day he could go and get her.

He walked into the cool darkness of the city gate. Water carriers, just outside, their barrows laden with great tubs of water, passed to and fro all day, the water splashing out of the tubs upon the stones. It was always wet and cool in the tunnel of the gate under the thick wall of earth and brick; cool even upon a summer's day, so that the melon vendors spread their fruits upon the stones, melons split open to drink in the moist coolness. There were none yet, for the season was too early, but baskets of small hard green peaches stood along the walls, and the vendors cried out,

"The first peaches of spring—the first peaches! Buy, eat, purge your bowels of the poisons of winter!"

Wang Lung said to himself,

"If she likes them, I will buy her a handful when we return." He could not realize that when he walked back through the gate there would be a woman walking behind him.

He turned to the right within the gate and after a moment was in the Street of Barbers. There were few before him so early, only some farmers who had carried their produce into the town the night before in order that they might sell their vegetables at the dawn markets and return for the day's work in the fields. They had slept shivering and crouching over their baskets, the baskets now empty at their feet. Wang Lung avoided them lest some recognize him, for he wanted none of their joking on this day. All down the street in a long line the barbers stood behind their small stalls, and Wang Lung went to the furthest one and sat down upon the stool and motioned to the barber who stood chattering to his neighbor. The barber came at once and began quickly to pour hot water, from a kettle on his pot of charcoal, into his brass basin.

"Shave everything?" he said in a professional tone.

"My head and my face," replied Wang Lung.

"Ears and nostrils cleaned?" asked the barber.

"How much will that cost extra?" asked Wang Lung cautiously.

"Four pence," said the barber, beginning to pass a black cloth in and out of the hot water.

"I will give you two," said Wang Lung.

"Then I will clean one ear and one nostril," rejoined the barber promptly. "On which side of the face do you wish it done?" He grimaced at the next barber as he spoke and the other burst into a guffaw. Wang Lung perceived that he had fallen into the hands of a joker, and feeling inferior in some unaccountable way, as he always did, to these town dwellers, even though they were only barbers and the lowest of persons, he said quickly,

"As you will—as you will—"

Then he submitted himself to the barber's soaping and rubbing and shaving, and being after all a generous fellow enough, the barber gave him without extra charge a series of skilful poundings upon his shoulders and back to loosen his muscles. He commented upon Wang Lung as he shaved his upper forehead,

"This would not be a bad-looking farmer if he would cut off his hair. The new fashion is to take off the braid."

His razor hovered so near the circle of hair upon Wang Lung's crown that Wang Lung cried out,

"I cannot cut it off without asking my father!" And the barber laughed and skirted the round spot of hair.

When it was finished and the money counted into the barber's wrinkled, water-soaked hand, Wang Lung had a moment of horror. So much money! But walking down the street again with the wind fresh upon his shaven skin, he said to himself,

"It is only once."

He went to the market, then, and bought two pounds of pork and watched the butcher as he wrapped it in a dried lotus leaf, and then, hesitating, he bought also six ounces of beef. When all had been bought, even to fresh squares of beancurd, shivering in a jelly upon its leaf, he went to a candlemaker's shop and there he bought a pair of incense sticks. Then he turned his steps with great shyness toward the House of Hwang.

Once at the gate of the house he was seized with terror. How had he come alone? He should have asked his father—his uncle—even his nearest neighbor, Ching—anyone to come with him. He had never been in a great house before. How could he go in with his wedding feast on his arm, and say, "I have come for a woman"?

He stood at the gate for a long time, looking at it. It was closed fast, two great wooden gates, painted black and bound and studded with iron, closed upon each other. Two lions made of stone stood on guard, one at either side. There was no one else. He turned away. It was impossible.

He felt suddenly faint. He would go first and buy a little food. He had eaten nothing—had forgotten food. He went into a small street restaurant, and putting two pence upon the table, he sat down. A dirty waiting boy with a shiny black apron came near and he called out to him, "Two bowls of noodles!" And when they were come, he ate them down greedily, pushing them into his mouth with his bamboo chopsticks, while the boy stood and spun the coppers between his black thumb and forefinger.

"Will you have more?" asked the boy indifferently.

Wang Lung shook his head. He sat up and looked about. There was no one he knew in the small, dark, crowded room full of tables. Only a few men sat eating or drinking tea. It was a place for poor men, and among them he looked neat and clean and almost well-to-do, so that a beggar, passing, whined at him,

"Have a good heart, teacher, and give me a small cash—I starve!"

Wang Lung had never had a beggar ask of him before, nor had any ever called him teacher. He was pleased and he threw into the beggar's bowl two small cash, which are one fifth of a penny, and the beggar pulled back with swiftness his black claw of a hand, and grasping the cash, fumbled them within his rags.

Wang Lung sat and the sun climbed upwards. The waiting boy lounged about impatiently. "If you are buying nothing more," he said at last with much impudence, "you will have to pay rent for the stool."

Wang Lung was incensed at such impudence and he would have risen except that when he thought of going into the great House of Hwang and of asking there for a woman, sweat broke out over his whole body as though he were working in a field.

"Bring me tea," he said weakly to the boy. Before he could turn it was there and the small boy demanded sharply,

"Where is the penny?"

And Wang Lung, to his horror, found there was nothing to do but to produce from his girdle yet another penny.

"It is robbery," he muttered, unwilling. Then he saw entering the shop his neighbor whom he had invited to the feast, and he put the penny hastily upon the table and drank the tea at a gulp and went out quickly by the side door and was once more upon the street.

"It is to be done," he said to himself desperately, and slowly he turned his way to the great gates.

This time, since it was after high noon, the gates were ajar and the keeper of the gate idled upon the threshold, picking his teeth with a bamboo sliver after his meal. He was a tall fellow with a large mole upon his left cheek, and from the mole hung three long black hairs which had never been cut. When Wang Lung appeared he shouted roughly, thinking from the basket that he had come to sell something.

"Now then, what?"

With great difficulty Wang Lung replied,

"I am Wang Lung, the farmer."

"Well, and Wang Lung, the farmer, what?" retorted the gateman, who was polite to none except the rich friends of his master and mistress.

"I am come—I am come—" faltered Wang Lung.

"That I see," said the gateman with elaborate patience, twisting the long hairs of his mole.

"There is a woman," said Wang Lung, his voice sinking, helplessly, to a whisper. In the sunshine his face was wet.

The gateman gave a great laugh.

"So you are he!" he roared. "I was told to expect a bridegroom today. But I did not recognize you with a basket on your arm."

"It is only a few meats," said Wang Lung apologetically, waiting for the gateman to lead him within. But the gateman did not move. At last Wang Lung said with anxiety,

"Shall I go alone?"

The gateman affected a start of horror. "The Old Lord would kill you!".

Then seeing that Wang Lung was too innocent he said, "A little silver is a good key."

Wang Lung saw at last that the man wanted money of him.

"I am a poor man," he said pleadingly.

"Let me see what you have in your girdle," said the gateman.

And he grinned when Wang Lung in his simplicity actually put his basket upon the stones and lifting his robe took out the small bag from his girdle and shook into his left hand what money was left after his purchases. There was one silver piece and fourteen copper pence.

"I will take the silver," said the gateman coolly, and before Wang Lung could protest the man had the silver in his sleeve and was striding through the gate, bawling loudly,

"The bridegroom, the bridegroom!"

Wang Lung, in spite of anger at what had just happened and horror at this loud announcing of his coming, could do nothing but follow, and this he did, picking up his basket and looking neither to the right nor left.

Afterwards, although it was the first time he had ever been in a great family's house, he could remember nothing. With his face burning and his head bowed, he walked through court after court, hearing that voice roaring ahead of him, hearing tinkles of laughter on every side. Then suddenly when it seemed to him he had gone through a hundred courts, the gateman fell silent and pushed him into a small waiting room. There he stood alone while the gateman went into some inner place, returning in a moment to say,

"The Old Mistress says you are to appear before her."

Wang Lung started forward, but the gateman stopped him, crying in disgust,

"You cannot appear before a great lady with a basket on your arm—a basket of pork and beancurd! How will you bow?"

"True—true—" said Wang Lung in agitation. But he did not dare to put the basket down because he was afraid something might be stolen from it. It did not occur to him that all the world might not desire such

delicacies as two pounds of pork and six ounces of beef and a small pond fish. The gateman saw his fear and cried out in great contempt,

"In a house like this we feed these meats to the dogs!" and seizing the basket he thrust it behind the door and pushed Wang Lung ahead of him.

Down a long narrow veranda they went, the roofs supported by delicate carven posts, and into a hall the like of which Wang Lung had never seen. A score of houses such as his whole house could have been put into it and have disappeared, so wide were the spaces, so high the roofs. Lifting his head in wonder to see the great carven and painted beams above him he stumbled upon the high threshold of the door and would have fallen except that the gateman caught his arm and cried out,

"Now will you be so polite as to fall on your face like this before the Old Mistress?"

And collecting himself in great shame Wang Lung looked ahead of him, and upon a dais in the center of the room he saw a very old lady, her small fine body clothed in lustrous, pearly grey satin, and upon the low bench beside her a pipe of opium stood, burning over its little lamp. She looked at him out of small, sharp, black eyes, as sunken and sharp as a monkey's eyes in her thin and wrinkled face. The skin of her hand that held the pipe's end was stretched over her little bones as smooth and as yellow as the gilt upon an idol. Wang Lung fell to his knees and knocked his head on the tiled floor.

"Raise him," said the old lady gravely to the gateman, "these obeisances are not necessary. Has he come for the woman?"

"Yes, Ancient One," replied the gateman.

"Why does he not speak for himself?" asked the old lady.

"Because he is a fool, Ancient One," said the gateman, twirling the hairs of his mole.

This roused Wang Lung and he looked with indignation at the gateman.

"I am only a coarse person, Great and Ancient Lady," he said. "I do not know what words to use in such a presence."

The old lady looked at him carefully and with perfect gravity and made as though she would have spoken, except that her hand closed upon the pipe which a slave had been tending for her and at once she seemed to forget him. She bent and sucked greedily at the pipe for a moment and the sharpness passed from her eyes and a film of forgetfulness came over them. Wang Lung remained standing before her until in passing her eyes caught his figure.

"What is this man doing here?" she asked with sudden anger. It was as though she had forgotten everything. The gateman's face was immovable. He said nothing.

"I am waiting for the woman, Great Lady," said Wang Lung in much astonishment.

"The woman? What woman? . . ." the old lady began, but the slave girl at her side stooped and whispered and the lady recovered herself. "Ah, yes, I forgot for the moment—a small affair—you have come for the slave called O-lan. I remember we promised her to some farmer in marriage. You are that farmer?"

"I am he," replied Wang Lung.

"Call O-lan quickly," said the old lady to her slave. It was as though she was suddenly impatient to be done with all this and to be left alone in the stillness of the great room with her opium pipe.

And in an instant the slave appeared leading by the hand a square, rather tall figure, clothed in clean blue cotton coat and trousers. Wang Lung glanced once and then away, his heart beating. This was his woman.

"Come here, slave," said the old lady carelessly. "This man has come for you."

The woman went before the lady and stood with bowed head and hands clasped.

"Are you ready?" asked the lady.

The woman answered slowly as an echo, "Ready."

Wang Lung, hearing her voice for the first time, looked at her back as she stood before him. It was a good enough voice, not loud, not soft, plain, and not ill-tempered. The woman's hair was neat and smooth and her coat clean. He saw with an instant's disappointment that her feet were not bound. But this he could not dwell upon, for the old lady was saying to the gateman,

"Carry her box out to the gate and let them begone." And then she called Wang Lung and said, "Stand beside her while I speak." And when Wang had come forward she said to him, "This woman came into our house when she was a child of ten and here she has lived until now, when she is twenty years old. I bought her in a year of famine when her parents came south because they had nothing to eat. They were from the north in Shantung and there they returned, and I know nothing further of them. You see she has the strong body and the square cheeks of her kind. She will work well for you in the field and drawing water and all else that you wish. She is not beautiful but that you do not need. Only men of leisure have the need for beautiful women to divert them. Neither is she clever. But she does well what she is told to do and she has a good temper. So far as I know she is a virgin. She has not beauty enough to tempt my sons and grandsons even if she had not been in the kitchen. If there has been anything it has been only a serving man. But with the innumerable and pretty slaves running freely about the courts, I doubt if there has been anyone. Take her and use her well. She is a good slave, although somewhat slow and stupid, and had I not wished to acquire merit at the temple for my future existence by bringing more life into the world I should have kept her, for she is good enough for the kitchen. But I marry my slaves off if any will have them and the lords do not want them."

And to the woman she said,

"Obey him and bear him sons and yet more sons. Bring the first child to me to see."

"Yes, Ancient Mistress," said the woman submissively.

They stood hesitating, and Wang Lung was greatly embarrassed, not knowing whether he should speak or what.

"Well, go, will you!" said the old lady in irritation, and Wang Lung, bowing hastily, turned and went out, the woman after him, and after her the gateman, carrying on his shoulder the box. This box he dropped down in the room where Wang Lung returned to find his basket and would carry it no further, and indeed he disappeared without another word.

Then Wang Lung turned to the woman and looked at her for the first time. She had a square, honest face, a short, broad nose with large black nostrils, and her mouth was wide as a gash in her face. Her eyes were small and of a dull black in color, and were filled with some sadness that was not clearly expressed. It was a face that seemed habitually silent and unspeaking, as though it could not speak if it would. She bore patiently Wang Lung's look, without embarrassment or response, simply waiting until he had seen her. He saw that it was true there was not beauty of any kind in her face—a brown, common, patient face. But there were no pock-marks on her dark skin, nor was her lip split. In her ears he saw his rings hanging, the gold-washed rings he had bought, and on her hands were the rings he had given her. He turned away with secret exultation. Well, he had his woman!

"Here is this box and this basket," he said gruffly.

Without a word she bent over and picking up one end of the box she placed it upon her shoulder and, staggering under its weight, tried to rise. He watched her at this and suddenly he said,

"I will take the box. Here is the basket."

And he shifted the box to his own back, regardless of the best robe he wore, and she, still speechless, took the handle of the basket. He thought of the hundred courts he had come through and of his figure, absurd under its burden.

"If there were a side gate—" he muttered, and she nodded after a little thought, as though she did not understand too quickly what he said. Then she led the way through a small unused court that was grown up with weeds, its pool choked, and there under a bent pine tree was an old round gate that she pulled loose from its bar, and they went through and into the street.

Once or twice he looked back at her. She plodded along steadily on her big feet as though she had walked there all her life, her wide face expressionless. In the gate of the wall he stopped uncertainly and fumbled in his girdle with one hand for the pennies he had left, holding the box steady on his shoulder with the other hand. He took out two pence and with these he bought six small green peaches.

"Take these and eat them for yourself," he said gruffly.

She clutched them greedily as a child might and held them in her hand without speech. When next he looked at her as they walked along the margin of the wheat fields she was nibbling one cautiously, but when she saw him looking at her she covered it again with her hand and kept her jaws motionless.

And thus they went until they reached the western field where stood the temple to the earth. This temple was a small structure, not higher in all than a man's shoulder and made of grey bricks and roofed with tile. Wang Lung's grandfather, who had farmed the very fields upon which Wang Lung now spent his life, had built it, hauling the bricks from the town upon his wheelbarrow. The walls were covered with plaster on the outside and a village artist had been hired in a good year once to paint upon the white plaster a scene of hills and bamboo. But the rain of generations had poured upon this painting until now there was only a faint feathery shadow of bamboos left, and the hills were almost wholly gone.

Within the temple snugly under the roof sat two small, solemn figures, earthen, for they were formed from the earth of the fields about the temple. These were the god himself and his lady. They wore robes of red and gilt paper, and the god had a scant, drooping mustache of real hair. Each year at the New Year Wang Lung's father bought sheets of red paper and carefully cut and pasted new robes for the pair. And each year rain and snow beat in and the sun of summer shone in and spoiled their robes.

At this moment, however, the robes were still new, since the year was but well begun, and Wang Lung was proud of their spruce appearance. He took the basket from the woman's arm and carefully he looked about under the pork for the sticks of incense he had bought. He was anxious lest they were broken and thus make an evil omen, but they were whole, and when he had found them he stuck them side by side in the ashes of other sticks of incense that were heaped before the gods, for the whole neighborhood worshipped these two small figures. Then fumbling for his flint and iron he caught, with a dried leaf for tinder, a flame to light the incense.

Together this man and this woman stood before the gods of their fields. The woman watched the ends of the incense redden and turn grey. When the ash grew heavy she leaned over and with her forefinger she pushed the head of ash away. Then as though fearful for what she had done, she looked quickly at Wang Lung, her eyes dumb. But there was something he liked in her movement. It was as though she felt that the incense belonged to them both; it was a moment of marriage. They stood there in complete silence, side by side, while the incense smouldered into ashes; and then because the sun was sinking, Wang Lung shouldered the box and they went home.

At the door of the house the old man stood to catch the last rays of the sun upon him. He made no movement as Wang Lung approached with the woman. It would have been beneath him to notice her. Instead he feigned great interest in the clouds and he cried,

"That cloud which hangs upon the left horn of the new moon speaks of rain. It will come not later than tomorrow night." And then as he saw Wang Lung take the basket from the woman he cried out again, "And have you spent money?"

Wang Lung set the basket on the table. "There will be guests tonight," he said briefly, and he carried the box into the room where he slept and set it down beside the box where his own clothes were. He looked at it strangely. But the old man came to the door and said volubly,

"There is no end to the money spent in this house!"

Secretly he was pleased that his son had invited guests, but he felt it would not do to give out anything but complaints before his new daughter-in-law lest she be set from the first in ways of extravagance. Wang Lung said nothing, but he went out and took the basket into the kitchen and the woman followed him there. He took the food piece by piece from the basket and laid it upon the ledge of the cold stove and he said to her,

"Here is pork and here beef and fish. There are seven to eat. Can you prepare food?"

He did not look at the woman as he spoke. It would not have been seemly. The woman answered in her plain voice,

"I have been kitchen slave since I went into the House of Hwang. There were meats at every meal."

Wang Lung nodded and left her and did not see her again until the guests came crowding in, his uncle jovial and sly and hungry, his uncle's son an impudent lad of fifteen, and the farmers clumsy and grinning with shyness. Two were men from the village with whom Wang Lung exchanged seed and labor at harvest time, and one was his next door neighbor, Ching, a small, quiet man, ever unwilling to speak unless he were compelled to it. After they had been seated about the middle room with demurring and unwillingness to take seats, for politeness, Wang Lung went into the kitchen to bid the woman serve. Then he was pleased when she said to him,

"I will hand you the bowls if you will place them upon the table. I do not like to come out before men."

Wang Lung felt in him a great pride that this woman was his and did not fear to appear before him, but would not before other men. He took the bowls from her hands at the kitchen door and he set them upon the table in the middle room and called loudly,

"Eat, my uncle and my brothers." And when the uncle, who was fond of jokes, said, "Are we not to see the moth-browed bride?" Wang Lung replied firmly, "We are not yet one. It is not meet that other men see her until the marriage is consummated."

And he urged them to eat and they ate heartily of the good fare, heartily and in silence, and this one praised the brown sauce on the fish and that one the well done pork, and Wang Lung said over and over in reply,

"It is poor stuff—it is badly prepared."

But in his heart he was proud of the dishes, for with what meats she had the woman had combined sugar and vinegar and a little wine and soy sauce and she had skillfully brought forth all the force of the meat itself, so that Wang Lung himself had never tasted such dishes upon the tables of his friends.

That night after the guests had tarried long over their tea and had done with their jokes, the woman still lingered behind the stove, and when Wang Lung had seen the last guest away he went in and she cowered there in the straw piles asleep beside the ox. There was straw in her hair when he roused her, and when he called her she put up her arm suddenly in her sleep as though to defend herself from a blow. When she opened her eyes at last, she looked at him with her strange speechless gaze, and he felt as though he faced a child. He took her by the hand and led her into the room where that morning he had bathed himself for her, and he lit a red candle upon the table. In this light he was suddenly shy when he found himself alone with the woman and he was compelled to remind himself,

"There is this woman of mine. The thing is to be done."

And he began to undress himself doggedly. As for the woman, she crept around the corner of the curtain and began without a sound to prepare for the bed. Wang Lung said gruffly,

"When you lie down, put the light out first."

Then he lay down and drew the thick quilt about his shoulders and pretended to sleep. But he was not sleeping. He lay quivering, every nerve of his flesh awake. And when, after a long time, the room went dark, and there was the slow, silent, creeping movement of the woman beside him, an exultation filled him fit to break his body. He gave a hoarse laugh into the darkness and seized her.

The Tulips

From MISS LULU BETT
By Zona Gale

Zona Gale was a pioneer in the realistic phase which American fiction entered about the year 1920, when Miss Lulu Bett was published. Her village characters, moving against a background of extreme drabness, provided a novelty for the American public, accustomed for many years to the distinguished and often glittering figures which were the fashion in fiction.

Lulu Bett, the forlorn but sensitive spinster, suffers through this tragic story of frustration from the incessant irritations inflicted upon her by her sadistic brother-in-law, Dwight Herbert Deacon. The cumulative effect of these thousands of tiny stings amounts, eventually, to the pressure of extreme cruelty. The author's gentle, ironic handling of her widely familiar characters in their narrow, sordid lives achieved an immediate response from a public surfeited with exotic or wishful-thinking romance.

THE Deacons were at supper. In the middle of the table was a small, appealing tulip plant, looking as anything would look whose sun was a gas jet. This gas jet was high above the table and flared, with a sound.

"Better turn down the gas jest a little," Mr. Deacon said, and stretched up to do so. He made this joke almost every night. He seldom spoke as a man speaks who has something to say, but as a man who makes something to say.

"Well, what have we on the festive board to-night?" he questioned,

eyeing it. "Festive" was his favourite adjective. "Beautiful," too. In October he might be heard asking "Where's my beautiful fall coat?"

"We have creamed salmon," replied Mrs. Deacon gently. "On toast," she added, with a scrupulous regard for the whole truth. Why she should say this so gently no one can tell. She says everything gently. Her "Could you leave me another bottle of milk this morning?" would wring a milkman's heart.

"Well, now, let us see," said Mr. Deacon, and attacked the principal dish benignly. "*Let* us see," he added, as he served.

"I don't want any," said Monona.

The child Monona was seated upon a book and a cushion, so that her little triangle of nose rose adultly above her plate. Her remark produced precisely the effect for which she had passionately hoped.

"What's this?" cried Mr. Deacon. "No salmon?"

"No," said Monona, inflected up, chin pertly pointed. She felt her power, discarded her "sir."

"Oh now, Pet!" from Mrs. Deacon, on three notes. "You liked it before."

"I don't want any," said Monona, in precisely her original tone.

"Just a little? A very little?" Mr. Deacon persuaded, spoon dripping.

The child Monona made her lips thin and straight and shook her head until her straight hair flapped in her eyes on either side. Mr. Deacon's eyes anxiously consulted his wife's eyes. What is this? Their progeny will not eat? What can be supplied?

"Some bread and milk!" cried Mrs. Deacon brightly, exploding on "bread." One wondered how she thought of it.

"No," said Monona, inflection up, chin the same. She was affecting indifference to this scene, in which her soul delighted. She twisted her head, bit her lips unconcernedly, and turned her eyes to the remote.

There emerged from the fringe of things, where she perpetually hovered, Mrs. Deacon's older sister, Lulu Bett, who was "making her home with us." And that was precisely the case. *They* were not making her a home, goodness knows. Lulu was the family beast of burden.

"Can't I make her a little milk toast?" she asked Mrs. Deacon.

Mrs. Deacon hesitated, not with compunction at accepting Lulu's offer, not diplomatically to lure Monona. But she hesitated habitually, by nature, as another is by nature vivacious or brunette.

"Yes!" shouted the child Monona.

The tension relaxed. Mrs. Deacon assented. Lulu went to the kitchen. Mr. Deacon served on. Something of this scene was enacted every day. For Monona the drama never lost its zest. It never occurred to the others to let her sit without eating, once, as a cure-all. The Deacons were devoted parents and the child Monona was delicate. She had a white, grave face, white hair, white eyebrows, white lashes. She was sullen, anæmic. They let her wear rings. She "toed in." The poor child was the late birth of a late marriage and the principal joy which she had provided them thus far was the pleased reflection that they had produced her at all.

"Where's your mother, Ina?" Mr. Deacon inquired. "Isn't she coming to her supper?"

"Tantrim," said Mrs. Deacon, softly.

"Oh, ho," said he, and said no more.

The temper of Mrs. Bett, who also lived with them, had days of high vibration when she absented herself from the table as a kind of self-indulgence, and no one could persuade her to food. "Tantrims," they called these occasions.

"Baked potatoes," said Mr. Deacon. "That's good—that's good. The baked potato contains more nourishment than potatoes prepared in any other way. The nourishment is next to the skin. Roasting retains it."

"That's what I always think," said his wife pleasantly.

For fifteen years they had agreed about this.

They ate, in the indecent silence of first savouring food. A delicate crunching of crust, an odour of baked-potato shells, the slip and touch of the silver.

"Num, num, nummy-num!" sang the child Monona loudly, and was hushed by both parents in simultaneous exclamation which rivalled this lyric outburst. They were alone at table. Di, daughter of a wife early lost to Mr. Deacon, was not there. Di was hardly ever there. She was at that age. That age, in Warbleton.

A clock struck the half hour.

"It's curious," Mr. Deacon observed, "how that clock loses. It must be fully quarter to." He consulted his watch. "It is quarter to!" he exclaimed with satisfaction. "I'm pretty good at guessing time."

"I've noticed that!" cried his Ina.

"Last night, it was only twenty-three to, when the half hour struck," he reminded her.

"Twenty-one, I thought." She was tentative, regarded him with arched eyebrows, mastication suspended.

This point was never to be settled. The colloquy was interrupted by the child Monona, whining for her toast. And the doorbell rang.

"Dear me!" said Mr. Deacon. "What can anybody be thinking of to call just at meal-time?"

He trod the hall, flung open the street door. Mrs. Deacon listened. Lulu, coming in with the toast, was warned to silence by an uplifted finger. She deposited the toast, tiptoed to her chair. A withered baked potato and cold creamed salmon were on her plate. The child Monona ate with shocking appreciation. Nothing could be made of the voices in the hall. But Mrs. Bett's door was heard softly to unlatch. She, too, was listening.

A ripple of excitement was caused in the dining-room when Mr. Deacon was divined to usher some one to the parlour. Mr. Deacon would speak with this visitor in a few moments, and now returned to his table. It was notable how slight a thing would give him a sense of self-importance. Now he felt himself a man of affairs, could not even have a quiet supper with his family without the outside world demanding him. He waved his hand to indicate it was nothing which they would know anything about, resumed his seat, served himself to a second spoon of salmon and remarked, "More roast duck, anybody?" in a loud voice and with a slow wink at his wife. That lady at first looked blank, as she always did in the presence of any humour couched with the least indirection, and then drew back her chin and caught her lower lip in her gold-filled teeth. This was her conjugal rebuking.

Swedenborg always uses "conjugial." And really this sounds more married. It should be used with reference to the Deacons. No one was ever more married than they—at least than Mr. Deacon. He made little conjugal jokes in the presence of Lulu who, now completely unnerved by the habit, suspected them where they did not exist, feared lurking *entendre* in the most innocent comments, and became more tense every hour of her life.

And now the eye of the master of the house fell for the first time upon the yellow tulip in the centre of his table.

"Well, *well!*" he said. "What's this?"

Ina Deacon produced, fleetly, an unlooked-for dimple.

"Have you been buying flowers?" the master inquired.

"Ask Lulu," said Mrs. Deacon.

He turned his attention full upon Lulu.

"Suitors?" he inquired, and his lips left their places to form a sort of ruff about the word.

Lulu flushed, and her eyes and their very brows appealed.

"It was a quarter," she said. "There'll be five flowers."

"You *bought* it?"

"Yes. There'll be five—that's a nickel apiece."

His tone was as methodical as if he had been talking about the bread.

"Yet we give you a home on the supposition that you have no money to spend, even for the necessities."

His voice, without resonance, cleft air, thought, spirit, and even flesh.

Mrs. Deacon, indeterminately feeling her guilt in having let loose the dogs of her husband upon Lulu, interposed: "Well, but, Herbert— Lulu isn't strong enough to work. What's the use. . . ."

She dwindled. For years the fiction had been sustained that Lulu, the family beast of burden, was not strong enough to work anywhere else.

"The justice business—" said Dwight Herbert Deacon—he was a justice of the peace—"and the dental profession—" he was also a dentist—"do not warrant the purchase of spring flowers in my home."

"Well, but, Herbert—" It was his wife again.

"No more," he cried briefly, with a slight bend of his head. "Lulu meant no harm," he added, and smiled at Lulu.

There was a moment's silence into which Monona injected a loud "Num, num, nummy-num," as if she were the burden of an Elizabethan lyric. She seemed to close the incident. But the burden was cut off untimely. There was, her father reminded her portentously, company in the parlour.

"When the bell rang, I was so afraid something had happened to Di," said Ina sighing.

"Let's see," said Di's father. "Where is little daughter to-night?"

He must have known that she was at Jenny Plow's at a tea party, for at noon they had talked of nothing else; but this was his way. And Ina played his game, always. She informed him, dutifully.

"Oh, ho," said he, absently. How could he be expected to keep his mind on these domestic trifles.

"We told you that this noon," said Lulu.

He frowned, disregarded her. Lulu had no delicacy.

"How much is salmon the can now?" he inquired abruptly—this was one of his forms of speech, the can, the pound, the cord.

His partner supplied this information with admirable promptness. Large size, small size, present price, former price—she had them all.

"Dear me," said Mr. Deacon. "That is very nearly salmoney, isn't it?"

"Herbert!" his Ina admonished, in gentle, gentle reproach. Mr. Deacon punned, organically. In talk he often fell silent and then asked some question, schemed to permit his vice to flourish. Mrs. Deacon's return was always automatic: "Herbert!"

"Whose Bert?" he said to this. "I thought I was your Bert."

She shook her little head. "You are a case," she told him. He beamed upon her. It was his intention to be a case.

Lulu ventured in upon this pleasantry, and cleared her throat. She was not hoarse, but she was always clearing her throat.

"The butter is about all gone," she observed. "Shall I wait for the butter-woman or get some creamery?"

Mr. Deacon now felt his little jocularities lost before a wall of the matter of fact. He was not pleased. He saw himself as the light of his home, bringer of brightness, lightener of dull hours. It was a pretty rôle. He insisted upon it. To maintain it intact, it was necessary to turn upon their sister with concentrated irritation.

"Kindly settle these matters without bringing them to my attention at mealtime," he said icily.

Lulu flushed and was silent. She was an olive woman, once handsome, now with flat, bluish shadows under her wistful eyes. And if only she would look at her brother Herbert and say something. But she looked in her plate.

"I want some honey," shouted the child, Monona.

"There isn't any, Pet," said Lulu.

"I want some," said Monona, eyeing her stonily. But she found that her hair-ribbon could be pulled forward to meet her lips, and she embarked on the biting of an end. Lulu departed for some sauce and cake. It was apple sauce. Mr. Deacon remarked that the apples were almost as good as if he had stolen them. He was giving the impression that he was an irrepressible fellow. He was eating very slowly. It added pleasantly to his sense of importance to feel that some one, there in the parlour, was waiting his motion.

At length they rose. Monona flung herself upon her father. He put her aside firmly, every inch the father. No, no. Father was occupied now. Mrs. Deacon coaxed her away. Monona encircled her mother's waist, lifted her own feet from the floor and hung upon her. "She's such an active child," Lulu ventured brightly.

"Not unduly active, I think," her brother-in-law observed.

He turned upon Lulu his bright smile, lifted his eyebrows, dropped his lids, stood for a moment contemplating the yellow tulip, and so left the room.

Lulu cleared the table. Mrs. Deacon essayed to wind the clock. Well now. Did Herbert say it was twenty-three to-night when it struck the half hour and twenty-one last night, or twenty-one to-night and last night twenty-three? She talked of it as they cleared the table, but Lulu did not talk.

"Can't you remember?" Mrs. Deacon said at last. "I should think you might be useful."

Lulu was lifting the yellow tulip to set it on the sill. She changed her mind. She took the plant to the wood-shed and tumbled it with force upon the chip-pile.

The dining-room table was laid for breakfast. The two women brought their work and sat there. The child Monona hung miserably about, watching the clock. Right or wrong, she was put to bed by it. She had eight minutes more—seven—six—five—

Lulu laid down her sewing and left the room. She went to the wood-shed, groped about in the dark, found the stalk of the one tulip flower in its heap on the chip-pile. The tulip she fastened in her gown on her flat chest.

Outside were to be seen the early stars. It is said that if our sun were as near to Arcturus as we are near to our sun, the great Arcturus would burn our sun to nothingness.

A Boy's Reverie

From THE WEB AND THE ROCK

By Thomas Wolfe

Throughout his work Thomas Wolfe proves that there are no rules in the writing of fiction which cannot be transcended. His contempt for dogmas of economy, for precepts against repetition often turn his prose to pure rhapsodic poetry. The Web and the Rock is done with the kind of impulse and power which carried Walt Whitman so far beyond all the limits of traditional pattern. In this passage Wolfe has used prose in the function of poetry to express the boy's thoughts, not as the boy would express them but in the full measure of the boy's feeling. The feeling is fury at the interruption of a vast and necessary dream. Anything short of Wolfe's full rhapsody would be inadequate to it. The technique recalls that of Kenneth Grahame's The Golden Age but Wolfe's success with it here is possibly unique in our time. Thomas Wolfe, whose understanding of his material is as bold and hardy as that of our toughest realists, occupies in his expression an island of exceptional beauty in the flood of objective writing which has inundated his era.

CHILD, child!—Where are you, child?"
So did he always know Aunt Maw was there!
"Son, son!—Where are you son?"
Too far for finding and too near to seek!
"Boy, boy!—Where *is* that boy?"
Where you, at any rate, or any other of the apron-skirted kind, can never come.
"You can't take your eye off him a minute. . . ."

Keep eye *on*, then; it will do no good.

"The moment that your back is turned, he's up and gone. . . ."

And out and off and far away from you—no matter if your back is turned or not!

"I can never find him when I need him. . . ."

Need me no needs, sweet dame; when I need you, you shall be so informed!

"But he can *eat*, all right. . . . He's Johnny-on-the-spot when it is time to eat. . . ."

And, pray, what is there so remarkable in *that*? Of course he *eats*— more power to his eating, too. Was Hercules a daffodil; did Adam toy with water cress: did Falstaff wax fat eating lettuces; was Dr. Johnson surfeited on shredded wheat; or Chaucer on a handful of parched corn? No! What is more, were campaigns fought and waged on empty bellies; was Kublai Khan a vegetarian; did Washington have prunes for breakfast, radishes for lunch; was John L. Sullivan the slave of Holland Rusk, or President Taft the easy prey of lady fingers? No! More—who drove the traffic of swift-thronging noon, perched high above the hauling rumps of horses; who sat above the pistoned wheels of furious day; who hurled a ribbon of steel rails into the West; who dug, drove through gulches, bored through tunnels; whose old gloved hands were gripped on the throttles; who bore the hammer, and who dealt the stroke?—did such of these grow faint with longing when they thought of the full gluttony of peanut-butter and ginger snaps? And finally, the men who came back from the town at twelve o'clock, their solid liquid tramp of leather on the streets of noon, the men of labor, sweat, and business coming down the street—his uncle, Mr. Potterham, Mr. Shepperton, Mr. Crane—were fence gates opened, screen doors slammed, and was there droning torpor and the full feeding silence of assuagement and repose—if these men had come to take a cup of coffee and a nap?

"He can *eat* all right! . . . He's always here when it is time to *eat!*"

It was to listen to such stuff as this that great men lived and suffered, and great heroes bled! It was for this that Ajax battled, and Achilles died; it was for this that Homer sang and suffered—and Troy fell! It was for this that Artaxerxes led great armies, it was for this that Caesar took his legions over Gaul; for this that Ulysses had braved strange seas, encompassed perils of remote and magic coasts, survived the Cyclops and Charybdis, and surmounted all the famed enchantments of Circean time—to listen to such damned and dismal stuff as this—the astonishing discovery by a woman that men *eat!*

Peace, woman, to your bicker—hold your prosy tongue! Get back into the world you know, and do the work for which you were intended; you intrude—go back, go back to all your kitchen scourings, your pots and

pans, your plates and cups and saucers, your clothes and rags and soaps
and sudsy water; go back, go back and leave us; we are fed and we are
pleasantly distended, great thoughts possess us; drowsy dreams; we would
lie alone and contemplate our navel—it is afternoon!

"Boy, boy!—Where has he got to now! . . . Oh, I could see him
lookin' round. . . . I saw him edgin' towards the door! . . . Aha, I
thought, he thinks he's very smart . . . but I knew exactly what he
planned to do . . . to slip out and to get away before I caught him . . .
and just because he was afraid I had a little work for him to do!"

A *little* work! Aye, there's the rub—if only it were not always just a
little work we had to do! If only in their minds there ever were a moment of *supreme occasion* or *sublime event!* If only it were not always
just a *little* thing they have in mind, a *little* work we had to do! If only
there were something, just a spark of joy to lift the heart, a spark of
magic to fire the spirit, a spark of understanding of the thing we want
to do, a grain of feeling, or an atom of imagination! But always it is just a
little work, a *little* thing we have to do!

Is it the little *labor* that she asks that we begrudge? Is it the little *effort*
which it would require that we abhor? Is it the little *help* she asks for
that we ungenerously withhold, a hate of work, a fear of sweat, a spirit
of mean giving? No! It is not this at all. It is that women in the early
afternoon are dull, and dully ask dull things of us; it is that women in
the afternoon are dull, and ask us always for a *little* thing, and do not
understand!

It is that at this hour of day we do not want them near us—we would
be alone. They smell of kitchen steam and drabness at this time of day:
the depressing moistures of defunctive greens, left-over cabbage, lukewarm boilings, and the dinner scraps. An atmosphere of sudsy water now
pervades them; their hands drip rinsings and their lives are grey.

These people do not know it, out of mercy we have never told them;
but their lives lack interest at three o'clock—we do not want them, they
must let us be.

They have some knowledge for the morning, some for afternoon, more
for sunset, much for night; but at three o'clock they bore us, they
must leave us be! They do not understand the thousand lights and
weathers of the day as we; light is just light to them, and morning
morning, and noon noon. They do not know the thing that comes and
goes—the way light changes, and the way things shift; they do not know
how brightness changes in the sun, and how man's spirit changes like a
flick of light. Oh, they do not know, they cannot understand, the
life of life, the joy of joy, the grief of grief unutterable, the eternity of
living in a moment, the thing that changes as light changes, as swift
and passing as a swallow's flight; they do not know the thing that

comes and goes and never can be captured, the thorn of Spring, the sharp and tongueless cry!

They do not understand the joy and horror of the day as we can feel it; they do not understand the thing we dread at this hour of the afternoon.

To them the light is light, the brief hour passing; their soaps-suds spirits do not contemplate the horror of hot light in afternoon. They do not understand our loathing of hot gardens, the way our spirits dull and sicken at hot light. They do not know how hope forsakes us, how joy flies away, when we look at the mottled torpor of hot light on the hydrangeas, the broad-leaved dullness of hot dock-weeds growing by the barn. They do not know the horror of old rusty cans filled into gaps of rubbish underneath the fence; the loathing of the mottled, hot, and torpid light upon a row of scraggly corn; the hopeless depth of torpid, dull depression which the sight of hot coarse grasses in the sun can rouse to a numb wakefulness of horror in our souls at three o'clock.

It is a kind of torpid stagnancy of life, it is a hopelessness of hope, a dull, numb lifelessness of life! It is like looking at a pool of stagnant water in the dull torpor of the light of three o'clock. It is like being where no green is, where no cool is, where there is no song of unseen birds, where there is no sound of cool and secret waters, no sound of rock-bright, foaming waters; like being where no gold and green and sudden magic is, to be called out to do little things at three o'clock.

Ah, Christ, could we make speech say what no speech utters, could we make tongue speak what no tongue says! Could we enlighten their enkitchened lives with a revealing utterance, then they would never send us out to do a little thing at three o'clock.

We are a kind that hate clay banks in afternoon, the look of cinders, grimy surfaces, old blistered clapboard houses, the train yards and the coaches broiling on the tracks. We loathe the sight of concrete walls, the fly-speckled windows of the Greek, the strawberry horror of the row of lukewarm soda-pop. At this hour of the day we sicken at the Greek's hot window, at his greasy frying plate that fries and oozes with a loathsome sweat in the full torpor of the sun. We hate the row of greasy frankfurters that sweat and ooze there on the torpid plate, the loathsome pans all oozing with a stew of greasy onions, mashed potatoes, and hamburger steaks. We loathe the Greek's swart features in the light of three o'clock, the yellowed pock-marked pores that sweat in the hot light. We hate the light that shines on motor cars at three o'clock, we hate white plaster surfaces, new stucco houses, and most open places where there are no trees.

We must have coolness, dankness, darkness; we need gladed green and gold and rock-bright running waters at the hour of three o'clock. We must go down into the coolness of a concrete cellar. We like dark shade, and cool, dark smells, and cool, dark, secret places, at the hour of three o'clock. We like cool, strong smells with some cool staleness at that hour. Man smells are good at three o'clock. We like to remember the smells of all things that were in our father's room: the dank, cool pungency of the plug of apple tobacco on the mantelpiece, bit into at one end, and stuck with a bright red flag; the smell of the old mantelpiece, the wooden clock, the old calf bindings of a few old books; the smell of the rocking chair, the rug, the walnut bureau, and the cool, dark smell of clothing in the closet.

At this hour of the day we like the smell of old unopened rooms, old packing cases, tar, and the smell of the grape vines on the cool side of the house. If we go out, we want to go out in green shade and gladed coolnesses, to lie down on our bellies underneath the maple trees and work our toes down into the thick green grass. If we have to go to town we want to go to places like our uncle's hardware store, where we can smell the cool, dark cleanliness of nails, hammers, saws, tools, T-squares, implements of all sorts; or to a saddle shop where we can get the smell of leather; or to our father's brick and lumber yard where we can get the smells of putty, glass, and clean white pine, the smell of the mule-teams, and the lumber sheds. It is also good to go into the cool glade of the drug store at this hour, to hear the cool, swift slatting of the wooden fans, and to smell the citrus pungency of lemons, limes, and oranges, the sharp and clean excitements of unknown medicines.

The smell of a street car at this hour of day is also good—a dynamic smell of motors, wood work, rattan seats, worn brass, and steel-bright flanges. It is a smell of drowsy, warm excitement, and a nameless beating of the heart; it speaks of going somewhere. If we go anywhere at this hour of day, it is good to go to the baseball game and smell the grandstand, the old wooden bleachers, the green turf of the playing field, the horsehide of the ball, the gloves, the mits, the clean resilience of the ash-wood bats, the smells of men in shirt-sleeves, and the sweating players.

And if there is work to do at three o'clock—if we must rouse ourselves from somnolent repose, and from the green-gold drowsy magic of our meditations—for God's sake give us something *real* to do. Give us great labors, but vouchsafe to us as well the promise of a great accomplishment, the thrill of peril, the hope of high and spirited adventure. For God's sake don't destroy the heart and hope and life and will, the brave and dreaming soul of man, with the common, dull, soul-sickening, mean transactions of these *little* things!

Don't break our heart, our hope, our ecstasy, don't shatter irrevoca-

bly some brave adventure of the spirit, or some brooding dream, by
sending us on errands which any stupid girl, or nigger wench, or soulless
underling of life could just as well accomplish. Don't break man's heart,
man's life, man's song, the soaring vision of his dream with—"Here, boy,
trot around the corner for a loaf of bread,"—or "Here, boy; the telephone company has just called up—you'll have to trot around there . . ."
—Oh, for God's sake, and my sake, please don't say 'trot around'—
". . . and pay the bill before they cut us off!"

Or, fretful-wise, be-flusteredlike, all of a twitter, scattered and de-
moralized, fuming and stewing, complaining, whining, railing against
the universe because of things undone you should have done yourself,
because of errors you have made yourself, because of debts unpaid you
should have paid on time, because of things forgotten you should have
remembered—fretting, complaining, galloping off in all directions, unable to get your thoughts together, unable even to call a child by his
proper name—as here:

"Ed, John, Bob—pshaw, boy! George, I mean! . . ."

Well, then for God's sake, mean it!

"Why, pshaw!—to think that that fool nigger—I could wring her
neck when I think of it—well, as I say now. . . ."

Then, in God's name, say it!

". . . why, you know . . ."

No! I do not know!

". . . here I was dependin' on her—here she told me she would come
—and all the work to be done—and here she's sneaked out on me after
dinner—and I'm left here in the lurch."

Yes, of course you are; because you failed to pay the poor wench
on Saturday night the three dollars which is her princely emolument
for fourteen hours a day of sweaty drudgery seven days a week; because
"it slipped your mind," because you couldn't bear to let it go in one
gigantic lump—could you?—because you thought you'd hang on to
the good green smell of money just a little longer, didn't you?—let it
sweat away in your stocking and smell good just a little longer—didn't
you?—break the poor brute's heart on Saturday night just when she
had her mind all set on fried fish, gin, and f——g, just because you
wanted to hold on to three wadded, soiled, and rumpled greenbacks just
a little longer—dole it out to her a dollar at a time—tonight a dollar,
Wednesday night a dollar, Friday night the same . . . and so are left
here strapped and stranded and forlorn, where my father would have
paid and paid at once, and kept his nigger and his nigger's loyalty.
And all because you are a woman, with a woman's niggard smallness
about money, a woman's niggard dealing towards her servants, a woman's
selfishness, her small humanity of feeling for the dumb, the suffering,

and afflicted soul of man—and so will fret and fume and fidget now, all flustered and undone, to call me forth with:

"Here, boy!—Pshaw, now!—To think that she would play a trick like this!—Why as I say, now—child! child!—I don't know what I shall do—I'm left here all alone—you'll have to trot right down and see if you can find someone at once."

Aye! to call me forth from coolness, and the gladed sweetness of cool grass to sweat my way through Niggertown in the dreary torpor of the afternoon; to sweat my way up and down that grassless, treeless horror of baked clay; to draw my breath in stench and sourness, breathe in the funky nigger stench, sour wash-pots and branch-sewage, nigger privies and the sour shambles of the nigger shacks; to scar my sight and soul with little snot-nosed nigger children fouled with dung, and so bowed out with rickets that their little legs look like twin sausages of fat, soft rubber; so to hunt, and knock at shack-door, so to wheedle, persuade, and cajole, in order to find some other sullen wench to come and sweat her fourteen hours a day for seven days a week—and for three dollars!

Or again, perhaps it will be: "Pshaw, boy!—Why to think that he would play me such a trick!—Why, I forgot to put the sign out—but I thought he knew I needed twenty pounds!—If he'd only asked!—but here he drove right by with not so much as by-your-leave, and here there's not a speck of ice in the refrigerator—and ice cream and iced tea to make for supper.—You'll have to trot right down to the ice-house and get me a good ten-cent chunk."

Yes! A good ten-cent chunk tied with a twist of galling twine, that cuts like a razor down into my sweaty palm; that wets my trouser's leg from thigh to buttock; that bangs and rubs and slips and cuts and freezes against my miserable knees until the flesh is worn raw; that trickles freezing drops down my bare and aching legs, that takes all joy from living, that makes me curse my life and all the circumstances of my birth —and all because you failed to "put the sign out," all because you failed to think of twenty pounds of ice!

Or is it a thimble, or a box of needles, or a spool of thread that you need now! Is it for such as this that I must "trot around" some place for baking powder, salt or sugar, or a pound of butter, or a package of tea!

For God's sake thimble me no thimbles and spool me no spools! If I must go on errands send me out upon man's work, with man's dispatch, as my father used to do! Send me out with one of his niggers upon a wagon load of fragrant pine, monarch above the rumps of two grey mules! Send me for a wagon load of sand down by the river, where I can smell the sultry yellow of the stream, and shout and holler to the boys in swimming! Send me to town to my father's brick and lumber yard, the Square, the sparkling traffic of bright afternoon. Send me for something

in the City Market, the smell of fish and oysters, the green, cool growth
of vegetables; the cold refrigeration of hung beeves, the butchers cleaving
and sawing in straw hats and gouted aprons. Send me out to life and
business and the glades of afternoon; for God's sake, do not torture me
with spools of thread, or with the sunbaked clay and shambling rickets
of black Niggertown!

"Son, son! . . . Where has that fool boy got to! . . . Why, as I say
now, boy, you'll have to trot right down to. . . ."

With baleful, brooding vision he looked towards the house. Say me no
says, sweet dame; trot me no trots. The hour is three o'clock, and I would
be alone.

So thinking, feeling, saying, he rolled over on his belly, out of sight,
on the "good" side of the tree, dug bare, luxurious toes in cool, green
grass, and, chin a-cup in his supporting hands, regarded his small universe of three o'clock.

Scene in the Surgery

From ACTION AT AQUILA
By Hervey Allen

Action at Aquila *is* named for a cavalry engagement of the Civil
War which was neither famous nor triumphant, but a bloody encounter marked by panic and confusion. War is shown in varying aspects;
a wasteful, hideous force yet a challenge to the human spirit in answer to which, under stress of battle, men reach heights of greatness
beyond their individual differences. The following scene in a farmhouse hastily converted to a field hospital proves the impersonal quality of human mercy.

EVENING approached, and with it the great cloud drifting up the
Valley.

In the old brick farmhouse by the river, Surgeon Holtzmaier and his
two hospital assistants were now completely and conclusively over-
whelmed. Up until two o'clock that afternoon they had done heroically
well. The casualties from the skirmishing of the night before and of
earlier in the day had been rapidly disposed of. They had been sub-
jected to rifle fire only, and their care was comparatively simple. As
soon as the bullets were extracted and the wounds dressed, Dr. Holtzmaier had had them carried to the vacant camp where they now lay in
the big mess tents, cared for by some of their least injured comrades.

Dr. Holtzmaier could see no difference between a Confederate and a
Union wound. A wounded man was to him an example of suffering
humanity. He took men as they came, in turn. So in the big tents in the
camp the wounded of both sides lay together and tended one another
as best they could. They, however, were the fortunate ones. They had

83

been hit early. After the action was joined, Surgeon Holtzmaier could no more cope with the influx of wounded than a man could put out a forest fire with a tumbler of water.

By five o'clock in the afternoon the little farmhouse was surrounded for hundreds of feet by the wounded. They lay on the grass, gasping, pale and silent or shivering and moaning, according to the nature of their endurance or misery. The farmhouse itself, where the operating and dressing were going on, sounded like the headquarters of the Inquisition. The men were laid out on the blanket-covered counters of Mr. Mann's now defunct canteen and the surgeon performed on them. There were four counters, and the blankets on all of them were red and sopping.

They brought cases in four at a time, so the counters were always full. Surgeon Holtzmaier moved from number one to number four, and then back to number one again. He was dealing with every possible form of injury in all parts of the human frame. Men trampled by horses, with crushed faces and broken bones; men with smashed and mangled limbs; men with frightful head wounds from shrapnel; men riddled by canister and drilled with rifle bullets; men with the oozing weals and raw meat of sabre slashes; poor lost bodies shot through the stomach, lungs, and bowels, men and boys.

These had dragged themselves, crawled, or staggered, or had been brought by comrades to the little dressing station by the river, the one place in all that area of destruction where some element of mercy and intelligent reconstruction still remained. Surgeon Holtzmaier was simply doing all that he could. After a while he would send out the stretcher-bearers for the worst cases that always remained helpless on the field.

Already he had more than he could do. He moved rapidly, his instruments in a bucket, from number one to number four. His hospital apprentices tried to chloroform the men ahead of him. Sometimes they just held them down, if it didn't take. The surgeon amputated, cut, sawed, sewed, probed, and bandaged. To men shot through the entrails he gave an opiate—and had them carried out behind the house on the river-bank. There was nothing more he could do for them.

Mr. Felix Mann had remained to help. He didn't want to leave the goods on the shelves of his canteen. Later on, the doctor used two hundred beautiful white shirts for bandages, and Mr. Mann said nothing. He organized a dozen men as stretcher-carriers. They were probably skulkers. Surgeon Holtzmaier didn't give "a goot gottam."

As the doctor started on his sixteenth round of the line of counters he was joined by a slight, middle-aged man in Vandyke beard and worn Confederate coat with faded medical insignia.

"Dr. Huger Wilson of Charleston," said the new-comer quietly. There was a certain dry, crisp quality to his voice. "May I be of assistance?"

"Ja!" said Holtzmaier. "Ve all need assizztance here! Vat?"

"I think we do," replied Dr. Wilson, and went to work. They divided the tables between them. The new-comer worked with incredible speed and skill.

"Vilson? Not Vilson of der Garolina Gollege?" said Dr. Holtzmaier after a while, wiping the sweat from his eyes. "You write dat pook?"

Dr. Wilson nodded.

"All I know iss from dat pook," said Dr. Holtzmaier humbly.

"But you do well, sir," replied Dr. Wilson.

It was the great moment of Dr. Holtzmaier's life.

Dr. Wilson removed a patella hanging by shreds from a young lad, who shrieked and went grey under the knife. He squeezed a spongeful of laudanum between his lips.

"Knees seldom heal," said Wilson as they removed the man, who had fainted. "Take off his leg later."

"Ja, und der gloroform is gone und der lint und pandages will soon be all. Und dem damn vools iss schtill gillin' each odder out dere!"

Both the surgeons stopped for a moment to listen. The artillery was silent, but a constant popping of rifle fire was going on. The action by this time had degenerated into nothing but a series of scattered skirmishes, each side having retired to its own woods. Occasionally an obstinate group of Confederates, Valley men, would make another rush. They were determined "to drive the strangehs back." Such efforts were received by a violent burst of fire, and foiled.

"Der damn vools!" repeated Dr. Holtzmaier, as the crash of a volley came to him from far up the field—and went back to his work. A frightfully wounded young Confederate expired under his knife.

"Take him away," said Dr. Holtzmaier, tears of chagrin in his eyes.

Dr. Wilson shook his head, as he probed. His man shrieked.

"Ja," said Dr. Holtzmaier. "It is der gottam boliticians do dat! Ven dese fellers vas schust babies already dey mak sbeeches in der Senate. Und now, py Gott, der gloroform is all!"

"Sbeeches," said Dr. Holtzmaier, "sbeeches!"—from time to time that afternoon.

The two surgeons bent themselves to the desperate work that is necessary when oratory fails. Presently the surgeon of the 23rd Illinois and his hospital assistants joined them. The stretcher cases began to come in.

"Have you any sperm oil?" asked Dr. Wilson.

"In der lamps."

"Take some of it and get it boiling."

Dr. Holtzmaier bellowed to Felix Mann to start oil boiling.

"Gauterize, eh?"

"Yes," said Dr. Wilson. "It's too bad they have given it up. I observe that there is less gangrene when you cauterize. No pus, generally. Pus is the foam on the lips of death. It is *not* a healthy sign."

"Ve gauterize!" said Dr. Holtzmaier. "Und irons, alzo."

He hustled Mann with his preparations for boiling the oil in a big pot, and thrust the poker into the flames. Smoke began to pour out of the old farmhouse where the doctors worked. Presently the shrieks of those whose stumps were thrust into the boiling oil came out of the chimney too. Dr. Wilson used the hot poker unsparingly to sear wounds. He knew it saved lives. Dr. Holtzmaier could hardly stand it. The smell of roasted flesh sickened him.

"Go out and get a breath of air," said Dr. Wilson afterwhile. "You've been at it longer than we have. It will do you good, man. Do it so you can keep on." He pushed Dr. Holtzmaier affectionately to the door.

"Ja, I go und schump in der ribber und come pack."

He stood just outside the door, covered with gore from the knees up. A scalpel dropped out of his hand. He filled his lungs with clean air and wiped the bloody sweat out of his eyes with the underside of his sleeve. All the wounded near by began to beg him to do something for them. Piled under a window, where they had been thrown out, and extending almost to the height of the sill itself was a pile of mixed legs, arms, and other things. Near the top a stiff hand stuck out and pointed at him.

A sickening spasm of disgust, for himself, for the species he belonged to, and for the scene in which he found himself, dragged downward on the doctor's bowels.

"Oh, scheet!" he exclaimed. "Du lieber Gott im Himmel!"—and began to run for the river-bank.

He tore his clothes off, plunged in, and rolled about. Presently he emerged again, puffing. The cold water had sobered him. The horrible reek of blood was gone. He actually felt clean. So sudden and so profound was his change of mood that he literally felt like another man.

Dr. Holtzmaier dressed slowly. He knew he must take this opportunity of a few minutes from his work, or he would go under. There would be no sleep for him tonight. The stretcher cases would be coming in for hours. They had not even begun to get to the wounded on the field yet, and it was only sunset. A lot of the boys would die out there in the dark. He went up the river-bank a bit and removed a coat from a dead man who had tried to crawl down to the water. It fitted him ill, but it was better than his own blood-soaked blouse. From where he stood he had a view over the fields past the camp and clear down the valley almost to Luray. The air was chill but bracing. He felt warm in the dead man's big coat. He took a drink from his flask and sat down for a moment. He wanted to get his hands steady again.

Twilight deepened. There was no firing from the field now. The lights of the farmhouse windows, where the surgeons were working, turned from pale white to yellow. The Valley was strangely silent except for a distant yelling, a kind of whispered complaint that came through the trees. It was the voices of the wounded scattered over the meadows. Suddenly, as if they had been turned on, the night-birds began. Dr. Holtzmaier shivered a little as he rose to go back, and as he climbed the river-bank he looked down the Valley again.

The great cloud was quite near now. Just before and above it was a patch of bright clean sky from the last reflected rays of the sun. It was still day up there. Darkness moved under the cloud coming southward fast. Its frontlet stretched clear across the Valley like the forehead of night. And before the advancing cloud wall, flashing up in great swooping gyres and circles into the light above, was a flock of buzzards and swifter-darting hawks, torn between their fear of the oncoming storm and darkness and the temptations of the table spread by man below.

So sinister, brooding, and threatening was the slow advance of the great storm cloud with the harpies before it that something melancholily German and primevally fearful was appealed to in the recesses of the doctor's simple soul.

Far down the Valley patches of white appeared here and there, touched by the last long rays of the sunset, and from where the cloud billowed lowest descended streaks of shining sleet and rain.

"Vinter, she comes at last!" he exclaimed, stifling an obscure suicidal impulse compounded of fatigue, disgust, and the solemnly-terrifying landscape. "Maype we get rest now? Ha, dis is not so goot for der poys on der field!" He hastened back to get the stretcher-bearers busy and organized.

But he had to wait. The powers of nature were not the only things loose that evening. The United States government was also manifesting its sovereignty in physical and visible form.

From the ford down the river road came the sharp note of a bugle. The black water turned to cream there under the feet of a squadron. Behind it as far as the eye could see were black masses of men stretching miles back towards Luray and moving swiftly up the river road, pouring themselves out unceasingly from under the winter and the darkness of the cloud. Averell's and Merritt's cavalry divisions were on the way south. The cloud and the buzzards followed them.

The doctor should have crossed the road immediately. As it was, he was just too late.

The roar and clatter of hoofs was upon him just as he got his legs over a worm fence at the roadside. He sat there watching. Squadron after squadron, regiment after regiment, and brigade by brigade, the dark masses of men moving at a fast trot streamed by him. There was never an interval to get through. As the darkness grew the squadrons seemed to become solid masses of darker darkness. Now and then a flag with its white stripes and stars glimmered by. Irons and sabres jingled. Sparks sprang from the iron shoes and cobbles. Before him there was a sharp outburst of firing, the sound of the thunder of galloping masses. The fight died away, raving down the pass. What was left of LaTouche's men streamed back southward or scattered madly into the forests at the foot of the hills. The action at Aquila was over. It was merely an incident of the cavalry movement that day. It was hardly well known enough even to be forgotten—it was scarcely remembered at all.

Dr. Holtzmaier sat for nearly an hour. Then he slipped through an interval. Averell's division had passed. Thundering down the road behind it, Merritt's was close behind.

The rifle fire died away in the distance up the Valley. Cautiously, one by one, as they became used to the stony roar of the passing of armies, the night-birds, which had been scared by the firing, resumed again. By eleven o'clock nothing was to be heard about Aquila but the desperate shouts and screams of the wounded lost in the woods and fields. Answering them out of the insane darkness came the long, babbled monosyllables of owls and the inane insistence of whippoorwill, whippoorwill. The stretcher-bearers worked frantically. The lights in the farmhouse glowed and the fire smoked under the boiling oil.

The Whipping

From STRANGE FRUIT
By Lillian Smith

The bitter racial problem of the American Southland is presented in this novel by a southerner intimate with all its detail. Blacks and whites are caught in the traditional web as this story of the town of Maxwell unfolds; the forces of pity and justice on both sides are helpless against its mesh. With true artistry the author presents the scene, making no attempt to resolve its tragic discord.

Tracy Deen, the son of a doctor, has come home from war to find that he cannot accept his family's piety, dull respectability and limited outlook. In his restlessness he has turned to the Negro girl, Nonnie, for solace and understanding of his alien position. In the chosen passage we find Tracy and Henry, the houseboy with whom he has grown up, in a scene which uncovers the basic inconsistencies of race relations and foreshadows the sudden tragedy which before the book ends has overtaken Tracy and then, in error, claimed the life of Henry in payment.

IT WAS a well-built but old one-room cabin that Henry lived in, set in the Deens' back yard, close to the woodshed and the old abandoned privy. A brick fireplace on the north end, a window on the south, were the only variants to the walls lined with funny papers.

Above the mantel hung an oval frame containing two small photographs of Mamie and Ten McIntosh, Henry's parents. The picture of Ten had been taken before his leg was crushed by a log at the Harris sawmill—and subsequently amputated—and showed him to be a stalwart, iron-muscled, bulletheaded, long-armed, sober Negro of whom his son was an exact replica, save for his smaller eyes and big laughing mouth. Ten McIntosh was never known to laugh much at white folks' doings. Mamie's face, more placid, more patient, smiled from its frame at the world, white and colored alike. Mamie always got on with folks. She had cooked for the Deens from the time they married; her boy had been born in their back yard six months before the Deens' son, and she had nursed them both, hardly knowing which was her own, as she used to say.

Tracy looked at Mamie's picture hanging there above the mantel. Mamie had one jagged tooth and a space where two had been knocked out by Ten in one of his gloom spells. And there was a scar on her hand where she had spilled scalding water when hurrying supper one night. Tracy remembered this even now, twenty years after. He remembered her faint clean body smell like a pile of fresh-ironed sheets and he remembered her rich sweet smell on Sundays, when dressed in black silk she left the yard to go to church-meeting. He remembered her deep full breasts. There had been a time when her lap was wide enough for him and her Henry both to crawl up in. She'd sit there, knees spread wide, jogging them from side to side, singing vague sounds, breaking off, taking up after a little where she had left off, sometimes reaching down for a corner of her big white petticoat to wipe one nose and the other. Knees jogging slowly, easing them back and forth, cradling them from time and its bitterness, glazing eyes with peace. Tune moving on, on, on, and body moving with it, and all the world no wider, no deeper than the space her knees enclosed—no wider than that, and no colder than the heat from her breast.

There had been a time when he was sick and no food would stay on his stomach, and Mamie had fixed little odd things, and sometimes had chewed them for him and slipped them into his mouth and he had felt better. He remembered his mother used to say after that, "The child won't eat for anybody but Mamie," or when he was hurt, "Nobody can quiet him but Mamie."

He remembered these things, as you look at clouds moving across a quiet sky, circling, coming close together, passing each other, moving in close again, almost making something of themselves, something that should have meaning for you; breaking apart suddenly and meaning nothing at all.

But he did not remember, though it waited for a day to come back to him, the bad time when she whipped her Henry.

Henry was eight then and Tracy seven.

They were racing up and down the sidewalk. They'd chalked a line across it and were running, sliding to base. A little white girl on a bicycle was wheeling down the walk, arms up, face flying through space and cool air.

"Move, move, move!" she shrieked. And Henry, feeling the rush of air, the sting of flying, the thrilling power of speed, shrieked back, "Move, move, move, yourself!" and blocked the way, colliding with wheel and girl.

She had fallen, scratching her leg against the pedal.

"How dare you!" she said low, all the flying, the whistling air gone, only heaviness to breathe now. "How dare you do that!"

"Ha," Henry laughed, "ha ha ha ha!" he laughed, knowing nothing else to do, "ha ha ha—"

And Tracy laughed too, glad to see a girl fall, glad to see it happen, though he did not know why.

Mamie was sitting on the side steps, cooling off, resting a spell before starting her supper. Now she saw something she had to tend to. "You— Henry McIntosh, come here!" she called, standing, ease gone from her placid face. "Come here dis minute!"

Henry came and Tracy came with him, unused to the sound in Mamie's voice.

"I got to whip you," she said and hushed. And the two children stood there in the back yard and waited while Mamie went out to the garden and cut her a good heavy sprout from the pecan tree. They stood there and watched her strong wide back move resistlessly through space that enclosed all they knew of living, moving now sharply, drawing new lines they had not known before. They waited until she came back with the switch, took Henry by the shirt, bent him over her knee and whipped him so hard that Tracy burst into sobs and covered his eyes from the sight though he could not make himself leave the sound of it.

Mamie whipped her boy. She whipped him, saying, "I got to learn it to you, you heah! I got to. You can't look at a white gal like dat, you can't tech one, you can't speak to one cep to say yes mam and thanky mam. Say it atter me. Say it!" And Henry, squalling and catching his breath in strangling gasps, said it after her, word for word, three times, as she urged him on, tapping his legs with the tip of the switch as he said it. Then black legs whitened by the lash of his lesson, snuffling and dazed, he ran into the cabin and like a shamed dog crawled under the bed.

Mamie's big brown hands took the switch and slowly broke it to pieces, and the sound of the breaking was something hard to listen to. Then she hurled them with sudden fury away from her. Her hands fell to her sides. She stood there staring across the roof of the big yellow house in front of her. Stared so long that the small white boy watching her thought she must not be able to find what she looked for. Slowly she sat down on the steps . . . wrapped her hands in her apron . . . lips pulled down with the weight of her thinking . . . slowly she laid her face in her lap.

"Mamie," Tracy had said the word with no idea behind it, "Mamie."

She looked up, brown face wet with her crying, and twisted. "Go!" she said, "go to your *own folks!*" she said. And he turned and ran quickly, cut to the bone by the new strange words.

But though he had run quickly he had not been able to get away from her words. They followed him into the house, drove him through the big rooms, made him wander, a lost thing, from side to side of a room, touching table, chair, wall, reaching down once to feel the floor though he didn't know why he was feeling it, stretching, until he ached all over, to fill the empty dimensions of a life he had not chosen and did not know the size of and into which her words told him he must go and stay forever. . . .

He stopped at his mother's room—hearing her voice—opened the door, stood waiting. Alma was reading a big picture book to his baby sister, who solemnly listened. Seemed she was always reading picture books.

"Come in, Son," she said quietly and smiled as he stood there. He went to her, leaned on her chair, uncertain, anxious to do what would please her.

"You reading?"

"Yes, would you like to listen?"

"Yes mam," he said and stared at the picture, trying to find in its lines and planes and colors what he looked for.

Alma went on reading, answering little Laura's questions, laughing with her, showing her the pictures. Their words and voices and movements began to shut out the emptiness, shut out the bigness he had felt lost in; and he leaned closer, hungry now to push through this wall of softness and warmth and get in there with them.

"Don't lean so hard, Son," Alma said kindly, "you're so hot and sticky. And smelly—when have you had a bath?"

"This morning."

"I don't see how you and Henry can get so dirty. You must take another at bedtime." She went on with her reading.

Tracy moved away. Went to his mother's dressing table, lifted a mirror, put it down; moved the brush, moved it back; picked up the comb, put it in the brush; picked up a box of hairpins and dropped it, spilling the pins over table and chair and floor.

"Oh, Tracy! Now pick them up. If you don't want to listen, dear, why not go out and play?"

"He bad boy," said Laura, nodding her head in solemn disapproval and Alma laughed softly at the child's prattle and went on with the reading.

Tracy picked up the pins, moved quickly to where his mother was sitting, jerked the book from her, threw it on the floor. "I hate books!" he said, "I don't like her either," he said and gave Laura a hard push, then rushed from the room, through the hall, out on the side porch and stood there, breathing heavily, expecting his mother to follow and punish him, hoping she would follow and whip him, whip him hard as Mamie had whipped Henry. But she did not come.

After a time he heard Mamie's heavy clump-clump on the back steps. He heard the screen door open and close, heard her put down a load of wood in the box behind the stove, lift the stove lid, scratch a match, start her fire for supper. And unable longer to endure, he ran into the kitchen, stopped short inside the door, suddenly could not go farther.

Mamie turned. She held a piece of pine kindling in her hand, and her skirt had caught on the corner of the wood box. They stood there, a distance great between them, terrifying and strange and measureless between them. A floor that would not bear their weight to cross it.

Words formed in his mind and he opened his mouth to say them. "Mamie!" he whispered. He couldn't remember the others.

She laid down the wood, turned toward him, took a slow step. And now he was running. He buried his face against her, trying to keep the sound of his trouble in the apron. Through dress and petticoat he felt her leg and held on to it.

They didn't try words. She ran her fingers through his hair, over his head. He clung to the old leg until she almost lost her balance with the weight of him against her.

The small flame crackled, licked the air above the pot opening, pushing wisps of smoke through the room.

"Go git him and make him play," she said after a little. "Go git him," she said softly.

Tracy was glad to be told what to do. He ran to the backyard cabin, and into the room, crawled under the bed. "Come on," he said, "we going to play." And Henry obeyed the voice and crawled out, swollen-faced and bleary-eyed and stiff-jointed, and they went back to the lane and gravely played, and slowly the blood moved as blood ought to move in young veins, and after a while they laughed and yelled at each other. And the evening was like any other evening by the time Mamie rang the bell for supper.

When Ten came home from the mill he saw Henry's swollen face and asked questions that had to be answered. Henry said his lesson, for he had learned it well; and Ten listened, glum and tired as twelve hours in the sawmill can make you tired.

So it was easy—when supper was over and they had come back to the cabin—to let first quiet questions to Mamie turn quickly into all the words that hate and shame can form on a man's tongue.

"So you beats yo boy half to death cause you thinks white folks like dat."

"I learn him how to behave."

"You beats yo boy like he trash to please white folks."

"I learn him how to behave, Ten. He got to learn. You know dat!"

Tracy and Henry, playing in the dark yard outside, drew near the words like bits of steel to a magnet.

"You beat da sperrit outn him. He won't be a man fit fo nothin."

"Ten—our boy sassed a white gal."

"What ef he did! She sassed him first, I reckon. He's a good boy," Ten said, "good as any white gal in this goddam town. Say a word and folks beat you to death. Gawd help us, his own ma turns on him an—"

"Ten, I wants my boy to live till he's grown," Mamie's low voice did not rise against the high brittle sound of Ten's words. "I want him to *live!* He got to learn. He got to learn how to git along. He got to learn what he can't do. He got to learn there's white folks and colored folks and things you can't do ef you wants to live. Jesus help me, I'm goin to learn it to him."

"You goin to keep yo hands offn him! You hear! You tetch him again count of white folks and I'll beat you till you can't git offn da floor. He good as anybody, you hear! Good as anybody!" Words so heavy they seemed to fall back on his own chest as he said them.

"He ain good as white folks. I got to learn him dat. I gotta do it, Ten!"

"Gawd Jesus, I hate the sight of one! Hate livin in Deen's back yard. Told you a hundard time it'd be better in the quarters where we'd be free to do as we like. I don want ma boy brung up wid no white boy— don want none of it!"

"They's good to us, Ten."

"Good to us!"

"Good as they knows *how* to be."

"Tell you, I hate the sight of one!" And Ten walked quickly to the mantel and picked up the blue and white glass vase that once had been in the Deens' parlor and was now Mamie's one fine house ornament and hurled it to the floor, smashing it into a hundred fragments. You could hear the ring of the broken pieces, clashing as they rolled on the floor.

"Lawd, Lawd," she cried and hushed quickly, and now her hands sought her apron, twisting it in a tight knot as she stood looking at her husband.

And Ten satisfied a little, eased a little now, walked out on the shed and squatted there, staring into the dark yard.

Mamie found the broom, slowly swept the pieces into a paper and put them in her apron, followed him to the shed. "Hit's easy to break things, Ten," she said, "mighty easy to break things. Ain't easy to mend em up again. Dat what I want my boy to learn early. Want him to learn early dat *no matter what,* white folks is always right! And you treats em *always respectful.*"

"It means I'm white," Tracy whispered, "and you're black," eyes never leaving the shed where the two stood talking, deep shadows against the lamplighted cabin. "It means," he went on and he felt a strange new swelling pride rising in him, "I'm always right, I reckon."

"How come?" asked Henry dully.

"Cause I'm white—you heard Mamie!"

"Do skin make the diffunce?"

"Reckon so," Tracy said, losing his new confidence a little, "yep, reckon it do."

Black boy and white boy stood there in the darkness, watching the grown folks' trouble, and slowly Henry turned and went to the cabin, and slowly Tracy went to the big yellow house.

After Ten lost his leg they moved to Baxley, for Mamie and Ten together could look after a little patch of cotton while Ten settin around in the Deens' back yard with nothin on his mind, as Mamie said, jes got black-sad bout things and made a grumblin world for everybody. They moved to Baxley when Henry was thirteen and left him living in the Deens' back yard. It was not easy to leave him there, for Ten was dead-set against it. Mamie made no argument, wanting only peace in her family, but she told Mrs. Deen she wished her boy could stay here where he could get a little schooling and be around folks who knows things. She made no argument with Ten, for all he would say is, "I ain leavin my boy in no white folks' yard." The day came for them to leave. Uncle Pete's wagon had been borrowed to cart their baskets and the old trunk and the boxes and Mamie's rocking-chair to the depot. Everything was piled high on it, Mamie was dressed in her good black dress, and Ten in his Sunday suit and Henry in his Sunday suit and his new shoes. Tracy was at the wagon, helping them put in the last box and suitcase. The two boys were strangely quiet as they ran back and forth, never looking at each other, lifting and loading and doing all the last things that a final leaving requires of folks. Suddenly Henry dropped the old suitcase he was lifting into the wagon, sat down on it and began to blubber; and Tracy began to cry too. Both of them like little children, with no attempt to hide their tears. Mamie was already on the wagon seat, sitting primly with her hat on, and her hands, in their black cotton gloves, folded in her lap. She looked at Ten, looked at the crying boys, looked at Ten, her placid face suddenly set in its rarely determined lines. She crawled down, pulled out the old box in which Henry's things had been packed, unfastened a basket, pulled out two quilts, handed them to Henry. She looked at Ten again, who looked away.

"You stayin here, Henry," she said firmly, "and you to mind Miz Deen. She to be the same as yo ma, you hear! She say somethin, you do it. You to tote in the wood, and do what she say and go to school when school takes in, come November. You to mind, you hear?" And firmly she kissed him and crawled back up to the seat of the wagon, eyed her husband sharply, turned back and waved at her son whom she had left to grow up in the Deens' back yard.

Henry had grown up there. He did what his mother told him to do. He toted wood, he went to school when school took in come November, he made the fires; and there was plenty of time for him and Tracy to play together. Sometimes they'd go fishing, and sometimes at nights, Tracy would go out and study his lessons in the little cabin by Henry's fireplace, to keep him company. But sometimes, if you happened to step out on the Deens' back porch, you'd see a boy lying on his stomach in a cabin all alone, staring into the fire, mouth a little open, eyes staring into the flames, as the light flickered across a face that looked as if it had never quite belonged to anybody.

The Fishing Trip

From A TREE GROWS IN BROOKLYN

By Betty Smith

The Nolans of Brooklyn might have lived their entire lives uneventfully on the same back street among tenement neighbors had not the failure of Johnny, the father, as a singing waiter brought them to acute poverty. But when, at the lowest ebb in their fortunes, Johnny dies, the family rallies. Led by their courageous mother, who is determined to give her children a chance, they begin the climb upward to a decent life of their own making.

This is the story of Betty Smith's warm and human novel. In the chosen passage Johnny the charming Irishman, always trying to provide for his family and always failing, dons his tuxedo—his only suit —and takes his children, Francie and Neeley, and a small friend to the seaside for a glimpse of the only great, wide, beautiful world he has to offer. Though this incident is rich in humor, it points the inevitable futility of Johnny's efforts as a father and as a man.

IN THE summer of that same year, Johnny got the notion that his children were growing up ignorant of the great ocean that washed the shores of Brooklyn. Johnny felt that they ought to go out to sea in a ship. So he decided to take them for a rowboat ride at Canarsie and do a little deep sea fishing on the side. He had never gone fishing and he'd never been in a rowboat. But that's the idea he got.

Weirdly tied up with this idea, and by a reasoning process known only to Johnny, was the idea of taking Little Tilly along on the trip. Little Tilly was the four-year-old child of neighbors whom he had never met. In fact, he had never seen Little Tilly but he got this idea that he had to make something up to her on account of her brother Gussie. It all tied up with the notion of going to Canarsie.

Gussie, a boy of six, was a murky legend in the neighborhood. A tough little hellion, with an over-developed underlip, he had been born like other babies and nursed at his mother's great breasts. But there, all resemblance to any child, living or dead, ceased. His mother tried to wean him when he was nine months old but Gussie wouldn't stand for it. Denied the breast, he refused a bottle, food or water. He lay in his crib and whimpered. His mother, fearful that he would starve, resumed nursing him. He sucked contentedly, refusing all other food, and lived off his mother's milk until he was nearly two years old. The milk stopped then because his mother was with child again. Gussie sulked and bided his time for nine long months. He refused cow's milk in any form or container and took to drinking black coffee.

Little Tilly was born and the mother flowed with milk again. Gussie went into hysterics the first time he saw the baby nursing. He lay on the floor, screaming and banging his head. He wouldn't eat for four days and he refused to go to the toilet. He got haggard and his mother got frightened. She thought it wouldn't do any harm to give him the breast just once. That was her big mistake. He was like a dope fiend getting the stuff after a long period of deprivation. He wouldn't let go.

He took all of his mother's milk from that time on and Little Tilly, a sickly baby, had to go on the bottle.

Gussie was three years old at this time and big for his age. Like other boys, he wore knee pants and heavy shoes with brass toe tips. As soon as he saw his mother unbutton her dress, he ran to her. He stood up while nursing, an elbow on his mother's knee, his feet crossed jauntily and his eyes roving around the room. Standing to nurse was not such a remarkable feat as his mother's breasts were mountainous and practically rested in her lap when released. Gussie was indeed a fearful sight nursing that way and he looked not unlike a man with his foot on a bar rail, smoking a fat pale cigar.

The neighbors found out about Gussie and discussed his pathological state in hushed whispers. Gussie's father got so that he wouldn't sleep with his wife; he said that she bred monsters. The poor woman figured and figured on a way to wean Gussie. He was too big to nurse, she decided. He was going for four. She was afraid his second teeth wouldn't come in straight.

One day she took a can of stove blackening and the brush and closed herself in the bedroom where she copiously blackened her left breast with the stove polish. With a lipstick she drew a wide ugly mouth with frightening teeth in the vicinity of the nipple. She buttoned her dress

and went into the kitchen and sat in her nursing rocker near the window. When Gussie saw her, he threw the dice, with which he had been
playing, under the washtubs and trotted over for feeding. He crossed his
feet, planted his elbow on her knee and waited.

"Gussie want tiddy?" asked his mother wheedlingly.

"Yup!"

"All right. Gussie's gonna get nice tiddy."

Suddenly she ripped open her dress and thrust the horribly made-up
breast into his face. Gussie was paralyzed with fright for a moment,
then he ran away screaming and hid under the bed where he stayed for
twenty-four hours. He came out at last, trembling. He went back to
drinking black coffee and shuddered every time his eyes went to his
mother's bosom. Gussie was weaned.

The mother reported her success all over the neighborhood. It started
a new fashion in weaning called, "Giving the baby the Gussie."

Johnny heard the story and contemptuously dismissed Gussie from
his mind. He was concerned about Little Tilly. He thought she had
been cheated out of something very important and might grow up
thwarted. He got a notion that a boat ride off the Canarsie shore might
wipe out some of the wrong her unnatural brother had done her. He
sent Francie around to ask could Little Tilly go with them. The harassed mother consented happily.

The next Sunday, Johnny and the three children set out for Canarsie.
Francie was eleven years old, Neeley ten and Little Tilly well past three.
Johnny wore his tuxedo and derby and a fresh collar and dicky. Francie
and Neeley wore their everyday clothes. Little Tilly's mother, in honor
of the day, had dressed her up in a cheap but fancy lace dress trimmed
with dark pink ribbon.

On the trolley ride out, they sat in the front seat and Johnny made
friends with the motorman and they talked politics. They got off at the
last stop which was Canarsie and found their way to a little wharf on
which was a tiny shack; a couple of water-logged rowboats bobbed up
and down on the frayed ropes which held them to the wharf. A sign
over the shack read:

"Fishing tackle and boats for rent."

Underneath was a bigger sign which said:

FRESH FISH TO TAKE HOME FOR SALE HERE.

Johnny negotiated with the man and, as was his way, made a friend of
him. The man invited him into the shack for an eye opener saying that
he himself only used the stuff for a night cap.

While Johnny was inside getting his eyes opened, Neeley and Francie
pondered how a night cap could also be an eye opener. Little Tilly stood
there in her lace dress and said nothing.

Johnny came out with a fishing pole and a rusty tin can filled with worms in mud. The friendly man untied the rope from the least sorry of the rowboats, put the rope in Johnny's hand, wished him luck and went back to his shack.

Johnny put the fishing stuff into the bottom of the boat and helped the children in. Then he crouched on the wharf, the bit of rope in his hand and gave instructions about boats.

"There is always a wrong and a right way to get on a boat," said Johnny, who had never been on any boat except an excursion boat once. "The right way is to give the boat a shove and then jump in it before it drifts out to sea. Like this."

He straightened up, pushed the boat from him, leaped . . . and fell into the water. The petrified children stared at him. A second before, papa had been standing on the dock above them. Now he was below them in the water. The water came to his neck and his small waxed mustache and derby hat were in the clear. His derby was still straight on his forehead. Johnny, as surprised as the children, stared at them a moment before he said:

"Don't any of you damned kids dare to laugh!"

He climbed into the boat almost upsetting it. They didn't dare laugh aloud but Francie laughed so hard inside that her ribs hurt. Neeley was afraid to look at his sister. He knew that if their eyes met, he'd burst out laughing. Little Tilly said nothing. Johnny's collar and dicky were a sodden paperish mess. He stripped them off and threw them overboard. He rowed out to sea waveringly, but with silent dignity. When he came to what he thought was a likely spot, he announced that he was going to "drop anchor." The children were disappointed when they discovered that the romantic phrase simply meant that you threw a lump of iron attached to a rope overboard.

Horrified, they watched papa squeamishly impale a muddy worm on the hook. The fishing started. It consisted in baiting the hook, casting it dramatically, waiting awhile, pulling it up minus worm and fish and starting the whole thing over again.

The sun grew bright and hot. Johnny's tuxedo dried to a stiff wrinkled greenish outfit. The children started to get a whopping case of sunburn. After what seemed hours, papa announced to their intense relief and happiness that it was time to eat. He wound up the tackle, put it away, pulled up the anchor and made for the wharf. The boat seemed to go in a circle which made the wharf get further away. Finally they made shore a few hundred yards further down. Johnny tied up the boat, told the children to wait in it and went ashore. He said he was going to treat them to a nice lunch.

He came back after a while walking sideways, carrying hot dogs, huckleberry pie and strawberry pop. They sat in the rocking boat tied to the rotting wharf, looked down into the slimy green water that smelled of decaying fish, and ate. Johnny had had a few drinks ashore which made him sorry that he had hollered at the kids. He told them they could laugh at his falling into the water if they wanted to. But somehow, they couldn't bring up a laugh. The time was past for that. Papa was very cheerful, Francie thought.

"This is the life," he said. "Away from the maddening crowd. Ah, there's nothing like going down the sea in a ship. We're getting away from it all," he ended up cryptically.

After their amazing lunch, Johnny rowed them out to sea again. Perspiration poured down from under his derby and the wax in the points of his mustache melted causing the neat adornment to change into disorganized hair on his upper lip. He felt fine. He sang lustily as he rowed:

Sailing, sailing, over the bounding main.

He rowed and rowed and kept going around in a circle and never did get out to sea. Eventually his hands got so blistered that he didn't feel like rowing any more. Dramatically he announced that he was going to pull for the shore. He pulled and pulled and finally made it by rowing in smaller and smaller circles and making the circles come nearer the wharf. He never noticed that the three children were pea green in the spots where they were not beet red from the sunburn. If he had only known it, the hot dogs, huckleberry pie, strawberry pop and worms squirming on the hook weren't doing them much good.

At the wharf, he leaped to the dock and the children followed his example. All made it excepting Tilly who fell into the water. Johnny threw himself flat on the dock, reached in and fished her out. Little Tilly stood there, her lace dress wet and ruined, but she said nothing. Although it was a broiling hot day, Johnny peeled off his tuxedo jacket, knelt down and wrapped it around the child. The arms dragged in the sand. Then Johnny took her up in his arms and strode up and down the dock patting her back soothingly and singing her a lullaby. Little Tilly didn't understand a thing of all that happened that day. She didn't understand why she had been put into a boat, why she had fallen into the water or why the man was making such a fuss over her. She said nothing.

When Johnny felt that she was comforted, he set her down and went into the shack where he had either an eye opener or a night cap. He bought three flounders from the man for a quarter. He came out with the wet fish wrapped in a newspaper. He told his children that he had promised to bring home some fresh-caught fish to mama.

"The principal thing," said papa, "is that I am bringing home fish that were caught at Canarsie. It makes no difference who caught them. The point is that we went fishing and we're bringing home fish."

His children knew that he wanted mama to think he caught the fish. Papa didn't ask them to lie. He just asked them not to be too fussy about the truth. The children understood.

They boarded one of those trolley cars that had two long benches facing each other. They made a queer row. First there was Johnny in green wrinkled salt stiff pants, an undershirt full of big holes, a derby hat and a disorderly mustache. Next came Little Tilly swallowed up in his coat with salt water dripping from under it and forming a brackish pool on the floor. Francie and Neeley came next. Their faces were brick red and they sat very rigid trying not to be sick.

People got on the car, sat across from them and stared curiously. Johnny sat upright, the fish in his lap, trying not to think of the holes in his exposed undershirt. He looked over the heads of the passengers pretending to study an Ex-Lax advertisement.

More people got on, the car got crowded but no one would sit next to them. Finally one of the fish worked its way out of the sodden newspaper and fell on the floor where it lay slimily in the dust. It was too much for Little Tilly. She looked into the fish's glazed eye, said nothing but vomited silently and thoroughly all over Johnny's tuxedo jacket. Francie and Neeley, as if waiting for that cue, also threw up. Johnny sat there with two exposed fish in his lap, one at his feet and kept staring at the ad. He didn't know what else to do.

When the grisly trip was ended, Johnny took Tilly home feeling that his was the responsibility of explaining. The mother never gave him a chance to explain. She screamed when she saw her dripping be-fouled child. She snatched the coat off, threw it into Johnny's face and called him a Jack-the-Ripper. Johnny tried and tried to explain but she wouldn't listen. Little Tilly said nothing. Finally Johnny got a word in edgewise.

"Lady, I think your little girl has lost her speech."

Whereupon the mother went into hysterics. "You did it, you did it," she screamed at Johnny.

"Can't you make her say something?"

The mother grabbed the child and shook her and shook her. "Speak!" She screamed. "Say something." Finally Little Tilly opened her mouth, smiled happily and said,

"T'anks."

Katie gave Johnny a tongue lashing and said that he wasn't fit to have children. The children in question were alternating between the chills and hot flashes of a bad case of sunburn. Katie nearly cried when she saw the ruin of Johnny's only suit. It would cost a dollar to get it cleaned, steamed and pressed and she knew it would never be the same again. As for the fish, they were found to be in an advanced state of decay and had to be thrown into the garbage can.

The children went to bed. Between chills and fever and bouts of nausea, they buried their head under the covers and laughed silently and bed-shakingly at the remembrance of papa standing in the water.

Johnny sat at the kitchen window until far into the night trying to figure out why everything had been so wrong. He had sung many a song about ships and going down to the sea in them with a heave ho and a heave to. He wondered why it hadn't turned out the way it said in songs. The children should have returned exhilarated and with a deep and abiding love for the sea and he should have returned with a fine mess of fish. Why, oh why hadn't it turned out the way it did in a song? Why did there have to be his blistered hands and his spoiled suit and sunburn and rotting fish and nausea? Why didn't Little Tilly's mother understand the intention and overlook the result? He couldn't figure it out— he couldn't figure it out.

The songs of the sea had betrayed him.

The Undoing of Jean Le Nègre

From THE ENORMOUS ROOM
By E. E. Cummings

During World War I the author of this novel, attached to an ambulance corps in France, was confined in error in the French detention camp La Ferté Macé. The vile-smelling, vaultlike room which he shared with some thirty fellow men prisoners provided the material for his first book. In this polluted atmosphere, like some prodigal bloom of marsh plants, scholarship and generosity and a wild humor flourished in defiance of corrupt authority and sanity was preserved.

To the inmates Jean Le Nègre, the Negro too primitive for neuroses and too strong for chains, represented a magnificent answer to their incarceration. Jean's childlike, irrepressible nature could not be contained within any prison. The author portrays him in heroic proportions and the book's crescendo reaches its peak in the stirring apostrophe which concludes the chosen passage.

NOW we come to the story of Jean's undoing, and may the gods which made Jean Le Nègre give me grace to tell it as it was.

The trouble started with Lulu. One afternoon, shortly after the telephoning, Jean was sick at heart and couldn't be induced either to leave his couch or to utter a word. Every one guessed the reason—Lulu had left for another camp that morning. The *planton* told Jean to come down with the rest and get *soupe*. No answer. Was Jean sick? "*Oui, me seek.*" And steadfastly he refused to eat, till the disgusted *planton* gave it up and locked Jean in alone. When we ascended after *la soupe* we found Jean as we had left him, stretched on his couch, big tears on his cheeks. I asked him if I could do anything for him; he shook his head.

We offered him cigarettes—no, he did not wish to smoke. As B. and I went away we heard him moaning to himself, "Jawnee no see Loo-Loo no more." With the exception of ourselves, the inhabitants of La Ferté Macé took Jean's desolation as a great joke. Shouts of Lulu! rent the welkin on all sides. Jean stood it for an hour; then he leaped up, furious; and demanded (confronting the man from whose lips the cry had last issued)—"Feeneesh Loo-Loo?" The latter coolly referred him to the man next to him; he in turn to some one else; and round and round the room Jean stalked, seeking the offender, followed by louder and louder shouts of Lulu! and Jawnee! the authors of which (so soon as he challenged them) denied with innocent faces their guilt and recommended that Jean look closer next time. At last Jean took to his couch in utter misery and disgust.—The rest of *les hommes* descended as usual for the promenade—not so Jean. He ate nothing for supper. That evening not a sound issued from his bed.

Next morning he awoke with a broad grin, and to the salutations of Lulu! replied, laughing heartily at himself, "FEENEESH LooLoo." Upon which the tormentors (finding in him no longer a victim) desisted; and things resumed their normal course. If an occasional Lulu! upraised itself, Jean merely laughed, and repeated (with a wave of his arm) "FEENEESH." Finished Lulu seemed to be.

But *un jour* I had remained upstairs during the promenade, both because I wanted to write and because the weather was worse than usual. Ordinarily, no matter how deep the mud in the *cour*, Jean and I would trot back and forth, resting from time to time under the little shelter out of the drizzle, talking of all things under the sun. I remember on one occasion we were the only ones to brave the rain and slough—Jean in paper-thin soled slippers (which he had recently succeeded in drawing from the *Gestionnaire*) and I in my huge sabots—hurrying back and forth with the rain pouring on us, and he very proud. On this day, however, I refused the challenge of the *boue*.

The promenaders had been singularly noisy, I thought. Now they were mounting to the room making a truly tremendous racket. No sooner were the doors opened than in rushed half a dozen frenzied friends, who began telling me all at once about a terrific thing which my friend *le noir* had just done. It seems that The Sheeney With The Trick Raincoat had pulled at Jean's handkerchief (Lulu's gift in other days) which Jean wore always conspicuously in his outside breast pocket; that Jean had taken the Sheeney's head in his two hands, held it steady, abased his own head, and rammed the helpless Sheeney as a bull would do—the impact of Jean's head upon the Sheeney's nose causing that well-known feature to occupy a new position in the neighbourhood of the right ear. B. corroborated this description, adding the Sheeney's nose

was broken and that everyone was down on Jean for fighting in an un-
sportsmanlike way. I found Jean still very angry, and moreover very hurt
because everyone was now shunning him. I told him that I personally
was glad of what he'd done; but nothing would cheer him up. The
Sheeney now entered, very terrible to see, having been patched up by
Monsieur Richard with copious plasters. His nose was not broken, he
said thickly, but only bent. He hinted darkly of trouble in store for *le
noir*; and received the commiserations of everyone present except Mexique, The Zulu, B. and me. The Zulu, I remember, pointed to his own
nose (which was not unimportant), then to Jean, then made a *moue* of
excruciating anguish, and winked audibly.

Jean's spirit was broken. The wellnigh unanimous verdict against him
had convinced his minutely sensitive soul that it had done wrong. He
lay quietly, and would say nothing to anyone.

Some time after the soup, about eight o'clock, The Fighting Sheeney
and The Trick Raincoat suddenly set upon Jean Le Nègre à propos
nothing; and began pommelling him cruelly. The conscience-stricken
pillar of beautiful muscle—who could have easily killed both his assail-
ants at one blow—not only offered no reciprocatory violence but refused
even to defend himself. Unresistingly, wincing with pain, his arms mechanically raised and his head bent, he was battered frightfully to the
window by his bed, thence into the corner (upsetting the stool in the
pissoir), thence along the wall to the door. As the punishment increased
he cried out like a child: "*Laissez-moi tranquille!*"—again and again; and
in his voice the insane element gained rapidly. Finally, shrieking in
agony, he rushed to the nearest window; and while the Sheeneys together pommelled him yelled for help to the *planton* beneath.—

The unparalleled consternation and applause produced by this one-
sided battle had long since alarmed the authorities. I was still trying to
break through the five-deep ring of spectators—among whom was The
Messenger Boy, who advised me to desist and got a piece of advice in
return—when with a tremendous crash open burst the door, and in
stepped four *plantons* with drawn revolvers, looking frightened to
death, followed by the *Surveillant* who carried a sort of baton and was
crying faintly: "*Qu'est-ce que c'est!*"

At the first sound of the door the two Sheeneys had fled, and were
now playing the part of innocent spectators. Jean alone occupied the
stage. His lips were parted. His eyes were enormous. He was panting as
if his heart would break. He still kept his arms raised as if seeing everywhere before him fresh enemies. Blood spotted here and there the wonderful chocolate carpet of his skin, and his whole body glistened with
sweat. His shirt was in ribbons over his beautiful muscles.

Seven or eight persons at once began explaining the fight to the *Sur-*

veillant, who could make nothing out of their accounts and therefore called aside a trusted older man in order to get his version. The two retired from the room. The *plantons,* finding the expected wolf a lamb, flourished their revolvers about Jean and threatened him in the insignificant and vile language which *plantons* use to anyone whom they can bully. Jean kept repeating dully, "*Laissez-moi tranquille. Ils voulaient me tuer.*" His chest shook terribly with vast sobs.

Now the *Surveillant* returned and made a speech, to the effect that he had received independently of each other the stories of four men, that by all counts *le nègre* was absolutely to blame, that *le nègre* had caused an inexcusable trouble to the authorities and to his fellow-prisoners by this wholly unjustified conflict, and that as a punishment *le nègre* would now suffer the consequences of his guilt in the *cabinot.*—Jean had dropped his arms to his sides. His face was twisted with anguish. He made a child's gesture, a pitiful hopeless movement with his slender hands. Sobbing, he protested: "*C'est pas ma faute, monsieur le surveillant! Ils m'attaquaient! J'ai rien fait! Ils voulaient me tuer! Demandez à lui*"—he pointed to me desperately. Before I could utter a syllable the *Surveillant* raised his hand for silence: *le nègre* had done wrong. He should be placed in the *cabinot.*

—Like a flash, with a horrible tearing sob, Jean leaped from the surrounding *plantons* and rushed for the coat which lay on his bed screaming—"AHHHHH—*mon couteau!*"—"Look out or he'll get his knife and kill himself!" some one yelled; and the four *plantons* seized Jean by both arms just as he made a grab for his jacket. Thwarted in this hope and burning with the ignominy of his situation, Jean cast his enormous eyes up at the nearest pillar, crying hysterically: "*Tout le monde me fout au cabinot parce que je suis noir.*"—In a second, by a single movement of his arms, he sent the four *plantons* reeling to a distance of ten feet; leaped at the pillar: seized it in both hands like a Samson, and (gazing for another second with a smile of absolute beatitude at its length) dashed his head against it. Once, twice, thrice he smote himself, before the *plantons* seized him—and suddenly his whole strength wilted; he allowed himself to be overpowered by them and stood with bowed head, tears streaming from his eyes—while the smallest pointed a revolver at his heart.

This was a little more than the *Surveillant* had counted on. Now that Jean's might was no more, the bearer of the *croix de guerre* stepped forward and in a mild placating voice endeavoured to soothe the victim of his injustice. It was also slightly more than I could stand, and slamming aside the spectators I shoved myself under his honour's nose. "Do you know," I asked, "whom you are dealing with in this man? A child. There are a lot of Jeans where I come from. You heard what he said? He is black, is he not, and gets no justice from you. You heard that. I saw the whole affair. He was attacked, he put up no resistance whatever, he was beaten by two cowards. He is no more to blame than I am."—The *Surveillant* was waving his wand and cooing, "*Je comprends, je comprends, c'est malheureux.*"—"You're god damn right it's *malheureux*," I said, forgetting my French. "*Quand même*, he has resisted authority." The *Surveillant* gently continued: "Now, Jean, be quiet, you will be taken to the *cabinot*. You may as well go quietly and behave yourself like a good boy."

At this I am sure my eyes started out of my head. All I could think of to say was: "*Attends, un petit moment.*" To reach my own bed took but a second. In another second I was back, bearing my great and sacred pelisse. I marched up to Jean. "Jean," I remarked with a smile, "*tu vas au cabinot, mais tu vas revenir tout de suite. Je sais bien que tu as parfaitement raison. Mets cela*"—and I pushed him gently into my coat. "*Voici mes cigarettes, Jean; tu peux fumer comme tu veux*"—I pulled out all I had, one full *paquet jaune* of Marylands and half a dozen loose ones, and deposited them carefully in the right-hand pocket of the pelisse. Then I patted him on the shoulder and gave him the immortal salutation—"*Bonne chance, mon ami!*"

He straightened proudly. He stalked like a king through the doorway. The astounded *plantons* and the embarrassed *Surveillant* followed, the latter closing the doors behind him. I was left with a cloud of angry witnesses.

An hour later the doors opened, Jean entered quietly, and the doors shut. As I lay on my bed I could see him perfectly. He was almost naked. He laid my pelisse on his mattress, then walked calmly up to a neighbouring bed and skilfully and unerringly extracted a brush from under it. Back to his own bed he tiptoed, sat down on it, and began brushing my coat. He brushed it for a half-hour, speaking to no one, spoken to by no one. Finally he put the brush back, disposed the pelisse carefully on his arm, came to my bed, and as carefully laid it down. Then he took from the right-hand outside pocket a full *paquet jaune* and six loose cigarettes, showed them for my approval, and returned them to their place. "*Merci*," was his sole remark. B. got Jean to sit down beside him on his bed and we talked for a few minutes, avoiding the subject of the recent struggle. Then Jean went back to his own bed and lay down.

It was not till later that we learned the climax—not till *le petit belge avec le bras cassé, le petit balayeur*, came hurrying to our end of the room and sat down with us. He was bursting with excitement, his well arm jerked and his sick one stumped about and he seemed incapable of speech. At length words came.

"*Monsieur Jean*" (now that I think of it, I believe some one had told

him that all male children in America are named Jean at their birth)
"*j'ai vu QUELQUE CHOSE! le nègre, vous savez?*—*il est FORT!
Monsieur Jean, c'est un GÉANT, croyez moi! C'est pas un homme, tu
sais? Je l'ai vu, moi*"—and he indicated his eyes.

We pricked our ears.

The *balayeur*, stuffing a pipe nervously with his tiny thumb said:
"You saw the fight up here? So did I. The whole of it. *Le noir avait
raison*. Well, when they took him downstairs, I slipped out too—*Je suis
le balayeur, savez-vous?* and the *balayeur* can go where other people
can't."

—I gave him a match, and he thanked me. He struck it on his trousers with a quick pompous gesture, drew heavily on his squeaky pipe,
and at last shot a minute puff of smoke into the air; then another, and
another. Satisfied, he went on; his good hand grasping the pipe between
its index and second fingers and resting on one little knee, his legs
crossed, his small body hunched forward, wee unshaven face close to
mine—went on in the confidential tone of one who relates an unbelievable miracle to a couple of intimate friends:

"Monsieur Jean, I followed. They got him to the *cabinot*. The door
stood open. At this moment *les femmes descendaient*, it was their *corvée
d'eau, vous savez*. He saw them, *le noir*. One of them cried from the
stairs, Is a Frenchman stronger than you, Jean? The *plantons* were
standing around him, the *Surveillant* was behind. He took the nearest
planton, and tossed him down the corridor so that he struck against the
door at the end of it. He picked up two more, one in each arm, and
threw them away. They fell on top of the first. The last tried to take
hold of Jean, and so Jean took him by the neck"—(the *balayeur* stran-
gled himself for our benefit)—"and that *planton* knocked down the
other three, who had got on their feet by this time. You should have
seen the *Surveillant*. He had run away and was saying, "Capture him,
capture him." The *plantons* rushed Jean; all four of them. He caught
them as they came and threw them about. One knocked down the *Surveillant*. The *femmes* cried "Vive, Jean," and clapped their hands. The
Surveillant called to the *plantons* to take Jean, but they wouldn't go
near Jean; they said he was a black devil. The women kidded them. They
were so sore. And they could do nothing. Jean was laughing. His shirt
was almost off him. He asked the *plantons* to come and take him, please.
He asked the *Surveillant*, too. The women had set down their pails and
were dancing up and down and yelling. The *Directeur* came down and
sent them flying. The *Surveillant* and his plantons were as helpless as if
they had been children. Monsieur Jean—*quelque chose*."

I gave him another match. "*Merci, Monsieur Jean*." He struck it,
drew on his pipe, lowered it, and went on:

"They were helpless, and men. I am little. I have only one arm, *tu sais*. I walked up to Jean and said, "Jean, you know me, I am your friend." He said, "Yes." I said to the *plantons*, "Give me that rope." They gave me the rope that they would have bound him with. He put out his wrists for me. I tied his hands behind his back. He was like a lamb. The *plantons* rushed up and tied his feet together. Then they tied his hands and feet together. They took the lacings out of his shoes for fear he would use them to strangle himself. They stood him up in an angle between two walls in the *cabinot*. They left him there for an hour. He was supposed to have been in there all night; but The *Surveillant* knew that he would have died, for he was almost naked, and *vous savez*, Monsieur Jean, it was cold in there. And damp. A fully-clothed man would have been dead in the morning. And he was naked . . . Monsieur Jean—*un géant!*"

—This same *petit belge* had frequently protested to me that *Il est fou, le noir*. He is always playing when sensible men try to sleep. The last few hours (which had made of the *fou* a *géant*) made of the scoffer a worshipper. Nor did *"le bras cassé"* ever from that time forth desert his divinity. If as *balayeur* he could lay hands on a *morceau de pain* or de *viande*, he bore it as before to our beds; but Jean was always called over to partake of the forbidden pleasure.

As for Jean, one would hardly have recognized him. It was as if the child had fled into the deeps of his soul, never to reappear. Day after day went by, and Jean (instead of courting excitement as before) cloistered himself in solitude; or at most sought the company of B. and me and *le petit belge* for a quiet chat or a cigarette. The morning after the three fights he did not appear in the *cour* for early promenade along with the rest of us (including The Sheeneys). In vain did *les femmes* strain their necks and eyes to find the *noir qui était plus fort que six français*. And B. and I noticed our bed-clothing airing upon the windowsills. When we mounted, Jean was patting and straightening our blankets, and looking for the first time in his life guilty of some enormous crime. Nothing however had disappeared. Jean said, "Me feeks, *lits tous les jours*." And every morning he aired and made our beds for us, and we mounted to find him smoothing affectionately some final ruffle, obliterating with enormous solemnity some microscopic crease. We gave him cigarettes when he asked for them (which was almost never) and offered them when we knew he had none or when we saw him borrowing from some one else whom his spirit held in less esteem. Of us he asked no favours. He liked us too well.

When B. went away, Jean was almost as desolate as I.

About a fortnight later, when the grey dirty snow-slush hid the black filthy world which we saw from our windows, and when people lived in their ill-smelling beds, it came to pass that my particular *amis*—The Zulu, Jean, Mexique—and I and all the remaining miserables of La Ferté descended at the decree of Cæsar Augustus to endure our biweekly *bain*. I remember gazing stupidly at Jean's chocolate-coloured nakedness as it strode to the tub, a rippling texture of muscular miracle. *Tout le monde* had *baigné* (including The Zulu, who tried to escape at the last minute and was nabbed by the *planton* whose business it was to count heads and see that none escaped the ordeal) and now *tout le monde* was shivering all together in the ante-room, begging to be allowed to go upstairs and get into bed—when *Le Baigneur*, Monsieur Richard's strenuous successor that is, set up a hue and cry that one *serviette* was lacking. The Fencer was sent for. He entered; heard the case; and made a speech. If the guilty party would immediately return the stolen towel, he, The Fencer, would guarantee that party pardon; if not, everyone present should be searched, and the man on whose person the *serviette* was found *va attraper quinze jours de cabinot*. This eloquence yielding no results, The Fencer exhorted the culprit to act like a man and render to Cæsar what is Cæsar's. Nothing happened. Everyone was told to get in single file and make ready to pass out the door. One after one we were searched; but so general was the curiosity that as fast as they were inspected the erstwhile bed-enthusiasts, myself included, gathered on the side-lines to watch their fellows instead of availing themselves of the opportunity to go upstairs. One after one we came opposite The Fencer, held up our arms, had our pockets run through and our clothing felt over from head to heel, and were exonerated. When Cæsar came to Jean, Cæsar's eyes lighted, and Cæsar's hitherto perfunctory proddings and pokings became inspired and methodical. Twice he went over Jean's entire body, while Jean, his arms raised in a bored gesture, his face completely expressionless, suffered loftily the examination of his person. A third time the desperate Fencer tried; his hands, starting at Jean's neck, reached the calf of his leg—and stopped. The hands rolled up Jean's right trouser leg to the knee. They rolled up the underwear on his leg—and there, placed perfectly flat to the skin, appeared the missing *serviette*. As The Fencer seized it, Jean laughed—the utter laughter of old days—and the onlookers cackled uproariously, while with a broad smile The Fencer proclaimed: "I thought I knew where I should find it." And he added, more pleased with himself than anyone had ever seen him—"*Maintenant, vous pouvez tous monter à la chambre.*" We mounted, happy to get back to bed; but none so happy as Jean Le Nègre. It was not that the *cabinot* threat had failed to materialize— at any minute a *planton* might call Jean to his punishment: indeed this was what everyone expected. It was that the incident had absolutely removed that inhibition which (from the day when Jean *le noir* became

Jean *le géant*) had held the child, which was Jean's soul and destiny, prisoner. From that instant till the day I left him he was the old Jean— joking, fibbing, laughing, and always playing—Jean L'Enfant.

And I think of Jean Le Nègre . . . you are something to dream over, Jean; summer and winter (birds and darkness) you go walking into my head; you are a sudden and chocolate-coloured thing, in your hands you have a habit of holding six or eight *plantons* (which you are about to throw away) and the flesh of your body is like the flesh of a very deep cigar. Which I am still and always quietly smoking: always and still I am inhaling its very fragrant and remarkable muscles. But I doubt if ever I am quite through with you, if ever I will toss you out of my heart into the sawdust of forgetfulness. Kid, Boy, I'd like to tell you: *la guerre est finie.*

O yes, Jean: I do not forget, I remember Plenty; the snow's coming, the snow will throw again a very big and gentle shadow into The Enormous Room and into the eyes of you and me walking always and wonderfully up and down. . . .

—Boy, Kid, Nigger with the strutting muscles—take me up into your mind once or twice before I die (you know why: just because the eyes of me and you will be full of dirt some day). Quickly take me up into the bright child of your mind, before we both go suddenly all loose and silly (you know how it will feel). Take me up (carefully; as if I were a toy) and play carefully with me, once or twice, before I and you go suddenly all limp and foolish. Once or twice before you go into great Jack roses and ivory—(once or twice Boy before we together go wonderfully down into the Big Dirt laughing, bumped with the last darkness).

The Passing of the Coastwise Steamer

From LIGHTSHIP

By Archie Binns

Here is a variant of the familiar sea novel in which men sail be-tween ports and endure perils in a life of action. A lightship is a float-ing lighthouse rather than a ship as it stands guard outside a reef. The vessel's isolation and static existence reduce its men to extreme levels of loneliness. When this loneliness is interrupted by a passing ship, all the individual yearnings and secret dreams of the lightship's crew are released and they become for a tantalizing moment within reach of the world they have left behind.

WHEN Clark went on deck at eight, he sensed the game was about up. It was blowing a full gale, and the lightship leaped and bucked and rolled her boats under in the great seas that marched out of the west, thundering and smoking as they came. The engine was turning over at half speed, taking some of the strain from the cable, but the shock was tremendous each time she brought up. Sooner or later, he thought, something would let go. Captain Lindstrom had made his choice between running the engine at half speed, on the chance of rid-ing it out or breaking loose with enough fuel to reach shelter—or run-ning at full speed until the coal was gone, and then going adrift for a certainty and piling helplessly on the reef.

The everlasting reef. Clark turned his face aft and saw the departing seas boil over the half-tide grinders and spout against the higher fangs. Wild white horses and geysering whales sporting on hell's bathing beach. The boil and leap and fall of white water down the long reef was sound-less because of the gale from seaward, and the noise about the ship.

113

Closer, the bellowing would be terrible. But if that was going to come, it would come. Clark turned his face seaward and did not look back again.

He cared and did not care about what might happen. His mind had admitted its defeat long ago, but his body was still powerful and terribly alive. It would go on fighting with strength and cunning as long as it had the spark of life. His body was already scheming; his muscles rehearsing the motions of fastening him to this or that flotsam if the ship foundered or broke up. They would be unerring in seizing the best chance; if anything living got through the reef, it would be Clark's body. And all the time his mind was scornful of the fight it would put up against destruction. His mind was quite ready to knock off and call it a day.

The lightship wasn't much of a life. At best, it preserved him, like salt junk, in brine. And it wasn't preserving him for anything in particular. He got ashore, sometimes, on liberty and when the ship was in drydock at Eagle Harbor. And he was tired of his search for prostitutes who were like Virginia. That was another defeat his body had never admitted. Wherever there were women, his body was trying to find her. After all these years, he couldn't make it understand she was dead. She had given herself to him so completely that she had taken him completely. His body could still feel her in every fiber and hear her sweet, ringing voice. It thought it had only to reach out and touch her. His body was like a great dog, too stupid and faithful to understand about death, searching for its lost mistress. Like the Great Dane after Mrs. Walters died. Like that, and his mind was chained to the brute; dragged after it, protesting against the ridiculous, tragic search.

In his mind, it was all over and done with. He wanted to forget Virginia as much as possible. That was the best thing to do. Sometimes he even cursed the unfair hold she had on him. She should have lived, or taken that wild, penetrating sweetness with her. He wanted to shake it off, but the terrible fidelity of his body defeated him. . . .

The sea was swept clean, except for one steamer. Those gray, smoking seas looked as if they could sweep everything clean, and start over again. One of the Commodore Line steamers from San Francisco, with passengers. Little single-screw tub, making heavy weather of it. She was standing out now, taking it on the nose. A long beat seaward, then she would run in for the Straits with a quartering sea. Handling a full-powered steamer like a sailing ship. She wasn't making much progress, though. None, it seemed. Hove-to, maybe, waiting for better weather. That would be a long wait. Better get more sea-room, Captain. She was four miles further from the reef than the lightship, but she was miles too close at that.

The lightship wasn't taking much solid water on board, riding high and empty, but she reared and bucked and rolled madly in the seas that came down on her like mountains gone adrift. Every now and then, one of the boats, double lashed to its spar, would be pushed clear under. Then it would flourish up against the sky, red and shining wet, as if newly painted. The snubbing gear was a big gun, fired at regular intervals. No gear could stand that forever.

"How is it, Clark?"

Harry, with his dirty apron on, and his game leg, came toiling up the companion stairs. Like a hopeful child going up to bed in a house with the roof blown off.

"Middling bad," Clark told him. "But we're holding on."

"Bad? I was afraid it would be. But isn't it wonderful!"

Clark was startled. Wonderful? He hadn't thought of it that way.

"It's very beautiful."

Harry hadn't expected death to come this way; to come on deck from peeling the last potatoes, with his apron still on, and see the gates opening in awful grandeur. He couldn't fight against it because the thing was so much greater than himself. He couldn't even be sorry, down in his heart where he was afraid. He was very tired, and while he had come near getting a great deal out of life, he had missed. He had worn himself out and didn't have much of anything to show for it. He didn't mind being broken up. In the morning, he thought, the Indians would find his body on the shore. There was a mysterious comfort in that. His body would be a sacrifice for the wrongs done by his arrogant race. He offered it gladly.

"God, look at her roll!" Clark's great voice called him back.

"Where?"

"Just off the port bow!" Clark shouted. "Come up here, and you can see her." He opened the iron companion door, and the messman stepped out on deck, where the wind slashed through his thin clothes and moulded his apron to his legs. "See her?"

The coatwise steamer had swung back on her course for the Straits, sluggishly, taking the sea directly on her beam. They saw her whole hurricane deck, with a row of toy lifeboats on each side, as she rolled to leeward. Then everything but the masts disappeared as she sank in the trough.

"They'll never hold that course," the seaman declared. "A few like that will do for her!"

The two watchers lost the steamer altogether as a great graybeard bore down on the lightship, shutting out everything to seaward. Rising, they saw her again, still a point off the port bow. Her position was unchanged, except that she was taking the sea more on the quarter.

"What are they doing?" Harry shouted, bewildered at the aimless maneuver.

"Broken down, by God! Tell the captain there's a ship out here in distress—and better get a coat before you come on deck again."

Within a minute, everyone but the chief and Allen was on deck. The steamer had swung still more and was approaching them head-on. The men ignored the wild motion of their own ship, and only cursed the sea when it rose, smoking, between them and the approaching vessel. It was a nice source of speculation as to what was wrong.

"Maybe a broken tail-shaft," Ben suggested boldly. He had once read about that happening to a ship.

"That's one thing she hasn't got," Captain Lindstrom answered firmly. "The drag of the propeller is what keeps her stern up to the sea."

"Maybe they got no coal," Oscar said. The joke was too grim and personal for anyone to smile.

"What will we do if she comes here?" Harry wanted to know.

"What could we do?" Ole demanded coolly.

"We must do something!" the messman cried passionately. "There are women and children on board. Think of the helpless ones!"

The captain looked at him, anxiously. "We're doing all we can by being on our station, Harry." The snubbing gear crashed heavily, and he turned his face toward the steamer again as the spray-lashed ship rose with the sea. "Her master knows his exact position, and how long he has to make repairs—if they can be made."

"Ha, me byes, what have we got here?" Mickey O'Rorke's gray, grimy cat's face popped up from the companionway. Ben moved nearer Oscar, making room for the chief, and Oscar shrank away from the boy, glaring.

"Well, Chief, it looks like a job for her engineers," the captain observed.

For the moment, Mickey ignored the gentle raillery against his department. " 'Tis their circulator," he decided, "or else a main bearing."

The steamer was looming big as she bore down on the lightship, a thin banner of smoke driving before her.

Mickey hitched up his disgraceful old pants, on the very point of falling off. "They're all on their knees by now, praying to the engineers," he said with relish.

"Let's hope their prayers are answered."

The lightship leaped up and fell, floundering, ducking her boats under, with the crash of snubbing gear striking through the noise of the sea and gale. Ole sheltered a little round tin in his hand, and put a pinch of snuff in his cheek, without taking his cool, shrewd eyes from the steamer. "It's the *Paul Jones*," he said.

"What a half-arsed world," the chief commented. "They have fuel and no engine, and we have an engine and no fuel!" He blinked at the disabled craft, with piratical intent. If there were only some way of plundering her as she went by!

"Big one coming!" Ole called sharply.

At the same instant, Clark broke through the group about the companionway and lunged toward the wheel-house.

"Ring full speed!" the captain roared after him, while the little chief scuttled below.

To Ben, the chance sea that alarmed the others did not seem much different from the ones that preceded it. Then, as it loomed nearer, he changed his mind and took shelter in the companionway. As the lightship sank in the trough, the gong clanged faintly in the engine room. The sea blotted out the horizon, all the other seas that followed, and even the masts of the *Paul Jones*. There was nothing yielding or liquid about that sea; it was like a solid mountain range, gray-green, flecked with dirty snow, booming and smoking with volcanic power. The lightship rose to it with gallant desperation, steeper and steeper. . . . Then the crest exploded over her bow in a great burst of white that swept aft like a snowstorm. The sea passed, thundering by in the white darkness, and the air cleared.

In the relative silence following, a new sound came from forward, something bumping and grating, painfully.

Mr. Gill put his hand on Ben's arm and stopped him as he was following the captain and Ole below. "Stay on deck and get some air while you can, Lad. We'll soon be on our way home, with no chance to come above."

"Do you think so?"

The portly old fireman was positive. "The chain stopper is breaking up," he said. "The first solid jerk after the springs are gone, and we'll be steaming hell-for-leather for the Straits."

"Do you suppose we'll make it?" the boy asked anxiously.

"We'll make it, Ben. We know a trick or two yet. Look how close she is."

The *Paul Jones* was coming down from windward, hardly a quarter of a mile away, heading close for the lightship.

"I'll give her until she gets abreast of us to make her repair," Mr. Gill announced, puffing comfortably at the pipe he had just lit in the shelter of the companionway.

"I do hope she makes it," Harry said fervently.

"She'll make it, Lads."

Captain Lindstrom and Ole came from below. The captain held a piece of the three-inch spiraled steel that had been driven through the side of the vegetable bin, denting one of the iron hull plates. The wonder was it hadn't gone clear through.

Mickey came up and looked at the fragment of spring. "How long will the other be lasting?" he wondered.

"Not long, with a real stress." The captain swept back his long, wet hair with one hand. "Steaming to our mooring like this, it should hold until we see what happens to that ship, God help her."

"And then God help us!" the chief answered.

The steamer was coming down fast. When a sea burst white against her stern, she yawed badly but was pushed along faster toward the reef. The light banner of smoke, whirled forward from the stack, showed she was still breathing; alive but unconscious. There was no one in sight but one oilskin figure, motionless on the high bridge. Below decks, there would be a crew of thirty or forty, and a hundred-odd passengers—to spill out horribly at the last moment, when the ship burst on the reef.

The lightship bounded and lunged and staggered, rolling her boats under, rolling them up against the gray, racing sky. Forward, the broken gear gnawed at her hold on life, grinding, tearing—something felt rather than heard. Harry had known something like it before: the ends of the broken bone in his leg working together as he dragged himself across the deck of the *Bloody Harvester*, after the mate had knocked him from the main yard. The grind and bump of broken gear went to his maimed leg, hurting it acutely.

The *Paul Jones* rolled abreast, fifty yards to port, drifting on toward destruction like a sleepwalker.

"God help her engineers!" Mickey said—and went below to look after his own engines.

"Wake up!" Ben shouted, as if the ship might hear and head up before it was too late.

Harry looked about, wildly, for some means of helping the disabled steamer. "Think of the helpless ones!" he cried, working his hands together. He was knocked down by a vicious roll of the lightship, and when Oscar helped him up, disgustedly, he was still shouting, "Think of the helpless ones!"

They had to look aft, now. The steamer was passing them. Her stern, thrown up by a sea, showed the rudder and four-bladed propeller, unbroken but lifeless. Three miles ahead, the white water of the reef leaped and spouted and beckoned: wild white horses and tall sirens, dancing their unholy welcome. A breaking sea exploded against the steamer's counter. It seemed to Ben that the thick, high-flung spray took the form of women with veiled white limbs. Impatient sirens who had swum out from the reef and were pushing the ship toward their rocks in triumph.

The crew turned until they were looking dead aft, staring after the ship as if their lives depended on her fate. She seemed to be closing with the reef more rapidly now. Beyond the veil of dancing white water, there were the hills and forests of the land, but they floated in grayness, cloudy and insubstantial, like the coast of another world. It was another world, since one would have to die to reach that shore.

"They're gone to hell," Oscar muttered. "It's rotten; everything is rotten!"

"Only one piece of machinery is rotten," Ole answered, impatiently.

Ben was wet through with spray, shivering violently.

"You should go below and warm up," the captain told him.

But he stayed on deck, doggedly, with chattering teeth.

The *Paul Jones* became a dark, receding bulk, outlined against bursting white. She looked like a ship steaming confidently toward a safe harbor. Now, it was hard to say how far she was from the reef. She appeared to be on top of it, but might have been half a mile away. At most, though, it could only be a matter of a few minutes. Time was measured by the heave and roll of the lightship, the boom of seas and the gnawing of broken gear.

"She's struck!" Oscar croaked.

The steamer's progress appeared to have stopped. Her stern swung toward the reef until she was broadside on. Then she rolled to leeward, farther and farther, until her superstructure disappeared.

"Holy Christ!" Allen had come above, with a sweatcloth about his neck, and was staring at the doomed ship.

Harry turned forward, clinging to the side of the companionway, unable to watch the white curtain of death fall over the ship. "Think of the helpless ones!"

"It will be quick," Ole said.

"She's under weigh!" the captain roared out.

The others held their breath, uncertain of the outcome. Harry took courage and looked. The steamer was turning still more, staggering wildly as she headed up.

"They're the boys!" Mr. Gill boomed, patting the surprised Oscar on his souwestered head.

The steamer's sharp bow divided a sea, head-on, in a great burst of snow. Black smoke raced aft from her stack. She was forging ahead now.

"Hooray for the engineers!" Mickey crowed, popping up from the companionway. A moment later, he spied the deserter from the fireroom. "Allen, Allen! Get below, ye tourist! You're fired! Do ye hear me, you're fired!"

"We'll be under weigh next," Mr. Gill confided to Ben, recognizing the familiar sign. " 'Ray for the old *Paul Jones!*"

Allen gave a final look and went below, grinning broadly under a shower of abuse from the chief.

The steamer was drawing away from the reef, rearing and diving and reeling under the blows of the sea, but forging ahead.

Captain Lindstrom drew Mickey out of the hearing of the others.

"How long will the coal last at this rate, Chief?"

"Two hours, at most."

"At half speed?"

"Short of five hours."

The captain's mild eyes narrowed. "You can stand by," he said. "When the *Jones* passes, I will ring for half speed."

"The gear will never stand it!" Mickey's old face was grim.

"It will have to stand it, or carry away."

"We've hung on so long we can't afford to be breaking loose!"

The captain smiled gently, still able to appreciate irony. "We can't choose the moment of our freedom," he said. "The best we can do is gamble for a little more time. I will ring for half speed."

Mickey knew it was useless to argue with him when he had that mystical smile. And it was just possible he might be right; his understanding of things wasn't bad, for a captain.

The *Paul Jones* was heading to pass to starboard, and the crew shifted to that side of the companionway. They would have strung out along the rail, only the sea wouldn't have left them there for long.

The steamer's bow overlapped the lightship's flourishing stern. The figure on the bridge waved, in a more expansive mood than on the trip to the reef. Mickey gave the engineers a cheer. The man on the bridge had stood there like a bold hero, after the manner of deck officers, while the engineers made their repairs in the midst of blood and sweat and burns—and brought the ship back from the mouth of hell. He gave them another cheer, and went below. It spoiled things a little that the steamer's safety should be the signal for the lightship's mortal danger.

The lightship leaped and twisted and fought, tearing at her mooring as if she too wanted her moment of freedom. The spray-drenched crew was unconscious of her antics, with their eyes fastened on the *Paul Jones*. She battled abreast of them. Not yet. . . . A door on the upper deck opened a little, slowly, and a woman came out. A tall young woman in a gray coat and a small hat. She kept one hand on the knob of the door, which the wind had forcibly shut behind her, and raised the other to her throat, with a quick, compassionate gesture. Startled, perhaps, at finding the sea-battered lightship so close.

The steamer was drawing ahead, passing. A disordered cheer went up from the crew and was dashed away by the wind and lost in the thunder of a breaking sea. The lightship's whistle wheezed croupily, then changed into a roar as Clark hung on the cord. Good-bye, and good luck! An answering burst of steam swirled about the stack of the *Paul Jones*. The tall girl was waving now, throwing kisses with impersonal ardor. The mellow blast of the whistle reached them, faint but pleasantly.

Ole waved to the young woman, with the others. She was the kind he had never known. If he had been good-looking or fortunate, he might have been with a woman like that for love, and he would have known what she was like. But it hadn't happened that way. He had only been with whores and paid for what he got. Beyond quick necessity, women hadn't played much part in his life. It was stupid of him to know so little about them, when men and women were going to work together to make the new world. Ole removed the quid of snuff from his cheek and waved respectfully to the woman he had never known.

Mr. Gill took off his padded black cap and brandished it gallantly at the end of one big arm, wishing the little woman good luck. While he was still waving, he recognized her: the girl he had once walked with at dusk by the shore of the sea. Beyond that, he still didn't know who she was. Distance and driven spray blurred her face, as the twilight had done then. But he remembered her white hands, and he could still hear the caress of her voice, telling him a secret that was lost through his own preoccupation and the sound of the sea. He was flattered to think that she remembered him. If he could only recall a little more of their other meeting. . . . It came to him that she might be Death—he had been close to that lady before—and if that was it, he would know her better before long. Whoever she was, it was pleasant to see her again. Good-bye, and good luck, and no regrets! He had kept his own integrity and had a good life.

Harry waved frantically, with his voice calling: "Jibby, Jibby!" At first, he didn't know why he said that. Then he remembered. The *Paul Jones* was from San Francisco, and it was natural Jibby should be on board. The conscious part of him hadn't recognized her at first, because he had only known her as an irresponsible child. But that was years ago, and perhaps she had grown up; she would be about that age.

Jibby was a playmate Martha invented when she was three: she wore "a shirt, and then a bunnit-hat," and she lived in San Francisco. But Jibby had no regard for distance. Sometimes she pattered into Martha's room in the evening, and kept her awake and hilarious when she should have been sleeping, and sometimes she descended recklessly on a rare sunbeam. Jibby got into a great deal of mischief, and even drew pictures on the title page of Catlin's *North American Indians*. Often, Martha had to drive her away with angry little shouts and much stamping of feet, but when she didn't appear for a few days the flat was lonely. Harry never quite saw Jibby, but she had always been very real to him. Now, he was seeing her at last. She had grown up, tall and lovely, and was leaving San Francisco. If she went to New York, she would see the Village—it had become a kind of show-place, Harry understood. When she walked along Greenwich Avenue, would she remember the red tenement, near Jane Street, and the fifth-floor flat where she used to fly in at the window? Thank you, Jibby. You did your best. Good-bye, and good luck!

Ben had grown bold and was throwing kisses. His mind was clear and he felt sure of himself at last. The beautiful young woman on the steamer had done something to him. She had answered the questions that tumbled about in his mind for so long. The tumbling pieces had come to rest, fitting in a perfect pattern, and he saw how it was. Women weren't all either cold angels or degraded prostitutes. No woman was either of her own choice. They were warm-hearted human beings, eager for life, and he should have known that before. Everyone would know, only religion and education told men and women lies about each other to keep them apart. Often, the lies worked because people tried to live up to them. When that happened a man and woman didn't find each other, even though they lived together.

That was what the tall girl on the steamer was telling Ben. "We're warm and human, and we're coming into our own. The ones who treat women as something more than human beings wrong them as much as those who treat them as something less."

Ben waved frantically, to say he understood and would remember.

Only Oscar did not wave. And he found it hard to refrain, with so many waving hands and caps about him. He didn't think the woman on the Paul Jones was a whore, but her behavior strengthened a dark suspicion in his mind: the suspicion that at heart, all women are whores. Her waving and throwing kisses showed what she was under her fine clothes and fine manners. She had practically offered to come on board the lightship.

Oscar looked down his nose, to where his paunch made an expectant bulge in his spray-drenched yellow slicker. He felt dreadfully ashamed, standing there among those waving, cheering men. His embarrassment grew until he became afraid to look up and see the woman, flaunting the dirty secret of life. And at the same time he wanted, terribly, to have another look at her.

Clark was in the wheel-house, waiting for the lightship to go adrift, and watching the Paul Jones battle her way seaward. As he pulled the whistle cord, wishing her good luck, his body told him that the graceful, tall girl was Virginia. And his mind half believed it. She was very like that, and she held her head that way, and there was something about her waving. . . .

He remembered the day after their swim in the starlit creek, when he was afraid she would never come back. Then he came out of the woods, and the flames shot through him when he saw her beside the cutter. She was mending the storm trys'l, with her hat beside her on the grass, turned so she would see him as soon as he appeared at the far end of the meadow. She had waved to him like that, dear and proud, to tell him that for her there was no turning back from love.

The girl was throwing kisses now, and the flames were going through him, telling him that for his body there was no turning back, either. Virginia was on the *Paul Jones*; she would be in Seattle before him. It couldn't be Virginia, that was impossible. But was it? No one knew what happened, afterward. There might be some way of escaping the backwaters of death. Maybe one learned how, after a while.

The *Paul Jones* drew away from the lightship, rolling and pitching, shouldering the gray, smoking seas into bursting white. Her stern was thrown up and the wet blades of the propeller spun madly in unsubstantial spray. They sank and took hold of the sea again, driving on toward safety. The ensign, inverted at the head of the mainmast as a signal of distress, descended, jerkily, on an invisible halliard. The steamer was confident of making her own way.

Captain Lindstrom went below to cut down the revolutions of the engine. Better to tell the chief, quietly, without using the gong. It was a great load off his mind to see the *Jones* clear of the reef. A close call, and a nice problem for her master. Another situation where letting go the anchors would have been the wrong thing. Perhaps commanding a lightship prejudiced a man against all anchors.

Anna. He mustn't think of her now. That young woman on the steamer had the making of a sailor, coming on deck in such a storm. Probably the stewards were too seasick or scared to stop her. A fine, healthy type. She reminded him of Anna. Not Anna, the woman, in childbed. He mustn't think of that now. Anna at twenty. Remember that last night in Finland? Pine and birch logs roaring in the fireplace. The cry of violins, loud-singing balalaikas and the stamping feet of the dance. Outside, the fields under snow; forest black in the iron cold, and the moon going down into Russia. Anna standing beside him, tall and strong and healthy, like that girl on the steamer. Flushed pink and gold, with the blue fires of her eyes flickering through him with countless meanings.

"Carl, we are going to the Promised Land!"

She had said that a hundred times before, always with thrilling wonder. Half her wonder was because he had been there before. People on the Oregon side of the Columbia River didn't know they were living in the Promised Land. Carl hadn't known, living there, when he planned to search for it in the South Seas.

Now Anna knew the Promised Land better than he, and the children didn't know any other. Young Carl was doing well in the fifth grade; Richard was in the third, and at the end of Anna's last letter Walter had ground out in great, lumpy letters: "I love my Daddy." Three fine, healthy children growing up to be Americans, and the fourth waiting to be born, or born already. Or would it be born the moment the lightship crashed on the reef? Mustn't think of Anna and the children now. Not until the ship was safe—if there was any safety. Until then, he belonged to his other family, the crew. They needed him—those hopeful, heartbreaking bastards the sea had brought him.

The Jew

From CIMARRON

By Edna Ferber

Oklahoma, the last territory to be settled, nevertheless reflected all the color and impulse of the pioneer era. Even in the 1890's the virtues and vices of the town of Osage are again primitive under the wilderness impress. Sol Levy, the alien Jew who meets there the full intolerance of the frontier, finds sympathy and understanding only in Dixie Lee, leader of the town's prostitutes—a social outcast like himself—and in Yancey Cravat, editor of the Osage newspaper, and his wife Sabra. Yancey's past, Miss Ferber explains earlier in the novel, "was clouded with myths and surmises. Rumor, romantic, unsavory, fantastic, shifting and changing like clouds on a mountain peak, floated about the head of Yancey Cravat. They say he has Indian blood in him . . . an Indian wife, somewhere, and a lot of papooses." But whatever his past, his defense of the Jew, as the symbol of the crucifixion is presented, shows a gentleness and sensitivity which is reflected in the Cravat household.

SLOWLY, slowly, the life of the community, in the beginning so wild, so unrelated in its parts, began to weave in and out, warp and woof, to make a pattern. It was at first faint, almost undiscernible. But presently the eye could trace here a motif, there a figure, here a motif, there a figure. The shuttle swept back, forward, back, forward.

"It's almost time for the Jew," Sabra would say, looking up from her sewing. "I need some number forty sewing-machine needles."

And then perhaps next day, or the day after, Cim, playing in the yard, would see a familiar figure, bent almost double, gnomelike and

125

grotesque, against the western sky. It was Sol Levy, the peddler, the Alsatian Jew. Cim would come running into the house, Donna, perhaps, trotting at his heels. "Mom, here comes the Jew!"

Sabra would fold up her work, brush the threads from her apron; or if her hands were in the dough she would hastily mold and crimp her pie crust so as to be ready for his visit.

Sol Levy had come over an immigrant in the noisome bowels of some dreadful ship. His hair was blue-black and very thick, and his face was white in spite of the burning Southwest sun. A black stubble of beard intensified this pallor. He had delicate blue-veined hands and narrow arched feet. His face was delicate, too, and narrow, and his eyes slanted ever so little at the outer corners, so that he had the faintly Oriental look sometimes seen in the student type of his race. He belonged in crowded places, in populous places, in the color and glow and swift drama of the bazaars. God knows how he had found his way to this vast wilderness. Perhaps in Chicago, or in Kansas City, or Omaha he had heard of this new country and the rush of thousands for its land. And he had bummed his way on foot. He had started to peddle with an oilcloth-covered pack on his back. Through the little hot Western towns in summer. Through the bitter cold Western towns in winter. They turned the dogs on him. The children cried, "Jew! Jew!" He was only a boy, disguised with that stubble of beard. He would enter the yard of a farmhouse or a dwelling in a town such as Osage. A wary eye on the dog. Nice Fido. Nice doggie. Down, down! Pins, sewing-machine needles, rolls of gingham and calico, and last, craftily, his Hamburg lace. Hamburg lace for the little girls' petticoats, for the aprons of the lady of the house; the white muslin apron edged with Hamburg lace, to be donned after the midday dinner dishes were done, the house set to rights, her hair tidied with a wet comb, the basket of mending got out, or the roll of strips for the rag rug, to be plaited in the precious hours between three and five. He brought news, too.

"The bridge is out below Gray Horse. . . . The Osages are having a powwow at Hominy. All night they kept me awake with their drums, those savages. . . . The Kid and his gang held up the Santa Fé near Wetoka and got thirty-five thousand dollars; but one of them will never hold up a train again. A shot in the head. Verdigris Bob, they call him. A name! They say the posse almost caught the Kid himself because this Verdigris Bob when he finds he is dying he begs the others to leave him and go on, but first they must stop to take his boots off. His boots he wants to have off, that murderer, to die a respectable man! The Kid stops to oblige him, and the posse in ten more minutes would have caught him, too. A feather in that sheriff's cap, to catch the Kid! . . . A country! My forefathers should have lived to see me here!"

His beautiful, civilized face, mobile as an actor's, was at once expressive of despair and bitter amusement. His long slender hands were spread in a gesture of wondering resignation.

Later he bought a horse—a quadruped possessed unbelievably of the power of locomotion—a thing rheumy-eyed, cadaverous, high rumped, like a cloth horse in a pantomime. Sol Levy was always a little afraid of it; timorous of those great square white teeth, like gravestones. He came of a race of scholars and traders. Horses had been no part of their experience. He had to nerve himself to wait on it, to give it the feed bag, an occasional apple or lump of sugar. With the horse and rickety wagon he now added kitchenware to his stock, coarse china, too; bolts of woollen cloth; and, slyly, bright colored silks and muslin flowers and ribbons. Dixie Lee and her girls fell upon these with feverish fingers and shrill cries, like children. He spread his wares for them silently. Sometimes they teased him, these pretty morons; they hung on his meager shoulders, stroked his beard. He regarded them remotely, almost sadly.

"Come on, Solly!" they said. "Why don't you smile? Don't you never have no fun? I bet you're rich, Jews is all rich. Ain't that the truth, Maude?"

His deep-sunk eyes looked at them. *Schicksas.* They grew uncomfortable under his gaze, then sullen, then angry. "Go on, get the hell out of here! You got your money, ain't you? Get, sheeny!"

He sometimes talked to Dixie Lee. There existed between these two a strange relation of understanding and something resembling respect. Outcasts, both of them, he because of his race, she because of her calling. "A smart girl like you, what do you want in such a business?"

"I've got to live, Solly. God knows why!"

"You come from a good family. You are young yet, you are smart. There are other ways."

"Ye-e-e-s? I guess I'll take up school teaching. Tell a lot of snotty-nosed brats that two and two make four and get handed eleven dollars at the end of the month for it. I tried a couple of things. Nix, nix!"

In a year or two he opened a little store in Osage. It was, at first, only a wooden shack containing two or three rough pine tables on which his wares were spread. He was the town Jew. He was a person apart. Sometimes the cowboys deviled him; or the saloon loungers and professional bad men. They looked upon him as fair game. He thought of them as savages. Yancey came to his rescue one day in the spectacular fashion he enjoyed. Seated at his desk in the *Wigwam* office Yancey heard hoots, howls, catcalls, and then the crack and rat-a-tat-tat of a fusillade. The porch of the Sunny Southwest Saloon was filled with grinning faces beneath sombreros. In the middle of the dusty road, his back against a Howe scale, stood Sol Levy. They had tried to force him to drink a great glass of whisky straight. He had struggled, coughed, sputtered; had succeeded in spitting out the burning stuff. They had got another. They were holding it up from their vantage point on the porch. Their six-shooters were in their hands. And they were shooting at him—at his feet, at his head, at his hands, expertly, devilishly, miraculously, never hitting him, but always careful to come within a fraction of an inch. He had no weapon. He would not have known how to use it if he had possessed one. He was not of a race of fighters.

"Drink it!" the yells were high and less than human. "You're a dead Jew if you don't. Dance, gol darn you! Dance for your drink!"

The bullets spat all about him, sang past his ears, whipped up the dust about his feet. He did not run. He stood there, facing them, frozen with fear. His arms hung at his sides. His face was deathly white. They had shot off his hat. He was bareheaded. His eyes were sunken, suffering, stricken. His head lolled a little on one side. His thick black locks hung dank on his forehead. At that first instant of seeing him as he rushed out of his office, Yancey thought, subconsciously, "He looks like —like—" But the resemblance eluded him then. It was only later, after the sickening incident had ended, that he realized of Whom it was that the Jew had reminded him as he stood there, crucified against the scale.

Yancey ran into the road. It is impossible to say how he escaped being killed by one of the bullets. He seemed to leap into the thick of them like a charmed thing. As he ran he whipped out his own ivory-handled guns, and at that half the crowd on the saloon porch made a dash for the door and were caught in it and fell sprawling, and picked themselves up, and crawled or ran again until they were inside. Yancey stood beside Sol Levy, the terrible look in his eyes, the great head thrust forward and down, like a buffalo charging. Here was a scene to his liking.

"I'll drill the first son of a bitch that fires another shot. I will, so help me God! Go on, fire now, you dirty dogs. You filthy loafers. You stinking spawn of a rattlesnake!"

He was, by now, a person in the community—he was, in fact, the person in the town. The porch loafers looked sheepish. They sheathed their weapons, or twirled them, sulkily.

"Aw, Yancey, we was foolin'!"

"We was only kiddin' the Jew. . . . Lookit him, the white-livered son of a gun. Lookit—Holy Doggie, look at him! He's floppin'."

With a little sigh Sol Levy slid to the dust of the road and lay in a crumpled heap at the foot of the Howe scale. It was at that moment, so curiously does the human mind work, that Yancey caught that elusive resemblance. Now he picked the man up and flung him over his great shoulder as he would a sack of meal.

"Yah!" hooted the jokesters, perhaps a little shamefaced now.

Yancey, on his way to his own house so near by, made first a small detour that brought him to the foot of the tobacco-stained saloon porch steps. His eyes were like two sword blades flashing in the sun.

"Greasers! Scum of the Run! Monkey skulls!"

His limp burden dangling over his shoulder, he now strode through the *Wigwam* office, into the house, and laid him gently down on the sitting-room couch. Revived, Sol Levy stopped to midday dinner with the Cravats. He sat, very white, very still, in his chair and made delicate pretense of eating. Sabra, because Yancey asked her to, though she was mystified, had got out her DeGrasse silver and a set of her linen. His long meager fingers dwelt lingeringly on the fine hand-wrought stuff. His deep-sunk haunting eyes went from Sabra's clear-cut features, with the bold determined brows, to Yancey's massive head, then to the dazzling freshness of the children's artless countenances.

"This is the first time that I have sat at such a table in two years. My mother's table was like this, in the old country. My father—peace to his soul!—lighted the candles. My mother—sainted—spread the table with her linen and her precious thin silver. Here in this country I eat as we would not have allowed a beggar to eat that came to the door for charity."

"This Oklahoma country's no place for you, Sol. It's too rough, too hard. You come of a race of dreamers."

The melancholy eyes took on a remote—a prophetic look. There was, suddenly, a slight cast in them, as though he were turning his vision toward something the others could not see. "It will not always be like this. Wait. Those savages to-day will be myths, like the pictures of monsters you see in books of prehistoric days."

"Don't worry about those dirty skunks, Sol. I'll see that they leave you alone from now on."

Sol Levy smiled a little bitter smile. His thin shoulders lifted in a weary shrug. "Those barbarians! My ancestors were studying the Talmud and writing the laws the civilized world now lives by when theirs were swinging from tree to tree."

A Child Is Lost

From THE TREES

By Conrad Richter

The forest is the dominating force of this novel of pioneer life in Ohio. To the settlers along the banks of the Conestoga River it remains a dark and mysterious presence in their lives, and they graze their cattle and till their fields in its shadow. Gradually it becomes like a primitive deity, providing them with meat for their tables, wood for their fires and logs for their homes, and demanding in the end a human sacrifice from the colony.

The following passage, in which a small child wandering in the forest is lost forever to her family, reiterates this theme. Sulie is the youngest of the Lucketts. Her mother has died of fever, and in her father's long absences hunting and digging roots prized by the Indians she is in the care of her grown sister Sayward. Louie Scurrah, whom Sayward has distrusted because of his attentions to her younger sister Genny, becomes the leader of the search for Sulie.

SAYWARD wished Buckman Tull had kept what day it was to himself. She would rather not have known that she and her father had made this out against Louie Scurrah on a Friday. The Tulls were bighead and always had to show they knew the most. They never let you forget they had an almanac and that it came all the way from the Bay State. Now Portius Wheeler came from down there himself and you'd never know it from him. But the Tulls couldn't pass the time without fetching in the day of the week .

"How are you, this fine Friday mornin'?" Buckman Tull had called out big as you please as he went by to the post.

Sayward didn't mind them telling her when it was the Lord's day. The better the day, the better the deed. Any washing she did on the Sabbath would be cleaner and sweeter-smelling and bleached whiter even though it had no sun handy to hang it in. But Fridays were not like other days of the week. No, Friday was the deil's day, for the Lord was massacred on it. Oh, it could be fair enough one place on a Friday, but other places in the world it would be black and bitter as death.

Never mind, Sayward told herself. If she couldn't change the day, she would have to let it go. It appeared fair enough here in this Northwest country today. Achsa's axe rang out like a man's while she chopped supper wood. Genny hummed while she roiled the leaves soft in their beds and lugged the bedding in. And Wyitt and Sulie ran off early on their chore of fetching the cows. When it got late and they didn't come in, Sayward didn't think much about it. She and the other girls pulled stools to their supper. But once it was dark, she reckoned she'd go over to the Covenhovens and see what was keeping them.

Then she looked up and saw Wyitt silent and pale as tallow at the door. His bare legs were black muddy to the knees.

"Whar's Sulie at?" Genny cried at him first.

"Ain't she here?" he said, but you could see the way his look went around the cabin that he didn't expect her.

"Whar'd you leave her?" Sayward asked sharply.

Wyitt stood just inside the doorway. He acted like he was scared to come in his own pappy's house. The cows, he said, had never been out so far. He and Sulie couldn't hear a bell till they climbed atop a sharp hill. Away down on the other side they found them in some gat brush off from the flies. But when they drove them out, the cows wouldn't make for the settlement. No, they had it in their heads to go the other way. He beat them over their stubborn horns with a club and still they would go away from home.

He promised Sulie they would get fagged after while and then he could turn them. But she was scared to go further in the Shawanee country. He could go on with them if he wanted, she said; she would take the path back and tell Mrs. Covenhoven.

The cows kept right on with Wyitt scrambling behind. They forded a river and wound through places he had never seen before. It was dark when he saw a light ahead. This was one of the Shawanee towns, he expected. He saw a strange log barn, and a strange white man came out with a light. Wyitt asked him could he tell him where he and his cows were at. The man looked at him. He said didn't he know where he was at? This was the Covenhoven improvement and these were their cows he had fetched home.

"It was Mister Covenhoven hisself!" Achsa jeered in her man's voice. "The cows fetched you home and you never knowed it."

"Then whar's Sulie?" Genny cried.

"I expect Sulie kin take keer of her own self," Sayward said, holding her voice and face calm. "You and Achsa stay here. Wyitt kin eat his supper. Then me and him'll go out and git her. If he kin show me the way."

"I kin show you the way we went out," the boy said. "But I kain't the way the cows brung me home."

Before Wyitt got up from the table, big John Covenhoven came stooping in the door. His wife sent him over to see if Sulie had shown up. He said he better go along. Sayward dropped some dry candlewood and pine knots in her greasy leather apron. Wyitt lit a stick at the fireplace and went ahead. Sometimes he whirled around a pine knot or a sliver of candlewood and sometimes a bunch of shellbark torn off on the way.

More than once he stopped to make sure he wasn't turned around again. Sayward told herself that never had she seen any of this strange black woods before tonight. They went over runs and wet places, up hill and down and up again till Wyitt said this was the knoll he and Sulie had heard the bells from. He was sure as could be and if they couldn't find his and Sulie's barefoot tracks in the soft ground, it must be the deil had his foot over them.

They built a fire there atop the hill and kept it going to guide Sulie's little feet through the night. One time or another they would go to the end of the firelight.

"Whoooo-hoooo!" Sayward would send her strong call into the black woods.

"Suuuu-lieeee!" Wyitt would yell as if splitting his throat would fetch her in.

All that answered were echoes, and that, they knew, was the woods mocking them. Out in the darkness they could hear the night birds and beasts going about their business like nothing had happened. The big-eared owl some called the Hill Hooter bit off his hoots calm and steady as always and his barred relation dragged out the last of his arrogantly. Now and then wolves howled far off and once came a distant wail through the woods like a panther or catamount. Or it might have been only the red fox that Worth said could give you the worst scare of any beast in the woods when it wanted. Oh, the wild creatures gave no notice at all that they saw the red light of the fire up on this hill. They went prowling their rounds as if no little tyke had been lost in the woods and didn't know the way home in the dark to her pappy's.

It started to rain and in her mind Sayward could see little Sulie, a bedraggled mite somewhere out in this wide bush. Where was she at, she would be asking herself, and would ever she see sisters and brother again? She couldn't take her sopping wet clothes off her little body tonight and snuggle down safe and dry in her loft bed under the roof her pappy had made with his axe, frow and augur. No, she must crawl in a dead, hollow tree like a bear or up a live one like a marten. Up a tree she might be safe enough, should she but recollect she is no young gabby bird that can hold on to a limb with its toes while it sleeps. If she as much as half-dozed, down she might come. And if her young legs snapped like kindling, she would have to sit on a rock and wait till they came and fetched her.

John Covenhoven said hadn't they better go home on account of the rain?

"I ain't sugar and salt. I won't melt," Sayward told him.

She was all for pushing further on, but the rain put out their torches. They had to wait for daylight to look for the place Sulie and Wyitt had parted, and then Wyitt couldn't find the gat brush where the cows had stood off from the flies. When they got home to the cabin, no tuckered-out and brier-scratched little tyke was waiting for them, but Genny and Achsa hadn't lacked someone to talk to. When her man didn't come, Mrs. Covenhoven had bridled a horse and ridden over. And when he wasn't back by early dawn, she had ridden on to the Tulls and Harbisons to sound the alarm.

The settlers answered the summons like the blowing of a great hunting horn. No church bell could have drawn them as hard as such a heartbreak thing. Jake Tench and the bound boy, almost the last to hear, were the first to come. Billy Harbison fetched his hounds and tied them to a young dogwood from where they made it ring around the cabin. Tod Wylder rode his dun ox over with his wife on behind. A gaunt Kentucky woman came on foot with her man and her fourth baby. She was nursing it as she stepped dark as an Indian woman across the doorway, her breast white as milk beside the brown face, her eyes deep in their hollow sockets. Little Mathias and his boy came. The MacWhirters and the McFalls tramped together through the woods with all their five or six boys. And there were some the Lucketts had only heard about and never seen before.

It made you feel better with so many around, Sayward thought. The littlest ones didn't know what it was all about and ripped and tore-like they were at a frolic. But the older ones stood here and yonder, quiet as could be, the boys with their pappies, the girls with their mams in the cabin. The women had lots to ask about this thing. Each time a fresh one came, they listened to the story over again, and their eyes kept stirred up and glowing.

Outside the men stood in a hard knot, making men's talk, chewing off tobacco, telling of bodies they knew had been lost. Their eyes were alive in their sober faces, and now and then when one of them rubbed over his mouth with his hand, rumpling his beard if he had any and spitting copiously, he would cast around to see if his own youngest was all right, making like a grimace to cover it up, but there was no humor in it.

Jake Tench put a brighter face on them after the MacWhirters and the McFalls came.

"Never you mind, Saird," he called in at the door. "Jude MacWhirter kin find a young'un for you. Now John Covenhoven couldn't find one behind his own choppin' block."

The men's mouths opened round to laugh at this joke on the childless Covenhovens. Judah MacWhirter had six or seven living and only God knew how many dead back in Kentucky. The women in the house laughed, too, pulling down their faces at each other, for behind the chopping log was where they told their youngest that babies came from. For a while now it was more like usual in the Luckett cabin and out. The men told lighter stories and slapped their legs. But the woods closed around this place too thick and dark to last. It hadn't a field here nor tame bush, not a clearing or patch of sky a human could call his own. No, this cabin was owned soul and body by the great woods that ran on and on to the prairies by the English Lakes and to the Spanish Settlements on the Illinois.

Buckman Tull was the first to hear and the last to come. Billy Harbison loosed his hounds and they were ready to start. It didn't seem they cared if Wyitt went along or not to show them the way. They would go out in the woods and find out for themselves what happened to this young one that she didn't come home. The women crowded out of the door to watch them go. They looked like Sinclair's army, men and boys, with rifles and clubs, in boots and bare feet, shoepacks and moccasins. Buckman Tull had on his soldier coat with his horn slung over one shoulder, and it was he who took charge.

"They'll fetch your young'un back," Ellen MacWhirter comforted Sayward. "If she hain't been killed by some wild creater."

But all they fetched back next day was news of a barefoot young one's track by a run. It might have been Sulie's toes in the black mud, and it might have been the youngest MacWhirter boy's. At the blast of the horn they had all run up and tramped it out before they could measure. The day after that they found nothing.

Oh where, Sayward cried in her mind, was her father? Why did he have to be off now when they needed him most? They were out of fresh meat with all these mouths to feed. And Sulie's bed in the loft was slept in by strangers. Didn't he know his favorite young one was lost out in the woods while he wandered around digging in the dirt for roots for the pigtail people!

When he did come home, she pitied him hard. The second evening little Hughie McFall ran in and said that a strange man was outside. Sayward thought one of the other women could talk to him. Then she looked up and Worth stood in the doorway, his bag of sang roots weighting his back, his rifle in his hand.

"What fetches all these folks?" he asked sternly of Genny who was nearest him in the crowded cabin.

When she shrank back and wouldn't answer, his eyes moved on past Wyitt and Achsa till he found Sayward at the fire.

"Whar's Sulie?" he asked louder.

"She never came home with the cows," Sayward told him.

He gave a start like a beast in a trap when it gets the first lick with the club.

"When was this?" And when Sayward told him, "She ain't out in the woods yit?"

The neighbor folks all watched him, pitying him as Sayward told the story. She had told it so often, the words were worn to her tongue like Worth's pipestem to his teeth. Several times he groaned, and Sayward guessed he was thinking how it might have been different if he had stayed to home. She and John Covenhoven and Wyitt had done what they could that first night, but Worth could find his way through the woods like a lynx in the dark. That first night little Sulie couldn't have been far off. Now only God knew where she had wandered and to what end she had come.

When she finished, he looked like he had been dram drinking.

"Whar's Louie?" he wanted to know.

She didn't answer.

"You'd better git him." He wouldn't meet her eyes. "Louie mought know. He mought a seed her."

Louie Scurrah came early next morning. He wore a buck tail like it was some kind of frolic.

"So you wouldn't git me before!" the hard look he gave Sayward said.

Oh, you could see he knew he had been slighted and now they'd had to send for him. It made him cocky as all get out. He set himself in charge and told the men why they hadn't got anywhere. It was plain Buckman Tull didn't like this. Today, Louie said, they would stretch a line with every man and boy six poles apart. They would whoop at each other to keep the line straight and when some body found a sign, Buckman Tull would blow his horn. Buckman Tull sat up and nodded. That, you could tell, satisfied him. And if they fired off their rifles, Louie went on, that would mean they had found the young one.

"Dead or alive," he said, looking hard at Sayward.

Wouldn't they need every human they could get, Achsa put to him. You could see she hankered to go along. Every last man and boy, Louie told her. But not women and girls. They were no good in the woods. They only made it harder. If women found a sign, they would run ahead and screech for the young one till it would hide, if it were around. No, the place for a girl was women's work at home.

Achsa's black eyes burned back at him. You could tell she reckoned it easy enough to be a man and go out in the woods whooping to keep in line and beating the bushes for a little tyke in a red dress that by this time the brush must have whipped halfways off her back. You did no whooping at women's work. No, you stooped by the fire till your face singed and your leg muscles ached so folks got enough to eat. And you heard no horn. All you listened to was women's talk from daylight to dark.

The women hardly stirred foot outside the cabin, yet it hadn't one who didn't have her own notion why they hadn't found little Sulie. Tod Wylder's woman told about a boy called Chris that had been lost in the woods back in York state. This was in the olden times. When they found him, a panther had scratched leaves over what was left of him till it would get back that way again, and that's why it took so long to find him. Then Sally Harbison was acquainted with a lost girl it took four years to find down in Virginia. An Indian had shot her for a deer and buried her so the whites wouldn't find out. But her grave fell in and when they dug it up, they found the bullet in her breast bone.

God help you, getting lost in the woods was a fearsome thing, old Granny MacWhirter said. She had toothless gums and on the back of her head a white knit cap that was all yellow with age and hair grease. She was lost once herself for forty-eight hours.

"They's only one word for it," she bobbed her head, "and that's lostness. Even a growed woman keeps a runnin' and stumblin' till she's wore out. The smartest man gits fogged. He kain't see straight any more. He goes crazy with bein' lost, that's what he does. If he comes on a trace he tromped every day, he don't know it any more. Let him take it, and his craziness takes the wrong end. He thinks his own tracks an hour past are the tracks of some man he never seed or knowed. Let him hear man, woman or young'un a comin', and he runs and hides. He ain't a human no more. He's nothin' but a wild creater. Git him home and the whole world's turned around end for end. The sun's in the wrong place. It rises in the west and sets in the east. The North Star's away down yonder."

She knew a case once in Kentucky pitiful to tell. A young boy was lost seventeen days. They found him digging up acorns like a squirrel

with its paws and wilder than anything in the woods. He tried to bite
the thumb off his own pappy and run off. Once he was home, they
reckoned he would come back to his old life, but he never owned his
own sister or mother. He wouldn't sleep in a bed, and he dirtied the
house like a hound. What end he came to she didn't hear, but the
doctors knew nothing to do for a case like that.

"Sometimes," Granny MacWhirter bobbed her cap and worked her
lips and drew down her face at you, "it's a good thing if you don't find
a lost young'un!"

"Once they're out too long," Mrs. McFall said, wiping her eyes,
"I'd as soon see them dead and buried. That's easier to stand than this
waitin' around and never knowin'."

But Sayward reckoned different. She wouldn't mind if their little
Sulie snapped at them like a pet fox for a while, just so they found her
alive. She always snapped some anyhow. A little more would be of no
account. And sooner never find her than see her dead and buried. So
long as you never knew, you could keep on hoping, if it was a score of
years. Once you saw a body put underground, that was an end to it and
to a little part inside of you that died, too.

How many times the horn blew that day they didn't know, for it was
too far to hear. The men must have camped out somewhere in the
woods that night. You could see this wasn't going to be over and done
with easy like Louie Scurrah thought. In the morning Achsa, Cora Mac-
Whirter and some of the other big girls made the rounds of the im-
provements that had stock to tend. They fetched back food and bedding. The men did not come back that night either. But a few nights
following, when they were all down on pallets on the floor like so many
logs jammed side by each at a rolling, they heard a whooping. Genny's
hands trembled so she could hardly pull on her shortgown. She thought
they had Sulie.

It was old Hugh McFall and Hen Giddings whooping before they
got to the cabin so the women and young ones wouldn't be scared.
They had come back to see if the women folk were all right and the
stock tended. They would take back some meal to the woods tomorrow.
Sayward threw wood on the fire for light and got them rations. After
their bellies were filled, they told what they knew.

No, they hadn't come on the young one yet. But that Louie Scurrah
had a lynx eye in the woods. You needn't be out long to know he'd been
raised by the Delawares. Between him and Worth they had no need of
Billy Harbison's hounds. The first day Louie found spicewood chewed
by some other creature than a deer, for it had teeth marks on the upper
side of the twig. And Worth picked up a red thread torn off by a black
haw.

Oh, those two could follow where you could see nothing. And every sign they came on, the young one was further and further from home. They found where she ate wild cherries and whortleberries and where she crossed the runs. You could see her foot plain as could be in the sand. The third day they came on a nest of old leaves where she spent the night. She must have camped here more than one day, for her little feet had beaten a path in a heavy stand of timber. Now what do you reckon she had in there?

Old Hugh, who was telling it, settled himself. He blinked solemn as an owl.

You'd never guess it, he said. Louie Scurrah found it himself and had Buckman Tull blow his horn. When they all came up, he took them in and asked did they see anything. So help him, if there wasn't a little bitty play house made of sticks in that big timber! It had bark on the roof and a doorway in the middle. Inside it had a bed of leaves and a block of wood for a trencher with a scrap off a young one's dress for a fancy trencher cloth. It even had a nosegay of flowers. Anybody could see right off a mite of a girl had done this. Away back here in the wilderness, far from any human's cabin, she had made herself a little house just like her pappy's. You might reckon a big bearded fellow like Jake Tench wouldn't mind looking at such. But when Worth raised up and called out to the woods, "Sulie! Sulie! Be you still alive?" Jake had to walk himself off in the bush.

Genny couldn't listen any more. She buried her head in the bed clothing. Achsa's brown face twisted up in cruel lumps. Sayward turned hard to the fire because like Jake she couldn't stop her eyes. "Sulie! Sulie! Be you still alive?" she called out in her mind with her father. Out there in the great woods, further than any of them had ever been except maybe one or two, their little Sulie had built a play house to recollect how she and Wyitt and Genny and Achsa had run and played together by this cabin. Wasn't it just like her? Who but little Sulie would put a nosegay in a play house or make up a trencher with a fine red cloth? She was ever saying grand things that no one dared think of but she and her Granmam Powelly who lived in a story-and-a-half chipped-log house across the road from Granpappy's gunsmith shop along the Conestoga.

Sayward wished she could see for herself that little play house Sulie had made. She'd give all she had if Hugh McFall and Hen Giddings would take her back with them when they went. Those men would need a woman if ever they found Sulie. God knows that after all these days she would be a poor little bag of bones. She would need special waiting on. Men would not know how.

But old Hugh McFall and Hen Giddings went back to the woods

without saying a word, no not a word. They went alone at daylight, and that was the last the women saw of them for a week.

Once upon a time Sayward wished she had a clock. Mrs. Covenhoven had one, and Portius Wheeler, the bound boy said, carried a pocket clock that struck the hours though it was no bigger around than his fist. A clock, Sayward reckoned, was almost human, for it had face, hands and sense to tell the time. No doubt it was a friendly face to have around and to hear it ticking sociably through the day and night. But a human could tell time the best, for some hours were fast and some were slow. Now you could tell nothing from Sayward's face, but the hours of this last week were the longest in all her born days. This was a time in her life, she thought, she would never want to go back to and live again.

You would expect, Genny said, that since they found Sulie's play house, it wouldn't take long till they found the little tyke herself. But it didn't work out that way. No, it seemed the deil had done it like this just to work up their hopes and then let them fall through. The men said there was a plain track of Sulie going into that place but none going out. Like a pack of hounds trying to find the lost scent, they made bigger and bigger circles around, but the one cold track was all they could find. It was almost like an eagle had swooped down by her play house and carried her off, leaving never a sign on the ground.

In worn-out bunches the men and boys straggled back. They said they had done all mortal man could do. They had tramped the woods from Dan to Beersheba. They had tramped it further than any young one could travel on its own shanks. They had raked it with a fine tooth comb. All they had found were horse tracks and a place where some strange Indians had made fire for the night.

"The young'un's a gone Josie," Jude MacWhirter shook his shaggy head. "They ain't no use a huntin' what ain't thar."

Now little Sulie's bed up in the loft lay empty and lonesome again. Only Worth and Louie Scurrah had not come back. No, they had stuck to the woods like stubborn hounds that can't be clubbed into giving up the scent. There wasn't a fresh bone or dust of meal left in the cabin, but Sayward reckoned they could make out by their selves. The young ones could pick berries and fish the river with whang leather outlines. Wyitt could snare rabbits, and she could cut out the summer worms. Maybe, too, a body could take a rock and keep still long enough in the woods to call a turkey or kill a cock pheasant when he came strutting to his log.

But the hungry young ones were glad enough to lay eyes on Louie Scurrah at the cabin door one morning. Flowers sprang out on Genny's white cheeks though it would be an hour before she should taste the venison slung in a red summer hide on his back. No meat ever came in handier but Sayward begrudged him sorely that it wasn't their Sulie he had fetched back. Never would she forgive him that.

He said he and Worth had followed the tracks of the horseback Indians till they separated and petered out. Back on the Miami River he had to give up, but Worth wouldn't come home. No, he said he couldn't look at his cabin now with his littlest gone. Now that he was out this far, he would keep on beating the woods for her till he reached the granddaddy of rivers. Always had Worth wanted to lay eyes on that long river frozen in winter at one end while the other end has flowers and palm trees on either bank.

"He said one man could keep his cabin in meat till he got back," Louie told her.

Sayward's face was tight-lipped and cruel. She had not a word to say as she got a roast ready, for what could you say to a man who had beat the woods for your littlest sister that was likely dead, then fetched meat home for your living sisters and brother to eat. Oh, she would feed their empty bellies with smoking, hot flesh till their cheeks stuck out again, but it would be bitter enough meat to her. Dinner done she scrubbed what little she had to scrub and took herself off by her lonesome to the woods where she could work this thing off with her legs.

Everywhere she went the trees stood around her like a great herd of dark beasts. Up and up shot the heavy butts of the live ones. Down and down every which way on the forest floor lay the thick rotting butts of the dead ones. Alive or dead, they were mostly grown over with moss. The light that came down here was dim and green. All day even in the cabin you lived in a green light. At night that changed. By day you looked paler than you really were. By night the fire gave you a ruddy glow. She always waited for night time when little Sulie had looked to be ailing. Likely it was only the woods light. By firelight she would be well again.

Oh, it was a cruel thing for the trees to do this to a little girl who had never harmed them more than to shinny up their branches or swing on a creeper. Some claimed the trees were softhearted as humans. They said the pole of the cross had been cut from pine and that's why the pine was always bleeding. The crosspiece, they claimed, was from quaking ash. The quaking ash has shook ever since, and never can it live now more than the thirty-three years of the Lord.

Likely as not, Sayward told herself, a tree might tremble and bleed for the son of the Almighty who could heave it out by its roots with His breath or smack it down with His thunder. But neither pine nor quaking ash would give a hait for a poor little girl body wandering around lost in the woods crying for her sisters and pappy who never came to answer. And the birds and beasts would be as bad. Oh, she heard Genny sing a catch once where the birds and beasts covered up the lost Babes in the Woods with leaves. But that was just a pretty song. Any woodsy knew that the corbies would sit around in a ring waiting to pick out the poor little Babes in the Woods's eyes. And if any beast covered them up with leaves it would be the panther so he could come back and munch at their starved little hams another day.

Back along the Conestoga the trees seemed tame enough. Out here they were wild trees. Even in the daytime you could feel something was watching you. When you went through the woods it followed sly as a fox and stealthy as a Shawanee. Leave your cabin for a season and it would choke it around with brush. Likely you would find trees growing out of your bed when you got back.

Once Sayward thought she heard voices, but it was only beetles in the air. The sound came stronger when she got to the riffles. Far off she swore she could hear Sulie calling. "Sairdy! Pappy!" her little voice came. Sayward knew it was no more than river water slopping and gargling over logs and stones, but it sounded real enough to make the sweat come and her knees to tremble.

The Bordello

From SANCTUARY
By William Faulkner

In this novel William Faulkner gives us the Deep South at one of its deepest and darkest levels. The story deals with the prejudices and corruption underlying the life of a Tennessee town and city and the more primitive corruption of a country group of moonshiners. Against these two backgrounds move a few characters of ·isolated goodness who are hopelessly caught in the social mesh.

Faulkner's complete understanding of the provincial character is made clear in the following passage, in which two country boys come to Memphis to attend the Barber College. Virgil is the nephew of Congressman Snopes, a cheap politician, and Fonzo is his friend. They represent the universal Hayseed in his first baffling, exciting experience of the Big City. ·

AS THE train neared Memphis Virgil Snopes ceased talking and began to grow quieter and quieter, while on the contrary his companion, eating from a parrafin-paper package of popcorn and molasses, grew livelier and livelier with a quality something like intoxication, seeming not to notice the inverse state of his friend. He was still talking away when, carrying their new, imitation leather suit cases, their new hats slanted above their shaven necks, they descended at the station. In the waiting room Fonzo said:

"Well, what're we going to do first?" Virgil said nothing. Someone jostled them; Fonzo caught at his hat. "What we going to do?" he said. Then he looked at Virgil, at his face. "What's the matter?"

"Aint nothing the matter," Virgil said.

"Well, what're we going to do? You been here before. I aint."

"I reckon we better kind of look around," Virgil said.

Fonzo was watching him, his blue eyes like china. "What's the matter with you? All the time on the train you was talking about how many times you been to Memphis. I bet you aint never bu—" Someone jostled them, thrust them apart; a stream of people began to flow between them. Clutching his suit case and hat Fonzo fought his way back to his friend.

"I have, too," Virgil said, looking glassily about.

"Well, what we going to do then? It wont be open till eight o'clock in the morning."

"What you in such a rush for, then?"

"Well, I don't aim to stay here all night. . . . What did you do when you was here before?"

"Went to the hotel," Virgil said.

"Which one? They got more than one here. You reckon all these folks could stay in one hotel? Which one was it?"

Virgil's eyes were also a pale, false blue. He looked glassily about. "The Gayoso hotel," he said.

"Well, let's go to it," Fonzo said. They moved toward the exit. A man shouted "taxi" at them; a redcap tried to take Fonzo's bag. "Look out," he said, drawing it back. On the street more cabmen barked at them.

"So this is Memphis," Fonzo said. "Which way is it, now?" He had no answer. He looked around and saw Virgil in the act of turning away from a cabman. "What you—"

"Up this way," Virgil said. "It aint far."

It was a mile and a half. From time to time they swapped hands with the bags. "So this is Memphis," Fonzo said. "Where have I been all my life?" When they entered the Gayoso a porter offered to take the bags. They brushed past him and entered, walking gingerly on the tile floor. Virgil stopped.

"Come on," Fonzo said.

"Wait," Virgil said.

"Thought you was here before," Fonzo said.

"I was. This hyer place is too high. They'll want a dollar a day here."

"What we going to do, then?"

"Let's kind of look around."

They returned to the street. It was five o'clock. They went on, looking about, carrying the suit cases. They came to another hotel. Looking in they saw marble, brass cuspidors, hurrying bellboys, people sitting among potted plants.

"That un'll be just as bad," Virgil said.

"What we going to do then? We can't walk around all night."

"Let's git off this hyer street," Virgil said. They left Main Street. At the next corner Virgil turned again. "Let's look down this-a-way. Git away from all that ere plate glass and monkey niggers. That's what you have to pay for in them places."

"Why? It's already bought when we got there. How come we have to pay for it?"

"Suppose somebody broke it while we was there. Suppose they couldn't ketch who done it. Do you reckon they'd let us out withouten we paid our share?"

At five-thirty they entered a narrow dingy street of frame houses and junk yards. Presently they came to a three storey house in a small grass-less yard. Before the entrance a latticework false entry leaned. On the steps sat a big woman in a mother hubbard, watching two fluffy white dogs which moved about the yard.

"Let's try that un," Fonzo said.

"That aint no hotel. Where's ere sign?"

"Why aint it?" Fonzo said. " 'Course it is. Who ever heard of any-body just living in a three storey house?"

"We cant go in this-a-way," Virgil said. "This hyer's the back. Dont you see that privy?" jerking his head toward the lattice.

"Well, let's go around to the front, then," Fonzo said. "Come on."

They went around the block. The opposite side was filled by a row of automobile salesrooms. They stood in the middle of the block, their suit cases in their right hands.

"I dont believe you was ever here before, noways," Fonzo said.

"Let's go back. That must a been the front."

"With the privy built onto the front door?" Fonzo said.

"We can ask that lady."

"Who can? I aint."

"Let's go back and see, anyway."

They returned. The woman and the dogs were gone.

"Now you done it," Fonzo said. "Aint you?"

"Let's wait a while. Maybe she'll come back."

"It's almost seven o'clock," Fonzo said.

They set the bags down beside the fence. The lights had come on, quivering high in the serried windows against the tall serene western sky.

"I can smell ham, too," Fonzo said.

A cab drew up. A plump blonde woman got out, followed by a man. They watched them go up the walk and enter the lattice. Fonzo sucked his breath across his teeth. "Durned if they didn't," he whispered.

"Maybe it's her husband," Virgil said.

Fonzo picked up his bag. "Come on."

"Wait," Virgil said. "Give them a little time."

They waited. The man came out and got in the cab and went away.

"Caint be her husband," Fonzo said. "I wouldn't a never left. Come on." He entered the gate.

"Wait," Virgil said.

"You can," Fonzo said. Virgil took his bag and followed. He stopped while Fonzo opened the lattice gingerly and peered in. "Aw, hell," he said. He entered. There was another door, with curtained glass. Fonzo knocked.

"Why didn't you push that ere button?" Virgil said. "Don't you know city folks dont answer no knock?"

"All right," Fonzo said. He rang the bell. The door opened. It was the woman in the mother hubbard; they could hear the dogs behind her.

"Got ere extra room?" Fonzo said.

Miss Reba looked at them, at their new hats and the suit cases.

"Who sent you here?" she said.

"Didn't nobody. We just picked it out." Miss Reba looked at him. "Them hotels is too high."

Miss Reba breathed harshly. "What you boys doing?"

"We come hyer on business," Fonzo said. "We aim to stay a good spell."

"If it aint too high," Virgil said.

Miss Reba looked at him. "Where you from, honey?"

They told her, and their names. "We aim to be hyer a month or more, if it suits us."

"Why, I reckon so," she said after a while. She looked at them. "I can let you have a room, but I'll have to charge you extra whenever you do business in it. I got my living to make like everybody else."

"We aint," Fonzo said. "We'll do our business at the college."

"What college?" Miss Reba said.

"The barber's college," Fonzo said.

"Look here," Miss Reba said, "you little whipper-snapper." Then she began to laugh, her hand at her breast. They watched her soberly while she laughed in harsh gasps. "Lord, Lord," she said. "Come in here."

The room was at the top of the house, at the back. Miss Reba showed them the bath. When she put her hand on the door a woman's voice said: "Just a minute, dearie" and the door opened and she passed them, in a kimono. They watched her go up the hall, rocked a little to their young foundations by a trail of scent which she left. Fonzo nudged Virgil surreptitiously. In their room again he said:

"That was another one. She's got two daughters. Hold me, big boy; I'm heading for the henhouse."

They didn't go to sleep for some time that first night, what with the strange bed and room and the voices. They could hear the city, evocative and strange, imminent and remote; threat and promise both—a deep, steady sound upon which invisible lights glittered and wavered: colored coiling shapes of splendor in which already women were beginning to move in suave attitudes of new delights and strange nostalgic promises. Fonzo thought of himself surrounded by tier upon tier of drawn shades, rose-colored, beyond which, in a murmur of silk, in panting whispers, the apotheosis of his youth assumed a thousand avatars. Maybe it'll begin tomorrow, he thought; maybe by tomorrow night . . . A crack of light came over the top of the shade and sprawled in a spreading fan upon the ceiling. Beneath the window he could hear a voice, a woman's, then a man's: they blended, murmured; a door closed. Someone came up the stairs in swishing garments, on the swift hard heels of a woman.

He began to hear sounds in the house: voices, laughter; a mechanical piano began to play. "Hear them?" he whispered.

"She's got a big family, I reckon," Virgil said, his voice already dull with sleep.

"Family, hell," Fonzo said. "It's a party. Wish I was to it."

On the third day as they were leaving the house in the morning, Miss Reba met them at the door. She wanted to use their room in the afternoons while they were absent. There was to be a detective's convention in town and business would look up some, she said. "Your things'll be all right. I'll have Minnie lock everything up before hand. Aint nobody going to steal nothing from you in my house."

"What business you reckon she's in?" Fonzo said when they reached the street.

"Don't know," Virgil said.

"Wish I worked for her, anyway," Fonzo said. "With all them women in kimonos and such running around."

"Wouldn't do you no good," Virgil said. "They're all married. Aint you heard them?"

The next afternoon when they returned from the school they found a woman's undergarment under the washstand . . . Fonzo picked it up. "She's a dress-maker," he said.

"Reckon so," Virgil said. "Look and see if they taken anything of yourn."

The house appeared to be filled with people who did not sleep at night at all. They could hear them at all hours, running up and down the stairs, and always Fonzo would be conscious of women, of female flesh. It got to where he seemed to lie in his celibate bed surrounded by women, and he would lie beside the steadily snoring Virgil, his ears strained for the murmurs, the whispers of silk that came through the walls and the floor, that seemed to be as much a part of both as the planks and the plaster, thinking that he had been in Memphis ten days, yet the extent of his acquaintance was a few of his fellow pupils at the school. After Virgil was asleep he would rise and unlock the door and leave it ajar, but nothing happened.

On the twelfth day he told Virgil they were going visiting, with one of the barber-students.

"Where?" Virgil said.

"That's all right. You come on. I done found out something. And when I think I been here two weeks without knowing about it—"

"What's it going to cost?" Virgil said.

"When'd you ever have any fun for nothing?" Fonzo said. "Come on."

"I'll go," Virgil said. "But I aint going to promise to spend nothing."

"You wait and say that when we get there," Fonzo said.

The barber took them to a brothel. When they came out Fonzo said "And to think I been here two weeks without never knowing about that house."

"I wisht you hadn't never learned," Virgil said. "It cost three dollars."

"Wasn't it worth it?" Fonzo said.

"Aint nothing worth three dollars you caint tote off with you," Virgil said.

When they reached home Fonzo stopped. "We got to sneak in, now," he said. "If she was to find out where we been and what we been doing, she might not let us stay in the house with them ladies no more."

"That's so," Virgil said. "Durn you. Hyer you done made me spend three dollars, and now you fixing to git us both throwed out."

"You do like I do," Fonzo said. "That's all you got to do. Dont say nothing."

Minnie let them in. The piano was going full blast. Miss Reba appeared in a door, with a tin cup in her hand. "Well, well," she said, "you boys been out mighty late tonight."

"Yessum," Fonzo said, prodding Virgil toward the stairs. "We been to prayer-meeting."

In bed, in the dark, they could still hear the piano.

"You made me spend three dollars," Virgil said.

"Aw, shut up," Fonzo said. "When I think I been here for two whole weeks almost . . ."

The next afternoon they came home through the dusk, with the lights winking on, beginning to flare and gleam, and the women on their twinkling blonde legs meeting men and getting into automobiles and such.

"How about that three dollars now?" Fonzo said.

"I reckon we better not go over night," Virgil said. "It'll cost too much."

"That's right," Fonzo said. "Somebody might see us and tell her."

They waited two nights. "Now it'll be six dollars," Virgil said.

"Don't come, then," Fonzo said.

When they returned home Fonzo said: "Try to act like something, this time. She near about caught us before on account of the way you acted."

"What if she does?" Virgil said in a sullen voice. "She caint eat us."

They stood outside the lattice, whispering.

"How you know she caint?" Fonzo said.

"She dont want to, then."

"How you know she dont want to?"

"Maybe she dont," Virgil said. Fonzo opened the lattice door. "I caint eat that six dollars, noways," Virgil said. "Wisht I could."

Opening the Sluice Gates

From STORM

By George Stewart

The heroine of this novel is a storm which begins as a little whorl of air southeast of Japan, strikes the Pacific Coast of the United States in a fury of wind and snow and dies out on the American desert after the Arctic and the Tropics have felt its power. A meteorologist in San Francisco, watching the storm's birth, names it Maria and feels a kind of private responsibility for her as she smashes ships, holds up trains and planes, threatens dams and has her way with human lives.

George Stewart has divided his book into the days of Maria's life, each day marked by men's struggles against her elemental strength. In the chosen passage Johnny Martley, a Dam Superintendent, races against time to release the flooding waters before they overflow.

OPENING the sluice-gates unaided was something of a job; when Martley had finished, he was tired. He listened for just a moment to the water sweeping through beneath him. Then he thought of the leak in his living-room, and the road washing away, and a dozen greater emergencies which might arise any moment. He turned and went rapidly along the narrow passageway leading to the hole up which he must climb. "Gotta hurry," he thought. "Sure is a busy day!"

The passageway was just high enough for a man to walk; now and then his shoulders brushed the sides. Seepage water dripped from the top and oozed through the walls; the air was so wet that he half seemed to be breathing water; he coughed. From above, from the sides, the concrete of the great dam—millions of tons—pressed in upon him.

Ahead in the passageway as far as the bottom of the hole one electric light after another sent out a feeble yellow gleam. Then—without a warning flicker—they all went out. Black as Hell's basement and the fires out!

The darkness stopped the man in his tracks like a blow. The unexpected loss of his best sense brought momentary panic, but he suppressed it so quickly that he hardly missed the time of two strides. In the narrow passageway there was no chance of getting lost; he knew the distances and the hazards. He remembered where he was when the lights went out; as he walked he methodically counted his paces to know when he should expect to arrive at the end of the passageway. What worried him was why the lights had gone. In the storm anything might happen from the breakage of a local wire up to some major disaster. He hurried even faster; his men would need him; the L.D. might be calling. "Sure is a busy day!"—And this time he unconsciously spoke out loud for company and courage; he started as the voice reverberated hollowly from the concrete walls.

Reaching ahead with his left hand he felt the end of the passageway. With his right hand, groping in the blackness, he found a steel rung —wet, cold, and slick. He began to climb upward into the narrow hole which he could not even see was there; it was as if he forced his way by will-power right into the concrete.

Not for nothing had he been Superintendent at French Bar for eleven years. He knew every detail of the dam. He had to climb upward two hundred thirty feet, and the rungs were ten and a half inches apart —two hundred sixty-nine rungs.

One—two—three—four. Counting to himself, he climbed by feel in the darkness—hand over hand, foot following foot. The water spattered upon him; he coughed in the dank air. Twenty-eight—twenty-nine— thirty—thirty-one. He was climbing as fast as he dared. Forty-five— forty-six. His heart began to pound. His feet grew heavy. Sixty-six— sixty-seven. The hole was too small to give him free action. He felt cramps in his loins. Eighty—eighty-one—eighty—! (His left hand missed a grip and threw him out of rhythm.) Eighty-two—eighty-three. There was a pain across his chest and his ankle tendons were numb. He kept on grimly. *One hundred!* Then he rested. He took the next hundred again without halting. On rung two hundred, as he rested, he saw the dim little circle of half-light still high above him.

His feet were heavy from the start, but he took the last sixty-nine rungs with a rush. He was wondering what had happened to his power-house. Were the dynamos still purring steadily like sleek happy cats? Had something smashed? Had the L.D. called? Exhausted, like a man finishing a race, he pulled himself out of the hole. Leaking in from the closed door was a dim halo of light. He stumbled toward it. He was suddenly conscious of some unusual roaring noise. He flung the door open;

the flood of light blinded him for the moment; he put one foot out—
and then paused. There was no wind, but only the strange roar, and
spray—not like rain—in his face.

In half a breath his sight came back to him, but for the moment he
was not sure that he saw aright. There was no canyon wall, no swirling
rain—only a solid wall of falling water. The dam was spilling; he was
trapped.

Perhaps it was the mere inrush of water from the streams swollen by
the cloudburst; perhaps a wind-shift had piled water against the dam
instead of the other direction. As he had feared, the opening of the
sluice-gates was not enough; but he had not realized that it would be
so soon.

Because of the overhang there was a space of five feet between the
doorway and the falling water. He looked one way and then the other,
seeking escape. To the left his view ended against the solid wall of a
concrete buttress. To the right his glance ran far along the sheer front
of the dam with the water pouring over it; a few feet from where he
stood the ground fell off and disappeared into the canyon.

He reached out, picked up a stone, and threw it. From long experience with flowing water he knew from the way the stone disappeared
that the solid-looking wall could not be more than an inch or so thick.
It was falling only fifteen feet from the top of the dam. Given level
and sure footing, a man could rush through such a waterfall, and no
harm done. But here he had only a rough trail on a sloping rock-face and
the precipice a few feet to one side. The best man in the world would
be swept down. Courage would be only foolishness. If he stayed where
he was, he would be safe; eventually the boys would come and pass a
life-line through to him, or the dam would quit spilling. The storm
wouldn't last much longer.

But not for a moment did Martley consider staying where he was—
tamely. He remembered his leaderless men, his dynamos, the leak in
the living-room, and the L.D. "I'm too busy to stay here," he thought.

He cast about for some means of escape. A few bits of junk lay in
the passageway. They were useless. But just outside the door he saw a
worn and rusted half-inch cable. Some construction boss had cast it
aside as no longer trustworthy; but even if it were nine-tenths rusted
through, the steel would still hold the weight of a man.

Martley grabbed the end and pulled. The cable extended through
somewhere beyond the wall of water. Martley dragged it in, hoping that
the other end was stuck firmly. But it yielded; he pulled the loose end
through the water, and found himself with thirty feet of cable.

"I can't stay here; I'm too busy," he thought again.

Martley looped one end of the cable around upon itself. He pounded it with a stone for a hammer. The rusty projecting ends of wire tore at his hands, but he fabricated a loop about three feet in diameter.

Just outside the doorway he dug his heels in for a firm footing. He was so close to the falling water that he could reach it with his fingertips. Like a cowboy on foot making ready to rope his pony, he stood with the awkward steel loop in his right hand. He cast it at the wall of water.

It struck flatways, and was flung back. He corrected his aim. This time it disappeared neatly through the water. He pulled hopefully, but the loop came back to him without much resistance. He gathered it to his hand, and stood for a moment judging distance and direction.

In eleven years he had come to know every detail about his dam. He knew that just beyond the water stood three rocks close together. If he could cast the looped cable among them it might stick.

The third attempt did not pierce the water. The fourth went through, seemed to stick, and then yielded as he pulled a little harder. He tried again and again—now with no luck at all, now with enough hint of success to keep him trying.

He was a methodical man and kept his count. The eleventh and fourteenth throws stuck momentarily. By now he knew exactly where the rocks must be. But the fifteenth try was a complete miss; his arm was tired.

On the sixteenth throw he was careful. He pulled in; the cable ran freely for a foot and then stuck with a sudden jam. He was sure he had it! He pulled hard; he rested a moment, and then strained with his full weight. The cable was solid.

There was, of course, a very good chance that, when he swung through an arc of more than a right angle, he would slip the loop off whatever projection held it. "I can't stay here all day," he thought.

He grasped the cable at a point which he knew was about eight feet from whatever (presumably the rocks) the loop was caught on. He did not plunge at the waterfall. He merely stuck his head and shoulders into it, and felt the rush take him from his feet. He held his breath and gripped the steel strands. The sluice of the water swept him across the sloping rock, but he knew that holding the cable he must swing in a circle. Beneath his left foot was nothing; he felt the void of the canyon sucking him down. He knew that he had been too reckless, but he gripped the cable.

Then, still gripping the cable, he was lying on the sloping rock with water rushing against his face and shoulders. The loop of the cable was holding. Under his feet was empty space. He raised his face above the foaming rush, and heard the thunder of water plunging into the canyon. He panted a moment before daring to move. Then he bent both elbows, and hunched himself half a foot forward. He pulled up his right knee, and felt the roughness of rock beneath his foot. Only then did he dare to loose one hand and move it up on the cable for a fresh grip. (Even at that moment he felt, more than heard, the hum of the dynamos, and knew that the failure of the lights inside the dam had been purely local; the water going over the dam must have caused it.) The rest was easy.

"Did the L.D. call?" he yelled at his wife from the doorway.

"No!" she yelled back from where she was washing the breakfast dishes. "What made you so long?"

"Oh—nothing much!"

He was glad she did not come to look at him. His face and hands were scraped and bleeding; his pants-knees were both torn out. He grabbed the shovel from where he had left it on the porch, and hurried off to see about the road.

Night Journey

From STATE FAIR

By Phil Stong

As they ride through the night toward a midwestern state fair, the Frake family are for a few hours suspended between two worlds. Behind them lies the farm, the familiar pattern of their lives. Ahead lies the Fair town, unsettling in its strangeness, filled with new faces and possibilities of new experience. In the following passage all the restlessness and conflicting moods of the family are absorbed by the impressionable minds of Margy and Wayne. Blue Boy alone is unmoved.

As ONE who carefully arranged life in the precise patterns which she selected, Mrs. Frake felt that the Iowa State Fair had probably been put off a few days too many. She very well knew the tensions and the urgencies of the week before the event, but this year it seemed to her that that final suspense had broken; that—if she had been a member of a boxing commission—her family was overtrained for the Fair.

For six days Wayne had been growling and sulking, and for six days Margy had been sulking and weeping on the very slightest pretexts— or on no pretext at all. Just—as Wayne protested—bawling.

Mrs. Frake had actually been too busy to be very much disturbed by these phenomena. Reflections on her own youth and observations of her children had taught her that the emotions of younger persons are very curious, very changeable, and not particularly important, outside of humanitarian considerations. So she had carefully estimated the number of days that butter for the trip could be expected to keep in Mason jars, and let these other, probably intricate and unreasonable, affairs take care of themselves.

Abel Frake had been too preoccupied with Blue Boy to notice anything of less than seismic consequence. Blue Boy had pointed up so considerately that it seemed that he would reach the very needle-point of his condition just as he lifted his snout at the judges in the stock pavilion at Des Moines. If Blue Boy proved to be the best Hampshire boar in Iowa, it followed that he would be the best Hampshire boar in the world. He would take the International sweepstakes at Chicago and Abel Frake, prosperous but obscure farmer and stock-breeder of Brunswick, Iowa, would be known far and wide as the owner of the finest hog in the universe. Moreover, Blue Boy's facile amours would be worth—whatever they were worth to him—a very substantial sum of money to Abel Frake.

"I wish I hadn't broken that cracked cup," Mrs. Frake told Margy, worriedly, when the tent, the canned provisions, the cooking utensils, the bedding, the linen, the clothes, were all packed beside Blue Boy's crate on the farm truck. "Now I've got to take one of the new set. One cup always gets cracked and it will be just my luck to have it be that one to break up the six."

The whole farm was crackling with preparation. The Hired Man had not marcelled Blue Boy, but only because the curl of the hair was not a judging point. He had manicured him; he had viewed more critically than a Corot the misty sunrise tint of his snout; no Park Avenue specialist knew one-half about any dowager's bowels what the Hired Man knew about Blue Boy's—in addition, the Hired Man was pleased with what he knew; Blue Boy's coat was curried and rubbed to enamelled perfection; Blue Boy's tail was curled so tightly that its tension would have alarmed uninformed persons; Blue Boy, as he lay and rocked upon his four legs, was the finest creature of his species that had ever existed in time and space.

Sunday passed quietly. Mrs. Frake had managed things so well that there was really nothing much to do on the day before the departure. Late in the morning the Storekeeper drove over with the last of the supplies which the family would need for Fair Week. While the family leaned on the fence he sat in his little Ford truck and talked.

"I wouldn't depend on this fine weather. If you'd get off right away you'd be sure to get to Ottumwa before it begins to rain."

Abel Frake tapped the ash off one cigar of the box which the Storekeeper had given him, explaining that the five dollars would cover it easily. "The paper says 'continued fair.' "

"Listen, Abel," said the Storekeeper, more conspicuously patient than ever, "what would you say about the weather, yourself?"

Abel looked at the skies, familiarly. "I'd say it was going to be good weather. A little bit hot, but clear."

"You see?" said the Storekeeper triumphantly. "That's what I'd say myself. Bet a cigar there'll be a thunderstorm yet this afternoon."

At noon the rain began and by three o'clock the family had heard lightning hit the rods twice. At four o'clock the black matted clouds began to split; at five o'clock the sun shone brightly. Blue Boy could not start until sunset at any rate, for he must not suffer and sweat in the heat.

The family waited beside the truck. Slowly the sun moved down until the ferocity of its heat was sensibly diminished. Mrs. Frake served the family with sandwiches from the first of three lunch kits she had prepared. There was hot coffee from the kitchen stove, there were some of her own cucumber, green tomato, and onion pickles—the jars dotted with cloves, mace, whole black pepper, and bay leaf.

A little later the sun had definitely set and Abel went around the house trying the doors and windows. The sky was rich with the sunset. There was a warm light over everything. It was with almost an eerie feeling that the family settled itself into the truck: Abel, his wife, and Margy in the big front seat; Wayne back on the folded tent and the bedding near the boar.

They looked back at the house and Abel pressed on the starter. The motor burst into an even grumble and Abel turned around the carriage-yard carefully. The Hired Man, his wife, and three children were lined up by the side of the driveway. As the truck turned its nose into the face of the disappearing sun they suddenly burst into frenzied shouts and wavings of the arms.

"Hooray! Hooray!" they shouted. " 'Ray," shouted the three-year-old, running around in circles until she fell down, laughing.

"Hooray for Blue Boy! Blue Boy!"

The family laughed and waved at the Hired Man's family.

"Oink!" said Blue Boy.

The familiar river road towards Brunswick suddenly seemed strange because at this time it led to strange and romantic places. When the truck passed Brunswick, the Storekeeper and the loafers, who had evidently set out scouts, suddenly rushed out from the store porch with cheers and admonitions.

"Bring him back with the bacon or as it," yelled the Storekeeper, who was sometimes capable of a classic reference.

The shouts died out behind them. The dusk had come upon the truck as it left Brunswick on the less familiar road to Ottumwa.

Mrs. Frake coughed. "I think I caught a little cold, Wednesday, when I took down the washing in the rain."

Abel Frake, guiding the car, took one hand from the wheel to pat her. "Take anything for it?"

"No, it didn't seem to set in and I hope it's going to pass off."

They passed through Douds, and, a little later, through Selma. The new electric lights were burning brilliantly in both places. The truck droned along at ten or twelve miles an hour. Every time that Blue Boy was disturbed, a few ounces were lost from his perfect condition. But the morning would see them pulling up within sight of the great gilded Capitol dome and the shining Fair Grounds. Abel Frake swayed the car over slight inequalities in the surfaced road.

Mrs. Frake coughed. "Maybe we better stop in Eldon and get you something for that cold," Abel suggested.

"Everything'll be closed. It doesn't amount to anything."

They passed through the smoky, dirty little railroad junction without pausing and found themselves again between the clean trees and hedgerows. Abel switched on his lights. Night had officially set in. A golden moon was well up towards the zenith and its light across the sky made all the wooded horizons seem remote and mysterious.

Over the road-bed of an old railroad right-of-way they came into Ottumwa, the principal city of the whole section. To avoid stops and starts which might disturb Blue Boy, Abel picked his way around the back streets of the city to his highway again.

Mrs. Frake coughed. "We'll reach Oskaloosa about midnight, Mamma. There'll be some drug-store open all night there where we can get you a little pine syrup. There might even be one open in Eddyville when we go through there."

"I don't want a thing! I'm all right. This cold is wearing off."

Abel Frake drew the car up beside the road and stopped the motor. "How's he coming along, Wayne?"

"He's fine. He's grunting a little at some of the bumps, but I think he's about half asleep. He's not worrying any."

"Good!" Abel dismounted from the high seat of the truck, walked around to the end of the car and inspected the hog. The somnolent animal sighed and gasped, breathed a soft oath and began to snore quietly again. "He's certainly standing the ride fine so far."

Abel started the truck quietly and slipped in the gears so gently that his human passengers hardly realised that they had started to move. Blue Boy, however, protested sharply. As they drove out from Ottumwa the traffic of cars to that city grew more scattered. Finally, they were almost alone upon a road which wound in slow turns and gentle grades between the perfumed hedges and stiff martial ranks of the ripening corn, the yellow light of the moon hanging and flowing upon the road before them.

"How are you doing back there, Wayne?"

Wayne stirred from the pallet of blankets and bedclothes he had made himself on top of Blue Boy's crate, at the sound of his mother's voice. "Oh, fine. Why are you all so quiet?"

"Got to let Blue Boy get his rest," said Abel, turning the car gently around a pit in the concrete. "You got your pickles, Melissa?"

"Here." She pointed at a cardboard carton between her feet. Along the wall of Melissa Frake's kitchen at home was a long row of yellow and red ribbons which she had won for angel's food, devil's food and layer cake; cherry preserves made by the old Stidger recipe which had come down in the family for generations uncounted; for chicken dressing; for raised bread; for doughnuts. There were two blue ribbons—one for candied cherries and for a mincemeat to which Mrs. Frake had surreptitiously added some sherry wine the doctor had once prescribed as a tonic for Margy.

The little drop that was left over, it seemed a shame to waste. The judges awarded Mrs. Frake's mincemeat a blue ribbon with a promptness and unanimity which had shocked her. Although she felt a very small twinge of conscience when she saw this blue ribbon, she felt somehow that she had won it fairly. She also felt a slight moral indignation against judges whose souls would not warn them of irreligious matters in mincemeat.

This year she had concocted pickles of such intricate and overwhelming delicacy that she hoped for another blue ribbon to add to the row. She had never entered pickles before. However, she realised that pickles were a small matter as compared with Blue Boy.

"Think they'll ride all right there?"

"They'll have a chance to settle before the judges see them. Besides, they're packed tight, in layers."

The truck struck the brick paving of Eddyville. Already many of the houses were dark, but from their by-road they could see the glow of Main Street. Again there were cars and companionship upon the road. After this, they realised, it would be a solitary drive, for it was nearly nine o'clock. Driving alone in time as their forefathers had driven in the space of the Iowa prairies, they felt a faint sense of adventure and the large *Sehnsucht* of a starry, slightly humid Iowa night.

"What are you thinking about, Margy?"

"I'm not thinking about anything. I wish we were there. I wish it was morning."

Mrs. Frake laughed uncomfortably. "We'll be there soon enough. And then there'll be plenty to do. You'd better try to get some sleep, you and Wayne."

"How can I sleep here, squashed between you and Papa?"

"Why don't you go back with Wayne?" Abel asked. "There's plenty of room on top of that crate and he's got some kind of a bed fixed up there."

"And sleep over that hog? No, thank you."

Abel laughed. "That's a special hog. It isn't everybody that gets a chance to sleep on the crate of a hog like that. Besides, he's been washed and curried till he's probably cleaner than any of us. We've been washed, but we haven't been curried."

"I don't like hogs," said Margy, decisively.

"Well," said her father, "maybe hogs don't like you, either, but you don't hear Blue Boy making a big fuss because you're riding in his car."

Now the farmhouses at each side of the road were frequently unlighted and relays of cicadas which lined all the roads from Brunswick to Des Moines could be heard above the even hum of the motor. A glimpse of another car upon the road was a rarity now, and a subject for speculation. The moon, last light of humanity, was sinking in the east.

The slow, droning truck seemed hardly to move, yet they had already come more than forty miles. Wayne stirred from his blankets in the back of the truck and sat bolt upright. "I can't sleep."

"It's a fact," his mother said. "It's my bedtime, but I don't feel the least bit sleepy. It seems as if we were the last people left in the world and we had to watch it. Ah, we're going west now! See the Big Dipper?"

"How can you tell by that?" Margy asked crossly.

"You don't know that? You take the last two stars in the bowl, and right beyond them, a little to the left, that's the Pole Star. That's north. My grandfather set his fences on that star."

"Doesn't it ever move?"

"Of course not—that's why it's the Pole Star," said Mrs. Frake a little inaccurately. Far ahead, across the hills and valleys, they could see a very faint smudge of light. That was Oskaloosa.

Wayne had subsided into another day-dream. He was imagining Eleanor now, just falling asleep, and laughing at him. For a moment he almost regretted that the State Fair had taken him away from her. They would have fixed everything up. He was sure he could have kissed her good night, if he'd just tried to kiss her good night.

Maybe a good-night kiss didn't seem very important to her. Maybe she had asked a lot of people up at that college to kiss her good night. Maybe they had. He clenched his fist so violently that there was a little pain on the inside of his wrist. The sensation transferred his attentions to his muscles. He felt the hard swelling of his biceps, already building up and down into a solid terraced dome from shoulder to elbow; he felt the cordy firmness of his forearm—if he had them here, the villainous seducers who had kissed Eleanor good night, he would teach them to take advantage of an innocent girl's unsophistication.

Twice he smacked his competent fist into the palm of his left hand. About two licks like that and those male schoolma'ams—

"Was that Blue Boy?"

Wayne gasped frantically for an explanation. "I—I guess I was asleep. I—thought I was having a fight with somebody. What are all of you doing up there?"

"Nothing," his mother answered. "Did you see them turn the lights off over there on that farm?"

"Wonder what they are doing up so late."

"Maybe somebody's sick. Maybe they've got a doctor in."

They were all silent, speculating. And the truck drove on. The night settled down rapidly. Once the moonset in the west had vanished, the darkness dropped down suddenly and blackly and the truck's headlights picked out a way, washed in colour, along the dim grey of the Iowa road.

Said Margy timidly, "Maybe somebody's dying. Maybe some woman is having a baby—"

It suddenly occurred to all of them that life went on, far outside their consciousnesses, in many places and at all times.

"Poor soul!" said Mrs. Frake, sympathetically. "If it's a baby I hope it comes right away. And if it's somebody sick that's going to die I hope they die quick."

"I been reading a thing in a magazine," said Wayne, "that proves that time is just a kind of space. You can see up and down and to both sides and in front and behind. This fellow thinks that if we were made different we could see tomorrow and yesterday just the same way—but we don't because we can only see three dimensions. But really, time is just a way of saying a direction we don't know."

Mrs. Frake laughed. "Was he married?"

"I don't know."

"Well, if he was, and he'd ask his wife, he wouldn't go in for such ideas. Time, you can't change. They can figure all they want to on what way twenty minutes from now is from here, but it takes just so long to darn a sock and just so long to bake a cake, and if you're at a fair or a church supper or something, it lasts just as long, no matter how you try to stretch it out."

"I suppose you know better than he does," said Wayne, disrespectfully.

"I guess I do," said Melissa Frake, good-naturedly. "I know better than to waste my time fooling with notions like that."

But Wayne, lying on his back on Blue Boy's crate, was stirred to speculation by the cold, bright, distant stars. After a while he imagined that if you went out towards such and such a star, and then turned a corner, like, you would probably be able to see to-morrow around the bend. The process worked, for the next thing that he saw was to-morrow.

They stopped at a little drug-store in Oskaloosa and bought Mrs. Frake some medicine for her cough. From the drug-store cooler, Abel got fresh cold water for Blue Boy, who was droning sleepily between downright snores and a sense of depression because his barn-lot seemed not so substantial and secure as he had thought it. Sometimes it bumped most objectionably.

"He's riding mighty fine," Abel reported in a subdued voice to Mrs. Frake, who was enjoying her cough syrup.

"He breathes so," said Margy, in a tone of simple loathing. They passed a little country graveyard, overgrown with weeds and bushes, white and stark enough in the moonlight, but devoid of the dignity and serenity of well-kept country graveyards.

"Looks unappetising," said Abel Frake, an orderly man.

And so, thought Margy, in a hundred years will my grave look, and there I'll be for good and all and nothing will have been any fun and nothing much ever will have happened. A silly business, living. And somehow she felt that in some manner Harry might have made it less silly, and had withheld something precious from her, selfishly or stupidly. A dim resentment turned vaguely and more vaguely in her mind, growing less tangible at every turn.

"You better take Blue Boy straight to the Stock Pavilion when we get there," said Mrs. Frake. "The youngsters are getting a good sleep and they'll be ready to help get the tent up and straighten things. Then you can take us up and leave us and go back and enter my pickles and tend to Blue Boy. You folks can get a bite at some stand and I'll take a nap before supper-time. After supper, we'll go out and see the Fair."

"No," said Abel, "I'll drop you and the children first and you can be working on things while I take Blue Boy down. I want you to get a good sleep and clear up that cold of yours. It'd be a shame if you didn't enjoy every minute of the Fair, after waiting for it all these months."

"But it'll make a difference to Blue Boy, standing there while the things are unloaded, and it'll only take a minute to get the crate out. There's always plenty to help around."

"Well," said Abel, uncertainly, "we'll see when we get there. We're making mighty good time now. These concrete roads certainly do make a big difference."

She'd see that they did get the hog off first, Mrs. Frake thought, for the one thing which could crown Fair Week and make its perfect joys ecstatic would be for Abel's hog to win.

Then she and Wayne could pitch the tent and it wouldn't take any time to spread the bedding and get a place to cook fixed outside. Then she could find out where the best grocery stand was and then she could get a little nap and after she woke up . . .

Only Abel felt the dews which came towards morning and saw the trees faintly begin to silhouette themselves against a dawning grey light.

A little later he could see the sunrise from the side door of the truck, and then he began to hear a rising chorus of farm animals from the farms which drifted by the car. Only Abel saw the freshly gilded dome of the Capitol suddenly shine out over Des Moines, and the newly whitewashed Fair Buildings which promised them carnival from the near side of the town. At the gates he halted and showed a sleepy watchman his entry slip for Blue Boy. Mrs. Frake started up.

"Wake up, children," she cried, "wake up! We're here! We're at the Fair!"

Prelude to Drowning

From AN AMERICAN TRAGEDY
By Theodore Dreiser

The action of An American Tragedy is determined by the character
of its central figure, young Clyde Griffiths. A sense of the inevitabil-
ity of life forces him into catastrophic channels; yet the reader recog-
nizes that every circumstance in the novel stems from the boy's own
weakness and his inability to resolve any conflict except by postpone-
ment or evasion. These devices fail, however, when Clyde's ambition
for wealth and social success as personified by Sondra is threatened.
Having neither the honesty nor the courage to face his predicament
squarely, he sees only one way out . . . the murder of the factory
girl, Roberta, who is about to bear his child.

   The passage represents the climax toward which the first half of the
book ascends and from which the last half evolves. The prominent
part which Clyde's bag occupies in his own disturbed thoughts represents his frenzied desire for escape. This bag, containing a new straw
hat marked "Utica" with which he hopes to prove an alibi, becomes
the symbol of flight from a whole chapter of his life.

IN A confused and turbulent state mentally, scarcely realizing the
clarity or import of any particular thought or movement or act now,
he took up his bag and led the way to the boathouse platform. And then,
after dropping the bag into the boat, asking of the boathouse keeper if
he knew where the best views were, that he wanted to photograph them.
And this done—the meaningless explanation over, assisting Roberta (an
almost nebulous figure, she now seemed, stepping down into an insubstantial rowboat upon a purely ideational lake), he now stepped in after
her, seating himself in the center and taking the oars.

Copyright, 1925, by Boni & Liveright, Inc.

The quiet, glassy, iridescent surface of this lake that now to both seemed, not so much like water as oil—like molten glass that, of enormous bulk and weight, resting upon the substantial earth so very far below. And the lightness and freshness and intoxication of the gentle air blowing here and there, yet scarcely rippling the surface of the lake. And the softness and furry thickness of the tall pines about the shore. Everywhere pines—tall and spearlike. And above them the humped backs of the dark and distant Adirondacks beyond. Not a rower to be seen. Not a house or cabin. He sought to distinguish the camp of which the guide had spoken. He could not. He sought to distinguish the voices of those who might be there—or any voices. Yet, except for the lock-lock of his own oars as he rowed and the voice of the boathouse keeper and the guide in converse two hundred, three hundred, five hundred, a thousand feet behind, there was no sound.

"Isn't it still and peaceful?" It was Roberta talking. "It seems to be so restful here. I think it's beautiful, truly, so much more beautiful than that other lake. These trees are so tall, aren't they? And those mountains. I was thinking all the way over how cool and silent that road was, even if it was a little rough."

"Did you talk to any one in the inn there just now?"

"Why, no; what makes you ask?"

"Oh, I thought you might have run into some one. There don't seem to be very many people up here to-day, though, does there?"

"No, I don't see any one on the lake. I saw two men in that billiard room at the back there, and there was a girl in the ladies' room, that was all. Isn't this water cold?" She had put her hand over the side and was trailing it in the blue-black ripples made by his oars.

"Is it? I haven't felt it yet."

He paused in his rowing and put out his hand, then resumed. He would not row directly to that island to the south. It was—too far—too early. She might think it odd. Better a little delay. A little time in which to think—a little while in which to reconnoiter. Roberta would be wanting to eat her lunch (her lunch!) and there was a charming looking point of land there to the west about a mile further on. They could go there and eat first—or she could—for he would not be eating to-day. And then—and then—

She was looking at the very same point of land that he was—a curved horn of land that bent to the south and yet reached quite far out into the water and combed with tall pines. And now she added:

"Have you any spot in mind, dear, where we could stop and eat? I'm getting a little hungry, aren't you?" (If she would only not call him *dear,* here and now!)

The little inn and the boathouse to the north were growing momentarily smaller,—looking now, like that other boathouse and pavilion on Crum Lake the day he had first rowed there, and when he had been wishing that he might come to such a lake as this in the Adirondacks, dreaming of such a lake—and wishing to meet such a girl as Roberta— then— And overhead was one of those identical woolly clouds that had sailed above him at Crum Lake on that fateful day.

The horror of this effort!

They might look for water-lilies here to-day to kill time a little, before —to kill time . . . to kill, (God)—he must quit thinking of that, if he were going to do it at all. He needn't be thinking of it now, at any rate.

At the point of land favored by Roberta, into a minute protected bay with a small, curved, honey-colored beach, and safe from all prying eyes north or east. And then he and she stepping out normally enough. And Roberta, after Clyde had extracted the lunch most cautiously from his bag, spreading it on a newspaper on the shore, while he walked here and there, making strained and yet admiring comments on the beauty of the scene—the pines and the curve of this small bay, yet thinking—thinking, thinking of the island farther on and the bay below that again some- where, where somehow, and in the face of a weakening courage for it, he must still execute this grim and terrible business before him—not allow this carefully planned opportunity to go for nothing—if—if—he were to not really run away and leave all that he most desired to keep.

And yet the horror of this business and the danger, now that it was so close at hand—the danger of making a mistake of some kind—if noth- ing more, of not upsetting the boat right—of not being able to—to—oh, God! And subsequently, maybe, to be proved to be what he would be— then—a murderer. Arrested! Tried. (He could not, he would not, go through with it. No, no, no!)

And yet Roberta, sitting here with him now on the sand, feeling quite at peace with all the world as he could see. And she was beginning to hum a little, and then to make advisory and practical references to the nature of their coming adventure together—their material and financial state from now on—how and where they would go from here—Syracuse, most likely—since Clyde seemed to have no objection to that—and what, once there, they would do. For Roberta had heard from her brother-in-law, Fred Gabel, of a new collar and shirt factory that was just starting up in Syracuse. Might it not be possible for Clyde, for the time being at least, to get himself a position with that firm at once? And then later, when her own worst trouble was over, might not she connect herself with the same company, or some other? And temporarily, since they had so little money, could they not take a small room together somewhere in some family home, or if he did not like that, since they were by no means so close temperamentally as they once had been, then two small adjoining rooms, maybe. She could still feel his unrelenting opposition under all this present show of courtesy and consideration.

And he thinking, Oh, well, what difference such talk now? And whether he agreed or whether he did not. What difference since he was not going—or she either—that way. Great God! But here he was talking as though to-morrow she would be here still. And she would not be.

If only his knees would not tremble so; his hands and face and body continue so damp.

And after that, farther on down the west shore of this small lake in this little boat, to that island, with Clyde looking nervously and wearily here and there to see that there was no one—no one—not anywhere in sight on land or water—no one. It was so still and deserted here, thank God. Here—or anywhere near here might do, really,—if only he had the courage so to do now, which he had not,—yet. Roberta trailing her hand in the water, asking him if he thought they might find some water-lilies or wild flowers somewhere on shore. Water-lilies! Wild flowers! And he convincing himself as he went that there were no roads, cabins, tents, paths, anything in the form of a habitation among these tall, close, ranking pines—no trace of any little boat on the widespread surface of this beautiful lake on this beautiful day. Yet might there not be some lone, solitary hunter and trapper or guide or fisherman in these woods or along these banks? Might there not be? And supposing there were one here now somewhere? And watching!

Fate!

Destruction!

Death! Yet no sound and no smoke. Only—only—these tall, dark, green pines—spear-shaped and still, with here and there a dead one—ashen pale in the hard afternoon sun, its gaunt, sapless arms almost menacingly outstretched.

Death!

And the sharp metallic cry of a blue-jay speeding in the depths of these woods. Or the lone and ghostly tap-tap-tap of some solitary woodpecker, with now and then the red line of a flying tanager, the yellow and black of a yellow-shouldered blackbird.

"Oh, the sun shines bright in my old Kentucky home."

It was Roberta singing cheerfully, one hand in the deep blue water. And then a little later—"I'll be there Sunday if you will," one of the popular dance pieces of the day.

And then at last, after fully an hour of rowing, brooding, singing, stopping to look at some charming point of land, reconnoitering some receding inlet which promised water-lilies, and with Roberta already saying that they must watch the time and not stay out too long,—the bay, south of the island itself—a beautiful and yet most funereally pine-encircled and land delimited bit of water—more like a smaller lake, connected by an inlet or passage to the larger one, and yet itself a respectable body of water of perhaps twenty acres of surface and almost circular in form. The manner in which to the east, the north, the south, the west, even, except for the passage by which the island to the north of it was separated from the mainland, this pool or tarn was encircled by trees! And cat-tails and water-lilies here and there—a few along its shores. And somehow suggesting an especially arranged pool or tarn to which one who was weary of life and cares—anxious to be away from the strife and contentions of the world, might most wisely and yet gloomily repair.

And as they glided into this, this still dark water seemed to grip Clyde as nothing here or anywhere before this ever had—to change his mood. For once here he seemed to be fairly pulled or lured along into it, and having encircled its quiet banks, to be drifting, drifting—in endless space where was no end of anything—no plots—no plans—no practical problems to be solved—nothing. The insidious beauty of this place! Truly, it seemed to mock him—this strangeness—this dark pool, surrounded on all sides by those wonderful, soft, fir trees. And the water itself looking like a huge, black pearl cast by some mighty hand, in anger possibly, in sport or phantasy maybe, into the bosom of this valley of dark, green plush—and which seemed bottomless as he gazed into it.

And yet, what did it all suggest so strongly? Death! Death! More definitely than anything he had ever seen before. Death! But also a still, quiet, unprotesting type of death into which one, by reason of choice or hypnosis or unutterable weariness, might joyfully and gratefully sink. So quiet—so shaded—so serene. Even Roberta exclaimed over this. And he now felt for the first time the grip of some seemingly strong, and yet friendly sympathetic, hands laid firmly on his shoulders. The comfort of them! The warmth! The strength! For now they seemed to have a steadying effect on him and he liked them—their reassurance—their support. If only they would not be removed! If only they would remain always—the hands of this friend! For where had he ever known this comforting and almost tender sensation before in all his life? Not anywhere —and somehow this calmed him and he seemed to slip away from the reality of all things.

To be sure, there was Roberta over there, but by now she had faded to a shadow or thought really, a form of illusion more vaporous than real. And while there was something about her in color, form that suggested reality—still she was very insubstantial—so very—and once more now he felt strangely alone. For the hands of the friend of firm grip had vanished also. And Clyde was alone, so very much alone and forlorn, in this somber, beautiful realm to which apparently he had been led, and then deserted. Also he felt strangely cold—the spell of this strange beauty overwhelming him with a kind of chill.

He had come here for what?

And he must do what?

Kill Roberta? Oh, no.

And again he lowered his head and gazed into the fascinating and yet treacherous depths of that magnetic, bluish, purple pool, which, as he continued to gaze, seemed to change its form kaleidoscopically to a large, crystalline ball. But what was that moving about in this crystal? A form! It came nearer—clearer—and as it did so, he recognized Roberta struggling and waving her thin white arms out of the water and reaching toward him! God! How terrible! The expression on her face! What in God's name was he thinking of anyway? Death! Murder!

And suddenly becoming conscious that his courage, on which he had counted so much this long while to sustain him here, was leaving him, and he instantly and consciously plumbing the depths of his being in a vain search to recapture it.

Kit, kit, kit, Ca-a-a-ah!
Kit, kit, kit, Ca-a-a-ah!
Kit, kit, kit, Ca-a-a-ah!

(The weird, haunting cry of that unearthly bird again. So cold, so harsh! Here it was once more to startle him out of his soul flight into a realization of the real or unreal immediate problem with all of its torturesome angles that lay before him.)

He must face this thing! He must!

Kit, kit, kit, Ca-a-a-ah!
Kit, kit, kit, Ca-a-a-ah!

What was it sounding—a warning—a protest—condemnation? The same bird that had marked the very birth of this miserable plan. For there it was now upon that dead tree—that wretched bird. And now it was flying to another one—as dead—a little farther inland and crying as it did so. God!

And then to the shore again in spite of himself. For Clyde, in order to justify his having brought his bag, now must suggest that pictures of this be taken—and of Roberta—and of himself, possibly—on land and water. For that would bring her into the boat again, without his bag, which would be safe and dry on land. And once on shore, actually pretending to be seeking out various special views here and there, while he fixed in his mind the exact tree at the base of which he might leave his bag against his return—which must be soon now—must be soon. They would not come on shore again together. Never! Never! And that in spite of Roberta protesting that she was getting tired; and did he not think they ought to be starting back pretty soon? It must be after five, surely. And Clyde, assuring her that presently they would—after he had made one or two more pictures of her in the boat with those wonderful trees—that island and this dark water around and beneath her.

His wet, damp, nervous hands!
And his dark, liquid, nervous eyes, looking anywhere but at her.

And then once more on the water again—about five hundred feet from shore, the while he fumbled aimlessly with the hard and heavy and yet small camera that he now held, as the boat floated out nearer the center. And then, at this point and time looking fearfully about. For now—now—in spite of himself, the long evaded and yet commanding moment. And no voice or figure or sound on shore. No road or cabin or smoke! And the moment which he or something had planned for him, and which was now to decide his fate at hand! The moment of action— of crisis! All that he needed to do now was to turn swiftly and savagely to one side or the other—leap up—upon the left wale or right and upset the boat; or, failing that, rock it swiftly, and if Roberta protested too much, strike her with the camera in his hand, or one of the oars free at his right. It could be done—it could be done—swiftly and simply, were he now of the mind and heart, or lack of it—with him swimming swiftly away thereafter to freedom—to success—of course—to Sondra and hap- piness—a new and greater and sweeter life than any he had ever known.

Death of a Deer

From THE YEARLING

By Marjorie Kinnan Rawlings

The Yearling is the account of a boy's coming of age. Jody Baxter, growing up in the backlands of Florida, longs like all children for a pet of his own. His dearest friend, the gentle cripple Fodder-wing Forrester, has always had pets, and though the roistering, gigantic Forrester sons have periodically created trouble for their neighbors, Jody has always been free to visit their home for the pleasure he brought their sickly young brother. When an orphaned fawn comes into Jody's life, his prayers seem answered, and he makes the creature his constant companion. After Fodder-wing's death, Flag the fawn is more cherished than ever.

In the following passage Jody meets the first, staggering tragedy of his life. As he feels his world falling around him, he loses faith even in his parents. In his bitter denunciation he is echoing the eternal "why" of all children in conflict with a world shaped by adult values.

PENNY did not recover. He lay suffering without complaint. Ma Baxter wanted Jody to ride for Doc Wilson, but Penny would not allow it.

"I owe him a'ready," he said. "I'll git easement direckly."

"You're likely ruptured."

"Even so— Hit'll clare up."

Ma Baxter lamented, "If you had a mite o' sense— But you'll try to do like as if you was big as a Forrester."

"My uncle Miles were a big man and he were ruptured. He got around all right. Please to hush, Ory."

"I'll not hush. I want you should learn your lesson and learn it good."

"I've done learned it. Please hush."

Jody was disturbed. Yet Penny was always having minor accidents, trying, with his small stout physique, to do the work of ten. Jody could remember dimly when a tree that Penny was felling had caught him, crushing one shoulder. His father.had carried his arm in a sling for long months, but he had recovered and been as strong as ever. Nothing could harm Penny for long. Not even a rattlesnake, he thought comfortingly, could kill him. Penny was inviolable, as the earth was inviolable. Only Ma Baxter fretted and fumed, but she would have done so if it were only a little finger that had been strained.

Shortly after Penny was laid up, Jody came in to report that the corn was up. The stand was perfect.

"Now ain't that fine!"

The pale face on the pillow was bright.

"Now if it so happen I ain't outen the bed, you're jest the feller to plow it out." He frowned. "Boy, you know as good as I do, you got to keep that yearlin' outen the fields."

"I'll keep him out. He ain't bothered nary thing."

"That's fine. That's jest fine. But you keep him out, religious."

Jody spent most of the next day on a hunt with Flag. They went nearly to Juniper Spring and returned with four squirrels.

Penny said, "Now that's what I call a son. Come in with rations for his old man."

Ma Baxter made a pilau of the squirrels for supper.

"They do eat good," she said.

"Why, the meat's so tender," Penny said, "you could kiss it off the bones."

Jody, and Flag with him, was in high favor.

A light rain fell in the night. In the morning he went to the cornfield at Penny's request to see whether the rain had pushed the corn and whether there was any sign of cutworms. He leaped the split-rail fence and set out across the field. He had gone some yards when it occurred to him that he should be seeing the pale green shoots of the corn. There were none. He was bewildered. He went farther. There was no corn visible. It was not until he reached the far end of the field that the delicate sprouts appeared. He walked back along the rows. Flag's sharp tracks were plain. He had pulled up the corn in the early morning as neatly as though it had been pulled by hand.

Jody was frightened. He dawdled about the field, hoping to have a miracle happen and the corn appear again when his back was turned. Perhaps he was having a nightmare in which Flag had eaten the corn crop, and when he awakened he would go out and find it growing, green and tender. He pushed a stick into one arm to make sure. The dull misery he felt was that of a bad dream, but the pain in his arm was as real as the destruction of the corn. He dragged back to the house with slow and heavy feet. He sat down in the kitchen and did not go to his father. Penny called him. He went to the bedroom.

"Well, boy? How's the crops?"

"The cotton's up. Hit looks like okry, don't it?" His enthusiasm was spurious. "The cow-peas is breakin' the ground."

He spread the toes of his bare feet and wriggled them. He was absorbed in them, as though they had developed an interesting new function.

"And the corn, Jody?"

His heart beat as fast as a humming-bird's wings. He swallowed and took the plunge.

"Somethin's et off most of it."

Penny lay silent. His silence was a nightmare, too. At last he spoke.

"Couldn't you tell what 'twas, done it?"

He looked at his father. His eyes were desperate and beseeching.

Penny said, "Ne' mind. I'll git your Ma to go look. She kin tell."

"Don't send Ma!"

"She's obliged to know."

"Don't send her!"

"Hit were Flag done it, wa'n't it?"

Jody's lips trembled.

"I reckon— Yes, sir."

Penny looked at him pityingly.

"I'm sorry, boy. I more'n half looked for him to do it. You go play a while. Tell your Ma to come here."

"Don't tell her, Pa. Please don't tell her."

"She's got to know, Jody. Now go on. I aim to do the best I kin for you."

He stumbled to the kitchen.

"Pa wants you, Ma."

He went out of the house. He called Flag, quaveringly. The deer came to him from the black-jack. Jody walked down the road with his arm across his back. He loved him more than ever, in his sin. Flag kicked up his heels and invited him to romp. He had no heart for play. He walked slowly as far as the sink-hole. It was lovely as a spring flower garden. The dogwood had not finished blooming. The last blossoms were white against the pale green of the sweet gums and the hickories. He was not even tempted to walk around it. He turned back to the house and went inside. His mother and father were still talking. Penny called to him to come in beside the bed. Ma Baxter's face was flushed. She was hot with defeat. Her mouth was a tight line.

Penny said quietly, "We've come to a agreement, Jody. What's happened is powerful bad, but we'll have a try at a remedy. I take it you're willin' to work extry hard to fix things."

"I'll jest do ary thing, Pa. I'll keep Flag shut up 'til the crops is made—"

"We got no earthly place to shut up a wild thing like that. Now listen to me. You go now and git corn from the crib. Pick the best ears. Your Ma'll he'p you shell it. You go then and plant it jest like we done before, right where the fust lot was put. Drill your holes like I done, and go back over and drop the seed and kiver it."

"I know jest how."

"Then time you git that done, likely along tomorrer mornin', you hitch Cæsar to the wagon and go yonder to the old clearin' on the way to the Forresters, where the road turns off. You tear down that old rail fence there and load the rails on the wagon. Not too heavy a load, for Cæsar cain't pull too much on that piece of up-grade. You make as many trips as you need to. Pile the rails here and yon along our fence. Dump your first loads along the south side o' the cornfield and along the east side, borderin' the house yard. Then you build up that fence—workin' first on them two sides—jest as high as you got the rails to do it. I been noticin' your yearlin' allus takes the fence on this end. If you kin keep him out up here, he'll mebbe stay out 'til you kin build up the rest."

It seemed to Jody that he had been shut up in a small black box and now the lid was off, and the sun and light and air came in across him, and he was free.

Penny said, "Now when you git your fence higher'n you kin reach, if I ain't on my feet by then, your Ma'll he'p you with the riders."

Jody turned joyously to embrace his mother. She was patting one foot ominously on the floor. She stared straight ahead and did not speak. He decided that it was probably best not to touch her. Nothing could alter his relief. He ran outside. Flag was feeding along the road near the gate. Jody threw his arms around him.

"Pa's fixed it," he told him. "Ma's pattin' her foot, but Pa's fixed it."

Flag's mind was on the tender sprigs of grass and he shook free. Jody went whistling to the crib and sorted over the corn for the ears with the largest kernels. It would take a good many ears of the remaining corn for seed for the second planting. He carried it in a sack to the back door and sat down on the stoop and began the shelling. His mother came and sat beside him. Her face was a frigid mask. She picked up an ear and went to work.

"Huh!" she snorted.

Penny had forbidden her outright to scold Jody. He had not forbidden her to talk to herself.

" 'Spare his feelin's!' Huh! And who's to spare our bellies this winter? Huh!"

Jody swung around so that his back was partly turned on her. He hummed under his breath, ignoring her.

"Hush that racket."

He left off his humming. It was no moment to be impudent or to argue. His fingers flew. The corn popped from the cobs. He wanted to be away from her and at his planting as quickly as possible. He gathered up the sack of seed and slung it over his shoulder and went to the field. It was nearly dinner time, but he could get in an hour's work. In the open field he was free to sing and whistle. A mocking-bird in the hammock sang, whether in competition or harmony, he could not tell. The March day was blue and gold. The feel of the corn in his fingers, the feel of the earth that reached out to enclose the corn, was good. Flag discovered him and joined him.

He said, "You do your rompin' right now, ol' feller. You goin' to git barred out."

He bolted his dinner at noon and hurried back to the planting. He worked so fast that a couple of hours would finish it the next morning. He sat at Penny's bedside after supper, chattering like a squirrel. Penny listened gravely, as always, but his responses were sometimes detached and vacant, and his thoughts were elsewhere. Ma Baxter kept stonily to herself. Dinner and supper had both been meager and indifferently cooked, as though she took her revenge from behind her own citadel, the cook-pot. Jody paused for breath. In the hammock, a whip-poor-will called. Penny's face brightened.

" 'When the first whip-poor-will calls, the corn had ought to be in the ground.' We still not too late, boy."

"Ever' last bit'll be in tomorrer mornin'."

"That's good."

He closed his eyes. Relief from acute agony had come, as long as he lay quiet. When he moved, the pain was excruciating. He was wracked constantly with his rheumatism.

He said, "You go on to bed now and git your rest."

Jody left him and washed his feet without being told. He went to bed, peaceful of mind and tired of body, and was asleep in an instant. He awakened before dawn with a feeling of responsibility. He got out of bed and dressed immediately.

Ma Baxter said, "Pity hit take a thing like this to make you put out."

In standing between her and Flag during the past months, he had learned the value of his father's trick of an unarguing silence. It annoyed his mother more for the moment, but she stopped scolding sooner. He ate heartily but hurriedly, slipped a handful of biscuits inside his shirt for Flag, and went at once to his work. He could scarcely see, at first, to plant. He watched the sun rise beyond the grape arbor. In the thin golden light the young leaves and tendrils of the Scuppernong were like Twink Weatherby's hair. He decided that sunrise and sunset both gave him a pleasantly sad feeling. The sunrise brought a wild, free sadness; the sunset, a lonely yet a comforting one. He indulged his agreeable melancholy until the earth under him turned from gray to lavender and then to the color of dried corn husks. He went at his work vigorously. Flag came to him from the woods where he had evidently spent the night. He fed him the biscuits and let him nose inside his shirt bosom for the crumbs. He tingled with the sensation of the soft wet nose against his bare flesh.

When the planting of the corn was finished in the early morning, he bounded back to the lot. Old Cæsar was pasturing south of it. He lifted his grizzled head from the grass with a mild astonishment. Jody had seldom had the harnessing of him. He behaved meekly for the hitching and stepped backward politely between the shafts of the wagon. It gave Jody an agreeable sense of authority. He made his voice as deep as possible and gave unnecessary orders. Cæsar obeyed humbly. Jody took his seat alone, slapped the reins and set off to the abandoned clearing to the west. Flag was pleased with the business and trotted ahead. Now and then he stopped dead in the middle of the road, for mischievousness, and Jody had to stop the horse and cajole the deer into moving.

"You mighty biggety now you're a yearlin'," he called to him.

He flicked the reins and made Cæsar jog-trot, then remembered that he would have many trips to make, and allowed the old animal to slow down to his usual walk. At the clearing, it was no job at all to pull the old split-rail fence apart. The stakes and riders collapsed conveniently. The loading seemed easy for a time, then his back and arms began to ache and he had to stop and rest. There was no danger of over-loading, because it was too difficult to pile the rails past a certain height. He tried to coax Flag to jump up on the seat beside him. The yearling eyed the narrow space and turned away and could not be induced. Jody tried to lift him in, but he was astonishingly heavy and he could no more than get his front legs over the wagon wheel. He gave it up and turned around and drove home. Flag went into a sprint and was waiting ahead of him when he reached there. He decided to begin dumping his piles at the fence corner near the house and working in both directions, alternately. In that way, when the rails gave out, he would have built up the fence highest across Flag's favorite crossing places.

The hauling and unloading took longer than he dreamed of. Midway, it seemed an endless and a hopeless task. The corn would be up before he had begun the fencing. The weather was dry and the corn was slow in germinating. Each morning he looked fearfully for the pale shoots. Each morning he found with relief that they were not yet showing. He was up each day in the dark before dawn and either ate a cold breakfast without disturbing his mother, or hauled a load before he came to the table. He worked at night until the sun had set, and the red and orange faded through the pines, and the split rails merged with the color of the earth. He had dark circles under his eyes for lack of enough sleep. Penny had not had time to cut his hair, and it hung shaggily in his eyes. He made no complaint when, his eyelids drooping after supper, his mother asked him to fetch in wood that she could easily have brought in herself during the day. Penny watched him with a pain keener than the rupture in his groin. He called him to the bed one night.

"I'm proud to see you workin' so hard, boy, but even the yearlin', much as you think of him, ain't wuth killin' yourself over."

Jody said doggedly, "I ain't killin' myself. Feel my muscle. I'm gittin' powerful strong."

Penny felt of the thin hard arm. It was true. The regular and heavy lifting and heaving of the rails were developing his arms and back and shoulders.

Penny said, "I'd give a year o' my life to be to where I could he'p you with this."

"I'll git it done."

On the fourth morning he decided to begin building up the fence at the end Flag had been using. Then if the corn was up before he had fin-.ished, Flag would not take him unaware. He would even tie him by the legs to a tree, day and night, and let him kick and flounder, if necessary, until the fence was done. He found to his relief that the work went rapidly. In two days, he had raised the south and east fence lines to a height of five feet. Ma Baxter, seeing the impossible materialize, softened. On the morning of the sixth day, she said, "I got nothin' to do today. I'll he'p you git another foot on that fence."

"Oh, Ma. You good ol' Ma—"

"Now ne' mind squeezin' the life outen me. I never figgered you had it in you to work this-a-way."

She gave out of breath easily, but the work itself, while arduous, was not heavy with a pair of hands at each end of the light rails. The swing of it was rhythmic, like the swing of the cross-cut saw. She grew red in the face and panted and sweat, but she laughed and stayed with him most of the day and part of the next. There were enough rails piled at the corner to go even higher, and they built it well over the six feet that Penny had said would be high enough to keep out the yearling.

"If 'twas a full-growed buck now," he said, "he could clear eight feet easy."

That night Jody discovered the corn breaking the ground. In the morning he tried to put a hobble on Flag. He tied a rope from one hind shin to the other, with a foot of play between. Flag bucked and kicked and threw himself on the ground in a frenzy. He stumbled to his knees and fought so wildly that it was plain he would break a leg if he were not released. Jody cut the rope and let him go. He galloped away to the woods and was gone all day. Jody worked furiously at the west fence line, for that would be the yearling's most logical line of attack on the field when the south and east ends turned him. Ma Baxter gave him two or three hours of help in the afternoon. He used up all the rails he had dumped to the west and north.

Two showers of rain pushed the corn. It was more than an inch high. On the morning that Jody was ready to return to the old clearing for more rails, he went to the new high fence and climbed to the top to look over the field. His eye caught sight of Flag, feeding on the corn near the north hammock. He jumped down and called his mother.

"Ma, will you go he'p me haul rails? I got to hurry. Flag's done come in the north end."

She hurried outside with him and climbed part-way up the fence until she could peer over.

"North end nothin'," she said. "He takened the fence right here at the highest corner."

He looked down where she pointed. The sharp tracks led to the fence and appeared again on the other side, inside the cornfield.

"And he's got this crop, too," she said.

Jody stared. Again, the shoots had been pulled up by the roots. The rows were bare. The yearling's tracks led regularly up and down between them.

"He ain't gone fur, Ma. Look, the corn's still there, yonder. He ain't et but a leetle ways."

"Yes, and what's to keep him from finishin' it?"

She dropped back to the ground and walked stolidly back into the house.

"This settles it," she said. "I was a fool to give in before."

Jody clung to the fence. He was numb. He could neither feel nor think. Flag scented him, lifted his head and came bounding to him. Jody climbed down into the yard. He did not want to see him. As he stood, Flag cleared, as lightly as a mocking-bird in flight, the high fence on which he had labored. Jody turned his back on him and went into the house. He went to his room and threw himself on his bed and buried his face in his pillow.

He was prepared for his father to call him. The talk between Penny and Ma Baxter this time had not taken long. He was prepared for trouble. He was prepared for something ominous that had dogged him for days. He was not prepared for the impossible. He was not prepared for his father's words.

Penny said, "Jody, all's been done was possible. I'm sorry. I cain't never tell you, how sorry. But we cain't have our year's crops destroyed. We cain't all go hongry. Take the yearlin' out in the woods and tie him and shoot him."

Jody wandered west with Flag beside him. He carried Penny's shotgun over his shoulder. His heart beat and stopped and beat again.

He said under his breath, "I'll not do it. I'll jest not."

He stopped in the road.

He said out loud, "They cain't make me do it."

Flag looked at him with big eyes, then bent his head to a wisp of grass by the roadside. Jody walked on again slowly.

"I'll not. I'll not. I'll jest not. They kin beat me. They kin kill me. I'll not."

He held imaginary conversations with his mother and father. He told them both that he hated them. His mother stormed and Penny was quiet. His mother whipped him with a hickory switch until he felt the blood run down his legs. He bit her hand and she whipped him again. He kicked her in the ankles and she whipped him once more and threw him in a corner.

He lifted his head from the floor and said, "You cain't make me. I'll not do it."

He fought them in his mind until he was exhausted. He stopped at the abandoned clearing. A short length of fence was left that he had not yet torn down. He threw himself in the grass under an old chinaberry tree and sobbed until he could sob no more. Flag nuzzled him and he clutched him. He lay panting.

He said, "I'll not. I'll jest not."

He was dizzy when he stood up. He leaned against the rough trunk of the chinaberry. It was in bloom. The bees buzzed in it and the fragrance was sweet across the spring air. He was ashamed of himself for having taken time to cry. It was no time to cry. He would have to think. He would have to study his way out of it, as Penny did out of things that threatened him. At first he conjectured wildly. He would build a pen for Flag. A pen ten feet tall. He would gather acorns and grass and berries and feed him there. But it would take all his time to gather feed for a penned animal— Penny was on his back in the bed— The crops would have to be worked— There was no one but himself to do it.

He thought of Oliver Hutto. Oliver would have come and helped him work the crops until Penny was better. But Oliver had gone to Boston and the China Sea, away from the treachery that had swooped down on him. He thought of the Forresters. He regretted bitterly that they were now the Baxters' enemies. Buck would have helped him. Even now— But what could Buck do? A thought struck him sharply. It seemed to him that he could endure to be parted from Flag if he knew that somewhere in the world the yearling was alive. He could think of him, alive and mischievous, carrying his flag-like tail high and merry. He would go to Buck and throw himself on his mercy. He would remind Buck of Fodder-wing, talk of Fodder-wing until Buck's throat choked. Then he would ask him to take Flag in the wagon, as he had taken the bear cubs, to Jacksonville. Flag would be taken to a broad park where people came to look at the animals. He would bound about and be given plenty of feed, and a doe, and every one would admire him. He, Jody, would raise money crops of his own, and once a year he would go and visit Flag. He would save his money and he would get a place of his own, and he would buy Flag back, and they would live together.

He was flooded with excitement. He turned from the clearing up the road to the Forresters', trotting. His throat was dry and his eyes were swollen and smarting. His hope refreshed him and in a little while, when he swung up the Forresters' trail under the live oaks, he felt all right again. He ran to the house and up the steps. He rapped at the open door and stepped inside. There was no one in the room but Pa and Ma Forrester. They sat immobile in their chairs.

He said breathlessly, "Howdy. Where's Buck?"

Pa Forrester turned his head slowly on his withered neck, like a turtle. "Been a long time since you was here," he said.

"Where's Buck, please, sir?"

"Buck? Why, Buck and the hull passel of 'em has rode off to Kentucky, hoss-tradin'."

"In plantin' time?"

"Plantin' time be tradin' time. They'd ruther trade than plow. They figgered they'd make enough, tradin', to buy our rations." The old man spat. "And likely, they will."

"They're all gone?"

"Ever' one of 'em. Pack and Gabby'll be back in April."

Ma Forrester said, "Heap o' good it do a woman to birth a mess o' young uns and raise 'em and then have 'em all go off to oncet. I will say, they left rations and stacked wood. We won't need nothin' 'til some of 'em's back in April."

"April—"

He turned dully from the door.

"Come set with us, boy. I'd be proud to cook dinner for you. Raisin puddin', eh? You and Fodder-wing allus loved my raisin puddin'."

"I got to go," he said. "I thank you."

He turned back.

He burst out desperately, "What would you do, did you have a yearlin' et up the corn and you couldn't keep it out no-way and your Pa told you to go shoot it?"

They blinked at him. Ma Forrester cackled.

Pa Forrester said, "Why, I'd go shoot it."

He realized that he had not made the matter clear.

He said, "Supposin' it was a yearlin' you loved like you-all loved Fodder-wing?"

Pa Forrester said, "Why, love's got nothin' to do with corn. You cain't have a thing eatin' the crops. Lessen you got boys like mine, has got other ways o' makin' a livin'."

Ma Forrester asked, "Hit that fawn you carried here last summer for Fodder-wing to put a name to?"

"That's him. Flag," he said. "Cain't you-all take him? Fodder-wing would of takened him."

"Why, we got no better way'n you o' keepin' him. He'd not stay here, no-how. What's four mile to a yearlin' deer?"

They too were a stone wall.

He said, "Well, good-by," and went away.

The Forrester clearing was desolate without the big men and their horses. They had taken most of the dogs with them. Only a mangy pair remained, chained at the side of the house, scratching themselves mournfully. He was glad to get away again.

He would walk to Jacksonville with Flag himself. He looked about for something to make a halter by which to lead him, so that he would not turn and run home, as he had done on the Christmas hunt. He hacked laboriously at a grapevine with his pocket knife. He looped a length of it around Flag's neck and set off to the northeast. The trail came out somewhere near Hopkins Prairie, he knew, on the Fort Gates road on which he and Penny had intercepted the Forresters. Flag was docile for a time under the leash, then grew impatient of the restraint and tugged against it.

Jody said, "How come you to grow up so unlawful?"

It wore him out, trying to coax the yearling into going willingly. At last he gave it up and took off the grapevine halter. Flag was then perversely content to keep in sight. In the afternoon, Jody found himself tired with a fatigue born of hunger. He had left the house without breakfast. He had wanted only to get away. He looked along the road for berries to eat, but it was too early and there were none. The blackberries had not yet finished blooming. He chewed some leaves, as Flag was doing, but they made him feel emptier than before. His feet dragged. He lay down by the road in the sun for a rest and induced Flag to lie beside him. He was drugged with hunger and misery and the strong March sun on his head. He fell asleep. When he awakened, Flag had gone. He followed his tracks. They led in and out of the scrub, then turned back to the road and continued evenly toward home.

There was nothing to do but follow. He was too weary to think further. He reached Baxter's Island after dark. A candle burned in the kitchen. The dogs came to him. He patted them to quiet them. He crept close silently and peered in. Supper was over. His mother sat in the candle-light, sewing her endless patchwork pieces. He was trying to make up his mind whether to go in or not, when Flag galloped across the yard. He saw his mother lift her head and listen.

He slipped hurriedly beyond the smoke-house and called Flag in a low voice. The yearling came to him. He crouched at the corner. His mother came to the kitchen door and threw it open. A bar of light lay across the sand. The door closed. He waited a long time until the light went out in the kitchen. He allowed time for her to go to bed and to sleep. He prowled inside the smoke-house and found the remainder of the smoked bear-meat. He hacked off a strip. It was hard and dry, but he chewed on it. He supposed Flag had fed on buds in the woods, but he could not bear to think of him hungry. He went to the corn-crib and took two ears of corn and shelled them and fed the kernels to him. He chewed some kernels himself. He thought longingly of the cold cooked food that must be in the kitchen safe but he dared not go in after it. He felt like a stranger and a thief. This was the way the wolves felt, he thought, and the wild-cats and the panthers and all the varmints, looking in at the clearing with big eyes and empty bellies. He made a bed in a stall at the lot with an armful of the scant remaining marsh-grass hay. He slept there with Flag beside him, not quite warm enough through the chill March night.

He awakened after sunrise, stiff and miserable. Flag was gone. He went reluctantly but compelled to the house. At the gate he heard his mother's voice raised in a storm of anger. She had discovered the shotgun where he had leaned it against the smoke-house wall. She had discovered Flag. She had discovered, too, that the yearling had made the most of the early hours and had fed, not only across the sprouting corn, but across a wide section of the cow-peas. He went helplessly to her to meet her wrath. He stood with his head down while she flailed him with her tongue.

She said finally, "Git to your Pa. For oncet, he's with me."

He went into the bedroom. His father's face was drawn.

Penny said gently, "How come you not to do what I told you?"

"Pa, I jest couldn't. I cain't do it."

Penny leaned his head back against the pillow.

"Come here clost to me, boy. Jody, you know I've done all I could to keep your leetle deer for you."

"Yes, sir."

"You know we depend on our crops to live."

"Yes, sir."

"You know they ain't a way in the world to keep that wild yearlin' from destroyin' 'em."

"Yes, sir."

"Then why don't you do what's got to be done?"

"I cain't."

Penny lay silent.

"Tell your Ma to come here. Go to your room and shut the door."

"Yes, sir."

There was a relief in following simple orders.

"Pa says to go to him."

He went to his room and closed the door. He sat on the side of the bed, twisting his hands. He heard low voices. He heard steps. He heard a shot. He ran from the room to the open kitchen door. His mother stood on the stoop with the shotgun smoking in her hands. Flag lay floundering beside the fence.

She said, "I didn't want to hurt the creetur. I cain't shoot straight. You know I cain't."

Jody ran to Flag. The yearling heaved to his three good legs and stumbled away, as though the boy himself were his enemy. He was bleeding from a torn left forequarter. Penny dragged himself from his bed. He sank on one knee in the doorway, clutching it for support.

He called, "I'd do it if I could. I jest cain't stand up— Go finish him, Jody. You got to put him outen his torment."

Jody ran back and snatched the gun from his mother.

He screamed, "You done it o' purpose. You allus hated him."

He turned on his father.

"You went back on me. You told her to do it."

He screeched so that his throat felt torn.

"I hate you. I hope you die. I hope I never see you agin."

He ran after Flag, whimpering as he ran.

Penny called, "He'p me, Ory. I cain't git up—"

Flag ran on three legs in pain and terror. Twice he fell and Jody caught up to him.

He shrieked, "Hit's me! Hit's me! Flag!"

Flag thrashed to his feet and was off again. Blood flowed in a steady stream. The yearling made the edge of the sink-hole. He wavered an instant and toppled. He rolled down the side. Jody ran after him. Flag lay beside the pool. He opened great liquid eyes and turned them on the boy with a glazed look of wonder. Jody pressed the muzzle of the gun barrel at the back of the smooth neck and pulled the trigger. Flag quivered a moment and then lay still.

Jody threw the gun aside and dropped flat on his stomach. He retched and vomited and retched again. He clawed into the earth with his fingernails. He beat it with his fists. The sink-hole rocked around him. A far roaring became a thin humming. He sank into blackness as into a dark pool.

Reunion

From THE DEEPENING STREAM
By Dorothy Canfield Fisher

The "deepening stream" of this novel is the maturing love of an American woman for her husband. Throughout the narrative the author has woven the threads of two encompassing emotions; one Matey's love for Adrian, the other her devotion to France. At the decisive moments of her life these strands become inevitably united and France stands as a symbol of change and growth in Matey's character.

When finally France faces desolation in 1914, these two loves find their highest expression. Matey's resolve to take her children and go with her husband to France's aid confirms the oneness of mind and spirit which is the essence of marriage. Adrian goes to the front and Matey devotes herself to war work and to caring for her old friend Madame Vinet, whose family is scattered by the war. In the following pages Matey prepares for her husband's return from the battle zone. This passage contains the properties of all homecomings, which are compounded of anxiety and joy and confusion. Underlying the reunion are the doubts of two people long separated, their fear of changes in each other and themselves—a fear that is allayed in the final paragraph.

SHE had lived to see it dawn, the day of Adrian's return for his first furlough. But the time from dawn until his train was due was almost as hard to live through as all those weeks and months. She had too carefully finished her work ahead of time so that she should be free for his visit. It would have been better to save some of those endless tasks for today rather than to wander around the apartment, looking in at the children's room, looking in at the kitchen, looking at her watch and thinking it must have been stopped.

"Sit down, child!" said Mme. Vinet finally. "You'll wear yourself out." She sat down and took the everlasting knitting from the older woman's hands.

"But what shall *I* do?"

"Go play something for me," implored Matey.

She sat knitting fast and listening to Bach, once more stating honestly the complexity of all things and once more showing that in the end they are but harmonious parts of the whole. The room was filled with the intelligent beauty of that comforting voice. At the end, "How it does one good!" breathed Mme. Vinet. They were painfully sensitive to music in those days.

"It's one of the things I owe to you," said Matey.

"You have repaid it—dear child," murmured the woman before the piano.

"Have you still, do you suppose, that old piano arrangement for the Fifth Symphony that you and Henri used to play years ago?" asked Matey.

"Why, certainly I have it. Come and play the bass with me."

They began bravely:

But they could get no further. Streaming up from the notes came the past—it was Henri who sat there beside his mother, Henri the other half of her soul. Back of them sat the little girls, Mimi gentle and loving, Ziza, ardent Ziza with her great gifts for joy and suffering. And the baby Paul slept in his cradle in the next room. The two women sat motionless, staring at the familiar notes on the page as if they were ghosts.

Dominiqua put her head in at the door, and asked, "Pardon, Madam Mété, does Monsieur like garlic with his leg of lamb?"

"*Non, non, non, non!*" cried Matey, springing up, horrified at the idea of something wrong in Adrian's first meal at home. "No garlic in anything!"

She looked at her watch again. It was really not too early to begin to get the children's wraps on. There were so many protections to be put on against this steady February rain.

They plodded from the Métro station into the Gare de l'Est, blue with soldiers ending or beginning their furloughs, camping out on the benches, smoking, eating, waiting for their trains. Matey put down her dripping umbrella and asked an employee which was the exit for soldiers returning en permission. He looked appraisingly at her bourgeois hat and gloves and asked, "Officer or common soldier?"

"Ambulance driver," said Matey. "An American driving an ambulance attached to the Third Army."

The man shrugged his shoulders, quite blank as to the status of an American. "Does he rank as an officer or a common soldier?"

"I haven't any idea," said Matey, surprised. "Why?"

"Officers come out this exit, common soldiers out of the side door around the corner," he announced and went his way.

Matey and Petella were thrown into helpless agitation by this news. Which door should they choose? Suppose he took the other one. It would be too horrible to miss him after all. If only they had brought Mme. Vinet! But it was too late to get her now.

Matey, undone with excitement, lost her head and was ready to cry. Petella took command. "I'll stay here, Mother, and you and Brother go round to the side door."

"But I can't leave you alone in such a crowd . . . in a city!" cried poor Matey. "You're only seven years old!"

"I'll be all right," said Petella. "I'll stand right here and hold on to this railing. And if he comes here, I'll holler to him and we'll go round and meet you."

Matey dared not agree and dared do nothing else. The train was almost due. She kissed Petella and told her, "Don't you stir from there on any account unless Father comes," and went away, looking back anxiously at the valiant little figure, lost in the midst of the great echoing hall and the crowds of roughly hurrying grown-ups.

Putting up her umbrella again, she ran hurriedly with Brother along the street to the side door, the slimy February mud spattering the little boy's leggings and his mother's skirts. There could be no doubt where to go. A silent crowd of women and children stood in the mud and rain, looking fixedly at a large door in the wall. Most of them were working-people who did not carry umbrellas but protected themselves from the rain sketchily with black woolen scarves over their heads, or the hoods of their dark-blue capes. Matey and her little son joined them. "It is here for common soldiers returning from the front?" she asked the woman next her, who nodded without taking her eyes from the dingy painted panels of the door.

They waited, stepping from one foot to the other, shifting babies from shoulder to shoulder. Matey began to tremble. She saw that an old woman near her was shaking so that she could scarcely stand. "Take my arm, Madame," she murmured, and stood more firmly herself then, steadied by Brother's pull at her hand and the weight of old age on the other arm.

"Will I know Adrian when I see him?" she thought. It seemed years since she had been his wife, had been a person at all.

She started when an employee flung the door open. The roar and clatter of a moving train poured out loudly as if the open door were a trumpet. The women fixed their eyes on it. Matey felt their silent patience rise to a passion. She too, for her life, could not have looked away.

Heavy, rapid footsteps were heard. An unshaven, unhandsome middle-aged little Frenchman stepped through the door, his ill-fitting uniform of coarse blue cloth smeared with yellow mud, his hulking shapeless shoes caked with it to their tops.

"Maurice!" cried a woman's voice hysterically, and "Oh, Papa! *Papa!*" a child's. A beautiful smile came over his insignificant face. He took one long step forward and was gone in the crowd. Another had appeared behind him, long and lean and rustic. "Pierre! *Ici!* Pierre!" some one called fervently from the back of the crowd, and every one stepped back to let a weeping woman in a shawl fling herself into his arms.

They came all at once then, three or four crowding through the door together. The crowd surged forward and back; there were cries and tears and laughter; babies were transferred from women's to men's shoulders; Matey and Brother and the old woman were jostled from side to side by heedless reunited couples.

And then it was over. The open door stood empty, only a trickle of small railroad noises coming from it, the slow rumble of a baggage-truck, the distant hoot of a train. A handful of women still stood waiting under the rain. An employee came to shut the door. "All out of that train," he said, adding not unkindly, "Next train in from the east front due at two o'clock tomorrow morning." He shut the door. The women turned away, two of them sobbing.

"Adrian is evidently not ranked as a common soldier," thought Matey.

"But where is my son!" said the old woman on her arm.

"Perhaps he came through the other exit," suggested Matey, trying not to show her impatience.

"No, he always comes through this door. I always meet him here."

Matey's heart contracted at that "always." Could she live through this *again!* She struggled against her impulse to drop the old arm and run to Petella. "Perhaps he will come on the next train?" she said.

"Perhaps," muttered the old woman tonelessly, dropping her head and standing motionless in the rain. Matey noticed that she looked very poor. "Won't you let me offer you a hot supper while you wait?" she asked, pointing to a restaurant across the street. "You could eat it by the window so that you would not lose sight of the door."

She hurried her to the table by the window, left a bill by her plate, shook hands with her, and, Brother galloping at her side, spattered around through the mud to the waiting-room. It was almost empty. Petella, a little pale, stood there steadfastly, her eyes, very wide, fixed eagerly on the door to the street.

"Oh, wasn't he at your door, either?" she cried quaveringly.

Matey's heart began to pound. Her suspense recoiled upon her in a sick reaction from hope. She felt driven half crazy by all these dependents on her, old women, little children—for whom she must show qualities she did not have. She would have given anything to be alone, free to weep aloud, to be weak and desperate as she was. It was frightful to be grown up.

"Oh, Father probably missed the train," she said lightly in a reassuring voice to Petella. "You know he's always late." It was in fact one of the family jokes.

With a crackle of her nerves it occurred to her that this might be true. Adrian must have been slow in getting ready, as he often was, and have missed the train. She flared with anger. How could he do such a thing when he knew how anxious they would be! To have missed such a train! All the times in the past when he had been late and she had been prompt rose up from oblivion and heaped themselves to a mountainous grievance.

"Well, what do you say, dears, shall we walk part way home and look in at the windows instead of taking the Métro here?" she asked the children in a cheerful tone.

But the first window displayed beaded funeral wreaths with "A mon mari, mort sur le champ d'honneur" on a good many of them. As if some one had struck her a blow in the chest Matey thought gaspingly, "Adrian may be dead this minute. May have been hit with a shell on his last trip to the front-line dressing-station. When I get back to the apartment I may find a telegram. . . ."

"Children, don't you think it would be fun to take a taxi, for a treat?" The cheerfulness of her voice was wearing thin. Petella looked at her anxiously. Darling little daughter! Matey, unstrung with anxiety, was afraid that in another moment she would lay her head on her little daughter's shoulder and burst into tears. She looked fixedly out of the cab window and let Petella restrain Brother from dashing himself out of the windows as he careered about, "playing bear."

But there was no telegram at the apartment. Only a rich unwonted odor of roast meat, and Mme. Vinet and Dominiqua running to welcome in the *permissionaire*, very much startled that he had not come. Matey read in Mme. Vinet's disappointed face another explanation of Adrian's non-appearance, something Matey had not thought of, although she was as familiar with the possibility now as Mme. Vinet. Another big offensive had perhaps started suddenly and again *permissions* indefinitely recalled. At this idea she sank down in a chair, all her strength gone. "I *couldn't* wait another month!" she thought. Dominiqua went back to the kitchen to change her plans for dinner, and Matey pulled Brother up on her lap to take off his muddy leggings. Her hands trembled so she could not unbutton them. "Sit *still*, Brother!" she said tearfully, although the weary child had not stirred.

"*I'll* unbutton them!" cried Petella, springing forward.

There was a knock on the outer door. Hearing Dominiqua step to open, they all froze into listening statues. The door opened, a murmur of voices, a "*Oui, Monsieur*" from Dominiqua. The door to the living-room opened. A slight, pale, unshaven man in a muddy uniform stood there, his great shoes caked with mud. As he looked at Matey and the children a beautiful smile came to his lips.

"Adrian!" cried Matey, incredulously, springing up from her seat.

"Father!" shouted Petella, running to throw her arms around his knees.

"*C'est mon papa*," explained Brother proudly, with a Gallic sweep of his little hand, to Mme. Vinet, who had snatched at him as his mother let him fall.

"But how *did* you get here without our seeing you!" demanded Matey breathlessly, her arms still around his neck. She hardly knew what she was saying.

"Two sections to the train," explained Adrian.

"Why didn't the man at the Gare tell us?"

"Didn't know, probably—I'll bet he didn't try to find out very hard."

Matey's taut nerves snapped. She cried out angrily, "Adrian, how *like* you to miss the first one! Can't you ever get anywhere on time!"

Before even the ugly echo of this greeting had time to reach her ears, she turned sick. What answer could a man make to such a woman save to turn and leave her forever!

Well, she had forgotten him, it seemed, had in her hysterical loss of any sense of proportion forgotten that he never lost his. His answer was not in the least to turn and leave her. It was given with a grin. "The stars in their courses, Matey, didn't seem to care as much about my *permission* as I did. It's been quite a day. First the *camionette* I started on bust a rear axle. I bummed a ride on a R.V.F. truck and bribed the driver with cigarettes to step on the gas. Got to Bar-le-Duc. More cigarettes to the Maréchal des Logis to stamp my papers in a hurry. Got out on the platform just in time to see the train I expected to take breezing through like the Empire State passing Rustdorf. Mob of *permissionaires* —me too—acting like the mob in *Julius Caesar*. Despair. Then along comes another train. Somebody calls out 'Chalons! Epernay! Paris!' and we all surge on, several hundred of us. Packed like sardines. First I stood on one foot and then on the other; there wasn't room for both. Anyway here I am." The clasp of his arms tightened about her. He had not even listened to her poor wrong words except to recognize them as part of the strain of her longing for him. Adrian was not a dream, after all.

He looked well, they began to say then, all talking at once—rather pale from driving at night and sleeping by day. But quite like himself. Quite like all men back from the front too, in that his first thought was for a bath. They had the flat tin tub ready in the little *cabinet de toilette*, the reservoir of the cookstove full of hot water. Matey laid out clean underwear—bought at the department store in Rustdorf!—and while he bathed went into the kitchen. For weeks she had been planning and replanning what to have for that first dinner and had run all over Paris to find the ingredients for the Boston brown bread and the pancakes.

But after all Adrian did not eat much of it. "I spoiled my appetite with bread and cheese in the train. I'm afraid I can't do justice to dinner," he said apologetically at the last.

Matey's heart sank in alarm. She lost her head again. She saw herself as perhaps she looked to Adrian with her elaborate dinner to celebrate his homecoming, trivial—or callous. He would despise her. From his letters it had been evident that he had been profoundly affected by what he saw at the front. Perhaps he had grown away from her, would feel that her wildness of longing for him was grasping and personal, indecorous in the midst of tragedy. In a flash she imagined him grown like his father, old, remote, disembodied, beyond passion, beyond her, lost to her . . . and because she imagined him so, she knew he was so. Mme. Vinet said, "You two haven't had a moment to yourselves yet. Let me put the children to bed."

Petella and Brother said hastily *merci bien, Bonnemaman*, but they *would* like Father too, because there were certain things he always did, a certain story he always told, the same, only different. . . . "Putting the children to bed is one of the things I'm here for," Adrian said.

"He doesn't *want* to be alone with me," thought Matey, wildly.

He helped the children undress with a great deal of noisy play, he tucked them up, told them an installment of a serial saga of his invention, in which Brother figured as an elephant tamer and Petella an explorer in African jungles, and afterward according to the tradition which dated before the beginning of the children's memories, said, "Now I'm going to sit here and hope you'll always be good children," and sat between their beds in the dark, holding in each of his hands the small warm hand of a drowsy child.

After a time, "This is a sort of 'Meeting,' Brother," Petella's voice came sleepily through the darkness.

"*J'aime ça alors*," murmured the little boy.

Their father stood up finally, felt his way to the door, and stepped out into the hallway. The apartment was quiet. No light in the living-room; Mme. Vinet had humanely gone to bed. He drew a long breath.

He turned out the gas in the hall and opened the door to his wife's room. At the sound she turned, tall in her white nightgown, her beautiful wide gray eyes, dark with emotion, fixed on his.

He gave a cry, "Why, it's true! I'm here!" And went toward her, trembling like a bridegroom.

She came into his arms like a bride.

The Death of Robert Jordan

From FOR WHOM THE BELL TOLLS

By Ernest Hemingway

Though the action of this novel moves within a few days, its thought reaches far back into the lives of a group of loyalist guerillas of the Spanish civil war, whose furtive and isolated existence is the foreground of the book. Robert Jordan, an American, joins this group of patriots, and it is through his eyes that we see the strange, fervent characters. The real leader of these underground fighters is Pilar, a woman whose immense spiritual strength completely dominates the nominal authority of her husband, Pablo. Into the little circle comes Maria, a girl who has been rescued from the revolutionary forces after brutal abuse by their soldiers.

The chosen passage is the end of the novel. Here Jordan's conflict between his love for Maria and his stern sense of the necessity of his mission is resolved. Severely wounded, Jordan watches the final fulfillment of his assignment—the blowing of a vital bridge. His thought in this suffering interval is, perhaps, the thought of all dying soldiers.

WHEN they heard the planes they all looked up and the planes were coming from Segovia very high in the sky, silvery in the high sky, their drumming rising over all the other sounds.

"Those!" Pilar said. "There has only lacked those!"

Robert Jordan put his arm on her shoulders as he watched them. "Nay, woman," he said. "Those do not come for us. Those have no time for us. Calm thyself."

"I hate them."

"Me too. But now I must go to Agustín."

He circled the hillside through the pines and all the time there was the throbbing, drumming of the planes and across the shattered bridge on the road below, around the bend of the road there was the intermittent hammering fire of a heavy machine gun.

Robert Jordan dropped down to where Agustín lay in the clump of scrub pines behind the automatic rifle and more planes were coming all the time.

"What passes below?" Agustín said. "What is Pablo doing? Doesn't he know the bridge is gone?"

"Maybe he can't leave."

"Then let us leave. The hell with him."

"He will come now if he is able," Robert Jordan said. "We should see him now."

"I have not heard him," Agustín said. "Not for five minutes. No. There! Listen! There he is. That's him."

There was a burst of the spot-spot-spotting fire of the cavalry submachine gun, then another, then another.

"That's the bastard," Robert Jordan said.

He watched still more planes coming over in the high cloudless blue sky and he watched Agustín's face as he looked up at them. Then he looked down at the shattered bridge and across to the stretch of road which still was clear. He coughed and spat and listened to the heavy machine gun hammer again below the bend. It sounded to be in the same place that it was before.

"And what's that?" Agustín asked. "What the unnameable is that?"

"It has been going since before I blew the bridge," Robert Jordan said. He looked down at the bridge now and he could see the stream through the torn gap where the center had fallen, hanging like a bent steel apron. He heard the first of the planes that had gone over now bombing up above at the pass and more were still coming. The noise of their motors filled all the high sky and looking up he saw their pursuit, minute and tiny, circling and wheeling high above them.

"I don't think they ever crossed the lines the other morning," Primitivo said. "They must have swung off to the west and then come back. They could not be making an attack if they had seen these."

"Most of these are new," Robert Jordan said.

He had the feeling of something that had started normally and had then brought great, outsized, giant repercussions. It was as though you had thrown a stone and the stone made a ripple and the ripple returned roaring and toppling as a tidal wave. Or as though you shouted and the echo came back in rolls and peals of thunder, and the thunder was deadly. Or as though you struck one man and he fell and as far as you

could see other men rose up all armed and armored. He was glad he was
not with Golz up at the pass.

Lying there, by Agustín, watching the planes going over, listening for
firing behind him, watching the road below where he knew he would
see something but not what it would be, he still felt numb with the surprise that he had not been killed at the bridge. He had accepted being
killed so completely that all of this now seemed unreal. Shake out of
that, he said to himself. Get rid of that. There is much, much, much to
be done today. But it would not leave him and he felt, consciously, all
of this becoming like a dream.

"You swallowed too much of that smoke," he told himself. But he
knew it was not that. He could feel, solidly, how unreal it all was
through the absolute reality and he looked down at the bridge and then
back to the sentry lying on the road, to where Anselmo lay, to Fernando
against the bank and back up the smooth, brown road to the stalled
truck and still it was unreal.

"You better sell out your part of you quickly," he told himself.
"You're like one of those cocks in the pit where nobody has seen the
wound given and it doesn't show and he is already going cold with it."

"Nuts," he said to himself. "You are a little groggy is all, and you have
a let-down after responsibility, is all. Take it easy."

Then Agustín grabbed his arm and pointed and he looked across the
gorge and saw Pablo.

They saw Pablo come running around the corner of the bend in the
road. At the sheer rock where the road went out of sight they saw him
stop and lean against the rock and fire back up the road. Robert Jordan
saw Pablo, short, heavy and stocky, his cap gone, leaning against the rock
wall and firing the short cavalry automatic rifle and he could see the
bright flicker of the cascading brass hulls as the sun caught them. They
saw Pablo crouch and fire another burst. Then, without looking back,
he came running, short, bow-legged, fast, his head bent down straight
toward the bridge.

Robert Jordan had pushed Agustín over and he had the stock of the
big automatic rifle against his shoulder and was sighting on the bend of
the road. His own submachine gun lay by his left hand. It was not accurate enough for that range.

As Pablo came toward them Robert Jordan sighted on the bend but
nothing came. Pablo had reached the bridge, looked over his shoulder
once, glanced at the bridge, and then turned to his left and gone down
into the gorge and out of sight. Robert Jordan was still watching the
bend and nothing had come in sight. Agustín got up on one knee. He
could see Pablo climbing down into the gorge like a goat. There had
been no noise of firing below since they had first seen Pablo.

"You see anything up above? On the rocks above?" Robert Jordan asked.

"Nothing."

Robert Jordan watched the bend of the road. He knew the wall just below that was too steep for any one to climb but below it eased and some one might have circled up above.

If things had been unreal before, they were suddenly real enough now. It was as though a reflex lens camera had been suddenly brought into focus. It was then he saw the low-bodied, angled snout and squat green, gray and brown-splashed turret with the projecting machine gun come around the bend into the bright sun. He fired on it and he could hear the spang against the steel. The little whippet tank scuttled back behind the rock wall. Watching the corner, Robert Jordan saw the nose just re-appear, then the edge of the turret showed and the turret swung so that the gun was pointing down the road.

"It seems like a mouse coming out of his hole," Agustín said. "Look, *Inglés.*"

"He has little confidence," Robert Jordan said.

"This is the big insect Pablo has been fighting," Agustín said. "Hit him again, *Inglés.*"

"Nay. I cannot hurt him. I don't want him to see where we are."

The tank commenced to fire down the road. The bullets hit the road surface and sung off and now they were pinging and clanging in the iron of the bridge. It was the same machine gun they had heard below.

"*Cabrón!*" Agustín said. "Is that the famous tanks, *Inglés?*"

"That's a baby one."

"*Cabrón.* If I had a baby bottle full of gasoline I would climb up there and set fire to him. What will he do, *Inglés?*"

"After a while he will have another look."

"And these are what men fear," Agustín said. "Look, *Inglés!* He's re-killing the sentries."

"Since he has no other target," Robert Jordan said. "Do not reproach him."

But he was thinking, Sure, make fun of him. But suppose it was you, way back here in your own country and they held you up with firing on the main road. Then a bridge was blown. Wouldn't you think it was mined ahead or that there was a trap? Sure you would. He's done all right. He's waiting for something else to come up. He's engaging the enemy. It's only us. But he can't tell that. Look at the little bastard.

The little tank had nosed a little farther around the corner.

Just then Agustín saw Pablo coming over the edge of the gorge, pull-ing himself over on hands and knees, his bristly face running with sweat.

"Here comes the son of a bitch," he said.

"Who?"

"Pablo."

Robert Jordan looked, saw Pablo, and then he commenced firing at the part of the camouflaged turret of the tank where he knew the slit above the machine gun would be. The little tank whirred backwards, scuttling out of sight and Robert Jordan picked up the automatic rifle, clamped the tripod against the barrel and swung the gun with its still hot muzzle over his shoulder. The muzzle was so hot it burned his shoulder and he shoved it far behind him turning the stock flat in his hand.

"Bring the sack of pans and my little *máquina*," he shouted, "and come running."

Robert Jordan ran up the hill through the pines. Agustín was close behind him and behind him Pablo was coming.

"Pilar!" Jordan shouted across the hill. "Come on, woman!"

The three of them were going as fast as they could up the steep slope. They could not run any more because the grade was too severe and Pablo, who had no load but the light cavalry submachine gun, had closed up with the other two.

"And thy people?" Agustín said to Pablo out of his dry mouth.

"All dead," Pablo said. He was almost unable to breathe. Agustín turned his head and looked at him.

"We have plenty of horses now, *Inglés*," Pablo panted.

"Good," Robert Jordan said. The murderous bastard, he thought. "What did you encounter?"

"Everything," Pablo said. He was breathing in lunges. "What passed with Pilar?"

"She lost Fernando and the brother—"

"Eladio," Agustín said.

"And thou?" Pablo asked.

"I lost Anselmo."

"There are lots of horses," Pablo said. "Even for the baggage."

Agustín bit his lip, looked at Robert Jordan and shook his head. Below them, out of sight through the trees, they heard the tank firing on the road and bridge again.

Robert Jordan jerked his head. "What passed with that?" he said to Pablo. He did not like to look at Pablo, nor to smell him, but he wanted to hear him.

"I could not leave with that there," Pablo said. "We were barricaded at the lower bend of the post. Finally it went back to look for something and I came."

"What were you shooting at, at the bend?" Agustín asked bluntly.

Pablo looked at him, started to grin, thought better of it, and said nothing.

"Did you shoot them all?" Agustín asked. Robert Jordan was thinking, keep your mouth shut. It is none of your business now. They have done all that you could expect and more. This is an inter-tribal matter. Don't make moral judgments. What do you expect from a murderer? You're working with a murderer. Keep your mouth shut. You knew enough about him before. This is nothing new. But you dirty bastard, he thought. You dirty, rotten bastard.

His chest was aching with the climbing as though it would split after the running and ahead now through the trees he saw the horses.

"Go ahead," Agustín was saying. "Why do you not say you shot them?"

"Shut up," Pablo said. "I have fought much today and well. Ask the *Inglés*."

"And now get us through today," Robert Jordan said. "For it is thee who has the plan for this."

"I have a good plan," Pablo said. "With a little luck we will be all right."

He was beginning to breathe better.

"You're not going to kill any of us, are you?" Agustín said. "For I will kill thee now."

"Shut up," Pablo said. "I have to look after thy interest and that of the band. This is war. One cannot do what one would wish."

"*Cabrón*," said Agustín. "You take all the prizes."

"Tell me what thou encountered below," Robert Jordan said to Pablo.

"Everything," Pablo repeated. He was still breathing as though it were tearing his chest but he could talk steadily now and his face and head were running with sweat and his shoulders and chest were soaked with it. He looked at Robert Jordan cautiously to see if he were really friendly and then he grinned. "Everything," he said again. "First we took the post. Then came a motorcyclist. Then another. Then an ambulance. Then a camion. Then the tank. Just before thou didst the bridge."

"Then—"

"The tank could not hurt us but we could not leave for it commanded the road. Then it went away and I came."

"And thy people?" Agustín put in, still looking for trouble.

"Shut up," Pablo looked at him squarely, and his face was the face of a man who had fought well before any other thing had happened. "They were not of our band."

Now they could see the horses tied to the trees, the sun coming down on them through the pine branches and then tossing their heads and kicking against the botflies and Robert Jordan saw Maria and the next thing he was holding her tight, tight, with the automatic rifle leaning against his side, the flash-cone pressing against his ribs and Maria saying, "Thou, Roberto. Oh, thou."

"Yes, rabbit. My good, good rabbit. Now we go."

"Art thou here truly?"

"Yes. Yes. Truly. Oh, thou!"

He had never thought that you could know that there was a woman if there was battle; nor that any part of you could know it, or respond to it; nor that if there was a woman that she should have breasts small, round and tight against you through a shirt; nor that they, the breasts, could know about the two of them in battle. But it was true and he thought, good. That's good. I would not have believed that and he held her to him once hard, hard, but he did not look at her, and then he slapped her where he never had slapped her and said, "Mount. Mount. Get on that saddle, guapa."

Then they were untying the halters and Robert Jordan had given the automatic rifle back to Agustín and slung his own submachine gun over his back, and he was putting bombs out of his pockets into the saddle-bags, and he stuffed one empty pack inside the other and tied that one behind his saddle. Then Pilar came up, so breathless from the climb she could not talk, but only motioned.

Then Pablo stuffed three hobbles he had in his hand into a saddle-bag, stood up and said, "Qué tal, woman?" and she only nodded, and then they were all mounting.

Robert Jordan was on the big gray he had first seen in the snow of the morning of the day before and he felt that it was much horse between his legs and under his hands. He was wearing rope-soled shoes and the stirrups were a little too short; his submachine gun was slung over his shoulder, his pockets were full of clips and he was sitting reloading the one used clip, the reins under one arm, tight, watching Pilar mount into a strange sort of seat on top of the duffle lashed onto the saddle of the buckskin.

"Cut that stuff loose for God's sake," Primitivo said. "Thou wilt fall and the horse cannot carry it."

"Shut up," said Pilar. "We go to make a life with this."

"Canst ride like that, woman?" Pablo asked her from the guardia-civil saddle on the great bay horse.

"Like any milk peddler," Pilar told him. "How do you go, old one?"

"Straight down. Across the road. Up the far slope and into the timber where it narrows."

"Across the road?" Agustín wheeled beside him, kicking his soft-heeled, canvas shoes against the stiff, unresponding belly of one of the horses Pablo had recruited in the night.

"Yes, man. It is the only way," Pablo said. He handed him one of the lead ropes. Primitivo and the gypsy had the others.

"Thou canst come at the end if thou will, *Inglés*," Pablo said. "We cross high enough to be out of range of that *máquina*. But we will go separately and riding much and then be together where it narrows above."

"Good," said Robert Jordan.

They rode down through the timber toward the edge of the road. Robert Jordan rode just behind Maria. He could not ride beside her for the timber. He caressed the gray once with his thigh muscles, and then held him steady as they dropped down fast and sliding through the pines, telling the gray with his thighs as they dropped down what the spurs would have told him if they had been on level ground.

"Thou," he said to Maria, "go second as they cross the road. First is not so bad though it seems bad. Second is good. It is later that they are always watching for."

"But thou—"

"I will go suddenly. There will be no problem. It is the places in line that are bad."

He was watching the round, bristly head of Pablo, sunk in his shoulders as he rode, his automatic rifle slung over his shoulder. He was watching Pilar, her head bare, her shoulders broad, her knees higher than her thighs as her heels hooked into the bundles. She looked back at him once and shook her head.

"Pass the Pilar before you cross the road," Robert Jordan said to Maria.

Then he was looking through the thinning trees and he saw the oiled dark of the road below and beyond it the green slope of the hillside. We are above the culvert, he saw, and just below the height where the road drops down straight toward the bridge in that long sweep. We are around eight hundred yards above the bridge. That is not out of range for the Fiat in that little tank if they have come up to the bridge.

"Maria," he said. "Pass the Pilar before we reach the road and ride wide up that slope."

She looked back at him but did not say anything. He did not look at her except to see that she had understood.

"*Comprendes?*" he asked her.

She nodded.

"Move up," he said.

She shook her head.

"Move up!"

"Nay," she told him, turning around and shaking her head. "I go in the order that I am to go."

Just then Pablo dug both his spurs into the big bay and he plunged down the last pine-needled slope and crossed the road in a pounding, sparking of shod hooves. The others came behind him and Robert Jordan saw them crossing the road and slamming on up the green slope and heard the machine gun hammer at the bridge. Then he heard a noise come sweeeish-crack-boom! The boom was a sharp crack that widened in the cracking and on the hillside he saw a small fountain of earth rise with a plume of gray smoke. Sweeeish-crack-boom! It came again, the swishing like the noise of a rocket and there was another up-pulsing of dirt and smoke farther up the hillside.

Ahead of him the gypsy was stopped beside the road in the shelter of the last trees. He looked ahead at the slope and then he looked back toward Robert Jordan.

"Go ahead, Rafael," Robert Jordan said. "Gallop, man!"

The gypsy was holding the lead rope with the pack-horse pulling his head taut behind him.

"Drop the pack-horse and gallop!" Robert Jordan said.

He saw the gypsy's hand extended behind him, rising higher and higher, seeming to take forever as his heels kicked into the horse he was riding and the rope came taut, then dropped, and he was across the road and Robert Jordan was knee-ing against a frightened pack-horse that bumped back into him as the gypsy crossed the hard, dark road and he heard his horse's hooves clumping as he galloped up the slope.

Wheeeeeeish-ca-rack! The flat trajectory of the shell came and he saw the gypsy jink like a running boar as the earth spouted the little black and gray geyser ahead of him. He watched him galloping, slow and reaching now, up the long green slope and the gun threw behind him and ahead of him and he was under the fold of the hill with the others.

I can't take the damned pack-horse, Robert Jordan thought. Though I wish I could keep the son of a bitch on my off side. I'd like to have him between me and that 47 mm. they're throwing with. By God, I'll try to get him up there anyway.

He rode up to the pack-horse, caught hold of the hackamore, and then, holding the rope, the horse trotting behind him, rode fifty yards up through the trees. At the edge of the trees he looked down the road past the truck to the bridge. He could see men out on the bridge and behind it looked like a traffic jam on the road. Robert Jordan looked around, saw what he wanted finally and reached up and broke a dead limb from a pine tree. He dropped the hackamore, edged the pack-horse up to the slope that slanted down to the road and then hit him hard across the rump with the tree branch. "Go on, you son of a bitch," he said, and threw the dead branch after him as the pack-horse crossed the road and started across the slope. The branch hit him and the horse broke from a run into a gallop.

Robert Jordan rode thirty yards farther up the road; beyond that the bank was too steep. The gun was firing now with the rocket whish and the cracking, dirt-spouting boom. "Come on, you big gray fascist bastard," Robert Jordan said to the horse and put him down the slope in a sliding plunge. Then he was out in the open, over the road that was so hard under the hooves he felt the pound of it come up all the way to his shoulders, his neck and his teeth, onto the smooth of the slope, the hooves finding it, cutting it, pounding it, reaching, throwing, going, and he looked down across the slope to where the bridge showed now at a new angle he had never seen. It crossed in profile now without foreshortening and in the center was the broken place and behind it on the road was the little tank and behind the little tank was a big tank with a gun that flashed now yellow-bright as a mirror and the screech as the air ripped apart seemed almost over the gray neck that stretched ahead of him, and he turned his head as the dirt fountained up the hillside. The pack-horse was ahead of him swinging too far to the right and slowing down and Robert Jordan, galloping, his head turned a little toward the bridge, saw the line of trucks halted behind the turn that showed now clearly as he was gaining height, and he saw the bright yellow flash that signalled the instant whish and boom, and the shell fell short, but he heard the metal sailing from where the dirt rose.

He saw them all ahead in the edge of the timber watching him and he said, "*Arre caballo!* Go on, horse!" and felt his big horse's chest surging with the steepening of the slope and saw the gray neck stretching and the gray ears ahead and he reached and patted the wet gray neck, and he looked back at the bridge and saw the bright flash from the heavy, squat, mud-colored tank there on the road and then he did not hear any whish but only a banging acrid smelling clang like a boiler being ripped apart and he was under the gray horse and the gray horse was kicking and he was trying to pull out from under the weight.

He could move all right. He could move toward the right. But his left leg stayed perfectly flat under the horse as he moved to the right. It was as though there was a new joint in it; not the hip joint but another one that went sideways like a hinge. Then he knew what it was all right and just then the gray horse knee-ed himself up and Robert Jordan's right leg, that had kicked the stirrup loose just as it should, slipped clear over the saddle and came down beside him and he felt with his two hands of his thigh bone where the left leg lay flat against the ground and his hands both felt the sharp bone and where it pressed against the skin.

The gray horse was standing almost over him and he could see his ribs heaving. The grass was green where he sat and there were meadow flowers in it and he looked down the slope across to the road and the bridge and the gorge and the road and saw the tank and waited for the next flash. It came almost at once with again no whish and in the burst of it, with a smell of the high explosive, the dirt clods scattering and the steel whirring off, he saw the big gray horse sit quietly down beside him as though it were a horse in a circus. And then, looking at the horse sitting there, he heard the sound the horse was making.

Then Primitivo and Agustín had him under the arm-pits and were dragging him up the last of the slope and the new joint in his leg let it swing any way the ground swung it. Once a shell whished close over them and they dropped him and fell flat, but the dirt scattered over them and the metal sung off and they picked him up again. And then they had him up to the shelter of the long draw in the timber where the horses were, and Maria, Pilar and Pablo were standing over him.

Maria was kneeling by him and saying, "Roberto, what hast thou?"

He said, sweating heavily, "The left leg is broken, guapa."

"We will bind it up," Pilar said. "Thou canst ride that." She pointed to one of the horses that was packed. "Cut off the load."

Robert Jordan saw Pablo shake his head and he nodded at him.

"Get along," he said. Then he said, "Listen, Pablo. Come here."

The sweat-streaked, bristly face bent down by him and Robert Jordan smelt the full smell of Pablo.

"Let us speak," he said to Pilar and Maria. "I have to speak to Pablo."

"Does it hurt much?" Pablo asked. He was bending close over Robert Jordan.

"No. I think the nerve is crushed. Listen. Get along. I am mucked, see? I will talk to the girl for a moment. When I say to take her, take her. She will want to stay. I will only speak to her for a moment."

"Clearly, there is not much time," Pablo said.

"Clearly."

"I think you would do better in the Republic," Robert Jordan said.

"Nay. I am for Gredos."

"Use thy head."

"Talk to her now," Pablo said. "There is little time. I am sorry thou hast this, Inglés."

"Since I have it—" Robert Jordan said. "Let us not speak of it. But use thy head. Thou hast much head. Use it."

"Why would I not?" said Pablo. "Talk now fast, *Inglés*. There is no time."

Pablo went over to the nearest tree and watched down the slope, across the slope and up the road across the gorge. Pablo was looking at the gray horse on the slope with true regret on his face and Pilar and Maria were with Robert Jordan where he sat against the tree trunk.

"Slit the trouser, will thee?" he said to Pilar. Maria crouched by him and did not speak. The sun was on her hair and her face was twisted as a child's contorts before it cries. But she was not crying.

Pilar took her knife and slit his trouser leg down below the left-hand pocket. Robert Jordan spread the cloth with his hands and looked at the stretch of his thigh. Ten inches below the hip joint there was a pointed, purple swelling like a sharp-peaked little tent and as he touched it with his fingers he could feel the snapped-off thigh bone tight against the skin. His leg was lying at an odd angle. He looked up at Pilar. Her face had the same expression as Maria's.

"*Anda*," he said to her. "Go."

She went away with her head down without saying anything nor looking back and Robert Jordan could see her shoulders shaking.

"*Guapa*," he said to Maria and took hold of her two hands. "Listen. We will not be going to Madrid—"

Then she started to cry.

"No, *guapa*, don't," he said. "Listen. We will not go to Madrid now but I go always with thee wherever thou goest. Understand?"

She said nothing and pushed her head against his cheek with her arms around him.

"Listen to this well, rabbit," he said. He knew there was a great hurry and he was sweating very much, but this had to be said and understood. "Thou wilt go now, rabbit. But I go with thee. As long as there is one of us there is both of us. Do you understand?"

"Nay, I stay with thee."

"Nay, rabbit. What I do now I do alone. I could not do it well with thee. If thou goest then I go, too. Do you not see how it is? Whichever one there is, is both."

"I will stay with thee."

"Nay, rabbit. Listen. That people cannot do together. Each one must do it alone. But if thou goest then I go with thee. It is in that way that I go too. Thou wilt go now, I know. For thou art good and kind. Thou wilt go now for us both."

"But it is easier if I stay with thee," she said. "It is better for me."

"Yes. Therefore go for a favor. Do it for me since it is what thou canst do."

"But you don't understand, Roberto. What about me? It is worse for me to go."

"Surely," he said. "It is harder for thee. But I am thee also now."

She said nothing.

He looked at her and he was sweating heavily and he spoke now, trying harder to do something than he had ever tried in all his life.

"Now you will go for us both," he said. "You must not be selfish, rabbit. You must do your duty now."

She shook her head.

"You are me now," he said. "Surely thou must feel it, rabbit.

"Rabbit, listen," he said. "Truly thus I go too. I swear it to thee."

She said nothing.

"Now you see it," he said. "Now I see it is clear. Now thou wilt go. Good. Now you are going. Now you have said you will go."

She had said nothing.

"Now I thank thee for it. Now you are going well and fast and far and we both go in thee. Now put thy hand here. Now put thy head down. Nay, put it down. That is right. Now I put my hand there. Good. Thou art so good. Now do not think more. Now art thou doing what thou should. Now thou art obeying. Not me but us both. The me in thee. Now you go for us both. Truly. We both go in thee now. This I have promised thee. Thou art very good to go and very kind."

He jerked his head at Pablo, who was half-looking at him from the tree and Pablo started over. He motioned with his thumb to Pilar.

"We will go to Madrid another time, rabbit," he said. "Truly. Now stand up and go and we both go. Stand up. See?"

"No," she said and held him tight around the neck.

He spoke now still calmly and reasonably but with great authority.

"Stand up," he said. "Thou art me too now. Thou art all there will be of me. Stand up."

She stood up slowly, crying, and with her head down. Then she dropped quickly beside him and then stood up again, slowly and tiredly, as he said, "Stand up, guapa."

Pilar was holding her by the arm and she was standing there.

"Vamonos," Pilar said. "Dost lack anything, Inglés?" She looked at him and shook her head.

"No," he said and went on talking to Maria.

"There is no good-by, guapa, because we are not apart. That it should be good in the Gredos. Go now. Go good. Nay," he spoke now still calmly and reasonably as Pilar walked the girl along. "Do not turn around. Put thy foot in. Yes. Thy foot in. Help her up," he said to Pilar. "Get her in the saddle. Swing up now."

He turned his head, sweating, and looked down the slope, then back toward where the girl was in the saddle with Pilar by her and Pablo just behind. "Now go," he said. "Go."

She started to look around. "Don't look around," Robert Jordan said. "Go." And Pablo hit the horse across the crupper with a hobbling strap and it looked as though Maria tried to slip from the saddle but Pilar and Pablo were riding close up against her and Pilar was holding her and the three horses were going up the draw.

"Roberto," Maria turned and shouted. "Let me stay! Let me stay!"

"I am with thee," Robert Jordan shouted. "I am with thee now. We are both there. Go!" Then they were out of sight around the corner of the draw and he was soaking wet with sweat and looking at nothing.

Agustín was standing by him.

"Do you want me to shoot thee, *Inglés?*" he asked, leaning down close. "*Quieres?* It is nothing."

"*No hace falta,*" Robert Jordan said. "Get along. I am very well here."

"*Me cago en la leche que me han dado!*" Agustín said. He was crying so he could not see Robert Jordan clearly. "*Salud, Inglés.*"

"*Salud,* old one," Robert Jordan said. He was looking down the slope now. "Look well after the cropped head, wilt thou?"

"There is no problem," Agustín said. "Thou hast what thou needest?"

"There are very few shells for this *máquina,* so I will keep it," Robert Jordan said. "Thou canst not get more. For that other and the one of Pablo, yes."

"I cleaned out the barrel," Agustín said. "Where thou plugged it in the dirt with the fall."

"What became of the pack-horse?"

"The gypsy caught it."

Agustín was on the horse now but he did not want to go. He leaned far over toward the tree where Robert Jordan lay.

"Go on, *viejo,*" Robert Jordan said to him. "In war there are many things like this."

"*Qué puta es la guerra,*" Agustín said. "War is a bitchery."

"Yes man, yes. But get on with thee."

"*Salud, Inglés,*" Agustín said, clenching his right fist.

"*Salud,*" Robert Jordan said. "But get along, man."

Agustín wheeled his horse and brought his right fist down as though he cursed again with the motion of it and rode up the draw. All the others had been out of sight long before. He looked back where the draw turned in the timber and waved his fist. Robert Jordan waved and then Agustín, too, was out of sight. . . . Robert Jordan looked down the green slope of the hillside to the road and the bridge. I'm as well this way as any, he thought. It wouldn't be worth risking getting over on my belly yet, not as close as that thing was to the surface, and I can see better this way.

He felt empty and drained and exhausted from all of it and from them going and his mouth tasted of bile. Now, finally and at last, there was no problem. However all of it had been and however all of it would be now, for him, no longer was there any problem.

They were all gone now and he was alone with his back against a tree. He looked down across the green slope, seeing the gray horse where Agustín had shot him, and on down the slope to the road with the timber-covered country behind it. Then he looked at the bridge and across the bridge and watched the activity on the bridge and the road. He could see the trucks now, all down the lower road. The gray of the trucks showed through the trees. Then he looked back up the road to where it came down over the hill. They will be coming soon now, he thought.

Pilar will take care of her as well as any one can. You know that. Pablo must have a sound plan or he would not have tried it. You do not have to worry about Pablo. It does no good to think about Maria. Try to believe what you told her. That is the best. And who says it is not true? Not you. You don't say it, any more than you would say the things did not happen that happened. Stay with what you believe now. Don't get cynical. The time is too short and you have just sent her away. Each one does what he can. You can do nothing for yourself but perhaps you can do something for another. Well, we had all our luck in four days. Not four days. It was afternoon when I first got there and it will not be noon today. That makes not quite three days and three nights. Keep it accurate, he said. Quite accurate.

I think you better get down now, he thought. You better get fixed around some way where you will be useful instead of leaning against this tree like a tramp. You have had much luck. There are many worse things than this. Every one has to do this, one day or another. You are not afraid of it once you know you have to do it, are you? No, he said, truly. It was lucky the nerve was crushed, though. I cannot even feel that there is anything below the break. He touched the lower part of his leg and it was as though it were not part of his body.

He looked down the hill slope again and he thought. I hate to leave it, is all. I hate to leave it very much and I hope I have done some good in it. I have tried to with what talent I had. *Have*, you mean. All right, *have*.

I have fought for what I believed in for a year now. If we win here we will win everywhere. The world is a fine place and worth the fighting for and I hate very much to leave it. And you had a lot of luck, he told himself, to have had such a good life. You've had just as good a life as grandfather's though not as long. You've had as good a life as any one because of these last days. You do not want to complain when you have been so lucky. I wish there was some way to pass on what I've learned, though. Christ, I was learning fast there at the end. I'd like to talk to Karkov. That is in Madrid. Just over the hills there, and down across the plain. Down out of the gray rocks and the pines, the heather and the gorse, across the yellow high plateau you see it rising white and beautiful. That part is just as true as Pilar's old women drinking the blood down at the slaughterhouse. There's no one thing that's true. It's all true. The way the planes are beautiful whether they are ours or theirs. The hell they are, he thought.

You take it easy, now, he said. Get turned over now while you still have time. Listen, one thing. Do you remember? Pilar and the hand? Do you believe that crap? No, he said. Not with everything that's happened? No, I don't believe it. She was nice about it early this morning before the show started. She was afraid maybe I believed it. I don't, though. But she does. They see something. Or they feel something. Like a bird dog. What about extra-sensory perception? What about obscenity? he said. She wouldn't say good-by, he thought, because she knew if she did Maria would never go. That Pilar. Get yourself turned over, Jordan. But he was reluctant to try it.

Then he remembered that he had a small flask in his hip pocket and he thought, I'll take a good spot of the giant killer and then I'll try it. But the flask was not there when he felt for it. Then he felt that much more alone because he knew there was not going to be even that. I guess I'd counted on that, he said.

Do you suppose Pablo took it? Don't be silly. You must have lost it at the bridge. "Come on now, Jordan," he said. "Over you go."

Then he took hold of his left leg with both hands and pulled on it hard, pulling toward the foot while he lay down beside the tree he had been resting his back against. Then lying flat and pulling hard on the leg, so the broken end of the bone would not come up and cut through the thigh, he turned slowly around on his rump until the back of his head was facing downhill. Then with his broken leg, held by both hands, uphill, he put the sole of his right foot against the instep of his left foot and pressed hard while he rolled, sweating, over onto his face and chest. He got onto his elbows, stretched the left leg well behind him with both hands and a far, sweating, push with the right foot and there he was. He felt with his fingers on the left thigh and it was all right. The bone end had not punctured the skin and the broken end was well into the muscle now.

The big nerve must have been truly smashed when that damned horse rolled on it, he thought. It truly doesn't hurt at all. Except now in certain changes of positions. That's when the bone pinches something else. You see? he said. You see what luck is? You didn't need the giant killer at all.

He reached over for the submachine gun, took the clip out that was in the magazine, felt in his pocket for clips, opened the action and looked through the barrel, put the clip back into the groove of the magazine until it clicked, and then looked down the hill slope. Maybe half an hour, he thought. Now take it easy.

Then he looked at the hillside and he looked at the pines and he tried not to think at all.

He looked at the stream and he remembered how it had been under the bridge in the cool of the shadow. I wish they would come, he thought. I do not want to get in any sort of mixed-up state before they come.

Who do you suppose has it easier? Ones with religion or just taking it straight? It comforts them very much but we know there is no thing to fear. It is only missing it that's bad. Dying is only bad when it takes a long time and hurts so much that it humiliates you. That is where you have all the luck, see? You don't have any of that.

It's wonderful they've got away. I don't mind this at all now they are away. It *is* sort of the way I said. It is really very much that way. Look how different it would be if they were all scattered out across that hill where that gray horse is. Or if we were all cooped up here waiting for it. No. They're gone. They're away. Now if the attack were only a success. What do you want? Everything. I want everything and I will take whatever I get. If this attack is no good another one will be. I never noticed when the planes came back. *God, that was lucky I could make her go.*

I'd like to tell grandfather about this one. I'll bet he never had to go over and find his people and do a show like this. How do you know? He may have done fifty. No, he said. Be accurate. Nobody did any fifty like this one. Nobody did five. Nobody did one maybe not just like this. Sure. They must have.

I wish they would come now, he said. I wish they would come right now because the leg is starting to hurt now. It must be the swelling.

We were going awfully good when that thing hit us, he thought. But it was only luck it didn't come while I was under the bridge. When a thing is wrong something's bound to happen. You were bitched when they gave Golz those orders. That was what you knew and it was probably that which Pilar felt. But later on we will have these things much better organized. We ought to have portable short wave transmitters. *Yes, there's a lot of things we ought to have.* I ought to carry a spare leg, too.

He grinned at that sweatily because the leg, where the big nerve had been bruised by the fall, was hurting badly now. Oh, let them come, he said. I don't want to do that business that my father did. I will do it all right but I'd much prefer not to have to. I'm against that. Don't think about that. Don't think at all. I wish the bastards would come, he said. I wish so very much they'd come.

His leg was hurting very badly now. The pain had started suddenly with the swelling after he had moved and he said, Maybe I'll just do it now. I guess I'm not awfully good at pain. Listen, if I do that now you wouldn't misunderstand, would you? *Who are you talking to?* Nobody, he said. Grandfather, I guess. No. Nobody. Oh bloody it, I wish that they would come.

Listen, I may have to do that because if I pass out or anything like that I am no good at all and if they bring me to they will ask me a lot of questions and do things and all and that is no good. It's much best not to have them do those things. So why wouldn't it be all right to just do it now and then the whole thing would be over with? Because oh, listen, yes, listen, *let them come now.*

You're not so good at this, Jordan, he said. Not so good at this. And who is so good at this? I don't know and I don't really care right now. But you are not. That's right. You're not at all. Oh not at all, at all. I think it would be all right to do it now? Don't you?

No, it isn't. Because there is something you can do yet. As long as you know what it is you have to do it. As long as you remember what it is you have to wait for that. *Come on. Let them come. Let them come. Let them come!*

Think about them being away, he said. Think about them going through the timber. Think about them crossing a creek. Think about them riding through the heather. Think about them going up the slope. Think about them O. K. tonight. Think about them travelling, all night. Think about them hiding up tomorrow. Think about them. God damn it, think about them. *That's just as far as I can think about them,* he said.

Think about Montana. *I can't.* Think about Madrid. *I can't.* Think about a cool drink of water. *All right.* That's what it will be like. Like a cool drink of water. *You're a liar.* It will just be nothing. That's all it will be. Just nothing. Then do it. *Do it.* Do it now. It's all right to do it now. Go on and do it now. *No, you have to wait.* What for? You know all right. *Then wait.*

I can't wait any longer now, he said. If I wait any longer I'll pass out. I know because I've felt it starting to go three times now and I've held it. I held it all right. But I don't know about any more. What I think is you've got an internal hemorrhage there from where that thigh bone's

cut around inside. Especially on that turning business. That makes the
swelling and that's what weakens you and makes you start to pass. It
would be all right to do it now. Really, I'm telling you that it would be
all right.

*And if you wait and hold them up even a little while or just get the
officer that may make all the difference. One thing well done can
make—*

All right, he said. And he lay very quietly and tried to hold on to himself that he felt slipping away from himself as you feel snow starting to
slip sometimes on a mountain slope, and he said, now quietly, then let
me last until they come.

Robert Jordan's luck held very good because he saw, just then, the
cavalry ride out of the timber and cross the road. He watched them coming riding up the slope. He saw the trooper who stopped by the gray
horse and shouted to the officer who rode over to him. He watched
them both looking down at the gray horse. They recognized him of
course. He and his rider had been missing since the early morning of
the day before.

Robert Jordan saw them there on the slope, close to him now, and
below he saw the road and the bridge and the long lines of vehicles below it. He was completely integrated now and he took a good long look
at everything. Then he looked up at the sky. There were big white
clouds in it. He touched the palm of his hand against the pine needles
where he lay and he touched the bark of the pine trunk that he lay
behind.

Then he rested as easily as he could with his two elbows in the pine
needles and the muzzle of the submachine gun resting against the trunk
of the pine tree.

As the officer came trotting now on the trail of the horses of the band
he would pass twenty yards below where Robert Jordan lay. At that
distance there would be no problem. The officer was Lieutenant Berrendo. He had come up from La Granja when they had been ordered
up after the first report of the attack on the lower post. They had ridden
hard and had then had to swing back, because the bridge had been
blown, to cross the gorge high above and come around through the
timber. Their horses were wet and blown and they had to be urged
into the trot.

Lieutenant Berrendo, watching the trail, came riding up, his thin face
serious and grave. His submachine gun lay across his saddle in the crook
of his left arm. Robert Jordan lay behind the tree, holding onto himself very carefully and delicately to keep his hands steady. He was waiting until the officer reached the sunlit place where the first trees of the
pine forest joined the green slope of the meadow. He could feel his
heart beating against the pine needle floor of the forest.

The Birth of a Child

From *LAMB IN HIS BOSOM*

By Caroline Miller

The Carvers are settlers in the back country of Georgia, five days by horse from the Coast. In this remote world where the first rumblings of the Civil War are not heard, Vince and Seen have raised their family, Cean the only daughter and Lias, Jasper and Jake the sons. Cean marries Lonzo and they move to their own farm, and Lias brings home from the Coast his bride, Margot, a half-Irish beauty whose city manners and dainty clothes set her apart. But beyond this surface strangeness, her early life makes her suspect in the family's eyes, for as a tavern keeper's daughter and helper she was thrown with men in an easy, offhand fashion which the Carvers do not condone.

The following scene, in which Cean awaits the birth of her first child, contains the elemental quality of the entire novel in which the human events of birth, marriage and death are allied with the cycles of nature and the earth itself.

WHEN the December moon was nigh onto fullin', Cean's mother came to be with her. And Lonzo's father brought Dicie, his wife, to help tend to Cean when she got down. The little un was due on the full of the moon; if it put off its coming on that day, it would wait on for another change; and what's more it would be a girl if it came on the shrinking moon. The child's grandmothers came in time for the full moon, hoping for a boy. Lonzo would need boys to help break ground and pull fodder; girls were good for but little, except to weave and pick cotton.

They waited about the fire, Lonzo and Cean and the two old women, while the moon moved across from east to west in its journey through each day's hours; at night it bulged out of the flat sky, heavy and yellow and full of knowledge. The moon was a powerful thing; she pulled the tides on invisible leashes; she governed the seasons somehow, lengthening or shortening them at her will; she let the rain fall, or she withheld it, just as she pleased; her light made the ground strong or weak, all according to some curious formula which men had learned long before Lonzo's or Cean's time (or Dicie's or Seen's, either). Peas will never grow if they are planted in the time of dark nights; potatoes must go into the ground only on a waning moon, so that the roots may grow downward—and so with all rooty things; bushy things must grow upward as the moon grows. . . . The moon has all power; it even governs women's ways, and who can explain that? It can muddle the wits of a child allowed to sleep in its full light. Now the sun will cut no didos, but the moon is a willful, changeable body, kind or hateful as she pleases, undependable as her face.

Cean spread her extry quilts as a pallet in front of the fire for Dicie and Seen to sleep on where the warmth could bake their gnarled old feet. They would mumble sometimes far into the night, discussing this or that childbed, or spell of fever, or cut that brought on proud flesh. Each had brought her sack of yerbs, saved each in its season, and tied separately in clean white rags; each had brought her best knowledge to serve the need of her child and the loved one of her child. Dicie lived ten miles off, two miles on yan side o' the river. She knew many people of whom these people had not heard in months, so she brought them news of a big hog, or the killing of a neighbor, a summer hailstorm that cut the corn to ribands, or a child that was born to Timothy Hall's wife, red-mottled, with one eye set high in its forehead. But it died, by God's mercy. Dicie had a bright, sharp wit about her; she talked fast and told many outrageous things, so that Cean laughed a lot at her. Lonzo never laughed much—nor cried, neither; it wasn't his way to show what he was thinking. Seen didn't have much to say, either; she was dreading this thing. Cean didn't know what she was getting into.

Lonzo dreaded it, too, but there wasn't nothin' to do about it. He had helped many an old sow bring forth her young. And once he had knocked a young heifer in the head because he had figured that she had hurt long enough; and she would have surely died, anyway.

Dicie chattered, wrinkling her thin nose when she cackled over a joke; when she laughed, she threw back her head that was pert and brown and a little like a peaceable hen's. Dicie thought little about this business. Cean was a strong girl; no foolishness about her; she'd get through in a hurry.

On the night of the third day after the old women had come Dicie would make syrup candy and there was much talking and laughing about the fireplace. Syrup blubbered in the iron pot over the coals, and had to be stirred with the long horn spoon to keep it from boiling over. Dicie's and Seen's and Lonzo's faces were well-nigh blistered from the heat. Finally Dicie tried the candy in a gourd of water one last time, and pronounced it nigh about ready to pull.

Lonzo sat in a chair with his hands ready-larded. Cean stood behind him, not allowed to pull. She leaned over the back of Lonzo's chair; his hair brushed against her breast; her hands lay on his shoulders; she moved her hands upward and laid them on his neck where she could feel the blood beat in his veins. Her fingers stroked downward on his beard and rested again on his neck. She could smile now to think that ever she had been afraid of him; for no cow with its first calf was ever any gentler with it than Lonzo was with her. . . .

Suddenly she pressed her hands hard about his neck; a heavy pain had fastened on her child and would not let go.

Lonzo turned and looked into her face. But just then the pain let go, and she smiled sheepishly at him. She was all right; it wasn't time, after all. But the blood beat heavier and faster in Lonzo's neck. He spoke to his mother, who was taking off the pot of boiling candy:

"Ma, ye'd better git things ready . . ."

Dicie whirled about, and the pot of candy turned over on the hearth. Cean heard her mother shout in terror, and saw the syrup bubbling on Seen's bony old feet as she moved them frantically up and down in the spreading pool of liquid that was hot as molten brimstone.

Cean sat in a chair, holding her breath on another pain, while Lonzo raked the blistering, brown mess from Seen's feet. Dicie poulticed them with soft mullein poultices, crooning in a monotonous undertone: "You pore child! . . . You pore child! . . . I'd ruther hit was me. I'd a sight ruther hit was me. . . ."

After the first shock of the fiery pain Seen never whimpered. She bared her teeth against her lips and sat patiently with her swathed feet away from the fire, while waves of fire soaked and washed and soaked them. She said to Cean:

"Take yore mind off yourself, honey. . . . Jest think about somethin' else. . . ."

Till long after midnight Cean walked back and forth across the room, as Dicie told her to do; she walked until she could take not one more-step, for Dicie would not let her rest; she must stay on her feet even when the last pains caused her body to tremble as though it were beset by the ague, when these pains that should have been the last pains dragged her down if Lonzo's arms did not hold her up. Back and forth, and forth and back, Dicie made her walk, and her face was green, and sweat and tears were mingled on her cheeks. And with any one of these pains she would have fallen and swounded away if Lonzo's hands had not held her up, if Lonzo had not wiped the wet from her face and talked into her ear, saying "little un," and such-like words. She would not complain, because her mother would not complain of her tormented feet; she would not complain even when she had to take to her bed in the hour before morning and lay tossing between Lonzo's hands on one side of the bed and Dicie's on the other. Seen, with her feet in a fiery hell, watched her child endure another hell, and thought that she would gladly have endured both.

By daylight, Lonzo was sick of it. He went out into the whipping wind to feed up, to milk Betsey and turn her out. But he hurried back into the house. He asked his Ma:

"What makes her git along s' slow?"

Dicie's face was sober now:

"Hit's natural . . . with a fust un. . . ."

Lonzo quarreled:

"This hain't natural. . . . They's somethin' wrong. Ye might ez well tell me. . . ."

"No. They hain't nothin' wrong. They 'most al'ays take longer with a fust un. . . ."

Lonzo turned his face away and growled:

"Well, they won't be no second un. . . ."

A pitiable smile caught at the corners of Dicie's mouth. How many times had she heard that! And always they called her back before another twelve months were out. . . . Her eyes sought Seen's eyes in gentle derision of a man's fool blustering. . . . But Seen's eyes were set on her child's face and would not let loose of it where it lay tossing back and forth; Cean's hair was matted, her eyes were shut and unnoticing; her hands were locked to the bedstead back of her head. It wasn't good for her to reach her hands back of her head like that, but Lonzo could not break her grip without hurting her.

Lonzo turned away and would help no more when Cean began breathing each of her breaths with a low, animal-like grunt. She sounded too much like the little heifer that he had knocked in the head because it had hurt long enough, and would surely die anyway.

He stood before the fire, gazing down into the heat, and great unlikely tears ran from his eyes down into his beard. Lonzo knew that his little un was going to die. He knew from the look in Seen's eyes that never let go of her child's face; he knew from Dicie's hard-folded hands that waited now, having done all that they knew to do; and he knew from the little un that grunted like a little dumb heifer that knows that it is time for it to die. Even as he listened, a-feared, her moaning quieted, her pains ceased, and she lay as though she were already dead.

The dogs made a clamor out in front, and a woman's voice commanded them to keep still. Nobody in the room stirred, for they hardly noted the sound. What did it matter who came or went, now that the little un was dying with nobody to help her?

After a minute there was a framming of a fist on the front door and Dicie opened it. Lias's Margot blew in, beating her hands and stamping her feet that were numb with the cold. She looked quickly around the room and went and stood for a moment beside the bed. She turned to Seen:

"I knew it. . . . I couldn't sleep. Something told me to come. . . . I made Jasper bring me. Lias thought I was the master fool. Jasper's out there in the cold now."

She threw her wraps off, and discussed with Dicie a hasty means of bringing this child to its birth before it killed its mother.

After that, Lonzo heaped up the fire and boiled great pots of water; he lifted Cean when she was a dead weight in his arms; he thought that she was already dead, because her eyelids did not even quiver when he called her little un . . . for she would have given some sign if she had heard. . . .

There was a baby's angry, repeated crying; the sound of it eased the agony in Seen's eyes. Lonzo laid Cean down; still her eyelids didn't flicker when he called her. He held the cord whence bright life had flowed from this woman's body into his child, until that flow stopped; then he cut the cord forever since its use was past. He tied the shred of the child's body back into itself, making it an entity, as one finishes something perfect. Cean had made this thing—a thing harder and prettier to do than weaving cloth or sewing a dress. She was not able to do this little last thing for it, so he did it for her. Then he sat down beside her, waiting for her face to regain its color and its meaning for him.

When she opened her eyes after a while, he could not answer a word to her fearful question. Nor did he know that she was afraid to look on the little thing that she had made so carefully. It was Lias's Margot who laughed away Cean's fears, saying:

"Just as fine as a fiddle. They don't make them any finer. . . ."

Lonzo learned from Margot that Cean's child was a girl, and all the women laughed at his stupidity—all, except Cean. Truth to tell, he had not known—nor cared.

Dicie brought the little thing to the bed for it to lie beside its mother. Margot asked:

"Now what is her name?"

Cean's eyes lifted from the baby to Lonzo.

"Whatever Lonzo says. . . ."

Her eyes went back to the little stranger in her arms, whom she had not expected and for whom she had no name. Her mind went all around and about this new thing in her arms as she lay there, while the other women hovered over the fireplace, a long way off, preparing a belated breakfast. Lonzo sat beside her, a part of her awakening from the dream that had encompassed all her life until now. . . . So it was a Her, like herself, to be a little girl—a big girl—a Woman, at last. . . . Cean's senses were drugged with her past pain; she was unable to believe so much wonder; never would she have believed that the boy-child that had filled her heart until now would go so quickly into thin air, and leave her arms feeling no emptiness or disappointment, but filled with this wondrous woman-child.

Lonzo's voice came from a long way off above her:

"You liked them magnolia flowers. . . ."

Cean's thoughts took up the words—magnolias—high and white—and sweet-smelling—too pretty to be broken and wither in her dark house. . . . But here was a little bloom of some kind, broken for her, given to her to keep, to wear upon her breast as Coast women wear gold breastpins.

She called to the strange white woman by the fire:

"Her name's Magnolia. . . ."

Margot turned and came to the bed, smiling; her long white hands smoothed the cover and the pillow and the child and its mother.

Lonzo said:

"Cean, this is Lias's Margot."

The two women greeted each other with their eyes. Cean said:

"Her name's Mary Magnolia. . . ."

They had forgotten Jasper out in the cold; now they called him in.

All their thoughts and all their desires were toward the little Mary Magnolia.

When Vince Carver had seen her, he went home and set down her name in the big Bible, with the day of her birth. Remembering the little puckered face of his first grandchild, he thought his first kind thought of Margot; for it was because of that woman's knowledge of Coast ways that the child now slept in Cean's arms instead of out there beside Eliza-beth. . . . And Cean, too. . . .

Not till days afterward, when her feet were white and withered under the oft-renewed poultices that Margot made, did Seen remember that it was Christmas morning when the baby was born—a day when back in Carolina they were riding from house to house over the countryside, eating syllabub and eggnog at neighbors' houses, and shrieking "Christmas gift" to every passer-by. She said to Margot:

"I reckon you don't like the sticks, where they don't even know when it's Christmas."

Margot drooped over the feet of her husband's mother, that were soft and white like boiled bacon. She said:

"I never cared for Coast ways. I wish folks would forget that ever I was there."

Boston Post Road

From SO LITTLE TIME

By John Marquand

The words "so little time" run through this novel like an insistent and terrifying refrain. Jeffrey Wilson, the book's central character, is hounded by them as he sees the European war threaten his traditional, civilized American world. In the face of danger, Jeffrey takes stock of his life and finds it wanting. Where he had once dreamed of being an important dramatist, he has become merely a successful "play-doctor." His attractive, literal wife Madge only half understands him, and his children seem already lost to him in their own generation's concerns. On every side he sees familiar, accepted institutions disintegrating and feels the despair of a man forsaken by his household gods. In the selected passage we see his nostalgia against a background which he comes to accept as symbolic of the change.

IT WAS very hard for Jeffrey to remember what he had been thinking that previous spring, now that it was October. So many of the days of that spring and summer were like the parts of one of those dreams, which you know are dreams even when you are asleep and the worst parts of which, your sleeping logic tells you, are not true. He was still not able to understand how the city, in October of 1940, could look as it always had, beautiful and indifferent, or how there could be new model cars, or how there could still be antiques and silver and flowers and saddles and bridles and tweeds for sale on Madison Avenue. Everyone was back in town again and there was the same feeling of anticipation in the air. You could not tell from externals that isolationists and interventionists were quarreling. There was no way of knowing whether aid to Britain would keep us out or get us into war that October morning. The voice of Wendell Willkie and the Willkie Campaign Kits made no impression on the weather. It was easy to forget that "A VOTE FOR WILLKIE IS A VOTE FOR HITLER," and, "IT'S MOVING DAY ELEANOR, THE WILLKIES ARE COMING." It was easy to forget the speeches and the fireside chats. It was another October morning, and he and Madge were going to Fred and Beckie's for that week end in the country.

The bags were in the elevator. The garage had delivered the coupé at the door and Madge had given Albert and Effie the telephone number where they were staying in case anything should happen, and now Madge was wondering whether there might still be anything important that she had forgotten and Jeffrey was telling her not to worry, that it was easy enough to telephone. It was possible to think of German bombers sweeping over London and at the same time it was possible to think about the suitcases. Madge had said that they could put all their clothes together in one suitcase. For years she had been suggesting this, because it was easier to have one piece of luggage than two. She could never understand that it was undignified and that her boxes of powder might get open and spill on Jeffrey's evening clothes and that Jeffrey could never possibly find anything in a woman's suitcase.

"Jeffrey," she asked, "did you pack your sport clothes? Have you got the keys to the car? Have you set your watch, Jeffrey?"

"Yes," Jeffrey answered, "everything's all right."

"Jeffrey, I'll drive," she said.

"No, that's all right," he answered, "I'll drive."

"Then keep your mind on it," Madge said, "and don't start thinking about the war."

Madge was looking in her bag to be sure that she had her lipstick and her compact, and then she asked if he had any money with him, and he told her that of course he had money, and she said that he never carried enough with him in case the car broke down or something, and the last time they were at Fred's and Beckie's he might remember that he had to borrow something from Fred so that he could leave something for the servants. Jeffrey said that he had enough money and he looked at his watch. It seemed to him that they were starting early. It was true that they were to stop on the way at Madge's Uncle Judson's for lunch, but there would be nothing to do if they got there early.

"And remember this, Madge," he said, "let's get away from there as soon as we can. It—you know the way it is."

Madge smiled her brightest smile.

"It won't be any problem," she said. "Uncle Judson always has his nap right after lunch, and we'll just say we can't wait until he wakes up. And Jeffrey dear, remember . . ."

"Remember what?" Jeffrey asked.

"Remember not to say you have any doubts about Wendell Willkie, and don't say you think it's funny that Mr. Ickes called him a 'barefoot boy from Wall Street' the way you did last night. Uncle Judson might think you weren't going to vote for him."

"Maybe I'm not," Jeffrey said, and he started the car. "Maybe that's just what he is—a 'barefoot boy from Wall Street.' "

And then she made an unexpected suggestion.

"Let's go out on the Post Road, the way we used to," she said. "We haven't been there for years."

"The Post Road?" Jeffrey repeated after her.

The Post Road had become an ugly highway of oil-spattered concrete, choked with trucks and bordered by hamburger heavens and filling stations. You could avoid it now and save twenty-five minutes by cutting across town to the West Side Highway and then taking the new Parkway and cutting back to the Sound, but all at once he felt the way Madge must have. He wanted to see the Post Road again.

It was hard to find the landmarks on it, and even the towns had changed, except for their names. The road seemed to have sucked a part of the city out with it, making the highway a little like a river full of driftwood. Mt. Vernon and New Rochelle were full of apartment houses and so were Pelham Manor, Larchmont and Mamaroneck. There had been fine country residences once along the Post Road, and now they had been turned into convalescent homes, or tourist homes, or roadhouses. They stood sadly behind gasoline pumps and roadside booths with their grounds and shrubbery uncouth.

The farther Madge and Jeffrey got from the city along the road the more familiar the sights became. Jeffrey had the sensation of having been dead for a hundred years, and of now being back and trying to orient himself in the land of the living, and of looking vainly for stone walls, close-cropped lawns and tree-shaded driveways. Of course everyone had left the Post Road years before, because of the roar of traffic which continued day and night along it, and because the houses were too old, or too ugly, and the city was crowding outwards.

The town where he had first met Madge was a place now where commuters lived. The lawns and meadows which had once surrounded it were cut by little roads that led into real estate developments made up of small houses, each with a garage attached. These stood now among the red of small maple trees and among the gold-yellow of poplars. The Willis place was gone and so was the Henderson place. As they started down the hill to what used to be the village, he could see the fieldstone Episcopal Church, but he could not recognize a single house near it.

The Roberts place was as completely gone as though it had never been there. There was no sign of the driveway or of the gray granite house or of the garage-stable or of the greenhouses. He was sure that this was just where it had stood beside the Post Road, but now he could not recognize a single tree.

"Jeff," Madge said, "go a little slowly. Here—do you remember this?"

An oil truck roared by them clanging a chain behind it on the concrete. To the right was a white house with two fir trees in front of it, and beneath the trees were wire cages filled with cocker spaniel pups for sale.

"Jeff," Madge said, "don't you remember? This was where you kissed me."

"What?" Jeffrey asked. "Where?"

"Right here," Madge said. "Jeff, can't you remember? It was the first time you ever kissed me—when we came back from the Golf Club dance. I had to drive you. It was the family's old Cadillac. You didn't know how to drive anything except a plane."

Then he remembered the white house and the fir trees. There had not been a sound, for it had been very late. There had not been another car on the Post Road that night, and all the houses had been sound asleep, but no one would ever select it again as a propitious spot in which to kiss a girl. It made him feel sad, exactly like a ghost.

"We're early," Madge said. "Let's drive through the village to the railroad station. Do you remember the first time I met you there when you came down to stay with us? I've thought about it all day. I didn't think you were glad to see me."

She was wrong there. He had not wanted her to know how glad he was to see her.

There was no past tense about that town, only a pushing present and a doubtful future. It was just a suburb now where commuters spent the night, where houses were leased and sublet as casually as apartments in New York. There was no permanence and no very tangible evidence that it was a town at all. One's children would not live there. The store names had changed on Purchase Street and all the façades were new, glittering with plate glass and neon lights and plastics, but the railroad station had not been touched. It was painted the same sickly buff yellow; and as they looked, an express train hurtled by it on its way to Boston.

"Well, we'd better turn around now," Madge said. "Jeffrey, it's queer, isn't it? It was so lovely once."

It was not exactly queer because it was a concrete fact to which one might as well adjust oneself. You thought things would remain the

same, and somehow nothing did. It was a picture of one generation
giving way to another, and the new one never wanted any longer what
the old one had to offer.

"You can't tell," Jeffrey said. "Maybe the people here think it's
lovely now."

He wished they had not come up the Post Road, and Madge must
have been thinking the same thing. As they drove toward the Sound
there were fewer small houses, but no one was living in the large ones
any longer. They stood ugly and unwanted on their uncut lawns, their
windows unwashed and blank. The weeds were growing on their drives,
but there were signs of hopeful real estate agents staked in front of
them. There was an amusement park on the old beach by the Sound
and no one wanted to live near an amusement park, and the water of
the Sound, which he always thought of as clear and bluish green, was
too polluted for bathing any longer. He wondered if it all struck Madge
in the same way. As a stranger, he had once thought the places along
the Sound were impregnable. It must have been more of a shock to
him than it was to her to see them now.

"No," Madge said, suddenly, "don't take Willow Road. Take Rock
Point Road, it's only a little longer."

He knew she did not want to see the house where she had lived on
Willow Road, and she did not want to see what had happened to the
privet hedge or to the wall garden or to the cutting garden, and he did
not want to either.

A few miles back in the country from the Massachusetts town where
Jeffrey had been born there had been plenty of deserted farms with
their barn roofs falling and with the saplings growing up in the hay-
fields, but these had been peaceful in their utter loneliness because there
had been no life around them. It was different here because there was
too much life. It all made him think of the place which he and Madge
owned in Connecticut, and of all the trees he had planted, and it filled
him with a sense of futility. There was no use thinking any longer that
someone who belonged to you might live in your house after you were
through with it. The rows of trees which he and Madge had planted on
the hill in the country would not look like much for another forty years
because elm trees seldom did, but Madge had said that they would
be nice for the children and their children. She must have known, if
she had faced it, that even if the children wanted it, they would never
be able to afford it, but still you went on hoping in that archaic way.
Madge's father and mother must have had some sort of belief that the
house on Willow Road would surely be owned by Madge, just as surely
as the coupons would be good on a gilt-edged bond. He wondered what
her uncle thought about it, for he was the only one who had not sold

and moved away, but then, perhaps the old gentleman was too old to
think at all. Jeffrey heard Madge sigh.

"Jeff," he heard her ask, "do you remember when I took you to see
him?"

He knew that she meant the time when she took him there to tell
her Uncle Judson and her Aunt Clara, who was living then, that they
were engaged.

Somehow it was discordant after all the rest of it that her uncle's
house and grounds should still be exactly as he first remembered them.
The lawn had been freshly mowed, although it was October. The crimson woodbine around the gateposts had been pruned back, and the turf
along the edges of the drive was freshly trimmed. There was the same
dark bank of rhododendrons, with the oak trees just behind them. The
leaves of the copper beech in the center of the lawn had not turned yet.
Two gardeners were cutting back the shrubbery and a third was mulch-
ing the rosebed. The sun was striking the roof of the greenhouse that
held the hothouse grapes. The stable door was open and the blue gravel
of the whole drive was raked smooth. The flower boxes on the edge of
the porte-cochère contained their familiar red geraniums and nastur-
tiums. The sun struck on the veranda with its green rocking chairs and
there was a smell of smoke in the air from burning autumn leaves.

"Do not leave anything to be done in the spring," Madge's uncle
had always said, "that can possibly be done in the autumn."

The house itself glistened with a fresh coat of gray paint and there
was not a slate missing on the mansard roof. As the coupé stopped beneath the shadow of the porte-cochère, the screen door at the top of
the granite steps was opened by old Lizzie who had been Madge's aunt's
maid. Lizzie's face was firmly set and her apron was freshly starched and
her hair, though it was sparser and whiter, was done up in the same tight
knot that Jeffrey remembered.

"Lizzie, dear," Madge said, "we're not late, are we?"

"No, Miss Madge," Lizzie answered, "he's just coming down the
stairs." And when she looked at Jeffrey he felt as he had that time when
he had first come to call. Lizzie must still be thinking of all the young
gentlemen whom Miss Madge might have married.

"Hello, Lizzie," he said.

"Good afternoon," she answered, "Mr. Wilson."

The hall seemed dark after the bright October sunlight, but he could
distinguish the long Kermanshah carpet, the seat that opened for rub-
bers with the mirror above it and racks for canes and umbrellas on
either side, the wide gaping arch of the fireplace with the head of a
moose over it and the oil painting of a grass-grown Roman ruin. He
could see the cool, waxed yellow-oak staircase curving upward two ways

from the landing—the design sometimes used on ocean liners. There was a tart, clean smell of chrysanthemums from the vases just below the landing window, and sure enough, just as Lizzie had said, Madge's Uncle Judson, clean and brushed for lunch, was walking down the stairs.

He walked deliberately but not feebly, resting his hand lightly on the golden-oak bannister. His face was long and thin and paler than it had been. His starched collar and his dark suit looked too large for him.

"Well, well," he said to Madge, when he kissed her, "if you want to tidy up, everything is ready in your Aunt Clara's room."

"No, no, Uncle Judson," Madge said, "I don't want to keep you waiting."

He moved his head sharply sideways when she spoke, toward the tall clock which was ticking beside the umbrella stand.

"You have time," he said, "you're early. There is everything in your Aunt Clara's room."

Then he moved another step down the hall, and Jeffrey moved toward him.

"How do you do, Jeffrey?" he said.

"How do you do, sir?" Jeffrey answered.

Uncle Judson cleared his throat.

"Do you want to wash your hands?"

"No thanks, sir," Jeffrey said.

From the way Uncle Judson looked at him, Jeffrey could not tell whether he was suspected of exhibiting exceptional strength or weakness. Time had nothing to do with it. Jeffrey felt the way he always had with Madge's uncle, that he was being dealt with according to the best rules of hospitality, but that it had all been a whim of Madge's—an accident.

"There's sherry in the library," Uncle Judson said.

The French doors of the library opened to a piazza, and from outside there was the same smell of chrysanthemums.

"Thank you, sir," Jeffrey said when the old man handed him a glass.

"Well," Uncle Judson said, and sipped his sherry, "well—"

It seemed to Jeffrey that there was nothing much more to say. Through an open window he could hear the metallic ring of a rake on the driveway.

"The place is looking very well, sir," Jeffrey said.

"They're busy now," Uncle Judson answered. "Never leave anything to be done in the spring that can possibly be done in the autumn."

"It's always one long fight," Jeffrey said, "to keep a garden going."

"You think so?" Uncle Judson asked. "Not if one is systematic. It's a matter of routine."

"I don't suppose I'm systematic," Jeffrey said.

"No," Uncle Judson answered, "I suppose you're not. Let me see, I haven't seen you for some time."

"No," Jeffrey answered, "not for quite a while."

"I hope," Uncle Judson said, "that everything has been going well with you. Have Madge and the children been well?"

"Yes, they've been all right, thanks," Jeffrey said.

"Jim is quite a boy," Uncle Judson said, "but it always strikes me queer—he looks like you."

"Well," Jeffrey said, "of course he can't help that."

"Let me see," Uncle Judson said, "you were an aviator in the last war, weren't you?"

"Yes, sir," Jeffrey answered.

"They seem to be driving the British back," Uncle Judson said, "in the air, I mean."

"That's true, the forward fields are too hot for the fighters now," Jeffrey answered.

"I see that they've bombed St. Paul's," Uncle Judson said.

"Yes," Jeffrey answered, "London's getting it."

"I'm glad that I won't have to see it later." The old man waved to the decanter. "Another glass of sherry?"

"No, thank you, sir," Jeffrey said.

The old man clasped his hands behind his back.

"I wonder what's keeping Madgie," he said. "Well, we must always wait as patiently as we can for the ladies. This morning—do you know what I've been thinking?"

"No, sir," Jeffrey answered.

"I've been thinking that I'm very pleased to be my age with the way the world's been going."

As far as Jeffrey could recall in all their meetings, that was the only remark that old Judson Mapes had ever made to him that was intentionally informal.

"I think you're right, sir," Jeffrey said, "but my age is the worst. Right now I'd rather be old or young."

Uncle Judson clasped his hands behind his back. His pale blue eyes met Jeffrey's squarely.

"Everything is changing—for the worse," he said, "for the worse. The lavatory's right here—are you sure you don't want to wash your hands?"

"Thanks, quite sure," Jeffrey said.

"Well," Uncle Judson said, "here comes Madge. Madge is like her mother. She always kept us waiting, but her Aunt Clara was punctual. Madge, will you lead the way?"

Jeffrey had always heard that one became set in one's opinions as time went on, but he could never see this working in himself. It seemed to him that his attitude toward people whom he had known for long was always undergoing alterations, so that personal relationships were nearly as impermanent as real estate values and liking kept changing to indifference and dislike merged into tolerance simply because of living. Nevertheless, he had always been sure that his attitude toward Madge's uncle would never undergo much change. He would always call him "Mr. Mapes" rather than "Uncle Judson," but now as they entered the dining room, he knew that they shared the experience of observing the passing of time.

Lizzie, assisted by another maid about her age, was waiting on the table. The ceiling of the room was high. The walls were done in a greenish artificial leather. The curtains which framed the tall windows were heavy blackish-green velvet bordered by tarnished gold tapes. The table was round, made of black fumed oak like the sideboard, and its legs had the same heavy ornate carving. The chairs were black oak too, upholstered in dark green leather that was held in place by elaborate brass-capped tacks. Lizzie was removing the place plates, which were gold-embossed and dark purple, each with a different flower in its center. The silver was a variation of the Crown pattern, a heavy elaborate contortion of motifs such as you saw sold by weight in those strange New York shops that collected bric-a-brac from liquidating estates. Lizzie was bringing in the clear pale consommé, and Mr. Mapes was picking up his spoon. There was nothing in that room that anyone in his right senses would want any more.

"You never come to see us, Uncle Judson," he heard Madge saying.

"I do not like New York now," he said, "and I am very busy here."

There was no way at all of telling what went on behind that pale façade. Jeffrey had never thought of him except as a pompous old stuffed shirt and a snob, but now he felt a faint glow of admiration for him. He was like a ship sinking with its guns still firing.

"You ought to see more people, Uncle Judson," Jeffrey heard Madge saying, and he wondered how her Uncle Judson liked it when she tried to run his life.

"There is no one I wish to see," Uncle Judson said. "No one lives here any longer."

"But you must be lonely, Uncle Judson."

"Lonely?" he answered. "No, not lonely."

He was running his own show, and perhaps that was all that anyone could do. Jeffrey was wondering what he would be like himself if he reached that age, and he hoped he would not reach it. The hothouse grapes with their silver scissors had scarcely been passed before the old man was pushing back his chair.

"It is time for my nap," he said, "if you'll excuse me. Shall I find you here when I come down?"

Jeffrey thought that Madge was going to say they would wait, and if she had, he was not sure that he could have stood it.

"I wish we could wait," Madge said, "but we can't. We're driving to Connecticut."

"Then good-by," Uncle Judson said. "It was kind of you to come. Gregory has put some chrysanthemums in your car." His pale eyes met Jeffrey's for a moment. "It was kind of you to come. There are cigars on my desk in the library, and the door to the right—in case you want to wash your hands."

The car now had that same clean acrid smell of chrysanthemums.

"Darling," Madge said, "thanks for going. I know it was an awful beating for you."

"Oh," Jeffrey said, "it wasn't bad."

"Well, it wasn't fun," Madge said.

"It wasn't fun," Jeffrey answered, "but he puts on quite a show."

"Jeffrey," Madge said, "drive a little faster, please let's hurry."

He knew what she wanted, because he wanted the same thing. Now that it was over, she wanted to get away. She wanted to get away from the Sound and the Post Road and memory, and she thought that she could do it by driving faster.

"Jeffrey," she said, "it's such a clear day, isn't it?" And then he saw that she was crying, but there was nothing that anyone could do about it.

"I'll be all right in a minute," she said, "I'm sorry."

"That's all right," Jeffrey answered, "go ahead and cry."

"I'm all right now," she said, "and Jeff, all week end we'll have fun."

He was not so sure of that. They would be moving up the Merritt Parkway to adjust themselves to something else, and at any rate he had never liked the word. He supposed it was an Anglo-Saxon monosyllable —"fun."

Hurricane

From THEIR EYES WERE WATCHING GOD

By Zora Neale Hurston

Janie, twice married before she meets Tea Cake, encounters love for the first time in this gay, "summer time" man twelve years younger than herself. With him she escapes the dreariness of the Georgia Negro town in which they live and finds real happiness in a happy Florida community on the edge of the great winter resorts. But the true quality of their love, dominating the circumstances of terror, appears when the hurricane breaks their home and drives them into a strange wilderness. The passage was chosen for its intimate picture of Negroes away from any white background, written by an author of their own race who feels and understands the poetic beauty of their thought which often raises them above the sordid drudgery of their lives.

SINCE Tea Cake and Janie had friended with the Bahaman workers in the 'Glades, they, the "Saws," had been gradually drawn into the American crowd. They quit hiding out to hold their dances when they found that their American friends didn't laugh at them as they feared. Many of the Americans learned to jump and liked it as much as the "Saws." So they began to hold dances night after night in the quarters, usually behind Tea Cake's house. Often now, Tea Cake and Janie stayed up so late at the fire dances that Tea Cake would not let her go with him to the field. He wanted her to get her rest.

So she was home by herself one afternoon when she saw a band of Seminoles passing by. The men walking in front and the laden, stolid women following them like burros. She had seen Indians several times in the 'Glades, in twos and threes, but this was a large party. They were headed towards the Palm Beach road and kept moving steadily. About an hour later another party appeared and went the same way. Then another just before sundown. This time she asked where they were all going and at last one of the men answered her.

"Going to high ground. Saw-grass bloom. Hurricane coming."

Everybody was talking about it that night. But nobody was worried. The fire dance kept up till nearly dawn. The next day, more Indians moved east, unhurried but steady. Still a blue sky and fair weather. Beans running fine and prices good, so the Indians could be, must be, wrong. You couldn't have a hurricane when you're making seven and eight dollars a day picking beans. Indians are dumb anyhow, always were. Another night of Stew Beef making dynamic subtleties with his drum and living, sculptural, grotesques in the dance. Next day, no Indians passed at all. It was hot and sultry and Janie left the field and went home.

Morning came without motion. The winds, to the tiniest, lisping baby breath had left the earth. Even before the sun gave light, dead day was creeping from bush to bush watching man.

Some rabbits scurried through the quarters going east. Some possums slunk by and their route was definite. One or two at a time, then more. By the time the people left the fields the procession was constant. Snakes, rattlesnakes began to cross the quarters. The men killed a few, but they could not be missed from the crawling horde. People stayed indoors until daylight. Several times during the night Janie heard the snort of big animals like deer. Once the muted voice of a panther. Going east and east. That night the palm and banana trees began that long distance talk with rain. Several people took fright and picked up and went in to Palm Beach anyway. A thousand buzzards held a flying meet and then went above the clouds and stayed.

One of the Bahaman boys stopped by Tea Cake's house in a car and hollered. Tea Cake came out throwin' laughter over his shoulder into the house.

"Hello Tea Cake."

"Hello 'Lias. You leavin', Ah see."

"Yeah man. You and Janie wanta go? Ah wouldn't give nobody else uh chawnce at uh seat till Ah found out if you all had anyway tuh go."

"Thank yuh ever so much, Lias. But we 'bout decided tuh stay."

"De crow gahn up, man."

"Dat ain't nothin'. You ain't seen de bossman go up, is yuh? Well all right now. Man, de money's too good on de muck. It's liable tuh fair off by tuhmorrer. Ah wouldn't leave if Ah wuz you."

"Mah uncle come for me. He say hurricane warning out in Palm

Beach. Not so bad dere, but man, dis muck is too low and dat big lake
is liable tuh bust."

"Ah naw, man. Some boys in dere now talkin' 'bout it. Some of 'em
been in de 'Glades fuh years. 'Tain't nothin' but uh lil blow. You'll
lose de whole day tuhmorrer tryin' tuh git back out heah."

"De Indians gahn east, man. It's dangerous."

"Dey don't always know. Indians don't know much uh nothin', tuh
tell de truth. Else dey'd own dis country still. De white folks ain't gone
nowhere. Dey oughta know if it's dangerous. You better stay heah, man.
Big jumpin' dance tuhnight right heah, when it fair off."

Lias hesitated and started· to climb out, but his uncle wouldn't let
him. "Dis time tuhmorrer you gointuh wish you follow crow," he
snorted and drove off. Lias waved back to them gaily.

"If Ah never see you no mo' on earth, Ah'll meet you in Africa."

Others hurried east like the Indians and rabbits and snakes and coons.
But the majority sat around laughing and waiting for the sun to get
friendly again.

Several men collected at Tea Cake's house and sat around stuffing
courage into each other's ears. Janie baked a big pan of beans and something she called sweet biscuits and they all managed to be happy enough.

Most of the great flame-throwers were there and naturally, handling
Big John de Conquer and his works. How he had done everything big
on earth, then went up tuh heben without dying atall. Went up there
picking a guitar and got all de angels doing the ring-shout round and
round de throne. Then everybody but God and Old Peter flew off on a
flying race to Jericho and back and John de Conquer won the race; went
on down to hell, beat the old devil and passed out ice water to everybody down there. Somebody tried to say that it was a mouth organ harp
that John was playing, but the rest of them would not hear that. Don't
care how good anybody could play a harp, God would rather to hear a
guitar. That brought them back to Tea Cake. How come he couldn't
hit that box a lick or two? Well, all right now, make us know it.

When it got good to everybody, Muck-Boy woke up and began to
chant with the rhythm and everybody bore down on the last word of
the line:

> Yo' mama don't wear no Draws
> Ah seen her when she took 'em Off
> She soaked 'em in alcoHol
> She sold 'em tuh de Santy Claus
> He told her 'twas aginst de Law
> To wear dem dirty Draws

Then Muck-Boy went crazy through the feet and danced himself and
everybody else crazy. When he finished he sat back down on the floor

and went to sleep again. Then they got to playing Florida flip and coon-can. Then it was dice. Not for money. This was a show-off game. Every-body posing his fancy shots. As always it broiled down to Tea Cake and Motor Boat. Tea Cake with his shy grin and Motor Boat with his face like a little black cherubim just from a church tower doing amazing things with anybody's dice. The others forgot the work and the weather watching them throw. It was art. A thousand dollars a throw in Madison Square Garden wouldn't have gotten any more breathless suspense. It would have just been more people holding in.

After a while somebody looked out and said, "It ain't gitting no fairer out dere. B'lieve Ah'll git on over tuh mah shack." Motor Boat and Tea Cake were still playing so everybody left them at it.

Sometime that night the winds came back. Everything in the world had a strong rattle, sharp and short like Stew Beef vibrating the drum head near the edge with his fingers. By morning Gabriel was playing the deep tones in the center of the drum. So when Janie looked out of her door she saw the drifting mists gathered in the west—that cloud field of the sky—to arm themselves with thunders and march forth against the world. Louder and higher and lower and wider the sound and motion spread, mounting, sinking, darking.

It woke up old Okechobee and the monster began to roll in his bed. Began to roll and complain like a peevish world on a grumble. The folks in the quarters and the people in the big houses further around the shore heard the big lake and wondered. The people felt uncomfortable but safe because there were the seawalls to chain the senseless monster in his bed. The folks let the people do the thinking. If the castles thought themselves secure, the cabins needn't worry. Their decision was already made as always. Chink up your cracks, shiver in your wet beds and wait on the mercy of the Lord. The bossman might have the thing stopped before morning anyway. It is so easy to be hopeful in the day time when you can see the things you wish on. But it was night, it stayed night. Night was striding across nothingness with the whole round world in his hands.

A big burst of thunder and lightning that trampled over the roof of the house. So Tea Cake and Motor stopped playing. Motor looked up in his angel-looking way and said, "Big Massa draw him chair upstairs."

"Ah'm glad y'all stop dat crap-shootin' even if it wasn't for money," Janie said. "Ole Massa is doin' *His* work now. Us oughta keep quiet."

They huddled closer and stared at the door. They just didn't use an-other part of their bodies, and they didn't look at anything but the door. The time was past for asking the white folks what to look for through that door. Six eyes were questioning God.

Through the screaming wind they heard things crashing and things hurtling and dashing with unbelievable velocity. A baby rabbit, terror ridden, squirmed through a hole in the floor and squatted off there in the shadows against the wall, seeming to know that nobody wanted its flesh at such a time. And the lake got madder and madder with only its dikes between them and him.

In a little wind-lull, Tea Cake touched Janie and said, "Ah reckon you wish now you had of stayed in yo' big house 'way from such as dis, don't yuh?"

"Naw."

"Naw?"

"Yeah, naw. People don't die till dey time come nohow, don't keer where you at. Ah'm wid mah husband in uh storm, dat's all."

"Thanky, Ma'am. But 'sposing you wuz tuh die, now. You wouldn't git mad at me for draggin' yuh heah?"

"Naw. We been tuhgether round two years. If you kin see de light at daybreak, you don't keer if you die at dusk. It's so many people never seen de light at all. Ah wuz fumblin' round and God opened de door."

He dropped to the floor and put his head in her lap. "Well then, Janie, you meant whut you didn't say, 'cause Ah never knowed you wuz so satisfied wid me lak dat. Ah kinda thought—"

The wind came back with triple fury, and put out the light for the last time. They sat in company with the others in other shanties, their eyes straining against crude walls and their souls asking if He meant to measure their puny might against His. They seemed to be staring at the dark, but their eyes were watching God.

As soon as Tea Cake went out pushing wind in front of him, he saw that the wind and water had given life to lots of things that folks think of as dead and given death to so much that had been living things. Water everywhere. Stray fish swimming in the yard. Three inches more and the water would be in the house. Already in some. He decided to try to find a car to take them out of the 'Glades before worse things happened. He turned back to tell Janie about it so she could be ready to go.

"Git our insurance papers tuhgether, Janie. Ah'll tote mah box mahself and things lak dat."

"You got all de money out de dresser drawer, already?"

"Naw, git it quick and cut uh piece off de tablecloth tuh wrap it up in. Us liable tuh git wet tuh our necks. Cut uh piece uh dat oilcloth quick fuh our papers. We got tuh go, if it ain't too late. De dish can't bear it out no longer."

He snatched the oilcloth off the table and took out his knife. Janie held it straight while he slashed off a strip.

"But Tea Cake, it's too awful out dere. Maybe it's better tuh stay heah in de wet than it is tuh try tuh—"

He stunned the argument with half a word. "Fix," he said and fought
his way outside. He had seen more than Janie had.

Janie took a big needle and ran up a longish sack. Found some newspaper and wrapped up the paper money and papers and thrust them in
and whipped over the open end with her needle. Before she could get it
thoroughly hidden in the pocket of her overalls, Tea Cake burst in again.

" 'Tain't no cars, Janie."

"Ah thought not! Whut we gointuh do now?"

"We got tuh walk."

"In all dis weather, Tea Cake? Ah don't b'lieve Ah could make it out
de quarters."

"Oh yeah you kin. Me and you and Motor Boat kin all lock arms and
hold one 'nother down. Eh, Motor?"

"He's sleep on de bed in yonder," Janie said. Tea Cake called without
moving.

"Motor Boat! You better git up from dere! Hell done broke loose in
Georgy. Dis minute! How kin you sleep at uh time lak dis? Water knee
deep in de yard."

They stepped out in water almost to their buttocks and managed to
turn east. Tea Cake had to throw his box away, and Janie saw how it
hurt him. Dodging flying missiles, floating dangers, avoiding stepping in
holes and warmed on the wind now at their backs until they gained comparatively dry land. They had to fight to keep from being pushed the
wrong way and to hold together. They saw other people like themselves
struggling along. A house down, here and there, frightened cattle. But
above all the drive of the wind and the water. And the lake. Under its
multiplied roar could be heard a mighty sound of grinding rock and timber and a wail. They looked back. Saw people trying to run in raging
waters and screaming when they found they couldn't. A huge barrier of
the makings of the dike to which the cabins had been added was rolling
and tumbling forward. Ten feet higher and as far as they could see the
muttering wall advanced before the braced-up waters like a road crusher
on a cosmic scale. The monstropolous beast had left his bed. The two
hundred miles an hour wind had loosed his chains. He seized hold of his
dikes and ran forward until he met the quarters; uprooted them like
grass and rushed on after his supposed-to-be conquerors, rolling the
dikes, rolling the houses, rolling the people in the houses along with
other timbers. The sea was walking the earth with a heavy heel.

"De lake is comin'!" Tea Cake gasped.

"De lake!" In amazed horror from Motor Boat, "De lake!"

"It's comin' behind us!" Janie shuddered. "Us can't fly."

"But we still kin run," Tea Cake shouted and they ran. The gushing
water ran faster. The great body was held back, but rivers spouted

through fissures in the rolling wall and broke like day. The three fugitives ran past another line of shanties that topped a slight rise and gained a little. They cried out as best they could, "De lake is comin'!" and barred doors flew open and others joined them in flight crying the same as they went. "De lake is comin'!" and the pursuing waters growled and shouted ahead, "Yes, Ah'm comin'!" and those who could fled on.

They made it to a tall house on a hump of ground and Janie said, "Less stop heah. Ah can't make it no further. Ah'm done give out."

"All of us is done give out," Tea Cake corrected. "We'se goin' inside out dis weather, kill or cure." He knocked with the handle of his knife, while they leaned their faces and shoulders against the wall. He knocked once more then he and Motor Boat went round to the back and forced a door. Nobody there.

"Dese people had mo' sense than Ah did," Tea Cake said as they dropped to the floor and lay there panting. "Us oughta went on wid 'Lias lak he ast me."

"You didn't know," Janie contended. "And when yuh don't know, yuh just don't know. De storms might not of come sho nuff."

They went to sleep promptly but Janie woke up first. She heard the sound of rushing water and sat up.

"Tea Cake! Motor Boat! De lake is comin'!"

The lake was coming on. Slower and wider, but coming. It had trampled on most of its supporting wall and lowered its front by spreading. But it came muttering and grumbling onward like a tired mammoth just the same.

"Dis is uh high tall house. Maybe it won't reach heah at all," Janie counselled. "And if it do, maybe it won't reach tuh de upstairs part."

"Janie, Lake Okechobee is forty miles wide and sixty miles long. Dat's uh whole heap uh water. If dis wind is shovin' dat whole lake disa way, dis house ain't nothin' tuh swaller. Us better go. Motor Boat!"

"Whut you want, man?"

"De lake is comin'!"

"Aw, naw it 'tain't."

"Yes, it is so comin'! Listen! You kin hear it way off."

"It kin jus' come on. Ah'll wait right here."

"Aw, get up, Motor Boat! Less make it tuh de Palm Beach road. Dat's on uh fill. We'se pretty safe dere."

"Ah'm safe here, man. Go ahead if yuh wants to. Ah'm sleepy."

"Whut you gointuh do if de lake reach heah?"

"Go upstairs."

"S'posing it come up dere?"

"Swim, man. Dat's all."

"Well, uh, Good bye, Motor Boat. Everything is pretty bad, yuh know. Us might git missed of one 'nother. You sho is a grand friend fuh uh man tuh have."

"Good bye, Tea Cake. Y'all oughta stay here and sleep, man. No use in goin' off and leavin' me lak dis."

"We don't wanta. Come on wid us. It might be night time when de water hem you up in heah. Dat's how come Ah won't stay. Come on, man."

"Tea Cake Ah got tuh have mah sleep. Definitely."

"Good bye, then, Motor. Ah wish you all de luck. Goin' over tuh Nassau fuh dat visit widja when all dis is over."

"Definitely, Tea Cake. Mah mama's house is yours."

Tea Cake and Janie were some distance from the house before they struck serious water. Then they had to swim a distance, and Janie could not hold up more than a few strokes at a time, so Tea Cake bore her up till finally they hit a ridge that led on towards the fill. It seemed to him the wind was weakening a little so he kept looking for a place to rest and catch his breath. His wind was gone. Janie was tired and limping, but she had not had to do that hard swimming in the turbulent waters, so Tea Cake was much worse off. But they couldn't stop. Gaining the fill was something but it was no guarantee. The lake was coming. They had to reach the six-mile bridge. It was high and safe perhaps.

Everybody was walking the fill. Hurrying, dragging, falling, crying, calling out names hopefully and hopelessly. Wind and rain beating on old folks and beating on babies. Tea Cake stumbled once or twice in his weariness and Janie held him up. So they reached the bridge at Six Mile Bend and thought to rest.

But it was crowded. White people had pre-empted that point of elevation and there was no more room. They could climb up one of its high sides and down the other, that was all. Miles further on, still no rest.

They passed a dead man in a sitting position on a hummock, entirely surrounded by wild animals and snakes. Common danger made common friends. Nothing sought a conquest over the other.

Another man clung to a cypress tree on a tiny island. A tin roof of a building hung from the branches by electric wires and the wind swung it back and forth like a mighty ax. The man dared not move a step to his right lest this crushing blade split him open. He dared not step left for a large rattlesnake was stretched full length with his head in the wind. There was a strip of water between the island and the fill, and the man clung to the tree and cried for help.

"De snake won't bite yuh," Tea Cake yelled to him. "He skeered tuh go intuh uh coil. Skeered he'll be blowed away. Step round dat side and swim off!"

Soon after that Tea Cake felt he couldn't walk anymore. Not right away. So he stretched long side of the road to rest. Janie spread herself between him and the wind and he closed his eyes and let the tiredness seep out of his limbs. On each side of the fill was a great expanse of water like lakes—water full of things living and dead. Things that didn't belong in water. As far as the eye could reach, water and wind playing upon it in fury. A large piece of tar-paper roofing sailed through the air and scudded along the fill until it hung against a tree. Janie saw it with joy. That was the very thing to cover Tea Cake with. She could lean against it and hold it down. The wind wasn't quite so bad as it was anyway. The very thing. Poor Tea Cake!

She crept on hands and knees to the piece of roofing and caught hold of it by either side. Immediately the wind lifted both of them and she saw herself sailing off the fill to the right, out and out over the lashing water. She screamed terribly and released the roofing which sailed away as she plunged downward into the water.

"Tea Cake!" He heard her and sprang up. Janie was trying to swim but fighting water too hard. He saw a cow swimming slowly towards the fill in an oblique line. A massive built dog was sitting on her shoulders and shivering and growling. The cow was approaching Janie. A few strokes would bring her there.

"Make it tuh de cow and grab hold of her tail! Don't use yo' feet. Jus' yo' hands is enough. Dat's right, come on!"

Janie achieved the tail of the cow and lifted her head up along the cow's rump, as far as she could above water. The cow sunk a little with the added load and thrashed a moment in terror. Thought she was being pulled down by a gator. Then she continued on. The dog stood up and growled like a lion, stiff-standing hackles, stiff muscles, teeth uncovered as he lashed up his fury for the charge. Tea Cake split the water like an otter, opening his knife as he dived. The dog raced down the back-bone of the cow to the attack and Janie screamed and slipped far back on the tail of the cow, just out of reach of the dog's angry jaws. He wanted to plunge in after her but dreaded the water, somehow. Tea Cake rose out of the water at the cow's rump and seized the dog by the neck. But he was a powerful dog and Tea Cake was over-tired. So he didn't kill the dog with one stroke as he had intended. But the dog couldn't free himself either. They fought and somehow he managed to bite Tea Cake high up on his cheek-bone once. Then Tea Cake finished him and sent him to the bottom to stay there. The cow relieved of a great weight was landing on the fill with Janie before Tea Cake stroked in and crawled weakly upon the fill again.

Janie began to fuss around his face where the dog had bitten him but he said it didn't amount to anything. "He'd uh raised hell though if he had uh grabbed me uh inch higher and bit me in mah eye. Yuh can't buy eyes in de store, yuh know." He flopped to the edge of the fill as if the storm wasn't going on at all. "Lemme rest awhile, then us got tuh make it on intuh town somehow."

It was next day by the sun and the clock when they reached Palm Beach. It was years later by their bodies. Winters and winters of hardship and suffering. The wheel kept turning round and round. Hope, hopelessness and despair. But the storm blew itself out as they approached the city of refuge.

Havoc was there with her mouth wide open. Back in the Everglades the wind had romped among lakes and trees. In the city it had raged among houses and men. Tea Cake and Janie stood on the edge of things and looked over the desolation.

"How kin Ah find uh doctor fuh yo' face in all dis mess?" Janie wailed.

"Ain't got de damn doctor tuh study 'bout. Us needs uh place tuh rest."

A great deal of their money and perseverance and they found a place to sleep. It was just that. No place to live at all. Just sleep. Tea Cake looked all around and sat heavily on the side of the bed.

"Well," he said humbly, "reckon you never 'spected tuh come tuh dis when you took up wid me, didja?"

"Once upon uh time, Ah never 'spected nothin' Tea Cake but bein' dead from the standin' still and tryin' tuh laugh. But you come 'long and made somethin' outa me. So Ah'm thankful fuh anything we come through together."

"Thanky, Ma'am."

"You was twice noble tuh save me from dat dawg. Tea Cake, Ah don't speck you seen his eyes lak Ah did. He didn't aim tuh jus' bite me, Tea Cake. He aimed tuh kill me stone dead. Ah'm never tuh fuhgit dem eyes. He wuzn't nothin' all over but pure hate. Wonder where he come from?"

"Yeah, Ah did see 'im too. It wuz frightenin'. Ah didn't mean tuh take his hate neither. He had tuh die uh me one. Mah switch blade said it wuz him."

"Po' me, he'd tore me tuh pieces, if it wuzn't fuh you, honey."

"You don't have tuh say, if it wuzn't fuh me, baby, cause Ah'm *heah,* and then Ah want yuh tuh know it's uh man heah."

The Breadline

From A BELL FOR ADANO

By John Hersey

John Hersey's novel gave the first light on liberation in Europe. Its
theme is the impress of the justice and mercy of democracy upon the
hearts of Italians after the long fascist persecution. Major Joppolo is
the American administrator of the town of Adano. He himself is of
Italian descent and he shares with the townspeople the simplest and
gentlest of Italian virtues. While other passages contain more drama
and action than the one selected, in this the author's sense of comedy
reaches its fullest expression, and nowhere in the book is his understanding of a simple, beaten people more evident. Throughout his
entire experience in Adano the Major is trying, by acts and words, to
define democracy for them in understandable terms. His speech to
the crowd in this passage crystallizes the whole underlying motive of
war against the Axis.

ON THE fifth day of the invasion a babel stood in line in front of
the shop of the baker Zapulla. There were many women, mostly
dressed in black, and a few men. They talked in loud voices, each clam-
oring for an audience.

"He has a furious energy," said Maria Carolina, the wife of the noisy
cartman Afronti. "He told small Zito to report for work at seven each
morning. Zito thought that no official would be up that early. Zito went
to work at seven and a half, and the Mister Major told him that there
would be a new usher unless the old usher could wake up on time in the
morning."

Carmelina, the wife of the lazy Fatta, who was at the head of the line, said loudly: "It would be pleasing if Zapulla the baker got up on time in the morning so that the bread would be ready."

Zapulla the baker, black with the wood coke of his oven, came out to the front of the shop and roared: "Zapulla the baker has been up since four in the morning. If Zapulla the baker hears remarks, he is liable to go back to bed and let the bread burn up."

"Do you remember," said Margherita, the fat Craxi's formidable wife, "do you remember how the Mayor Nasta used to hold office hours from noon until one, each day, the hour when we were all busy with our children? And how we had to apply in writing to see him? And how we had to wait ten days? And how he would treat us when we did see him? Now it is different. You can walk in any time all day." She paused. "He stands up when you enter," she said impressively.

"Is that so?" said Laura Sofia, who was not the wife of anyone and at her age was not likely to be ever. "I think I shall go and see him."

"On what pretext?" jibed Maria Carolina, wife of the noisy cartman Afronti. "To make eyes at him?"

"Oh," said Laura Sofia, "I have my complaints, just like the rest of you—even if I haven't litters of children grunting like pigs on my floor."

Carmelina, wife of the lazy Fatta, said: "My children are hungry. It would be nice if they could get their bread on time."

From the depths of his shop Zapulla the baker shouted: "The children of certain people may stay hungry if certain people do not hold their tongues."

Mercurio Salvatore, crier of the town of Adano, was near the end of the line, but even though he toned his voice down to his conversational whisper, the whole line could hear him when he said: "I wish to tell you something. I asked him if I could listen to my radio.

"He said: 'Why not, crier?'

"I asked him what station I would be permitted to listen to. I asked: 'Should it be the Radio of Algiers, or should it be the Radio of London which is called B.B.C.?'

"He said: 'Reception here is best for Radio Roma. Why don't you listen to the one you can hear the best?'

"I said: 'Can you mean it? Radio Roma is anti-American. It has nothing but slander for the Americans.'

"And he said to me: 'Crier, I love the truth, and I want you to love it too. You listen to Radio Roma. You will hear that it is three fourths lies. I want you to judge for yourself and to want the truth. Then perhaps you will want to listen to the other broadcasts which you cannot hear quite so clearly.' "

Margherita, the formidable wife of Craxi, said: "Have you listened, crier?"

Mercurio Salvatore said: "I have listened. I could detect only one lie yesterday, but it was a big one. Radio Roma said that Italian forces in the city of Vicinamare threw back three vicious Allied attacks. We all knew that Vicinamare was in the hands of the Americans late on the first day of the disembarkation."

Carmelina, the wife of the lazy Fatta, said: "It will be late on the fifth day before we get bread from this baker Zapulla."

Zapulla was impolite to Carmelina because of what she said. He came forward and threw a piece of woodcoke at her head and roared: "Silence, whore!"

The woodcoke missed Carmelina's head, but hit the stomach of the formidable Margherita. She advanced, shaking her large fists. Zapulla went back to his ovens, as if he had not noticed where his woodcoke went.

At this angry moment, Gargano, Chief of the Carabinieri, came up to the line. This man was called by the people The Man With Two Hands, because of his continuous and dramatic gesturing. He was, he seemed to think, an actor, and he could not say two words without gesturing with both hands. He possessed and exercised all the essentially Italian gestures: the two forefingers laid side by side, the circle of thumb and forefinger, the hands up in stop position, the sign of the cuckold and of the genitals, the salute to the forehead with palm forward, the fingertips of the two hands placed tip to tip, the fingers linked, the hands flat and downward as if patting sand, the hands up heel to heel and pulled toward the chest, the attitude of prayer, the pointing forefinger of accusation, the V as if for victory or smoking cigarets, the forefinger on the chin, the rolling of the hands. All, he used them all.

When he approached the line, everyone thought that he was coming to restore order. There was a question in some people's minds whether he still had authority, but they did not feel that this was a good time to flout the question. It would be better to see first whether he made any arrests.

He did not make any arrests. He merely went up to Carmelina, wife of the lazy Fatta, and squeezed between her and the door of Zapulla's shop, and stood there. The people could see that he was merely taking his place at the head of the line to wait for bread.

Carmelina, who was annoyed by having had woodcoke thrown at her, said truculently: "Mister Gargano, you were Chief of the Carabinieri under the old regime, and that entitled you to stand at the head of the line. I am not sure that you are still Chief of the Carabinieri."

Gargano said: "I am the Chief," and he made a kind of Fascist salute with both hands.

Carmelina said: "I doubt it. Where is the proof?"

The Breadline

Gargano said: "See my uniform," and he ran his two forefingers from his shoulders to his knees.

Carmelina said: "That is no proof. The Americans do not care how we dress. I could dress as a rabbit and the Americans would not arrest me."

Gargano said: "Woman, stop your shouting, or I will arrest you," and he gripped his own left wrist with his own right hand, signifying arrest.

Carmelina said: "Where is your authority?"

Margherita, the formidable wife of Craxi, said: "I believe that this man is still Chief, since the Mister Major is keeping many Fascist scoundrels in office until they prove themselves bad. But I do not believe that under American law he has the right to go to the head of the line. That is where I think you are right, Carmelina."

Gargano said: "I have always come to the head of the line. I shall continue to do so," and he ran his forefinger along the length of the line until he came to the head, where he stood, then he pointed the finger at the ground.

Maria Carolina, the wife of the noisy cartman Afronti, who had once been arrested by Gargano, shouted: "You have no right, Two-Hands. The Americans would not permit it." This was the first time Gargano had ever been called Two-Hands to his face. He did not understand the reference.

Gargano stepped out of the line. "Who questions my right?" he roared, and he pounded one clenched fist on the other clenched fist.

Carmelina, wife of the lazy Fatta, standing right beside him, startled him by whispering in his ear: "I question it, Two-Hands."

Up to this time Zapulla the baker, standing in the front of his shop, had been torn between the two authorities, the old and the new. But he was so annoyed with Carmelina for having prodded him that he now said: "Arrest her, Mister Chief, if you have any courage."

Up to this time Gargano the Chief, somewhat unsure of his ground, had been trying to think of a way of retiring gracefully. But now his manhood, as well as his authority, was challenged. He moved toward Carmelina and said: "Woman, you are under arrest."

Carmelina shouted: "Keep your two active hands off me, Gargano."

Zapulla said: "Will you let this woman shriek down your courage?"

Gargano clapped his hands on Carmelina. She screamed. All up and down the line women shouted: "Out with the Fascist Chief of Carabinieri. Out with Two-Hands. Out with men who push themselves to the head of a line ahead of women who have been waiting three hours."

Gargano dragged Carmelina off screaming and kicking, and the anti-Gargano, anti-Fascist screams in the line grew louder and louder. Even Mercurio Salvatore, although as crier he was more or less an official and should have remained neutral or even taken the side of Gargano, raised his huge voice in a careful shout: "Down with injustice!"

When Gargano pulled Carmelina into Major Joppolo's office, she was still screaming. But the Major jumped to his feet and said sharply: "Silence, shrew," and she fell quiet at once.

"What is this all about?" the Major asked.

Gargano said: "This woman questioned my authority," and he pointed at her with both forefingers.

Carmelina said: "There is more to it than that."

Major Joppolo said: "Your authority to do what, Gargano?"

Carmelina shouted: "To push his way to the head of the line in front of Zapulla's bread shop."

Gargano said: "It is a privilege the officials of the town have always enjoyed."

Major Joppolo said: "Is that so?"

Gargano said: "I charge this woman with disturbing the peace and questioning authority." Gargano was shrewd in saying this, for he saw that things were going against him, and now he had put the matter on an official rather than a personal basis. The Major would have to decide the case officially.

The Major decided with a speed which dazzled Gargano. He decided that the woman was right but that he could not say so, because if he did the Chief would never regain his authority, and the Major wanted to keep him in office. Therefore he said: "I sentence this woman to one day in jail, suspended sentence. Let her go, Gargano, and gather all the officials of Adano for me at once."

When Carmelina got outside, she ran straight back to the bread shop. The bread was not ready yet, and the people gave her back her place at the head of the line and shouted to her: "What happened, Carmelina? What did they do to you?"

Carmelina told what had happened and she said: "Did you ever hear of such a light sentence in Adano? I believe in my heart that the Mister Major thought I was right. And what was the meaning of assembling the officials? I believe that he was for me."

In the Major's office, the officials gradually assembled. Some were held-over Fascists, some were new appointments to take the place of Fascists who had fled to the hills. In whispers, and with ample gestures, Gargano described to them the humiliation he had suffered, until Major Joppolo said: "Silence, please."

The officials drew up in a circle around the Major's desk. The Major stood up.

"I want you to be my friends," he said. "As my friends, I will consider it my duty to tell you everything I think, for we do not want Adano to be a town of mysteries and a place of suspicion.

"Adano has been a Fascist town. That is natural, because the country was Fascist, therefore the town was also. But now that the Americans have come, we are going to run the town as a democracy.

"Perhaps you do not know what a democracy is. I will tell you.

"Democracy is this: democracy is that the men of the government are no longer the masters of the people. They are the servants of the people. What makes a man master of another man? It is that he pays him for his work. Who pays the men in the government? The people do, for they pay the taxes out of which you are paid.

"Therefore you are now the servants of the people of Adano. I too am their servant. When I go to buy bread, I shall take my place at the end of the line, and I will wait my turn. You too must behave now as servants, not as masters. You must behave as the servant of the man without shoes just as much as of the baron. If I find that any of you are not giving the type of service that I desire, I shall have to remove you from office.

"Remember: you are servants now. You are servants of the people of Adano. And watch: this thing will make you happier than you have ever been in your lives."

The Sick Child

From HOLD AUTUMN IN YOUR HAND
By George Sessions Perry

Sam Tucker, a Texas dirt farmer, has for years been a sharecropper, managing only at terrific physical cost to keep his family alive. But in his mind lies the recurring hope of "getting somewhere" and he persuades Ruston, a large landowner, to let him work sixty-eight acres of rich bottom lands. The agreement is for a year and Sam, faced by the hardest work of his life, tackles it as a challenge to his skill and self-esteem.

In this year, Sam learns the real worth of his friends, Old Man Hewitt who rises in stature far above his own son Finley, Russell who owns a market in town and Dr. White. When the unvaried winter diet of cornbread, salt pork and molasses upon which he and his wife, Nona, and Granny and the children subsist finally strikes down their little boy, Sam discovers the meaning of neighborliness again.

THE land was crusted over, gray-black and ready, still too cold to germinate seed, but by no means too cold for breaking.

Ruston came and walked over it and crumbled a handful, like stale chocolate-cake crumbs, in his hand.

"It's just waiting on us," he said. "Let's see you do your stuff."

As they stood there, they had a feeling about each other. Though Ruston knew he ought to know better, he kept feeling that Sam had some stuff to do, and Sam felt that Ruston would keep out of his way.

Next day tools came. A cutter to chop last year's cotton stalks, which were bigger at their base than your thumb and tougher than seasoned willow. Long blades, the cutter was, fashioned into a cylinder that rolled

244

against the dead stalks, pushing them over and cutting them. There was a rake for pulling the cut stalks to the end of the rows to be burnt, a sweep for center-furrowing, and a middle-buster for sundering the old rows, for lifting their bottom dirt to sun and light and air. Finally there were two great black mules named Weaver and Frisno Emma, and corn to feed them with.

But the cutting and raking, even the center-furrowing, were but preliminary things in which the mules coasted and the man rode. Not until this was done was it time for the main event, for ramming the great middle-buster into the old rows, which were knitted into a greater formidableness, into a kind of reinforced earthwork, by the forever downgoing roots of last year's cotton. Into these he must drive the steel point, drive it down a foot into the row-ridge and plow, sunder earth, send the great clods tumbling stubbornly, but tumbling, out the rusty plow wings, which soon would be gleaming. He must guide the plow's snout evenly down the line it would be least inclined to go, breaking land.

Now farming had begun. The long, cumulative act of creation had begun, and not in the sand. Here something would come of it, something beautiful and substantial. And the nights were dead with sleeping, and the days, from edge to edge, were packed with labor, and there was no hiding from accomplishment. Each hour the bright, rough black area of new-plowed land grew larger, and that part of the land which was still unawakened decreased.

Your arms also told you you were getting the job done, especially in the shoulders, where the joints seemed to get shaken loose, and the small of your back, which the winter had softened, would keep thinking of going somewhere to lie down, and your legs were inhabited by shaftlike pains. The clods tried to bury your feet alive.

But the mules took it. You had the plow slammed in deep, but they were going on and you had to go too; you had hold of something you couldn't turn loose.

And as your legs grew more weary still, you were hammered by how much more there was to do, how many million steps were yet to be taken, how many thousand rocks and roots would send the plow, charged with mule strength, lurching off its course.

You combated these thoughts by thinking that when you really got hardened, it didn't matter how long the rows or days were. Once you really got in shape, you could plow to Kingdom Come and after the first couple of hours not get much tireder.

Sometimes it became necessary to play tricks on this animal you lived in. You treated it like a child. Or a drunk man uptown.

The first hour you didn't tell it anything, because it was doing all right. It was feeding on the decreasing stiffness in itself that a night's sleep had lodged there. During that first hour each step, each row, became more comfortable, more normal.

But nine o'clock thoughts were bad ones. They said you were still going downhill into the valley of the day. You hadn't done much of anything yet and you were already getting a little tired. You thought: If I had any sense I wouldn't be here. You thought about how much fun people had who worked in gangs. They weren't ever lonesome.

So you began pretending days didn't count, that dinner was the thing you were working toward. You ignored the afternoon and thought why, hell, the morning's over half finished. This was cheating because you'd started a little after seven, when good daylight came, yet you pretended you had started at six, like in big summer. And if you had begun to get hungry, you didn't have to pretend so hard that dinner was what you were aiming at, because you were. But those first few days with the middle-buster you weren't, because it was such a wild, surging thing, by the time you'd wrestled it all morning your guts were screwed up in such a knot that you weren't hungry.

But when noon finally came, and you unhitched and watered the mules and put them in the little mule pasture, you really felt like going home and sitting around and smoking, and maybe being tempted by a piece of hot bread and a few sirup.

And the babble of Granny was pleasant and lively with its fast-changing moods which might range from expansiveness through petulance to fury to an amusingly exaggerated but serious portrayal of martyrdom. You realized it was entertaining only because you were too tired to pay much attention and hadn't been hearing it all morning. However, it took a little something out of you to look at Nona's face. She had been listening all morning, and Granny didn't pour off Nona's back like she did off yours.

Lots of times listening to the old woman would be really funny to you. For example, the time when she was late getting to the table, which was so unlike her that you made some remark about it, and she explained, "I taken a dose of salts, Sammy boy, and slept right smack through em. I just been out there wrenchin out these old drawers. Person gets old, they haven't got such a good holt on theirselves as when they're younger."

But Granny was a human, or almost one, and not the thing that was frightening Sam and Nona. Granny, when she became absolutely intolerable, could be switched. This other matter wasn't so simple.

It was the thing that was happening to Jot that was taking the sap out of them all. Other people might not have noticed the difference in Nona, but Sam did, and knew why it was there.

Hardly had the weather turned off fine, and the tools come, when a little sore appeared in the corner of Jot's mouth. In every other way he seemed healthy, but the little sore came, and spread, just slowly and steadily, until it was the size of his hand and was still spreading. All of every day Nona had been watching it spread, knowing there was no reason for it, that Jot had not been sick, but that the sore had simply come and spread and was going to possess him.

It was a thing that the gods had fastened on him before your very eyes. The unknown was there in your house, and the way you recognized its presence was by seeing it devouring one of your babies.

Finally Nona said, "Sam, we got to get him to town and have him doctored."

A doctor, especially one of those who had let all your family that were dead die, was a trivial defender against the gods, but there was no other.

"I'll take him Sunday," Sam said. "I know it ain't hardly possible, but if you can, I'd try to keep his face and hands about half-way clean. We sure don't want no worms to get in him."

"All right," Nona said.

Sam made a cigarette and went back to the field.

Early Sunday morning, which was frosty, Sam left the house, carrying Jot on his shoulder. The baby was wrapped in the half-blanket left from Daisy's coat and was happy to be going somewhere with his father.

By nine o'clock, having caught a ride with some Mexicans after the first mile, Sam and Jot were in Dr. White's office.

Dr. White was an old man who still appeared to have the leathery, physical toughness of a ranch hand, and was always full of a kind of nervous impatience. He looked as if he had taken an uncommon amount of weatherbeating in his life, and could take a great deal more.

"Well, well . . ." the doctor said in a kind of detached flurry which usually hovered about him, though it was plainly somewhat less than skin-deep.

He had followed Sam into the office, which was always left open. It was neither very dirty nor very clean, but you could get a leg set there, or get sewed up after a fight, or get your claps doctored. If you were going to have a baby, you had that at home.

"I sure hate to bother you, Doctor," Sam said. "I tried to get some of them others, but they wouldn't come downtown."

The old doctor smiled shortly but warmly at Sam. What Sam had said conveyed considerable information and respect: Sam had known Dr. White would come to anybody who was sick, and he also knew there would be no money in it for whoever treated Jot. He had tried to save Dr. White the trouble of coming downtown on a profitless journey. But it hadn't worked.

The other two doctors in the town were younger, more progressive, and had acquired most of the pay practice. They were trying to make a living and were succeeding, which was all right. But Dr. White seemed to think he was there to treat the sick, and that was what he did. You could look at his face and tell he was not a man who just did something for a fee.

The doctor didn't look at Jot. He looked at Sam. Just now, he didn't bother with Jot's temperature or pulse or when did his bowels move.

"You don't have a cow, do you, Sam?"

"No, sir."

"Well, you better get one."

"I ain't got no way to get one."

"Raise a heifer for somebody. Meantime, borrow milk. I don't care where you live, some neighbor will let you have enough for this child. At least a pint a day. Much better, a quart."

"All right, sir. And what medicine?"

"He don't need any medicine. What vegetables have you all been eating this winter?"

"Why, not any, hardly."

Sam didn't think it would be necessary to explain that vegetables didn't grow in the wintertime.

"You got any money at all?"

"Yes, sir; sixty cents."

Dr. White exhaled and looked at nothing out the window.

"Go spend it on some vegetables," he said. "Get some lemons and give the baby a glass of lemonade twice a day."

The nervous impatience returned to the old man and lifted him out of the chair.

"That's all," he said. "Let's go."

As they went down the stairs (the office was on the second floor, over the drug store) Sam recalled that his own middle name was White, after the doctor, and that that had been the only pay the old man had ever got for making the delivery at his birth.

"Let me know how he gets along," the doctor said mechanically, but meaning it, and left Sam at the bottom step before Sam could even thank him.

Then Sam remembered he hadn't asked the doctor how sick Jot was.

From the back of the drug store, Sam phoned Russell and told him his plight, and that he'd have to ask somebody to open a store to sell him a measly sixty cents' worth of vegetables.

"Would you feel like doin it, Russell?"

"Hell, yes. Wait on the corner."

Russell was another one of those nervous ones.

As he unlocked the store ten minutes later, he said, "Your folks aren't too high-toned to eat a few wilted vegetables, are they, Sam?"

"Course not."

"Then get that tow-sack and come on."

When the sack was filled with wilted cabbage and turnips and sprouting onions and soft bananas and shriveled lemons and the like, Russell put some garden seeds in a sack and said, "Now God damn it, Sam, go plant a garden. Here, put some of these seed potatoes in your sack."

"Gosh," Sam said when Russell refused the proffered sixty cents, "how come you to do this nice thing to me, Russell?"

Russell ran his fingers through his hair with a kind of tense helplessness.

"I don't know," he said. "Don't worry me about it. Come on and I'll haul you home."

Russell's car rattled because he went all over the country trying to collect bills and to trade for anything he thought he could make money on.

He was so energetically moody that when he didn't say something, it was hard for you to either. A mile out in the country, he broke the silence.

"Why don't you gripe?" he said baldly.

"I don't know," Sam said, mystified.

Russell went back into himself.

He put Sam out at home, turned the car with a kind of furiousness expressed not by his face but by the car, and left.

Late that afternoon Sam went over to the Hewitts', where he found the old man dressing a home-made ax handle with a rasp. Sam told him what the doctor had said, that somehow milk must be obtained for Jot.

"I haven't come beggin and I haven't come borrowin," Sam said. "If you could let me have a little pan o milk every day, I'd keep track of it like it was money, and work it out."

"I don't reckon we'd have any trouble about that," the old man said. "We got it for the chickens most of the time, anyway."

Sam squatted against the barn while the old man went on working.

"It may seem funny," Sam said, "me comin to you like this for milk when my next-door neighbor's got six cows and you ain't got but two, but we're already usin out of his well and he don't like that none too much."

"Glad you came to me," the old man said. "First place, he probably wouldn't of let you had it."

"What's wrong with that sucker?" Sam asked, perplexed.

"Sometimes I've wondered if maybe it ain't cause he ain't got no confidence in hisself nor nobody else," the old man said. "He's the worst scared feller of not gettin his share I ever saw. Lessen he gets about eight times the best of a trade, seems like he's scared to make it. I been knowin that boy a long time an I'm mighty fraid he's what you'd call a mean, jealous-hearted son of a bitch. I could be mistaken bout that . . . but I ain't."

"I give him a fish one day," Sam said, "and he just knowed he was gettin some kind of round-house friggin."

The old man put down his work and took a chew of tobacco.

"You had any experience with idiots?" he asked Sam.

"You mean about Henry?"

"Come on into the barn."

Sam followed him to a stall where there were a brown cow and a scrawny little calf. About both of them there was an air of melancholy resignation.

"That calf," the old man said, "ain't even got sense enough to suck. Ain't somethin done about it mighty quick, it's gonna die. If you want to undertake to raise it for me, take em both. If you raise that calf, you'll more'n repay me for what milk you get out of the cow. If you don't, I'm gonna knock it in the head. I ain't got time to be runnin no lunatic asylum for addle-headed calves."

Sam didn't say anything. He was too concerned with the problem before him. He slid the calf under the cow, held its mouth open with one hand and squirted a little milk into it with the other.

Once its gullet seemed to work half-heartedly.

"Its nose is goin to have to be helt," the old man said. "I never expected to see a livin creature with less git-up-an-go than Finley, but looks like that calf's got it."

Then Sam saw the old man was ashamed of himself for saying what he had, and Sam looked back at the calf and picked it up.

"I got plenty of pasture along the river for the cow," Sam said. "Just winter grass and rescue grass now, but enough o that to hold her. We'll keep the calf up at the house. One o these days it's liable to catch onto what its jaws is for. I guess ole Brownie'll follow us on over there."

"Sure she will," the old man said. "I reckon she likes the thing cause it's hern. I wish you luck on the calf."

"I sure thank you for the use of the cow. I know the kids'll make a heap over this here runty calf, and Nona too, for that."

When Sam came up to the house, the family was already in the yard, standing in awe before him and Brownie and the calf.

"That boy!" Granny exclaimed. "Was he to come waggin in one of these days with a bokinstrictor I wouldn't be one bit surprised."

While Sam milked Brownie and Zoonie barked at her, the children tied a bright rag around the calf's neck and named it Snookums. The cow they named Uncle Walter, after a favorite relative.

When Sam held the calf's nose to choke the warm milk down its throat, the others held their breaths.

The feeding was a success.

"Why, shuckins," Granny exclaimed, "all he needs is a little practice! Fore long he'll be a-eatin the very posties outen the fence."

Daisy ran in circles around Jot singing, "Snookums et! Snookum zet!"

And Jot got down on all fours and said to Daisy, "I'm Snookums. I'm Jot, Snookums calf."

Then Nona brought some cups and Sam filled them from the bucket and said, "Now let's see if y'all got more sense than that calf."

The Death of Grampa

From THE GRAPES OF WRATH

By John Steinbeck

The migrant people in the aftermath of the depression of the 1930's is the theme of Steinbeck's novel. The Joad family, "tractored" off their land in Oklahoma by an impersonal company which sought to consolidate small farms worked by tenants into large tracts for mechanized cultivation, is the story's protagonist. Grampa and Granma, too old for the burdens of the hard trek, Pa and Ma and their children—Tom, Al, Noah and Rose of Sharon, already pregnant with the first of the fourth generation; Rose of Sharon's husband Connie, Pa's brother Uncle John, the youngsters Ruthie and Winfield, still only half conscious of the family sorrow, make up the family caravan moving on its overloaded truck toward the "paradise" of California. Casy, once a preacher, has been invited for his moral support. In the passage following, the family's fear of the law when Grampa dies is deepened by the haunting shadow of Tom's parole from prison where he has spent four years for a defense killing. The scene was chosen because it reflects the full sense of the broken social scheme which still menaces our people and for its implications of the simple, basic, American courage which has won all our victories.

THEY went through Bethany and out on the other side. In a ditch, where a culvert went under the road, an old touring car was pulled off the highway and a little tent was pitched beside it, and smoke came out of a stove pipe through the tent. Tom pointed ahead. "There's some folks campin'. Looks like as good a place as we seen." He slowed his motor and pulled to a stop beside the road. The hood of the old touring car was up, and a middle-aged man stood looking down at the motor. He wore a cheap straw sombrero, a blue shirt, and a black, spotted vest, and his jeans were stiff and shiny with dirt. His face was lean, the deep cheek-lines great furrows down his face so that his cheek bones and chin stood out sharply. He looked up at the Joad truck and his eyes were puzzled and angry.

Tom leaned out of the window. "Any law 'gainst folks stoppin' here for the night?"

The man had seen only the truck. His eyes focused down on Tom. "I dunno," he said. "We on'y stopped here 'cause we couldn't git no further."

"Any water here?"

The man pointed to a service-station shack about a quarter of a mile ahead. "They's water there they'll let ya take a bucket of."

Tom hesitated. "Well, ya 'spose we could camp down 'longside?"

The lean man looked puzzled. "We don't own it," he said. "We on'y stopped here 'cause this goddamn ol' trap wouldn' go no further."

Tom insisted. "Anyways you're here an' we ain't. You got a right to say if you wan' neighbors or not."

The appeal to hospitality had an instant effect. The lean face broke into a smile. "Why, sure, come on off the road. Proud to have ya." And he called, "Sairy, there's some folks goin' ta stay with us. Come on out an' say how d'ya do. Sairy ain't well," he added. The tent flaps opened and a wizened woman came out—a face wrinkled as a dried leaf and eyes that seemed to flame in her face, black eyes that seemed to look out of a well of horror. She was small and shuddering. She held herself upright by a tent flap, and the hand holding onto the canvas was a skeleton covered with wrinkled skin.

When she spoke her voice had a beautiful low timbre, soft and modulated, and yet with ringing overtones. "Tell 'em welcome," she said. "Tell 'em good an' welcome."

Tom drove off the road and brought his truck into the field and lined it up with the touring car. And people boiled down from the truck; Ruthie and Winfield too quickly, so that their legs gave way and they shrieked at the pins and needles that ran through their limbs. Ma went quickly to work. She untied the three-gallon bucket from the back of the truck and approached the squealing children. "Now you go git water —right down there. Ask nice. Say, 'Please, kin we git a bucket a water?' and say, 'Thank you.' An' carry it back together helpin', an' don't spill none. An' if you see stick wood to burn, bring it on." The children stamped away toward the shack.

By the tent a little embarrassment had set in, and social intercourse had paused before it started. Pa said, "You ain't Oklahomy folks?"

And Al, who stood near the car, looked at the license plates. "Kansas," he said.

The lean man said, "Galena, or right about there. Wilson, Ivy Wilson."

"We're Joads," said Pa. "We come from right near Sallisaw."

"Well, we're proud to meet you folks," said Ivy Wilson. "Sairy, these is Joads."

"I knowed you wasn't Oklahomy folks. You talk queer kinda—that ain't no blame, you understan'."

"Ever'body says words different," said Ivy. "Arkansas folks says 'em different, and Oklahomy folks says 'em different. And we seen a lady from Massachusetts, an' she said 'em differentest of all. Couldn' hardly make out what she was sayin'."

Noah and Uncle John and the preacher began to unload the truck. They helped Grampa down and sat him on the ground and he sat limply, staring ahead of him. "You sick, Grampa?" Noah asked.

"You goddamn right," said Grampa weakly. "Sicker'n hell."

Sairy Wilson walked slowly and carefully toward him. "How'd you like ta come in our tent?" she asked. "You kin lay down on our mattress an' rest."

He looked up at her, drawn by her soft voice. "Come on now," she said. "You'll git some rest. We'll he'p you over."

Without warning Grampa began to cry. His chin wavered and his old lips tightened over his mouth and he sobbed hoarsely. Ma rushed over to him and put her arms around him. She lifted him to his feet, her broad back straining, and she half lifted, half helped him into the tent.

Uncle John said, "He must be good an' sick. He ain't never done that before. Never seen him blubberin' in my life." He jumped up on the truck and tossed a mattress down.

Ma came out of the tent and went to Casy. "You been aroun' sick people," she said. "Grampa's sick. Won't you go take a look at him?"

Casy walked quickly to the tent and went inside. A double mattress was on the ground, the blankets spread neatly; and a little tin stove stood on iron legs, and the fire in it burned unevenly. A bucket of water, a wooden box of supplies, and a box for a table, that was all. The light of the setting sun came pinkly through the tent walls. Sairy Wilson knelt on the ground, beside the mattress, and Grampa lay on his back. His eyes were open, staring upward, and his cheeks were flushed. He breathed heavily.

Casy took the skinny old wrist in his fingers. "Feeling kinda tired, Grampa?" he asked. The staring eyes moved toward his voice but did not find him. The lips practiced a speech but did not speak it. Casy felt the pulse and he dropped the wrist and put his hand on Grampa's forehead. A struggle began in the old man's body, his legs moved restlessly and his hands stirred. He said a whole string of blurred sounds that were not words, and his face was red under the spiky white whiskers.

Sairy Wilson spoke softly to Casy. "Know what's wrong?"

He looked up at the wrinkled face and the burning eyes. "Do you?"

"I—think so."

"What?" Casy asked.

"Might be wrong. I wouldn' like to say."

Casy looked back at the twitching red face. "Would you say—maybe —he's workin' up a stroke?"

"I'd say that," said Sairy. "I seen it three times before."

From outside came the sounds of camp-making, wood chopping, and the rattle of pans. Ma looked through the flaps. "Granma wants to come in. Would she better?"

The preacher said, "She'll jus' fret if she don't."

"Think he's awright?" Ma asked.

Casy shook his head slowly. Ma looked quickly down at the struggling old face with blood pounding through it. She drew outside and her voice came through. "He's awright, Granma. He's jus' takin' a little res'."

And Granma answered sulkily, "Well, I want ta see him. He's a tricky devil. He wouldn't never let ya know." And she came scurrying through the flaps. She stood over the mattresses and looked down. "What's the matter'th you?" she demanded of Grampa. And again his eyes reached toward her voice and his lips writhed. "He's sulkin'," said Granma. "I tol' you he was tricky. He was gonna sneak away this mornin' so he wouldn't have to come. An' then his hip got a-hurtin'," she said disgustedly. "He's jus' sulkin'. I seen him when he wouldn't talk to nobody before."

Casy said gently, "He ain't sulkin', Granma. He's sick."

"Oh!" She looked down at the old man again, "Sick bad, you think?"

"Purty bad, Granma."

For a moment she hesitated uncertainly. "Well," she said quickly, "why ain't you prayin'? You're a preacher, ain't you?"

Casy's strong fingers blundered over to Grampa's wrist and clasped around it. "I tol' you, Granma. I ain't a preacher no more."

"Pray anyway," she ordered. "You know all the stuff by heart."

"I can't," said Casy. "I don' know what to pray for or who to pray to."

Granma's eyes wandered away and came to rest on Sairy. "He won't pray," she said. "D'I ever tell ya how Ruthie prayed when she was a little skinner? Says, 'Now I lay me down to sleep. I pray the Lord my soul to keep. An' when she got there the cupboard was bare, an' so the poor dog got none. Amen.' That's jus' what she done." The shadow of someone walking between the tent and the sun crossed the canvas.

Grampa seemed to be struggling; all his muscles twitched. And suddenly he jarred as though under a heavy blow. He lay still and his breath was stopped. Casy looked down at the old man's face and saw that it was turning a blackish purple. Sairy touched Casy's shoulder. She whispered, "His tongue, his tongue, his tongue."

Casy nodded. "Get in front a Granma." He pried the tight jaws apart and reached into the old man's throat for the tongue. And as he lifted it clear, a rattling breath came out, and a sobbing breath was indrawn. Casy found a stick on the ground and held down the tongue with it, and the uneven breath rattled in and out.

Granma hopped about like a chicken. "Pray," she said. "Pray, you. Pray, I tell ya." Sairy tried to hold her back. "Pray, goddamn you!" Granma cried.

Casy looked up at her for a moment. The rasping breath came louder and more unevenly. "Our Father who art in Heaven, hallowed be Thy name—"

"Glory!" shouted Granma.

"Thy kingdom come, Thy will be done—on earth—as it is in Heaven."

"Amen."

A long gasping sigh came from the open mouth, and then a crying release of air.

"Give us this day—our daily bread—and forgive us—" The breathing had stopped. Casy looked down into Grampa's eyes and they were clear and deep and penetrating, and there was a knowing serene look in them.

"Hallelujah!" said Granma. "Go on."

"Amen," said Casy.

Granma was still then. And outside the tent all the noise had stopped. A car whished by on the highway. Casy still knelt on the floor beside the mattress. The people outside were listening, standing quietly intent on the sounds of dying. Sairy took Granma by the arm and led her outside, and Granma moved with dignity and held her head high. She walked for the family and held her head straight for the family. Sairy took her to a mattress lying on the ground and sat her down on it. And Granma looked straight ahead, proudly, for she was on show now. The tent was still, and at last Casy spread the tent flaps with his hands and stepped out.

Pa asked softly, "What was it?"

"Stroke," said Casy. "A good quick stroke."

Life began to move again. The sun touched the horizon and flattened over it. And along the highway there came a long line of huge freight trucks with red sides. They rumbled along, putting a little earthquake in the ground, and the standing exhaust pipes sputtered blue smoke from the Diesel oil. One man drove each truck, and his relief man slept in a bunk high up against the ceiling. But the trucks never stopped; they thundered day and night and the ground shook under their heavy march.

The family became a unit. Pa squatted down on the ground, and Uncle John beside him. Pa was the head of the family now. Ma stood beside him. Noah and Tom and Al squatted, and the preacher sat down, and then reclined on his elbow. Connie and Rose of Sharon walked at a distance. Now Ruthie and Winfield, clattering up with a bucket of water held between them, felt the change, and they slowed up and set down the bucket and moved quietly to stand with Ma.

Granma sat proudly, coldly, until the group was formed, until no one looked at her, and then she lay down and covered her face with her arm. The red sun set and left a shining twilight on the land, so that faces were bright in the evening and eyes shone in reflection of the sky. The evening picked up light where it could.

Pa said, "It was in Mr. Wilson's tent."

Uncle John nodded. "He loaned his tent."

"Fine friendly folks," Pa said softly.

Wilson stood by his broken car, and Sairy had gone to the mattress to sit beside Granma, but Sairy was careful not to touch her.

Pa called, "Mr. Wilson!" The man scuffed near and squatted down, and Sairy came and stood beside him. Pa said, "We're thankful to you folks."

"We're proud to help," said Wilson.

"We're beholden to you," said Pa.

"There's no beholden in a time of dying," said Wilson, and Sairy echoed him, "Never no beholden."

Al said, "I'll fix your car—me an' Tom will." And Al looked proud that he could return the family's obligation.

"We could use some help." Wilson admitted the retiring of the obligation.

Pa said, "We got to figger what to do. They's laws. You got to report a death, an' when you do that, they either take forty dollars for the undertaker or they take him for a pauper."

Uncle John broke in, "We never did have no paupers."

Tom said, "Maybe we got to learn. We never got booted off no land before, neither."

"We done it clean," said Pa. "There can't no blame be laid on us. We never took nothin' we couldn' pay; we never suffered no man's charity. When Tom here got in trouble we could hold up our heads. He only done what any man would a done."

"Then what'll we do?" Uncle John asked.

"We go in like the law says an' they'll come out for him. We on'y got a hundred an' fifty dollars. They take forty to bury Grampa an' we won't get to California—or else they'll bury him a pauper." The men stirred restively, and they studied the darkening ground in front of their knees.

Pa said softly, "Grampa buried his pa with his own hand, done it in dignity, an' shaped the grave nice with his own shovel. That was a time when a man had the right to be buried by his own son an' a son had the right to bury his own father."

"The law says different now," said Uncle John.

"Sometimes the law can't be foller'd no way," said Pa. "Not in decency, anyways. They's lots a times you can't. When Floyd was loose an' goin' wild, law said we got to give him up—an' nobody give him up. Sometimes a fella got to sift the law. I'm sayin' now I got the right to bury my own pa. Anybody got somepin to say?"

The preacher rose high on his elbow. "Law changes," he said, "but 'got to's' go on. You got the right to do what you got to do."

Pa turned to Uncle John. "It's your right too, John. You got any word against?"

"No word against," said Uncle John. "On'y it's like hidin' him in the night. Grampa's way was t'come out a-shootin'."

Pa said ashamedly, "We can't do like Grampa done. We got to get to California 'fore our money gives out."

Tom broke in, "Sometimes fellas workin' dig up a man an' then they raise hell an' figger he been killed. The gov'ment's got more interest in a dead man than a live one. They'll go hell-scrapin' tryin' to fin' out who he was and how he died. I offer we put a note of writin' in a bottle an' lay it with Grampa, tellin' who he is an' how he died, an' why he's buried here."

Pa nodded agreement. "Tha's good. Wrote out in a nice han'. Be not so lonesome too, knowin' his name is there with 'im, not jus' a old fella lonesome underground. Any more stuff to say?" The circle was silent.

Pa turned his head to Ma. "You'll lay 'im out?"

"I'll lay 'im out," said Ma. "But who's to get supper?"

Sairy Wilson said, "I'll get supper. You go right ahead. Me an' that big girl of yourn."

"We sure thank you," said Ma. "Noah, you get into them kegs an' bring out some nice pork. Salt won't be deep in it yet, but it'll be right nice eatin'."

"We got a half sack a potatoes," said Sairy.

Ma said, "Gimme two half-dollars." Pa dug in his pocket and gave her the silver. She found the basin, filled it full of water, and went into the tent. It was nearly dark in there. Sairy came in and lighted a candle and stuck it upright on a box and then she went out. For a moment Ma looked down at the dead old man. And then in pity she tore a strip from her own apron and tied up his jaw. She straightened his limbs, folded his hands over his chest. She held his eyelids down and laid a silver piece on each one. She buttoned his shirt and washed his face.

Sairy looked in, saying, "Can I give you any help?"

Ma looked slowly up. "Come in," she said. "I like to talk to ya."

"That's a good big girl you got," said Sairy. "She's right in peelin' potatoes. What can I do to help?"

"I was gonna wash Grampa all over," said Ma, "but he got no other clo'es to put on. An' 'course your quilt's spoilt. Can't never get the smell a death from a quilt. I seen a dog growl an' shake at a mattress my ma died on, an' that was two years later. We'll wrop 'im in your quilt. We'll make it up to you. We got a quilt for you."

Sairy said, "You shouldn' talk like that. We're proud to help. I ain't felt so—safe in a long time. People needs—to help."

Ma nodded. "They do," she said. She looked long into the old whiskery face, with its bound jaw and silver eyes shining in the candlelight. "He ain't gonna look natural. We'll wrop him up."

"The ol' lady took it good."

"Why, she's so old," said Ma, "maybe she don't even rightly know what happened. Maybe she won't really know for quite a while. Besides, us folks takes a pride holdin' in. My pa used to say, 'Anybody can break down. It takes a man not to.' We always try to hold in." She folded the quilt neatly about Grampa's legs and around his shoulders. She brought the corner of the quilt over his head like a cowl and pulled it down over his face. Sairy handed her half-a-dozen big safety pins, and she pinned the quilt neatly and tightly about the long package. And at last she stood up. "It won't be a bad burying," she said. "We got a preacher to see him in, an' his folks is all aroun'." Suddenly she swayed a little, and Sairy went to her and steadied her. "It's sleep—" Ma said in a shamed tone. "No, I'm awright. We been so busy gettin' ready, you see."

"Come out in the air," Sairy said.

"Yeah, I'm all done here." Sairy blew out the candle and the two went out.

A bright fire burned in the bottom of the little gulch. And Tom, with sticks and wire, had made supports from which two kettles hung and bubbled furiously, and good steam poured out under the lids. Rose of Sharon knelt on the ground out of range of the burning heat, and she had a long spoon in her hand. She saw Ma come out of the tent, and she stood up and went to her.

"Ma," she said. "I got to ask."

"Scared again?" Ma asked. "Why, you can't get through nine months without sorrow."

"But will it—hurt the baby?"

Ma said, "They used to be a sayin', 'A chile born outa sorrow'll be a happy chile.' Isn't that so, Mis' Wilson?"

"I heard it like that," said Sairy. "An' I heard the other: 'Born outa too much joy'll be a doleful boy.' "

"I'm all jumpy inside," said Rose of Sharon.

"Well, we ain't none of us jumpin' for fun," said Ma. "You jes' keep watchin' the pots."

On the edge of the ring of firelight the men had gathered. For tools they had a shovel and a mattock. Pa marked out the ground—eight feet long and three feet wide. The work went on in relays. Pa chopped the earth with the mattock and then Uncle John shoveled it out. Al chopped and Tom shoveled, Noah chopped and Connie shoveled. And the hole drove down, for the work never diminished in speed. The shovels of dirt flew out of the hole in quick spurts. When Tom was shoulder keep in the rectangular pit, he said, "How deep, Pa?"

"Good an' deep. A couple feet more. You get out now, Tom, and get that paper wrote."

Tom boosted himself out of the hole and Noah took his place. Tom went to Ma, where she tended the fire. "We got any paper an' pen, Ma?"

Ma shook her head slowly, "No-o. That's one thing we didn' bring." She tooked toward Sairy. And the little woman walked quickly to her tent. She brought back a Bible and a half pencil. "Here," she said. "They's a clear page in front. Use that an' tear it out." She handed book and pencil to Tom.

Tom sat down in the firelight. He squinted his eyes in concentration, and at last wrote slowly and carefully on the end paper in big clear letters: "This here is William James Joad, dyed of a stroke, old old man. His fokes bured him becaws they got no money to pay for funerls. Nobody kilt him. Jus a stroke an he dyed." He stopped. "Ma, listen to this here." He read it slowly to her.

"Why, that soun's nice," she said. "Can't you stick on somepin from Scripture so it'll be religious? Open up an' git a-sayin' somepin outa Scripture."

"Got to be short," said Tom. "I ain't got much room lef' on the page."

Sairy said, "How 'bout 'God have mercy on his soul'?"

"No," said Tom. "Sounds too much like he was hung. I'll copy somepin." He turned the pages and read, mumbling his lips, saying the words under his breath. "Here's a good short one," he said. " 'An' Lot said unto them, Oh, not so, my Lord.' "

"Don't mean nothin'," said Ma. "Long's you're gonna put one down, it might's well mean somepin."

Sairy said, "Turn to Psalms, over further. You kin always get somepin outa Psalms."

Tom flipped the pages and looked down the verses. "Now here *is* one," he said. "This here's a nice one, just blowed full a religion: 'Blessed is he whose transgression is forgiven, whose sin is covered.' How's that?"

"That's real nice," said Ma. "Put that one in."

Tom wrote it carefully. Ma rinsed and wiped a fruit jar and Tom screwed the lid down tight on it. "Maybe the preacher ought to wrote it," he said.

Ma said, "No, the preacher wan't no kin." She took the jar from him and went into the dark tent. She unpinned the covering and slipped the fruit jar in under the thin cold hands and pinned the comforter tight again. And then she went back to the fire.

The men came from the grave, their faces shining with perspiration. "Awright," said Pa. He and John and Noah and Al went into the tent, and they came out carrying the long, pinned bundle between them. They carried it to the grave. Pa leaped into the hole and received the bundle in his arms and laid it gently down. Uncle John put out a hand and helped Pa out of the hole. Pa asked, "How about Granma?"

"I'll see," Ma said. She walked to the mattress and looked down at the old woman for a moment. Then she went back to the grave. "Sleepin'," she said. "Maybe she'd hold it against me, but I ain't a-gonna wake her up. She's tar'd."

Pa said, "Where at's the preacher? We oughta have a prayer."

Tom said, "I seen him walkin' down the road. He don't like to pray no more."

"Don't like to pray?"

"No," said Tom. "He ain't a preacher no more. He figgers it ain't right to fool people actin' like a preacher when he ain't a preacher. I bet he went away so nobody wouldn' ast him."

Casy had come quietly near, and he heard Tom speaking. "I didn' run away," he said. "I'll he'p you folks, but I won't fool ya."

Pa said, "Won't you say a few words? Ain't none of our folks ever been buried without a few words."

"I'll say 'em," said the preacher.

Connie led Rose of Sharon to the graveside, she reluctant. "You got to," Connie said. "It ain't decent not to. It'll jus' be a little."

The firelight fell on the grouped people, showing their faces and their eyes, dwindling on their dark clothes. All the hats were off now. The light danced, jerking over the people.

Casy said, "It'll be a short one." He bowed his head, and the others followed his lead. Casy said solemnly, "This here ol' man jus' lived a life an' jus' died out of it. I don' know whether he was good or bad, but that don't matter much. He was alive, an' that's what matters. An' now he's dead, an' that don't matter. Heard a fella tell a poem one time, an' he says 'All that lives is holy.' Got to thinkin', an' purty soon it means more than the words says. An' I wouldn' pray for a ol' fella that's dead. He's awright. He got a job to do, but it's all laid out for 'im an' there's on'y one way to do it. But us, we got a job to do, an' they's a thousan' ways, an' we don' know which one to take. An' if I was to pray, it'd be for the folks that don' know which way to turn. Grampa here, he got the easy straight. An' now cover 'im up and let 'im get to his work." He raised his head.

Pa said, "Amen," and the others muttered, "A-men." Then Pa took the shovel, half filled it with dirt, and spread it gently into the black hole. He handed the shovel to Uncle John, and John dropped in a shovelful. Then the shovel went from hand to hand until every man had his turn. When all had taken their duty and their right, Pa attacked the mound of loose dirt and hurriedly filled the hole. The women moved back to the fire to see to supper. Ruthie and Winfield watched, absorbed.

Ruthie said solemnly, "Grampa's down under there." And Winfield looked at her with horrified eyes. And then he ran away to the fire and sat on the ground and sobbed to himself.

Pa half filled the hole, and then he stood panting with the effort while Uncle John finished it. And John was shaping up the mound when Tom stopped him. "Listen," Tom said. " 'F we leave a grave, they'll have it open in no time. We got to hide it. Level her off an' we'll strew dry grass. We got to do that."

Pa said, "I didn' think a that. It ain't right to leave a grave unmounded."

"Can't he'p it," said Tom. "They'd dig 'im right up, an' we'd get it for breakin' the law. You know what I get if I break the law."

"Yeah," Pa said. "I forgot that." He took the shovel from John and leveled the grave. "She'll sink, come winter," he said.

"Can't he'p that," said Tom. "We'll be a long ways off by winter. Tromp her in good, an' we'll strew stuff over her."

When the pork and potatoes were done the families sat about on the ground and ate, and they were quiet, staring into the fire. Wilson, tearing a slab of meat with his teeth, sighed with contentment. "Nice eatin' pig," he said.

"Well," Pa explained, "we had a couple shoats, an' we thought we might's well eat 'em. Can't get nothin' for them. When we get kinda use' ta movin' an' Ma can set up bread, why, it'll be pretty nice, seein' the country an' two kags a' pork right in the truck. How long you folks been on the road?"

Wilson cleared his teeth with his tongue and swallowed. "We ain't been lucky," he said. "We been three weeks from home."

"Why, God Awmighty, we aim to be in California in ten days or less."

Al broke in, "I dunno, Pa. With that load we're packin', we maybe ain't never gonna get there. Not if they's mountains to go over."

They were silent about the fire. Their faces were turned downward and their hair and foreheads showed in the firelight. Above the little dome of the firelight the summer stars shone thinly, and the heat of the day was gradually withdrawing. On her mattress, away from the fire, Granma whimpered softly like a puppy. The heads of all turned in her direction.

Ma said, "Rosasharn, like a good girl go lay down with Granma. She needs somebody now. She's knowin', now."

Rose of Sharon got to her feet and walked to the mattress and lay beside the old woman, and the murmur of their soft voices drifted to the fire. Rose of Sharon and Granma whispered together on the mattress.

Noah said, "Funny thing is—losin' Grampa ain't made me feel no different than I done before. I ain't no sadder than I was."

"It's just the same thing," Casy said. "Grampa an' the old place, they was jus' the same thing."

Al said, "It's a goddamn shame. He been talkin' what he's gonna do, how he gonna squeeze grapes over his head an' let the juice run in his whiskers, an' all stuff like that."

Casy said, "He was foolin', all the time. I think he knowed it. An' Grampa didn' die tonight. He died the minute you took 'im off the place."

"You sure a that?" Pa cried.

"Why, no. Oh, he was breathin'," Casy went on, "but he was dead. He was that place, an' he knowed it."

Uncle John said, "Did you know he was a-dyin'?"

"Yeah," said Casy. "I knowed it."

John gazed at him, and a horror grew in his face. "An' you didn' tell nobody?"

"What good?" Casy asked.

"We—we might of did somepin."

"What?"

"I don' know, but—"

"No," Casy said, "you couldn' a done nothin'. Your way was fixed an' Grampa didn' have no part in it. He didn' suffer none. Not after fust thing this mornin'. He's jus' stayin' with the lan'. He couldn' leave it."

Uncle John sighed deeply.

Wilson said, "We hadda leave my brother Will." The heads turned toward him. "Him an' me had forties side by side. He's older'n me. Neither one ever drove a car. Well, we went in an' we sol' ever'thing. Will, he bought a car, an' they give him a kid to show 'im how to use it. So the afternoon 'fore we're gonna start, Will an' Aunt Minnie go a-practicin'. Will, he comes to a bend in the road an' he yells "Whoa' an' yanks back, an' he goes through a fence. An' he yells 'Whoa, you bastard,' an' tromps down on the gas an' goes over into a gulch. An' there he was. Didn't have nothin' more to sell an' didn't have no car. But it were his own damn fault, praise God. He's so damn mad he won't come along with us, jus' set there a-cussin' an' a-cussin'."

"What's he gonna do?"

"I dunno. He's too mad to figger. An' we couldn' wait. On'y had eighty-five dollars to go on. We couln' set an' cut it up, but we et it up anyways. Didn' go a hundred mile when a tooth in the rear end bust, an' cost thirty dollars to get her fix', an' then we got to get a tire, an' then a spark plug cracked, an' Sairy got sick. Had ta stop ten days. An' now the goddamn car is bust again, an' money's gettin' low. I dunno when we'll ever get to California. 'F I could on'y fix a car, but I don' know nothin' about cars."

Al asked importantly, "What's the matter?"

"Well, she jus' don't run. Starts an' farts an' stops. In a minute she'll start again, an' then 'fore you can git her goin', she peters out again."

"Runs a minute an' then dies?"

"Yes, sir. An' I can't keep her a-goin' no matter how much gas I give her. Got worse an' worse, an' now I cain't get her a-movin' a-tall."

Al was very proud and very mature, then. "I think you got a plugged gas line. I'll blow her out for ya."

And Pa was proud too. "He's a good hand with a car," Pa said.

"Well, I'll sure thank ya for a han'. I sure will. Makes a fella kinda feel—like a little kid, when he cain't fix nothin'. When we get to California I aim to get me a nice car. Maybe she won't break down."

Pa said, "When we get there. Gettin' there's the trouble."

"Oh, but she's worth it," said Wilson. "Why, I seen han'bills how they need folks to pick fruit, an' good wages. Why, jus' think how it's gonna be, under them shady trees a-pickin' fruit an' takin' a bite ever' once in a while. Why, hell, they don't care how much you eat 'cause they got so much. An' with them good wages, maybe a fella can get hisself a little piece a land an' work out for extra cash. Why, hell, in a couple years I bet a fella could have a place of his own."

Pa said, "We seen them han'bills. I got one right here." He took out his purse and from it took a folded orange handbill. In black type it said, "Pea Pickers Wanted in California. Good Wages All Season. 800 Pickers Wanted."

Wilson looked at it curiously. "Why, that's the one I seen. The very same one. You s'pose—maybe they got all eight hunderd awready?"

Pa said, "This is jus' one little part a California. Why, that's the secon' biggest State we got. S'pose they did get all them eight hunderd. They's plenty places else. I rather pick fruit anyways. Like you says, under them trees an' pickin' fruit—why, even the kids'd like to do that."

Suddenly Al got up and walked to the Wilsons' touring car. He looked in for a moment and then came back and sat down.

"You can't fix her tonight," Wilson said.

"I know. I'll get her in the morning."

Tom had watched his young brother carefully. "I was thinkin' somepin like that myself," he said.

Noah asked, "What you two fellas talkin' about?"

Tom and Al went silent, each waiting for the other. "You tell 'em," Al said finally.

"Well, maybe it's no good, an' maybe it ain't the same thing Al's thinking. Here she is, anyways. We got a overload, but Mr. and Mis' Wilson ain't. If some of us folks could ride with them an' take some of their light stuff in the truck, we wouldn't break no springs an' we could git up hills. An' me an' Al both knows about a car, so we could keep that car a-rollin'. We'd keep together on the road an' it'd be good for ever'body."

Wilson jumped up. "Why, sure. Why, we'd be proud. We certain'y would. You hear that, Sairy?"

"It's a nice thing," said Sairy. "Wouldn' be a burden on you folks?"

"No, by God," said Pa. "Wouldn't be no burden at all. You'd be helpin' us."

Wilson settled back uneasily. "Well, I dunno."

"What's a matter, don' you wanta?"

"Well, ya see— I on'y got 'bout thirty dollars lef', an' I won't be no burden."

Ma said, "You won't be no burden. Each'll help each, an' we'll all git to California. Sairy Wilson he'ped lay Grampa out," and she stopped. The relationship was plain.

Al cried, "That car'll take six easy. Say me to drive, an' Rosasharn an' Connie and Granma. Then we take the big light stuff an' pile her on the truck. An' we'll trade off ever' so often." He spoke loudly, for a load of worry was lifted from him.

They smiled shyly and looked down at the ground. Pa fingered the dusty earth with his fingertips. He said, "Ma favors a white house with oranges growin' around. They's a big pitcher on a calendar she seen."

Sairy said, "If I get sick again, you got to go on an' get there. We ain't a-goin' to burden."

Ma looked carefully at Sairy, and she seemed to see for the first time the pain-tormented eyes and the face that was haunted and shrinking with pain. And Ma said, "We gonna see you get through. You said yourself, you can't let help go unwanted."

Sairy studied her wrinkled hands in the firelight. "We got to get some sleep tonight." She stood up.

"Grampa—it's like he's dead a year," Ma said.

The families moved lazily to their sleep, yawning luxuriously. Ma sloshed the tin plates off a little and rubbed the grease free with a flour sack. The fire died down and the stars descended. Few passenger cars went by on the highway now, but the transport trucks thundered by at intervals and put little earthquakes in the ground. In the ditch the cars were hardly visible under the starlight. A tied dog howled at the service station down the road. The families were quiet and sleeping, and the field mice grew bold and scampered about among the mattresses. Only Sairy Wilson was awake. She stared into the sky and braced her body firmly against pain.

The Heroism of Ensign Schiff

From DELILAH

By Marcus Goodrich

The heroine of this novel is an old destroyer of the United States Navy. The scene is the Pacific before the first World War. For months Delilah's overtaxed captain and crew have driven her through tropic waters on various missions and are finally ordered into the Philippines for overhauling. Two of her men, Mendel and Warrington, are assigned to a submarine for temporary duty and Lieutenant Fitzpatrick, Delilah's engineering officer, envies them the transfer as he watches the submarine fleet put out to sea. Because of his strong affection for Warrington, despite the barrier of rank, he feels a personal loss in the boy's departure.

Every page of this novel is powerful evidence that only a man who has lived aboard a warship at sea can properly write of its men and the secret life they share. The chosen passage is important because its portrait of a heroic naval officer is not sentimentalized. Ensign Schiff, the submarine's skipper, has been schooled like all good naval officers in the belief that "the ship comes first." His heroism, and his magnificent performance of his duty, spring from this conviction.

LIEUTENANT FITZPATRICK, at a quarter to nine the next morning, stood at the end of the dock, near Delilah's stern, and watched the little submarines lumber out through the breakwater toward Corregidor. There were four of them, one behind the other at about hundred yard intervals, struggling and foaming along in the quiet brown water of the bay like over-fat grey pigs with awninged howdahs on their slightly awash backs. To Lieutenant Fitzpatrick, they appeared some-

how clean and definite out there under the sun-blue morning sky. He
glanced around at the greasy, splintered dock on which he stood, now
completely denuded of the greenery that had transformed it, and then
at the dishevelled ship alongside him. It looked rusty and deserted
despite the animal-like little workmen crawling about it. He moved his
shoulders restlessly. He would, he thought, like to serve in a submarine
. . . "not in one of those Noah's Arks out there . . . they could barely
creep along . . . but in a capable, modern one . . . like one of those
fast K-Boats at Pearl Harbour . . . That would be real Navy . . . on
one's own with a handful of picked men in the depths of the sea." He
glanced reluctantly at his own ship. ". . . just a God damn coal barge
when you came right down to it . . . ferrying back and forth." With
a sense of futility that spread in calm malignancy into every reach of
his being, he glanced out again over the muddy glitter of the bay. The
last submarine in line had fallen a considerable distance behind. He
watched mechanically as it gradually lost headway and relaxed into a
stupid rolling and drifting with the almost invisible motion of the
placid water. "Break-down," he guessed, ". . . The whole, stinking,
antiquated Fleet is breaking down." He wondered if any of the men he
had transferred were on her. "Must be hot as hell drifting out there in
that blistering calm . . . A lot of help Warrington would be to them
in this fix if that was the one he was on." The water splashed restively
around the piling beneath his feet. Through the wide cracks in the plank-
ing a stench of some floating dead thing thrust vaguely up at him. "Every
man on those boats has to fit in and do more than his share . . . no
room for excess baggage there . . . only twelve or so men . . . and all
of them crowded into one little compartment along with everything else,
torpedoes, engines, tools, ballast, periscope, storage batteries, men . . ."
     The submarine, which now had been left far behind by the others in
the assurance that if she could not continue on she could signal the
Base for a tow, drifted into such position that Lieutenant Fitzpatrick
could make out the number on her. "Schiff's boat . . . Ensign Schiff,
phooey! . . . it would be his boat that broke down . . . a Jew had no
business being a naval officer . . . much less in command of a vessel
. . . Schiff was clever as hell, you had to hand him that . . . but their
guts and blood were sour . . . no iron in them . . . they . . ." Lieutenant Fitzpatrick's hand had come quickly up to shade his eyes, which
had levelled in a stare of amazement. Out there three men had been
spat abruptly up into the air from the conning-tower in the most ridiculous fashion. Like acrobatic clowns in a vaudeville act, they sprawled
laughably for a moment in the air between the submarine and the
blazing sun. Then they splashed successively into the water. He watched
for them to swim back to the submarine; but there seemed to be no

movement where they had fallen. There was no movement on the submarine either, not a sign of a man between the four stanchions that had held the small awning. The awning had disappeared too: Only a ragged wisp hung at the tip of each stanchion where its corners had been fastened. The submarine was moving, moving uncertainly and very slowly in a meaningless direction, moving, he thought, through the still heat like an abandoned derelict in a light breeze. Suddenly Lieutenant Fitzpatrick began to shout, nearly screaming as if under the assault of some desperate awakening.

"Man overboard! . . . Man overboard! . . . Get away the lifeboat!"

"No, by God, that wasn't it," he told himself. "Explosion! . . . that's what it was . . . that thing had exploded without a sound, without a puff of smoke!" Lieutenant Fitzpatrick swung around and faced the men that were springing toward him along the dock.

"Get away the Rescue Party! . . . Explosion on submarine six hundred yards due north!"

A number of men automatically followed him as he leapt from the dock onto Delilah and made for the starboard whaleboat, which still hung forlornly at its davits. Most of the men on the dock, however, had been thrown into helpless confusion by the officer's shouts. Nobody knew what to do marooned there out of the ship on the cluttered dock. The regularly organized Rescue Party had been broken up by the tranfers . . . "Who goes? . . . Where's the boat? . . . What gear? . . . What tools?" Cruck, the Chief Boatswain's Mate, had swung out, in response to the officer's order, "A-w-a-y-y-y the Rescue Party!" in a chant that had been heard clearly far beyond the limits of the dock and which had alarmed that whole section of the Base into concerned alertness; but around him men did nothing but shout back uncertainly and mill towards a view of the bay. Cruck grabbed Wright by the throat and flung him ferociously towards Delilah. The Seaman's pimpled face crashed stunningly against a railing stanchion as he grabbed frantically to keep himself from falling into the narrow crevice between the ship and the dock. His dirty hands groped childishly at his straw-coloured hair as his stunned senses struggled with the meaning in the bellowing behind him:

"Lay aft the Rescue Party! . . . Lay aft all hands! . . . The starboard whaleboat, you dirty bastards! . . . *move!*"

The men had stood there, a sweating, wildly disturbed mob, frustrated in the face of Cruck's uninforming violence, until he uttered the words, "all hands" and "starboard whaleboat." Then they charged at the ship as if, like Wright, they had been flung there.

Lieutenant Fitzpatrick and those who had followed him had gotten the boat down in the water. Forsythe, the Seaman, stood in the bow fending her off with a boat-hook. Easterly, the Fireman, Second-Class, was at the stern, awkwardly holding her in by clutching at one of Delilah's open port-holes. The officer, a thick streak of grease disfiguring his white cap-cover, balanced himself on spread legs in the middle of the whaleboat and with grim impatience fixed his eyes in the direction from which, on the other side of the ship, came the fury of Cruck's shouting. All at once the whole ship's company flooded across the ship and massed at the railing above him, a great, arrested wave of staring eyes. His gaze met, for an instant, that of a man in the crowd. He lashed an order at these eyes, an order that was fatalistic rather than calm:

"Get an axe" . . . Then to another pair of eyes: "Get a fire extinguisher" . . . Another: "Get a bucket" . . . "sledge" . . . "bar" . . . "line" . . . But he was thinking: "Warrington's on that boat . . . it couldn't be any other way . . . that's the way life works . . . Christ!"

After Chief Machinist's Mate Stengle had climbed down, armed with a Stillson wrench and a hacksaw, the boat started to pull away; but when Lieutenant Fitzpatrick saw Heller, the Pharmacist's Mate, fighting his way through the crowd at the rail, he ordered the boat to back water . . . "Got to have this man, God damn him." The Pharmacist's Mate, who evidently had been taking a bath, was wet and naked save for a pair of drawers and his emergency kit slung by a strap over his shoulder. Even at that, for two or three minutes Delilah's boat, badly manned and overloaded, was the only one on the way to the submarine, which still was circling slowly in the smooth water like a small whale tortured into imbecile helplessness by the relentless sun.

When they were some three hundred yards from the stricken craft, the atmosphere of being abandoned that pervaded it was abruptly dissipated by the figure of a man emerging from the small, black hole of the conning-tower hatch. Out waist high, he bent at the middle in an eerie manner and writhed face down across the bulge of the submarine's top-side into the water. Those pulling at the oars in the whaleboat could not, of course, see this; but the cry that arose from the others in the boat, a cry of consternation and discovery, empowered their pulling with furious desperation. That helpless figure sliding awkwardly, blindly into the sea there had slugged through the abstraction of disaster with the personal reality of tortured men trying to claw their way up out of frightful confinement. Another blind figure arose from the submarine's hatch, tottered around for an instant as if trying to locate the water, then leapt insanely as if trusting to chance. The unseen splash of his body, counterpointed by the involuntary sounds this tore from the mouths of men who could see it, shattered the self-control of some of those at the oars. Easterly, the Fireman, Second-Class, missed the water altogether with his blade. Confusion swept the stroke of the six oarsmen behind whose backs something horrible was happening. Easterly fought viciously with the oar defying his sweaty, blistering hands and screamed silently against the injustice of his own incompetence and the fate that had driven him into this intolerable corner: He never had touched an oar more than a dozen times in his life.

Lieutenant Fitzpatrick had begun to shout the stroke:

"Pull! . . . Pull! . . . Pull! . . ." The officer's eyes were clutching at the figures in the water. ". . . Stroke! . . . Stroke! . . . (He probably was pinned inside the thing) . . . Stroke! . . ."

It occurred to Easterly to heave the oar that was defeating him over the side. As he did so, he flung his head around in a reckless, relieving gesture that permitted him to see behind him . . . "The hell with the God damn oar! . . . Doing more harm than good with it anyway." However, the instant he had adjusted himself to the scene behind him, he semi-consciously leapt at the idea of some compensatory act, something that would assuage his own agony under the pressure of the horror only a few yards away there that he just had betrayed by flinging away his oar. As a result of his defection the boat had swung off its course, almost broadside to the direction in which the submarine slowly was moving. In the intervening strip of water, near the whaleboat, his searching eyes found a head and an arm. Further disrupting the efforts of the oarsmen to get reorganized, he stood up in the boat pointing wildly and trying to shout above the roar of recrimination that rose around him. He prepared to jump overboard after the man barely afloat in the water. Somebody knocked him back on the thwart. He arose again, was knocked back once more; and as the whaleboat was oared toward the figure in the water he crouched there, half out of the boat, every feature alive with frustration because he could not jump overboard after that man.

It was Lieutenant Fitzpatrick, leaning authoritatively far out from the stern, both hands extended eagerly, who got hold of the man. Mendel's head was denuded completely of hair, and the flesh of his skull and face had turned a strange, parboiled white. His hawklike nose was bulged out of shape, and the closed lids of his eyes had become very thick and purple. The officer grasped him violently under the armpits and shook him.

"Mendel! . . . Mendel!"

The line of the Jew's wide, sensuous mouth slowly changed its shape, like a small, torpid serpent that had been disturbed. His breath was coming and going with the sound of a jet of air fluttering a loose strip of membrane. Lieutenant Fitzpatrick half lifted him out of the water and, putting his mouth close to the Jew's ear, said:

"Where's Warrington? . . . Is he inside? . . . Did he get out?"

The Jew's wet face was a mask of unrestrained resignation and sub-mission, like the face of an invalid who has had enough of pain and of life. He partially opened his eyes for a moment to look at this face close to his as he said:

"He's on another boat."

In the spasm of exquisite relief and comfort that struck through Lieutenant Fitzpatrick, his hands and arms unconsciously relaxed, per-mitting Mendel to slip back into the muddy water. He simply sank beneath it without another movement, as if he somehow had expended the last fateful vestige of a pretext for remaining above it. The momen-tum of the whaleboat carried it several yards past where the Jew sank before those in the stern of the boat, including Lieutenant Fitzpatrick, himself, fully realized that nobody any longer had hold of him. The moment this generally was perceived, the oarsmen began to swing the boat back toward the spot. With a kind of ferocity Easterly once more prepared to dive into the water. Lieutenant Fitzpatrick now, however, insuperably was possessed with his obligation to the disaster as a whole; and from the depths of this obligation his voice, irresistible and calm, rose to hold the men back from their excited effort to return to Mendel. Into the face of their confused, unexpressed averseness he shouted, as he pointed astern at other small boats that were coming up swiftly:

"They'll get him."

When the whaleboat, dominated by the first real semblance of order that had prevailed since it had left Delilah's side, was almost upon the submarine, Lieutenant Fitzpatrick was astonished to see the stricken craft suddenly increase its speed. As if this had been a symptom of further disaster, he stared belligerently at the ominous little conning-tower expecting to see its dark mouth vomit more victims. The cry went up:

"It's going under!"

What it was doing was careening erratically around a turn of its un-guided course before the thrust of its greater speed. "If it would only turn this way," thought Lieutenant Fitzpatrick, "a man could jump onto her deck and take the wheel . . . steer her into the dock." He tried to direct the whaleboat across the submarine's new course, but in the very moment he thought he finally was intercepting her, she changed direction once more. If those other boats would only get up they could corner it! He glanced helplessly in their direction. The nearest boats had stopped to pick up the men in the water. One was hauling in a man whose glinting leg bone had been stripped of flesh by the plunge from the searing heat of the explosion into the water.

"Lay on those oars, damn you!" yelled Lieutenant Fitzpatrick.

The oarsmen did not hear him. They were semi-conscious under the desperation of their sustained effort. Their faces were red and dripping perspiration. Their teeth were clenched. They heaved at each stroke as if it were the last act of their lives. Lieutenant Fitzpatrick fixed his gaze in an agony of intensity on the small surface-steering-wheel, swinging helplessly first one way and then the other, on the deserted deck of that grey death-trap fleeing through the muddy water . . . If he watched its swing he might get an idea which way the thing was going to turn . . . it was getting farther and farther away . . . If only he could get a man at that wheel!

As if the fury of the wish he shot along his gaze at that forlorn little steering-wheel had a power too strong for reality and fate to resist, an apparition, a long, distorted object of blood and rags, and flesh that looked unreal in the sunlight, rose from the hatch of the submarine and crawled fumblingly on all fours to the steering post. Grasping the spokes of the wheel, it pulled itself upright, a horrible caricature sharply out-lined against the luminous background of the sky. It even straightened its shoulders in a grim and ridiculous gesture as if bracing itself for an ordeal; then it swung the wheel and the submarine headed for the break-water. A veritable scream of relief rose from the boats struggling to come up with him. Those nearest him shouted his name in frantic encourage-ment:

"Straight ahead, Mr. Schiff!" . . . "Stay with it, Schiff, old boy!" . . . "Schiff . . ."

Ensign Schiff did "stay with it." He stayed there at that wheel, a tall, gaunt figure, stiff and appalling, and steered his vessel through the breakwater entrance and straight at the Submarine Dock, steered her on and on in some miraculous fashion, the soiled, glistening skull his youthful head had become, in which only the aquiline nose still seemed to live, bent far back so that the eye sockets were aimed rigidly, sight-lessly up into the topmost depths of the glaring and pitiless sunshine.

The crowd of watchers lining the shore-lines of the Base, and those in the welter of boats in its wake, grunted spasmodically when the sub-marine finally crashed bow on into the Submarine Dock, grunted as if they had been a single individual struck violently in the stomach. Those on the dock grappled the submarine and made her fast. Then, for an instant, the rush aboard her of a Rescue Party was checked by the stench, acrid, fleshy, nauseating, that poured from the hole in that steel maw. In that instant, Ensign Schiff turned, holding onto the wheel behind him with one hand, and said to the people on the dock, speaking as a man speaks who has fought to hold his breath for a long time:

"Batteries . . . hydrogen . . . Get the men out please."

Then he swung slowly about and faced in the direction of the bunga-
low, not far away, where he lived with his wife. It seemed for a moment
as if he were about to walk off in that direction right across the intervening strip of water; but instead he sank reluctantly to his knees, then
onto his side, and pillowed his head on the odious thing that had been
his arm.

The Baby-Killer

From *THE HEART IS A LONELY HUNTER*

By Carson McCullers

The scene of The Heart is a Lonely Hunter is a southern mill town. Its chief character is a deaf-mute, Mr. Singer, a boarder in the Kelly home. Gradually this remarkable man becomes a reference point of serenity for the whole turbulent community and the lives of all the characters inevitably revolve around him.

The chosen passage is a crisis which brings disaster to the whole Kelly family. Mick, the oldest child, whose sensitiveness is disguised by her boy's clothes and tomboy manner, has a secret love for music and a mystic admiration for Mr. Singer. She is burdened and harassed by her three brothers, Ralph, Bubber and Bill for whom she feels responsible, and by her handicapped father and overworked mother. The arrogance of Mrs. Wilson, the Kelly's nearest neighbor, who constantly parades her "wonder-child" before the town, has bred a long bitterness among the poverty-stricken Kellys.

MICK," Bubber said. "I come to believe we all gonna drown."

It was true that it like to never quit raining. Mrs. Wells rode them back and forth to school in her car, and every afternoon they had to stay on the front porch or in the house. She and Bubber played Parcheesi and Old Maid and shot marbles on the living-room rug. It was nearing along toward Christmas time and Bubber began to talk about the Little Lord Jesus and the red bicycle he wanted Santa Claus to bring him. The rain was silver on the windowpanes and the sky was wet and cold and gray. The river rose so high that some of the factory

---

Copyright, 1940, by Carson Smith McCullers.

people had to move out of their houses. Then when it looked like the rain would keep on and on forever it suddenly stopped. They woke up one morning and the bright sun was shining. By afternoon the weather was almost warm as summer. Mick came home late from school and Bubber and Ralph and Spareribs were on the front sidewalk. The kids looked hot and sticky and their winter clothes had a sour smell. Bubber had his slingshot and a pocketful of rocks. Ralph sat up in his wagon, his hat crooked on his head, and he was fretful. Spareribs had his new rifle with him. The sky was a wonderful blue.

"We waited for you a long time, Mick," Bubber said. "Where you been?"

She jumped up the front steps three at a time and threw her sweater toward the hat rack. "Practicing on the piano in the gym."

Every afternoon she stayed after school for an hour to play. The gym was crowded and noisy because the girls' team had basketball games. Twice today she was hit on the head with the ball. But getting a chance to sit at a piano was worth any amount of knocks and trouble. She would arrange bunches of notes together until the sound came that she wanted. It was easier than she had thought. After the first two or three hours she figured out some sets of chords in the bass that would fit in with the main tune her right hand was playing. She could pick out almost any piece now. And she made up new music too. That was better than just copying tunes. When her hands hunted out these beautiful new sounds it was the best feeling she had ever known.

She wanted to learn how to read music already written down. Delores Brown had taken music lessons for five years. She paid Delores the fifty cents a week she got for lunch money to give her lessons. This made her very hungry all through the day. Delores played a good many fast, runny pieces—but Delores did not know how to answer all the questions she wanted to know. Delores only taught her about the different scales, the major and minor chords, the values of the notes, and such beginning rules as those.

Mick slammed the door of the kitchen stove. "This all we got to eat?"

"Honey, it the best I can do for you," Portia said.

Just cornpones and margarine. As she ate she drank a glass of water to help wash down the swallows.

"Quit acting so greedy. Nobody going to snatch it out your hand."

The kids still hung around in front of the house. Bubber had put his slingshot in his pocket and now he played with the rifle. Spareribs was ten years old and his father had died the month before and this had been his father's gun. All the smaller kids loved to handle that rifle. Every few minutes Bubber would haul the gun up to his shoulder. He took aim and made a loud *pow* sound.

"Don't monkey with the trigger," said Spareribs. "I got the gun loaded."

Mick finished the cornbread and looked around for something to do. Harry Minowitz was sitting on his front porch banisters with the newspaper. She was glad to see him. For a joke she threw up her arm and hollered to him, "Heil!"

But Harry didn't take it as a joke. He went into his front hall and shut the door. It was easy to hurt his feelings. She was sorry, because lately she and Harry had been right good friends. They had always played in the same gang when they were kids, but in the last three years he had been at Vocational while she was still in grammar school. Also he worked at part-time jobs. He grew up very suddenly and quit hanging around the back. and front yards with kids. Sometimes she could see him reading the paper in his bedroom or undressing late at night. In mathematics and history he was the smartest boy at Vocational. Often, now that she was in high school too, they would meet each other on the way home and walk together. They were in the same shop class, and once the teacher made them partners to assemble a motor. He read books and kept up with the newspapers every day. World politics were all the time on his mind. He talked slow, and sweat stood out on his forehead when he was very serious about something. And now she had made him mad with her.

"I wonder has Harry still got his gold piece," Spareribs said.

"What gold piece?"

"When a Jew boy is born they put a gold piece in the bank for him. That's what Jews do."

"Shucks. You got it mixed up," she said. "It's Catholics you're thinking about. Catholics buy a pistol for a baby soon as it's born. Some day the Catholics mean to start a war and kill everybody else."

"Nuns give me a funny feeling," Spareribs said. "It scares me when I see one on the street."

She sat down on the steps and laid her head on her knees. She went into the inside room. With her it was like there was two places—the inside room and the outside room. School and the family and the things that happened every day were in the outside room. Mister Singer was in both rooms. Foreign countries and plans and music were in the inside room. The songs she thought about were there. And the symphony. When she was by herself in this inside room the music she had heard that night after the party would come back to her. This symphony grew slow like a big flower in her mind. During the day sometimes, or when she had just waked up in the morning, a new part of the symphony would suddenly come to her. Then she would have to go into the inside room and listen to it many times and try to join it into the parts of the symphony she remembered. The inside room was a very private place. She could be in the middle of a house full of people and still feel like she was locked up by herself.

Spareribs stuck his dirty hand up to her eyes because she had been staring off at space. She slapped him.

"What is a nun?" Bubber asked.

"A Catholic lady," Spareribs said. "A Catholic lady with a big black dress that comes up over her head."

She was tired of hanging around with the kids. She would go to the library and look at pictures in the *National Geographic*. Photographs of all the foreign places in the world. Paris, France. And big ice glaciers. And the wild jungles in Africa.

"You kids see that Ralph don't get out in the street," she said.

Bubber rested the big rifle on his shoulder. "Bring me a story back with you."

It was like that kid had been born knowing how to read. He was only in the second grade but he loved to read stories by himself—and he never asked anybody else to read to him. "What kind you want this time?"

"Pick out some stories with something to eat in them. I like that one a whole lot about them German kids going out in the forest and coming to this house made out of all different kinds of candy and the witch. I like a story with something to eat in it."

"I'll look for one," said Mick.

"But I'm getting kinda tired of candy," Bubber said. "See if you can't bring me a story with something like a barbecue sandwich in it. But if you can't find none of them I'd like a cowboy story."

She was ready to leave when suddenly she stopped and stared. The kids stared too. They all stood still and looked at Baby Wilson coming down the steps of her house across the street.

"Ain't Baby cute!" said Bubber softly.

Maybe it was the sudden hot, sunny day after all those rainy weeks. Maybe it was because their dark winter clothes were ugly to them on an afternoon like this one. Anyway Baby looked like a fairy or something in the picture show. She had on her last year's soirée costume—with a little pink-gauze skirt that stuck out short and stiff, a pink body waist, pink dancing shoes, and even a little pink pocketbook. With her yellow hair she was all pink and white and gold—and so small and clean that it almost hurt to watch her. She prissed across the street in a cute way, but would not turn her face toward them.

"Come over here," said Bubber. "Lemme look at your little pink pocketbook—"

Baby passed them along the edge of the street with her head held to one side. She had made up her mind not to speak to them.

There was a strip of grass between the sidewalk and the street, and when Baby reached it she stood still for a second and then turned a handspring.

"Don't pay no mind to her," said Spareribs. "She always tries to show off. She's going down to Mister Brannon's café to get candy. He's her uncle and she gets it free."

Bubber rested the end of the rifle on the ground. The big gun was too heavy for him. As he watched Baby walk off down the street he kept pulling the straggly bangs of his hair. "That sure is a cute little pink pocketbook," he said.

"Her Mama always talks about how talented she is," said Spareribs. "She thinks she's gonna get Baby in the movies."

It was too late to go look at the *National Geographic*. Supper was almost ready. Ralph tuned up to cry and she took him off the wagon and put him on the ground. Now it was December, and to a kid Bubber's age that was a long time from summer. All last summer Baby had come out in that pink soirée costume and danced in the middle of the street. At first the kids would flock around and watch her, but soon they got tired of it. Bubber was the only one who would watch her as she came out to dance. He would sit on the curb and yell to her when he saw a car coming. He had watched Baby do her soirée dance a hundred times—but summer had been gone for three months and now it seemed new to him again.

"I sure do wish I had a costume," Bubber said.

"What kind do you want?"

"A real cool costume. A real pretty one made out of all different colors. Like a butterfly. That's what I want for Christmas. That and a bicycle!"

"Sissy," said Spareribs.

Bubber hauled the big rifle up to his shoulder again and took aim at a house across the street. "I'd dance around in my costume if I had one. I'd wear it every day to school."

Mick sat on the front steps and kept her eyes on Ralph. Bubber wasn't a sissy like Spareribs said. He just loved pretty things. She'd better not let old Spareribs get away with that.

"A person's got to fight for every single thing they get," she said slowly. "And I've noticed a lot of times that the farther down a kid comes in the family the better the kid really is. Youngest kids are always the toughest. I'm pretty hard 'cause I've a lot of them on top of me. Bubber—he looks sick, and likes pretty things, but he's got guts underneath that. If all this is true Ralph sure ought to be a real strong one when he's old enough to get around. Even though he's just seventeen months old I can read something hard and tough in that Ralph's face already."

Ralph looked around because he knew he was being talked about. Spareribs sat down on the ground and grabbed Ralph's hat off his head and shook it in his face to tease him.

"All right!" Mick said. "You know what I'll do to you if you start him to cry. You just better watch out."

Everything was quiet. The sun was behind the roofs of the houses and the sky in the west was purple and pink. On the next block there was the sound of kids skating. Bubber leaned up against a tree and he seemed to be dreaming about something. The smell of supper came out of the house and it would be time to eat soon.

"Lookit," Bubber said suddenly. "Here comes Baby again. She sure is pretty in the pink costume."

Baby walked toward them slowly. She had been given a prize box of popcorn candy and was reaching in the box for the prize. She walked in that same prissy, dainty way. You could tell that she knew they were all looking at her.

"Please, Baby—" Bubber said when she started to pass them. "Lemme see your little pink pocketbook and touch your pink costume."

Baby started humming a song to herself and did not listen. She passed by without letting Bubber play with her. She only ducked her head and grinned at him a little.

Bubber still had the big rifle up to his shoulder. He made a loud pow sound and pretended like he had shot. Then he called to Baby again— in a soft, sad voice like he was calling a little kitty. "Please Baby—Come here, Baby—"

He was too quick for Mick to stop him. She had just seen his hand on the trigger when there was the terrible *ping* of the gun. Baby crumpled down to the sidewalk. It was like she was nailed to the steps and couldn't move or scream. Spareribs had his arm up over his head.

Bubber was the only one that didn't realize. "Get up, Baby," he hollered. "I ain't mad with you."

It all happened in a second. The three of them reached Baby at the same time. She lay crumpled down on the dirty sidewalk. Her skirt was over her head, showing her pink panties and her little white legs. Her hands were open—in one there was the prize from the candy and in the other the pocketbook. There was blood all over her hair ribbon and the top of her yellow curls. She was shot in the head and her face was turned down toward the ground.

So much happened in a second. Bubber screamed and dropped the gun and ran. She stood with her hands up to her face and screamed too. Then there were many people. Her Dad was the first to get there. He carried Baby into the house.

"She's dead," said Spareribs. "She's shot through the eyes. I seen her face."

Mick walked up and down the sidewalk, and her tongue stuck in her mouth when she tried to ask was Baby killed. Mrs. Wilson came running down the block from the beauty parlor where she worked. She went into the house and came back out again. She walked up and down in the street, crying and pulling a ring on and off her finger. Then the ambulance came and the doctor went in to Baby. Mick followed him. Baby was lying on the bed in the front room. The house was quiet as a church.

Baby looked like a pretty little doll on the bed. Except for the blood she did not seem hurt. The doctor bent over and looked at her head. After he finished they took Baby out on a stretcher. Mrs. Wilson and her Dad got into the ambulance with her.

The house was still quiet. Everybody had forgotten about Bubber. He was nowhere around. An hour passed. Her Mama and Hazel and Etta and all the boarders waited in the front room. Mister Singer stood in the doorway. After a long time her Dad came home. He said Baby wouldn't die but that her skull was fractured. He asked for Bubber. Nobody knew where he was. It was dark outside. They called Bubber in the back yard and in the street. They sent Spareribs and some other boys out to hunt for him. It looked like Bubber had gone clear out of the neighborhood. Harry went around to a house where they thought he might be.

Her Dad walked up and down the front porch. "I never have whipped any of my kids yet," he kept saying. "I never believed in it. But I'm sure going to lay it onto that kid as soon as I get my hands on him."

Mick sat on the banisters and watched down the dark street. "I can manage Bubber. Once he comes back I can take care of him all right."

"You go out and hunt for him. You can find him better than anybody else."

As soon as her Dad said that she suddenly knew where Bubber was. In the back yard there was a big oak and in the summer they had built a tree house. They had hauled a big box up in this oak, and Bubber used to love to sit up in the tree house by himself. Mick left the family and the boarders on the front porch and walked back through the alley to the dark yard.

She stood for a minute by the trunk of the tree. "Bubber—," she said quietly. "It's Mick."

He didn't answer, but she knew he was there. It was like she could smell him. She swung up on the lowest branch and climbed slowly. She was really mad with that kid and would have to teach him a lesson. When she reached the tree house she spoke to him again—and still there wasn't any answer. She climbed into the big box and felt around the edges. At last she touched him. He was scrouged up in a corner and his legs were trembling. He had been holding his breath, and when she touched him the sobs and the breath came out all at once.

"I—I didn't mean Baby to fall. She was just so little and cute—seemed to me like I just had to take a pop at her."

Mick sat down on the floor of the tree house. "Baby's dead," she said. "They got a lot of people hunting for you."

Bubber quit crying. He was very quiet.

"You know what Dad's doing in the house?"

It was like she could hear Bubber listening.

"You know Warden Lawes—you heard him over the radio. And you know Sing Sing. Well, our Dad's writing a letter to Warden Lawes for him to be a little bit kind to you when they catch you and send you to Sing Sing."

The words were so awful-sounding in the dark that a shiver came over her. She could feel Bubber trembling.

"They got little electric chairs there—just your size. And when they turn on the juice you just fry up like a piece of burnt bacon. Then you go to Hell."

Bubber was squeezed up in the corner and there was not a sound from him. She climbed over the edge of the box to get down. "You better stay up here because they got policemen guarding the yard. Maybe in a few days I can bring you something to eat."

Mick leaned against the trunk of the oak tree. That would teach Bubber all right. She had always managed him and she knew more about that kid than anybody else. Once, about a year or two ago, he was always wanting to stop off behind bushes and pee and play with himself awhile. She had caught on to that pretty quick. She gave him a good slap every time it happened and in three days he was cured. Afterwards he never even peed normal like other kids—he held his hands behind him. She always had to nurse that Bubber and she could always manage him. In a little while she would go back up to the tree house and bring him in. After this he would never want to pick up a gun again in all his life.

There was still this dead feeling in the house. The boarders all sat on the front porch without talking or rocking in the chairs. Her Dad and her Mama were in the front room. Her Dad drank beer out of a bottle and walked up and down the floor. Baby was going to get well all right, so this worry was not about her. And nobody seemed to be anxious about Bubber. It was something else.

"That Bubber!" said Etta.

"I'm ashamed to go out of the house after this," Hazel said.

Etta and Hazel went into the middle room and closed the door. Bill was in his room at the back. She didn't want to talk with them. She stood around in the front hall and thought it over by herself.

Her Dad's footsteps stopped. "It was deliberate," he said. "It's not like the kid was just fooling with the gun and it went off by accident. Everybody who saw it said he took deliberate aim."

"I wonder when we'll hear from Mrs. Wilson," her Mama said.

"We'll hear plenty, all right!"

"I reckon we will."

Now that the sun was down the night was cold again like November. The people came in from the front porch and sat in the living-room— but nobody lighted a fire. Mick's sweater was hanging on the hat rack, so she put it on and stood with her shoulders bent over to keep warm. She thought about Bubber sitting out in the cold, dark tree house. He had really believed every word she said. But he sure deserved to worry some. He had nearly killed that Baby.

"Mick, can't you think of some place where Bubber might be?" her Dad asked.

"He's in the neighborhood, I reckon."

Her Dad walked up and down with the empty beer bottle in his hand. He walked like a blind man and there was sweat on his face. "The poor kid's scared to come home. If we could find him I'd feel better. I've never laid a hand on Bubber. He oughtn't be scared of me."

She would wait until an hour and a half was gone. By that time he would be plenty sorry for what he did. She always could manage that Bubber and make him learn.

After a while there was a big excitement in the house. Her Dad telephoned again to the hospital to see how Baby was, and in a few minutes Mrs. Wilson called back. She said she wanted to have a talk with them and would come to the house.

Her Dad still walked up and down the front room like a blind man. He drank three more bottles of beer. "The way it all happened she can sue my britches off. All she could get would be the house outside of the mortgage. But the way it happened we don't have any comeback at all."

Suddenly Mick thought about something. Maybe they would really try Bubber in court and put him in a children's jail. Maybe Mrs. Wilson would send him to reform school. Maybe they would really do something terrible to Bubber. She wanted to go out to the tree house right away and sit with him and tell him not to worry. Bubber was always so thin and little and smart. She would kill anybody that tried to send that kid out of the family. She wanted to kiss him and bite him because she loved him so much.

But she couldn't miss anything. Mrs. Wilson would be there in a few minutes and she had to know what was going on. Then she would run out and tell Bubber that all the things she said were lies. And he would really have learned the lesson he had coming to him.

A ten-cent taxicab drove up to the sidewalk. Everybody waited on the front porch, very quiet and scared. Mrs. Wilson got out of the taxi with Mister Brannon. She could hear her Dad grinding his teeth together in a nervous way as they came up the steps. They went into the front room and she followed along after them and stood in the doorway. Etta and Hazel and Bill and the boarders kept out of it.

"I've come to talk over all this with you," Mrs. Wilson said.

The front room looked tacky and dirty and she saw Mister Brannon notice everything. The mashed celluloid doll and the beads and junk Ralph played with were scattered on the floor. There was beer on her Dad's workbench, and the pillows on the bed where her Dad and Mama slept were right gray.

Mrs. Wilson kept pulling the wedding ring on and off her finger. By the side of her Mister Brannon was very calm. He sat with his legs crossed. His jaws were blue-black and he looked like a gangster in the movies. He had always had this grudge against her. He always spoke to her in this rough voice different from the way he talked to other people. Was it because he knew about the time she and Bubber swiped a pack of chewing gum off his counter? She hated him.

"It all boils down to this," said Mrs. Wilson. "Your kid shot my Baby in the head on purpose."

Mick stepped into the middle of the room. "No, he didn't," she said. "I was right there. Bubber had been aiming that gun at me and Ralph and everything around there. He just happened to aim it at Baby and his finger slipped. I was right there."

Mister Brannon rubbed his nose and looked at her in a sad way. She sure did hate him.

"I know how you all feel—so I want to come to the point right now."

Mick's Mama rattled a bunch of keys and her Dad sat very still with his big hands hanging over his knees.

"Bubber didn't have it in his mind beforehand," Mick said. "He just—"

Mrs. Wilson jabbed the ring on and off her finger. "Wait a minute.

I know how everything is. I could bring it to court and sue you for every cent you own."

Her Dad didn't have any expression on his face. "I tell you one thing," he said. "We don't have much to sue for. All we got is—"

"Just listen to me," said Mrs. Wilson. "I haven't come here with any lawyer to sue you. Bartholomew—Mister Brannon—and I talked it over when we came and we just about agree on the main points. In the first place, I want to do the fair, honest thing—and in the second place, I don't want Baby's name mixed up in no common lawsuit at her age."

There was not a sound and everybody in the room sat stiff in their chairs. Only Mister Brannon halfway smiled at Mick, but she squinted her eyes back at him in a tough way.

Mrs. Wilson was very nervous and her hand shook when she lighted a cigarette. "I don't want to have to sue you or anything like that. All I want is for you to be fair. I'm not asking you to pay for all the suffering and crying Baby went through with until they gave her something to sleep. There's not any pay that would make up for that. And I'm not asking you to pay for the damage this will do to her career and the plans we had made. She's going to have to wear a bandage for several months. She won't get to dance in the soirée—maybe there'll even be a little bald place on her head."

Mrs. Wilson and her Dad looked at each other like they was hypnotized. Then Mrs. Wilson reached around to her pocketbook and took out a slip of paper.

"The things you got to pay are just the actual price of what it will cost us in money. There's Baby's private room in the hospital and a private nurse until she can come home. There's the operating room and the doctor's bill—and for once I intend the doctor to be paid right away. Also, they shaved all Baby's hair off and you got to pay me for the permanent wave I took her to Atlanta to get—so when her hair grows back natural she can have another one. And there's the price of her costume and other little extra bills like that. I'll write all the items down just as soon as I know what they'll be. I'm trying to be just as fair and honest as I can, and you'll have to pay the total when I bring it to you."

Her Mama smoothed her dress over her knees and took a quick, short breath. "Seems to me like the children's ward would be a lot better than a private room. When Mick had pneumonia—"

"I said a private room."

Mister Brannon held out his white, stumpy hands and balanced them like they was on scales. "Maybe in a day or two Baby can move into a double room with some other kid."

Mrs. Wilson spoke hard-boiled. "You heard what I said. Long as your kid shot my Baby she certainly ought to have every advantage until she gets well."

"You're in your rights," her Dad said. "God knows we don't have anything now—but maybe I can scrape it up. I realize you're not trying to take advantage of us and I appreciate it. We'll do what we can."

She wanted to stay and hear everything that they said, but Bubber was on her mind. When she thought of him sitting up in the dark, cold tree house thinking about Sing Sing she felt uneasy. She went out of the room and down the hall toward the back door. The wind was blowing and the yard was very dark except for the yellow square that came from the light in the kitchen. When she looked back she saw Portia sitting at the table with her long, thin hands up to her face, very still. The yard was lonesome and the wind made quick, scary shadows and a mourning kind of sound in the darkness.

She stood under the oak tree. Then just as she started to reach for the first limb a terrible notion came over her. It came to her all of a sudden that Bubber was gone. She called him and he did not answer. She climbed quick and quiet as a cat.

"Say! Bubber!"

Without feeling in the box she knew he wasn't there. To make sure she got into the box and felt in all the corners. The kid was gone. He must have started down the minute she left. He was running away for sure now, and with a smart kid like Bubber it was no telling where they'd catch him.

She scrambled down the tree and ran to the front porch. Mrs. Wilson was leaving and they had all come out to the front steps with her.

"Dad!" she said. "We got to do something about Bubber. He's run away. I'm sure he left our block. We all got to get out and hunt him."

Nobody knew where to go or how to begin. Her Dad walked up and down the street, looking in all the alleys. Mister Brannon telephoned for a ten-cent taxi for Mrs. Wilson and then stayed to help with the hunt. Mister Singer sat on the banisters of the porch and he was the only person who kept calm. They all waited for Mick to plan out the best places to look for Bubber. But the town was so big and the little kid was so smart that she couldn't think what to do.

Maybe he had gone to Portia's house over in Sugar Hill. She went back into the kitchen where Portia was sitting at the table with her hands up to her face.

"I got this sudden notion he went down to your house. Help us hunt him."

"How come I didn't think of that! I bet a nickel my little scared Bubber been staying in my home all the time."

Mister Brannon had borrowed an automobile. He and Mister Singer and Mick's Dad got into the car with her and Portia. Nobody knew what Bubber was feeling except her. Nobody knew he had really run away like he was escaping to save his life.

Portia's house was dark except for the checkered moonlight on the floor. As soon as they stepped inside they could tell there was nobody in the two rooms. Portia lighted the front lamp. The rooms had a colored smell, and they were crowded with cut-out pictures on the walls and the lace table covers and lace pillows on the bed. Bubber was not there.

"He been here," Portia suddenly said. "I can tell somebody been in here."

Mister Singer found the pencil and piece of paper on the kitchen table. He read it quickly and then they all looked at it. The writing was round and scraggly and the smart little kid hadn't misspelled but one word. The note said:

> Dear Portia,
>   I gone to Florada. Tell every body.
> Yours truly,
Bubber Kelly

They stood around surprised and stumped. Her Dad looked out the doorway and picked his nose with his thumb in a worried way. They were all ready to pile in the car and ride toward the highway leading south.

"Wait a minute," Mick said. "Even if Bubber is seven years old he's got brains enough not to tell us where he's going if he wants to run away. That about Florida is just a trick."

"A trick?" her Dad said.

"Yeah. There only two places Bubber knows very much about. One is Florida and the other is Atlanta. Me and Bubber and Ralph have been on the Atlanta road many a time. He knows how to start there and that's where he's headed. He always talks about what he's going to do when he gets a chance to go to Atlanta."

They went out to the automobile again. She was ready to climb into the back seat when Portia pinched her on the elbow. "You know what Bubber done?" she said in a quiet voice. "Don't you tell nobody else, but my Bubber done also taken my gold earrings off my dresser. I never thought my Bubber would have done such a thing to me."

Mister Brannon started the automobile. They rode slow, looking up and down the streets for Bubber, headed toward the Atlanta road.

It was true that in Bubber there was a tough, mean streak. He was acting different today than he had ever acted before. Up until now he was always a quiet little kid who never really done anything mean.

When anybody's feelings were hurt it always made him ashamed and nervous. Then how come he could do all the things he had done today?

They drove very slow out the Atlanta road. They passed the last line of houses and came to the dark fields and woods. All along they had stopped to ask if anyone had seen Bubber. "Has a little barefooted kid in corduroy knickers been by this way?" But even after they had gone about ten miles nobody had seen or noticed him. The wind came in cold and strong from the open windows and it was late at night.

They rode a little farther and then went back toward town. Her Dad and Mister Brannon wanted to look up all the children in the second grade, but she made them turn around and go back on the Atlanta road again. All the while she remembered the words she had said to Bubber. About Baby being dead and Sing Sing and Warden Lawes. About the small electric chairs that were just his size, and Hell. In the dark the words had sounded terrible.

They rode very slow for about half a mile out of town, and then suddenly she saw Bubber. The lights of the car showed him up in front of them very plain. It was funny. He was walking along the edge of the road and he had his thumb out trying to get a ride. Portia's butcher knife was stuck in his belt, and on the wide, dark road he looked so small that it was like he was five years old instead of seven.

They stopped the automobile and he ran to get in. He couldn't see who they were, and his face had the squint-eyed look it always had when he took aim with a marble. Her Dad held him by the collar. He bit with his fists and kicked. Then he had the butcher knife in his hand. Their Dad yanked it away from him just in time. He fought like a little tiger in a trap, but finally they got him into the car. Their Dad held him in his lap on the way home and Bubber sat very stiff, not leaning against anything.

They had to drag him into the house, and all the neighbors and the boarders were out to see the commotion. They dragged him into the front room and when he was there he backed off into a corner, holding his fists very tight and with his squinted eyes looking from one person to the other like he was ready to fight the whole crowd.

He hadn't said one word since they came into the house until he began to scream: "Mick done it! I didn't do it. Mick done it!"

There were never any kind of yells like the ones Bubber made. The veins in his neck stood out and his fists were hard as little rocks.

"You can't get me! Nobody can get me!" he kept yelling.

Mick shook him by the shoulder. She told him the things she had said were stories. He finally knew what she was saying but he wouldn't hush. It looked like nothing could stop that screaming.

"I hate everybody! I hate everybody!"

They all just stood around. Mister Brannon rubbed his nose and looked down at the floor. Then finally he went out very quietly. Mister Singer was the only one who seemed to know what it was all about. Maybe this was because he didn't hear that awful noise. His face was still calm, and whenever Bubber looked at him he seemed to get quieter. Mister Singer was different from any other man, and at times like this it would be better if other people would let him manage. He had more sense and he knew things that ordinary people couldn't know. He just looked at Bubber, and after a while the kid quieted down enough so that their Dad could get him to bed.

In the bed he lay on his face and cried. He cried with long, big sobs that made him tremble all over. He cried for an hour and nobody in the three rooms could sleep. Bill moved to the living-room sofa and Mick got into bed with Bubber. He wouldn't let her touch him or snug up to him. Then after another hour of crying and hiccoughing he went to sleep.

She was awake a long time. In the dark she put her arms around him and held him very close. She touched him all over and kissed him everywhere. He was so soft and little and there was this salty, boy smell about him. The love she felt was so hard that she had to squeeze him to her until her arms were tired. In her mind she thought about Bubber and music together. It was like she could never do anything good enough for him. She would never hit him or even tease him again. She slept all night with her arms around his head. Then in the morning when she woke up he was gone.

But after that night there was not much of a chance for her to tease him any more—her or anybody else. After he shot Baby the kid was not ever like little Bubber again. He always kept his mouth shut and he didn't fool around with anybody. Most of the time he just sat in the back yard or in the coal house by himself. It got closer and closer toward Christmas time. She really wanted a piano, but naturally she didn't say anything about that. She told everybody she wanted a Mickey Mouse watch. When they asked Bubber what he wanted from Santa Claus he said he didn't want anything. He hid his marbles and jack-knife and wouldn't let anyone touch his story books.

After that night nobody called him Bubber any more. The big kids in the neighborhood started calling him Baby-Killer Kelly. But he didn't speak much to any person and nothing seemed to bother him. The family called him by his real name—George. At first Mick couldn't stop calling him Bubber and she didn't want to stop. But it was funny how after about a week she just naturally called him George like the others did. But he was a different kid—George—going around by himself always like a person much older and with nobody, not even her, knowing what was really in his mind.

She slept with him on Christmas Eve night. He lay in the dark without talking. "Quit acting so peculiar," she said to him. "Less talk about the wise men and the way the children in Holland put out their wooden shoes instead of hanging up their stockings."

George wouldn't answer. He went to sleep.

She got up at four o'clock in the morning and waked everybody in the family. Their Dad built a fire in the front room and then let them go in to the Christmas tree and see what they got. George had an Indian suit and Ralph a rubber doll. The rest of the family just got clothes. She looked all through her stocking for the Mickey Mouse watch but it wasn't there. Her presents were a pair of brown Oxford shoes and a box of cherry candy. While it was still dark she and George went out on the sidewalk and cracked nigger-toes and shot firecrackers and ate up the whole two-layer box of cherry candy. And by the time it was daylight they were sick to the stomach and tired out. She lay down on the sofa. She shut her eyes and went into the inside room.

Forest Fire

From THE WAVE
By Evelyn Scott

This is a novel of panoramic scope, embracing the spectacle of a whole nation divided against itself in the Civil War. In a series of vivid narratives, it moves from the Negro shack to the bivouac, the mansion to the steel foundry, the battleground to the depot. Its characters are Americans, eminent or insignificant, eager or resentful, caught up in the full tide of conflict.

Bob, a Confederate soldier, is one of these. In the sweeping drama of the war he is a tiny figure, expendable and replaceable. Yet in his desperate will to live and his dread of an unrecorded, meaningless death in the forest fire which follows a battle he is the embodiment of all soldiers. It is the intensity of the following scene which keeps it long in the reader's memory.

AT FIRST, the heat was no more than is blown out by an oven, warming the face. Then it began to penetrate the clothing most uncomfortably. Mingled with the ache in his slightly wounded leg, Bob felt the scorched sensation which made retreat involuntary. In the glassy wall of flames, he could see men running. Then, like creatures imprisoned in some ruddy amber, they were trying vainly to get out. He could see them wriggling on charred stumps of ankles, waving shrivelled arms at him. Their blistered faces seemed to melt, and their twisted mouths were mobile scars, uttering soundless words of agony. Fortunately for Bob's self-control, the rushing, crackling noises of the fire consumed, as in a great wind, all those other noises. He clung to the colours, and still, when he was abandoned, would not let them go. They seemed to him, in some vague way, to supply his sanity. If he cast them aside, upon the sizzling earth, it would be because he hoped no longer. It was as if the dingy flag itself opposed this wilderness. As long as his physical sensations remained quite clear, he could at least imagine himself avoiding a death so obscure and hideous that it would leave, for another's reading, no indication of his "fine" last thoughts. It was not death that he seemed to be afraid of, but the way he had to die. It was a cruel circumstance which could demand of him a thing like this, with no recompense. When a shout for assistance did, finally, reach him, through the *blat-blat* of the fire, beating like flapping blankets, he hurried on to offer succour relievedly.

He had just opportunity to reach, again, the smutty edges of the conflagration, when the cries were exhausted. All he could discern in the smoke was a body inert as an old sack—the face was hidden—and a limp arm, fire running in the sleeve, eating the flesh under it, the sooted cloth all edged with the aliveness seen in embers, as though embroidered with rosy threads. The dying man was not precisely in the centre of the blaze, but as if surrounded by it. The sappy burble in the fuming twigs did not menace him directly. Rather, the haste of the flames ignored him purposely, protected him from any other approach. The seething flicker, leaping from one suddenly ignited object to another, left the huddled shape undisturbed, intact, in a mirror of heat.

Bewildered, Bob ran backward for twenty yards or more, but halted again. He was trapped here, in an inner acre, where the sun, only slightly shadowed by the dusk of the fire, continued to dazzle freshly the untouched earth. But he could not get out.

Twice, he gestured to toss away his flag. But, if he lost his flag, if he was here "for nothing," the whole stunning predicament would seem "like foolishness."

He retreated carefully toward the middle of the encircled plot. Fallen horses hummocked the grass. The dead here had not yet been made hideous, and he was not afraid of them. Indeed he considered their postures those of people in mysterious security. But the fire was encroaching. It would torture even that drab, stolid countenance which he noted enviously. He, Bob, was yet aware and on his guard. The dead were listless. The dead stared mindlessly at the down-pouring sun. They had no sense of the hell in store. Bob, because he had a conviction that suffering would surprise those fellows, feared death, and felt his own advantage.

A big grey, on its side, was a swollen mountain. Not an insect crawled upon its crusted nostrils. There was a pit gouged in that horse's breast, and the blood stood there, unflowing, thickening, as in a brimming cup.

All at once Bob understood the absence of insect life for what it meant. A dead sparrow, lying in the twigs, was so doubly dead. How instantly it would shrink to the weight of its draggled, lime-soiled feathers, when the breath went out of it. The air was full of hot currents, flooding from the burning trees. Bob felt a hectic chill, and drew the jacket of his uniform tight across his chest. The rain of sparks was perpetual. Now and then, a brand, spouted from the furnace, twirled rottenly to earth near him. He had already been over the whole free space, but he began to run about in circles, and to call out desperately for some answering voice.

It was the monotonous character of sound which he found hardest to endure—that, and the fact that the prostrate forms against which he stumbled, over which he had to hurdle, would not run with him. The wall of vapours was rising higher. Through the aqueous appearing curtain, drifting upward, he could discover no stirring animal. The woods were given over to the constant motions of strange lifelessness.

A tree, on the outskirts of purgatory, after waving its branches for a moment, wanly, toppled, with a thwack; and, where new showers of cinders scattered, other wildfire started.

Bob was choking. His chest strained with a breath he could not utter. He had come to the end of his rope. This was more than any man could stand. Then fear revived him. This is how you feel when you suffocate, he said to himself quickly. Again he ran. Again he was searching, going nowhere. Again he clung the tighter to the colours which explained his sanity.

Oh, he was *really* choking! Not merely to *think* of being dead—but to *be* dead. He had always welcomed suffering a little morbidly, but only because he so much dreaded it.

If he could make up his mind to run right into the fire, all would be over. Or would it? If you held back, if you held back till the final instant —there was still a hope. You couldn't see yourself as you had seen those grovelling men. *They* had not been forewarned as you were. But it was crazy to stand here passively waiting on disaster. The way to evade it— it *must* be evaded—was to be doing something.

Bob's lungs swelled achingly. He opened his mouth and tried to draw into him that clean breath that was above the trees. The air that he panted after would not come, and all that he was obliged to breathe made his wretchedness more ponderous.

It was hot everywhere now. If only in the beginning he had been more desperate. If he had ignored pride and had tried to flee. His feeling for the state of mind that had made his bravery was turned to useless hate.

The very ground was warming. The change in temperature penetrated his boots. Even the growth concealed under the dead leaves was smouldering furtively. From where a horse was spraddled, oozed the stink of singeing mane and hair. Sunshine was failing in haze. The flames, seen clearly while the fire was distant, were only purling intermittently. A pine toward the centre of the clearing had become alight. It bounded in branches that were sizzling torches. The needles evaporated, leaving limber bone exposed. Everything was catching. The whole forest was catching. Yet how could woods burn in a circle? When people quenched prairie fires, they laid the trails in opposition till the two fires met. Bob suspected some aberration of the usual. This gave importance to his danger, and was passing comfort. Then he grew exasperated with the fact that contradicted theory. He was vexed, he was rebellious, as a child is vexed when its will is thwarted. It was all the while as though he were gazing through a defective window pane of rutilant glass. Out of the aspirant fragrance of the smoke, slowly tormenting his sense of smell to dulness, darted a stiff ripple like thin blood. It attacked him. It pursued him. He escaped it frenziedly. All at once the zooming of the conflagration became a terror to the ears. Spirals, swift as lightning, but more suave, began to edge the dry vines and creepers looping the forest. Green foliage, fresh with May, wrinkled, shed cracked edges, and tightened, until each stem glowed with a tip of bud like a minute coal, all raging-hot.

Another dead bird tumbled from a fork. The straw nest from which it reeled vanished utterly, leaving a little mat of hairs of an ashless red. A hurled twig Bob caught on the cheek, and branded him to a more tremulous indignation. He wanted to exclaim with some awful cry. That it was not possible for him to do so, was due to the conviction he would not yield—that he could be seen, could be heard, that it would not be possible for him to die alone, and without a trace, folk forgetting him utterly.

The charred sticks of the farther wood now stood in the deep, vibrating atmosphere as in a pool. He searched for the corpses he had before evaded. He could not endure an acceptance of their eternal inattentiveness. O God, hear me. O God, all you people hear me, know I done my best this afternoon. O God, *damn* the heat!

A branch close over him crackled. Flaunting fire, it swung and danced as though a sudden wind had been aroused for it. The spread flame, in its lambency, encased the whole bough. From it, thinned a gauze of radiations. Miraculously, twigs yards higher, and out of contact, spurted an iteration of the blaze. On and on hurried the fire, lapping, with its suspended tide of glare, at a sustained distance above the woods, all the air at which it snapped. Bob, still eluding its enchanted rush, was moving dazedly.

There was no time to lose. He felt faint, depressed with a misery which effort could not surmount. His drunken feet caught in the folds of his smoky banner, and he flung it down viciously, with a despairing heedlessness. But he had no more than done so, when he felt its loss superstitiously, sank on his hands and knees, tore the silk from the staff, and hastened on with it. That was what they *had* to know—he had kept the flag. But you couldn't climb a pine and reach the outer, clearer atmosphere encumbered with three yards of stick.

He had decided to try a tree. Beneath one, he could yet gaze into the blue sky as into a garden. It was a pine with low projections. If he could once climb through it and suck in one untainted breath, he would believe that he defied the fate which drew so ruthlessly upon him. The knot tightening in his chest cramped his very bowels. The glow around him made his face tingle rawly, and, for some reason, he was already certain that his features were turning black. He threw the flag across his shoulders, and sprang for an armhold, determined to ignore his flabby wrists that, in the first instant, scarcely supported him. His physical self, as if it betrayed his pride, was what he loathed. But he was secret about it, even in his mind. *They* would never find it out. He had never hinted an alarm to anybody.

As he clambered, his fierce hands teased by the scratching bark, the boles around him seemed to float by in the haze. Droves of trees, wriggling stiffly in methodic outline, each an exact distance from its fellow, pushed by him. The smoke was heavy, low and arrested. The oaks and pines cavorted, in their rooted gliding, while he struggled with his dizziness. Rankly, they escaped the holocaust, and rose up as though to smite him from the branch. He hung, teetered in a higher space, and crawled on, upward. Flat on his face, watching, with blood-congested brow, he joyed suddenly in some triumph over the treacherous soil, while twigs pressed stubbornly into his belly. The drifting earth rolled on beneath him, so close, so close, and yet, already, like some danger passed—earth that was guttered with little winding, spiral fires, and could offer pain, but no substantiality.

Bob's lungs remained locked. Effortlessness was itself causing added torture. He was no more afraid of torment, but afraid of effortlessness, afraid of an insidious indifference to his victory. Keep alive, keep alive, it don't matter how, but you must keep alive, he felt. There was no particular person whom he was longing to impress; yet there was something he must "prove." He was here, not because he was a fool, he kept insisting, but for some good reason, though he couldn't remember.

Then he stood, bold at last, and, with his hands against the upright trunk, steadied himself. There was a strange undulance in every contour on which his vision fell; and in his seared eyes the trees were yet advancing as monotonously as boats in the pale current of the smoke. He looked down on their constant passage almost resentfully. The pine swayed, as it spindled, and his weight seemed all that it could bear. His thoughts, also, were swaying slightly, in peculiar dreaminess. It was as though he were climbing on a mast to a lookout over strange, bright waters. He had gone as far as he was able. Clasping a pricking spout of clean, damp needles, he gaped his mouth for the hardest trial of his endurance, and drew a breath of choked eagerness.

The wind was of piercing clarity. At the first giddying inhalation, he nearly succumbed to pain. Relief was so complete that it was like debauchery, inviting him to utter heedlessness. With reviving staunchness, he had to fight the peculiar temptation to let himself go, and drop forever and forever, out of peace too perfect. He choked with the lovely attempt at breathing, and was inclined to vomit. Then his mind was stirred with quick intelligence, and he began to fear again.

The May afternoon was bitter. The pure intolerable atmosphere seemed to stretch his every thought wide. His body lived even beyond his mind. The pinnacle of the pine had only a young, tufty growth to bear him, and, as he moved, rotated supply. It smelled with its rusty bloom, so he was vaguely conscious, as did no tree on earth. The sky astonished him. It was valid blue and cloud. A faint sun, coiled in a smoke-dappled horizon, had just begun to sink. There was the world, spread out, real and usual, beyond the insignificant smudges of the fire. There were miles of forest, quiet and green, and farther, somewhere, there were soldiers marching. A tenuous, glinting line of agitation broke the happy stillness—artillery, or infantry, or, maybe, cavalry, he could not make it out. They were men—they were "Uncle Robert's" men—if they could only see him. He *had* to feel that they would see him. On death that was being merely dead, he now refused to dwell, but he could not allow it, in contradiction of some awful hope, that the whole universe of beings he had tried to please refused him final notice.

Hysterically, he tried to shred a strip from the flag that he might knot his banner to the pine, for he was unreasonably convinced that, doing this, when he should fall, there would remain a mark to show to others what he had attempted. Doubt overcame him. The doubt was in his arms and legs and body, in his feebleness; and was like the doubt of some one very old. He swayed, his feet slipped, he clattered to a lower bough; then retrieved himself. He tried to wave. His fatigued signal fluttered for a second's space above all the acres of sun-rosied and unobservant solitudes on which the tree, as it was islanded above the fire, could yet give his eye egress.

He was slipping toward the smoke which was like a mildew in the leaves below him. He was slipping toward the resignation of that other singeing flesh. His youth rejected this abdication.

But when protest came, it was more the irritation of accumulating pain than any confirmed thought: Why did they make me do it? Why did they make me do it? But I done it, damn it— Oh, I love them boys— O, God damn these people. Oh, they've got to look!

The Patrol

From A WALK IN THE SUN

By Harry Brown

In clear and calm prose, Private Brown tells the story of a platoon in the invasion of Italy. His war is a war of patience and self-control, in which danger is commonplace and the sight of death familiar, and in which victory and defeat are accompanied by a certain comforting fatalism.

The platoon is assigned to take an Italian farmhouse, as quickly and with as few losses as possible. In the first few hours of the attack two of its leaders are killed, and Sergeant Porter, its third commander, has broken under the strain of too many campaigns, and turned his authority over to Corporal Tyne, the one man he thinks may successfully complete the mission. A German plane has strafed the file of men as they push inland, and they have engaged an enemy tank in a gun battle. Behind them are their dead and wounded. Ahead, across a sunlit field, lies the farmhouse, as Corporal Tyne leads his men out of the covering woods.

THE field was a hill that stretched a hundred and fifty yards up to a farmhouse with a red tile roof. Here and there a boulder marred its surface, and there were patches where the grass lay flat. It looked as though it had been trampled. Tyne counted four outbuildings; it was quite a large farm. The house had been painted or whitewashed quite recently. He could see no movement around the buildings. "I wish to God I had those binoculars now," he said.

"Can you see anything?"

"Not a damned thing."

297

"How about the windows?"

"Sun's on them."

To the right the wood curved around, along what evidently was the bank of the river. The wall seemed to stop down there. "I wish I knew," Tyne said. "I wish to God I knew."

"Knew what?" Archimbeau asked.

"Nothing. Let's go back."

They moved back on their stomachs. After a while Tyne stood up. Archimbeau also rose, and they broke into a fast walk. The platoon was waiting for them. Half the men were sitting or lying down; the rest were leaning against trees or just standing around. "How's it look?" Ward said.

"Quiet. But I don't like it. Too quiet."

Ward nodded. "They're bad when they're too quiet."

"Craven," Tyne said. He fell on his knees and picked up a stick. Craven came over to where he was kneeling, and Tyne drew a rough line along the ground. "There's a stone wall that runs along here for about two or three hundred yards, probably between the road and the river. There's a clear slope up to the farmhouse from the wall. Not much cover. The wall seems to stop where the river curves around the farm, but there are trees running along the river bank. There doesn't seem to be any movement among the farm buildings. It's hard to tell just what the story is. If I had a pair of binoculars I'd have been able to see more."

"Think there's anyone there?" Craven asked.

"That's what I don't know," said Tyne. "Anyway, we aren't going to take any chances. We'll send a patrol up first, four or five guys."

"I'll take it," Ward said suddenly.

"I may need you here," Tyne said.

"I want to take it," Ward said.

Tyne studied his face. "Okay," he said. "You take it. Pick yourself four men."

"I'll go," Rivera said.

"No, you won't, doughfoot," Tyne said. "I need your little instrument."

"I want four volunteers," Ward said. "Four Congressional-Medal-of-Honor-with-ten-oak-leaf-clusters volunteers."

"Any extra pay?" Rankin wanted to know.

"Naw."

"Then I'll go anyway," Rankin said. "Just to make them feel ashamed."

"I'm a hero," Cousins said. "I been up front all day. I might as well stay there."

"I'll go along," Tranella said.

"The first guys that get to that house will get the wine," Tinker said. "I'll go."

"Okay," Ward said. "That's four."

"Pass out the Purple Hearts, mother," Rivera said.

"All right," Tyne said. "We'll go up to the wall in column, then fan out when we get there. The wall's three feet high. There's plenty of room. But don't let me catch any son of a bitch sticking his head up in the air. When you fan out keep about five yards apart. Craven, you take your squad down toward the road. Riddle, you take Ward's squad down toward the river. My squad will stay in the center. Rivera, you take your popgun down by the road, so you can keep your eye on the farmhouse and the road at the same time. Got that, doughfoot?"

"It's in my head," Rivera said.

"Keep it there. And remember to cover if anyone needs it."

"Okay, chief."

"Let's go." Tyne moved through the woods. The platoon straggled after him, moving as silently as Indians. As Tyne came nearer to the field he was struck with the same feeling of the wood's unfolding like a flower that he had had the first time. He hit the dirt at almost the same place as before. One by one the men flopped down after him.

He stopped at the wall and directed traffic, to right and left. The men wiggled along the wall or moved at a crouch, careful not to hunch their backs too high. Ward and his volunteers hugged the wall near Tyne. "Might as well go over right here," Ward said.

Tyne considered a minute. "I guess so," he said. "Maybe we're getting worried for nothing. Maybe there's no one up there after all."

"I think there is," Ward said.

"What are you going to do?"

"Well," Ward said, "if we can get within grenade-throwing distance we'll be all right. Let me take a look and see." He raised his head a little over the wall and studied the terrain. When he pulled his head down again he was frowning. "Don't look too good at that," he said. "A few boulders, but not a hell of a lot else. That grass won't do much good."

"It'll help," Tyne said.

"Yeah, it'll help."

Most of the men were in position. "We'll wait till Rivera gets his gun up," Tyne said. "Give him five minutes. If anything goes wrong he'll cover you."

"If anything goes wrong, shoot for the windows," Ward said. "That's where they'll be. They like the windows."

"I know."

Warily Tyne took another look over the wall. Things did not seem to have changed. Nothing had moved around the farmhouse. The windows still reflected the sun. Certainly there was nothing about the farm to arouse suspicion. But that was the way it always was. The things to watch out for were the things that looked innocent. That was the principle of booby traps.

"Why are you so anxious to take a patrol?" Tyne asked.

"I don't know," Ward said. "I just am."

Down at the far end of the woods, by the road, Rivera and Friedman were finishing setting up the gun. "You can hit anything from here," Friedman said. "They ought to have portable walls to go with every war."

"I'll see they have them next time," Rivera said. "I wouldn't want you to be disappointed."

"This is a pretty good spot."

"It'll do for awhile. I ain't planning to raise a family here."

"How's the farm look?"

"I'll rake that joint."

"I think it's okay," Tyne said. "Got enough grenades?"

"Yeah," Ward said. He studied the four men who were to go with him. "We'll stay five yards apart," he said. "And keep on your gut, for God's sake. Spread out, now."

The four men strung themselves along behind the wall. "Good luck," Tyne said.

"The same to you," Ward said. He looked to the right and left. "Over," he said. He leaped over the wall and lay flat in the grass. The other men followed him.

All up and down the line of the wall there was silence. Silence hung over the farmhouse, too. Far away could be heard the dull rumble of artillery, but it was cut off in great measure by the intervening woods. Ward hugged the ground, listening. He could see none of the other members of the patrol because of the high grass. Now he wished he had not had them stay five yards apart. A guy could wander away, especially if he was on the end. Stiffly Ward began to move forward.

The patrol had a long way to go. He moved fast. Near him he could hear the other men moving forward. Beneath the grass the ground was rough. It stuck to his sweat-soaked fatigues. He seemed to grate on the earth as he crawled along. A boulder reared before him, and he skirted it. As he did so he caught sight of Tinker in a bare patch. He winked at him. Tinker licked his lips with his tongue and made a half-wave.

Tyne slowly raised his head over the wall. The patrol was moving steadily up the slope. He could see two figures; the other three he could locate only by the waving of the grass. One of the figures was in a bare patch, the other was behind a boulder. They had gone perhaps fifty yards.

Suddenly, as though by instinct, he knew that something was going to happen. It was like those times when people see a man who is actually dying a thousand miles away. One moment everything was all right, and the next Tyne wanted to yell out for the patrol to come back.

He saw smoke drift from one of the windows of the house, and the next minute the noise of a machine-gun came to his ears. The Germans had opened up. The farm was occupied, all right, very well occupied. Tyne jerked his head down, looked at the man nearest him, and shook his head. "God damn," he said over and over again. "God damn. God damn. God damn."

The machine-gun had started up so suddenly that it had taken Ward by surprise. Off to his left he could hear bullets hitting the ground and singing away. It was too hot a place, much too hot. "Go back," he yelled. "Patrol back." He turned around and began to crawl down the slope. He could see the wall beckoning to him. It was hard to believe that anything so near could be so far away. He passed the boulder again and saw Tinker again, crawling back with him. This time he did not wink. He hugged the ground as a line of bullets parted the air over his head.

Slowly Tyne peered over the wall again. Why the hell didn't they come back? But they were coming. Good. He could see the grass waving as they worked their way toward the wall, and he could see the grass swaying as the machine-gun traversed it. "Tell Rivera to let her go," he said to the man on his left. The word went down the line.

Ward was wondering why Rivera didn't open up. He was cut off from the rest of the patrol, and he didn't know whether or not any of them had been hit. He was conscious only of his own efforts and the wall luring him on. His mouth was very dry, and he regretted coming out with the patrol. There had been just a chance that the farm had been unoccupied. He had known the chance was slim—he hadn't believed it himself, but he had wanted to take it. He dug dirt again as a row of bullets passed over him.

"Jesus Christ, here goes," Rivera said. The gun jumped and shivered before him. Far away, along the wall of the house, Friedman could see dust rise as the slugs cut into the mortar. "Get that bloody window," he said. Rivera obligingly lowered the muzzle of the gun an almost imperceptible distance. Bullets smashed through the window and into the house. The German machine-gun went suddenly silent.

"Let me be the first to congratulate you," Friedman said solemnly. He held out his hand.

Ward heard Rivera's gun go into action. It was home and music to him. He stopped and listened. He was almost certain he could hear Rivera's slugs smash into the side of the house. Behind him the German machine-gun went dead. He raised his head and took a quick look over his shoulder. Dust and mortar were flying from the house and glass spattered from the windows as Rivera raked it back and forth. Ward grinned mirthlessly. Rivera kept his finger on the trigger. Might as well make a run for it, Ward said to himself.

He calculated the distance to the wall. It was perhaps twenty yards, an easy run. Ward did not bother to think the situation out in any detail. There wasn't time. He suddenly stood upright in the field. "Cousins, Rankin," he shouted. "Everybody over the wall." Three figures rose up from the grass. They all bolted for the long wall. Rivera's gun chattered on. Five yards from the wall Sergeant Ward heard rifle fire from the house. He leaped to the right and zigzagged back again. He went over the wall head first, in a giddy dive. Cousins and Tranella leaped after him. Tinker was slow, at least two yards behind the others. He wasn't zigzagging. As he reached the wall there were three scattered shots from the house. Tinker tossed his rifle in the air and fell forward against the wall, his body half crawling up the rough stone. His hand hung over the top. Far away, on the left, Rivera's gun stopped firing.

Ward lay flat for a moment. His leap had nearly knocked the wind out of him, and he gasped, trying to catch his breath. Tyne crawled over to him. He patted Ward's sweat-soaked back. "You shouldn't have tried it," he said. "You just shouldn't have tried it."

Ward sat up. "Everyone get back?" he asked. He took a deep breath and looked around him.

"They got Tinker," Tyne said. "And I think they got Rankin. Rankin didn't come back."

"I thought there was only three," Ward said. "Jesus, is that Tinker?" He was looking at the hand that appeared over the wall.

Tyne nodded.

"Why don't you pull him in?"

"What's the use? He's dead."

"How do you know he's dead?"

"I can tell when a man's dead."

"Oh, hell," Ward said. "What a god-damned mess. What a bloody, god-damned mess."

"It could have been worse. They could have waited until you were all up there and then let you have it. It could have been a hell of a lot worse."

"It's bad enough," said Ward.

Tyne looked at Cousins and Tranella. "You all right?"

"In the pink," Tranella said. Cousins nodded.

"Tough luck," Tyne said. He turned back to Ward. "Now we've really got a job on our hands."

"Yeah," Ward said.

"There's no element of surprise, and they've got us cold. They know where we are and where we want to get to, and they probably know every way we'll use to try and get where we want to go. They've probably got a machine-gun in every window of that house. No one could get near enough to use a grenade."

"I wish to Christ we had a mortar," Ward said.

"It never happens the way you want it to happen," said Tyne. "If we had a mortar there'd be nothing to it."

"But we haven't got a mortar."

"No."

"How about waiting till dark?"

"We can't wait till dark," Tyne said. "We've got to get in there and get in there fast. I wish to God I could make them think we've got a mortar."

"Yeah," Ward said. "But how?"

"Nothing we can do."

Rivera spat on the barrel of his gun. The spittle rolled down, sizzling. "I'm a marksman," he said. "A marksman first class."

"I wonder who they knocked off," Friedman said. "Too damn far away to see."

"I hope it's Ward," Rivera said. "Ward gives me a pain in the pratt. All the sergeants give me a pain in the pratt."

"Tyne's all right," Friedman said.

"Yeah, Tyne's all right. But he ain't a sergeant."

"He probably will be."

"Then he'll give me a pain in the pratt."

Friedman stared down along the wall. The figure lying against it puzzled him. Within him he had a desperate urge to know who it was. He liked some men in the platoon better than others; he didn't want the body to be that of someone he liked. As a matter of fact, he didn't want it to be the body of anyone he knew, anyone he had worked with. "He's a big guy, whoever he is," he said.

"There's somebody else out in the field," Rivera said noncommittally.

"I know it. Didn't see him get hit, though."

"Ah, it was beautiful. The way I messed up that house was beautiful. I could do that fifty times a day."

"You'd better keep your eyes open," Friedman said, "or they'll be sending a halfback around this end with a grenade stuck in his mitt. They'll only have to do that once a day."

"The hell with it," said Rivera. "I've seen them coming around my end by the millions. They never gained a yard around my end. I'm indestructible. Nobody dies."

"Okay, corpse," said Private Friedman.

It was up to Tyne. Responsibility weighed on his shoulders and creased his forehead. Cautiously he raised his head over the wall, behind Tinker's hand. The farmhouse was quiet again. It might have been a farm on a normal busy day, with all the men out in the fields and all the women in the kitchen. It did not look like a theater of war. It seemed quiet, peaceful. It reminded Tyne vaguely of pictures he had seen on calendars in garages and grocery stores. You could sit in that place on the side of the road and be a friend to man.

T-z-i-n-g-g-g. He hit the ground as a bullet ricocheted from the wall and went whizzing off in the woods. "Close," he said. "Somebody up there's careless with firearms." Cousins grinned appreciatively, and Tyne felt better. The joke was an old one, but he supposed it was what he should say under the circumstances.

"They've got us cold," he said to Ward. "Pretty and cold."

"It's no place for a gentleman," Tranella said. He held up one hand. "Please, teacher, can I leave the room?"

"You and Tinker," Ward said. Tranella's hand came suddenly down, and he swallowed.

"We should have given you some cover too," Tyne said.

Ward shrugged. "What the hell, it wouldn't have made any difference. All I hope is they haven't put through a call to send a couple of tanks. That would really screw us."

The thought of tanks chilled Tyne. He caught himself. "I don't think they will," he said. "We've got a lot of planes around here. They're probably afraid the planes would see the tanks."

"What makes you think so?" Ward asked.

"I just got a feeling."

"I just got a feeling, too," Ward admitted. "I wonder if Rankin's dead."

For a moment Tyne had forgotten Rankin. Now he found himself remembering him with some embarrassment. "God, I don't know," he said.

"He's safe where he is, I guess. He can hang on."

"Yeah, if anyone can hang on Rankin can hang on."

Privates Carraway and James were lying on their stomachs, talking about nature. Private James had a leaf in his hand. They had developed, over a period of months, a core of hardness to anything that might happen. Already they had forgotten Rankin and Tinker. It was as though they had never existed. "Now take this leaf," Private James said. "Look at the complications. Think of all the trouble it took to make this leaf. You never saw nothing as complicated as that."

"I'm as complicated as that," said Private Carraway. "The human body is the god-damned most complicated thing in the world."

"It ain't no more complicated than this leaf."

"Ah, sure it is. That leaf's just a little thing. The human body's a lot bigger."

"That's what I mean," said Private James. "It's got a lot more to be complicated about. This leaf ain't got anything to be complicated about when you come right down to it."

"What's so fancy about it?"

"Look at the veins, for instance."

"You mean to tell me that leaves' veins is more fancy than human veins?"

"I didn't say that. I only said look at them."

"All right," Carraway said. "I'm looking at them. So what?"

"They're fancy."

"Ah, for Christ's sake," Carraway said. "I got no time for nature study. There's a war on."

"Never heard of it," said Private James innocently. But he threw his leaf away.

The map came out again, and again was spread on the ground. "The trouble with this map is that there's no detail about the farm," Tyne said. "It says the wall stops down by the river, but we knew that anyway. It doesn't show anything new at all. We might just as well toss it away."

Craven had crawled over to see what was going on. "How about the river?" he asked.

"What about it?" Tyne wanted to know. He ran his finger over the blue line on the map that marked it off, as though by the mere pressure of the flesh it could actually become water.

"Maybe we can circle the farm by the river," Craven said. "We can crawl along the bank."

The map once more became the object of study. How dead the symbols are! Tyne thought. They are meaningless, like flies crawling on a wall. He looked at the little black rectangles that signified the farm buildings, then at the elliptical lines that stood for the wall. They were cold and empty. "The only thing is," he said, "we don't know what they've got on that side of the farm."

"There's one way to find out," Ward said.

"What's that?"

"Send a patrol."

Tyne shook his head violently. "No," he said. "There isn't time any more. We've got to get in there, that's all."

"How about forgetting the farm entirely?" Craven said. "How about just crawling down the wall, then wading along this bank of the river until we get to the bridge and then blow her?"

It sounded good. "Idea," Ward said. Tyne stared at the map without speaking. He was looking at the location of the bridge. Whether it had been blown or not would make little difference to its position. If it had been blown the Germans would have put up some sort of pontoon affair right beside the old one, so that they could run back on to the road again. It looked as though there might be a bit of rock between the farm and the bridge; there was just a chance that it couldn't be seen from the windows. And there was also the chance that the Germans had no defences around the bridge. Perhaps they thought the farmhouse was enough protection. The Germans were so methodical that they always left something undone. They were too methodical. "It doesn't sound bad," he said.

"Hell, no," Ward said. "Best thing we can do."

"We've got to work fast," Tyne said. He looked at his watch. "Damned fast."

"Well, let's go," said Ward. "Best thing's a patrol. Four or five men."

Tyne was dubious. "I don't know," he said. "Perhaps there ought to be more. If there is anyone on the bridge four or five men can get tied up very nicely. I'd rather send two big patrols. Say ten men in each. Send them one after the other. Then if the first one gets jammed up the second one can pitch in. That's the most logical thing."

"Whatever you want," Ward said.

Tyne folded the map very carefully. "The best thing would be a diversion. How long do you think it would take to get over around the farm, Ward?"

Ward thought for a moment. "Ought to allow about half an hour," he said. "Yeah, just about a half an hour."

"That's fast moving," Craven said.

"All right." Tyne nodded agreement. "What we'll do is this. Ward, you take one patrol and go first. Craven, you take the other one. I'll stay here with the rest of the platoon. We'll give you exactly a half an hour. Then we'll hop over the wall and head for the house. You'll know when we start, because I'll put Rivera to work. You can't help but know. The Krauts will think we're coming up on this side, and they'll pay us all the attention. Then you blow the bridge. As soon as we hear you blow it we'll all get up and rush the joint. How does that sound?"

Two vertical lines appeared at the bridge of Ward's nose. He was running the idea over in his head. "Yeah," he said finally. "It sounds right. How about you, Craven?"

"I don't know," Craven said. "I think they ought to start after twenty minutes. Then the Heinies might not pay so much attention to what's going on behind the house."

"You're right," Tyne said. "I never thought of it. Well, that's the story, then. I guess it's about the best we can do."

"You've cut yourself out a tough job," said Ward.

"Suicide," Tyne said. "I'm a hero. We're all heroes. This'll mean the Good Conduct Medal."

"What the hell," Craven said. "It might be a breeze."

"It might be," said Tyne. "But I don't think so."

The men were lounging behind the wall, taking it easy. They didn't seem very much concerned about what was going to happen. Some of them were at their rations. A man can get hungry almost anywhere, under almost any circumstances. The stomach is a sensitive instrument, the seat of many things besides hunger, but it is still a very demanding instrument. Condemned men can eat a hearty breakfast, at least for the benefit of the yellow press. The soldier, who does not necessarily consider himself condemned to anything more than utter boredom, can eat a hearty meal at any time. The men were not even interested in Tinker's hand, poised above the wall. They had seen such things before. It was very much like going to a bad movie for the second time. It was wonderful what could bore them after a year of battle.

They thought of the farmhouse dispassionately. When Ward came among them, picking out his patrol, they were not moved one way or another. What they were about to do was merely a job, and they had probably been on worse jobs before. That, in itself, was one way to make things seem better. Cousins, for instance, swore that none of the action he had seen—and he had seen a great deal—had been comparable to the Louisiana maneuvers. The idea was to convince yourself that nothing that could come could possibly be as bad as what had gone before. You could last that way; you could last a long time that way. They went with Ward and they went with Craven, and the men who were to go with Tyne went to him calmly. It was the war. It was the job. It was *their* job. Get it done and then relax, that was the thing to do.

Tyne talked to them and they listened. The plan was simple, beautifully simple, the sort of simple thing that could easily go wrong. They listened carefully, nodding their heads occasionally, letting Tyne's words sink in. And when he was through they sat looking at him or studied their rifles or rubbed their hands slowly together as though the joints were aching.

Night School

From THE EDUCATION OF H*Y*M*A*N K*A*P*L*A*N
By Leonard Q. Ross

Mr. Parkhill, teacher of an evening class in Americanization, finds his students often perplexing but seldom dull as they struggle with the irregularities of English and the Articles of the Constitution. In this class of adults, many of whom are of central European background, the bright particular star is Hyman Kaplan, a Polish Jew. Mr. Kaplan, whose cheerful confidence and sheer eagerness are the instructor's chief problems, is at once a touching and humorous figure. Behind his desire to succeed brilliantly in the class we see the deeper desire of the newcomer to America for opportunity and a share in this country's future.

FOR two weeks Mr. Parkhill had been delaying the inescapable: Mr. Kaplan, like the other students in the beginners' grade of the American Night Preparatory School for Adults, would have to present a composition for class analysis. All the students had had their turn writing the assignment on the board, a composition of one hundred words, entitled "My Job." Now only Mr. Kaplan's rendition remained.

It would be more accurate to say Mr. K*A*P*L*A*N's rendition of the assignment remained, for even in thinking of that distinguished student, Mr. Parkhill saw the image of his unmistakable signature, in all its red-blue-green glory. The multicolored characters were more than a trade-mark; they were an assertion of individuality, a symbol of singularity, a proud expression of Mr. Kaplan's Inner Self. To Mr. Parkhill, the signature took on added meaning because it was associated with the man who had said his youthful ambition had been to become "a physician and sergeant," the Titan who had declined the verb "to fail": "fail, failed, bankropt."

One night, after the two weeks' procrastination, Mr. Parkhill decided to face the worst. "Mr. Kaplan, I think it's your turn to—er—write your composition on the board."

Mr. Kaplan's great, buoyant smile grew more great and more buoyant. "My!" he exclaimed. He rose, looked around at the class proudly as if surveying the blessed who were to witness a linguistic *tour de force*, stumbled over Mrs. Moskowitz's feet with a polite "Vould you be so kindly?" and took his place at the blackboard. There he rejected several pieces of chalk critically, nodded to Mr. Parkhill—it was a nod of distinct reassurance—and then printed in firm letters:

My Job A Cotter In Dress Faktory
Comp. by
H*y*

"You need not write your name on the board," interrupted Mr. Parkhill quickly. "Er—to save time . . ."

Mr. Kaplan's face expressed astonishment. "Podden me, Mr. Pockheel. But de name is by me *pot* of mine composition."

"Your name is *part* of the composition?" asked Mr. Parkhill in an anxious tone.

"Yassir!" said Mr. Kaplan with dignity. He printed the rest of H*y*m*a*n K*a*p*l*a*n for all to see and admire. You could tell it was a disappointment for him not to have colored chalk for this performance. In pale white the elegance of his work was dissipated. The name, indeed, seemed unreal, the letters stark, anemic, almost denuded.

His brow wrinkled and perspiring, Mr. Kaplan wrote the saga of A Cotter In Dress Faktory on the board, with much scratching of the chalk and an undertone of sound. Mr. Kaplan repeated each word to himself softly, as if trying to give to its spelling some of the flavor and originality of his pronunciation. The smile on the face of Mr. Kaplan had taken on something beatific and imperishable: it was his first experience at the blackboard; it was his moment of glory. He seemed to be writing more slowly than necessary as if to prolong the ecstasy of his Hour. When he had finished he said "Hau Kay" with distinct regret in his voice, and sat down. Mr. Parkhill observed the composition in all its strange beauty:

My Job A Cotter In Dress Faktory
Comp. by
H*y*m*a*n K*a*p*l*a*n

Shakspere is saying what fulls man is and I am feeling just the same
way when I am thinking about mine job a cotter in Dress Faktory on
38 st. by 7 av. For why should we slafing in dark place by laktric lights
and all kinds hot for $30 or maybe $36 with overtime, for Boss who is
fat and driving in fency automobil? I ask! Because we are the deprassed
workers of world. And are being exployted. By Bosses. In mine shop is
no difference. Oh how bad is laktric light, oh how is all kinds hot. And
when I am telling Foreman should be better conditions he hollers, Kaplan you redical!!

At this point a glazed look came into Mr. Parkhill's eyes, but he
read on.

So I keep still and work by bad light and always hot. But somday will
the workers making Bosses to work! And then Kaplan will give to them
bad laktric and positively no windows for the air should come in! So
they can know what it means to slafe! Kaplan will make Foreman a cotter like he is. And give the most bad dezigns to cot out. Justice.

Mine job is cotting Dress dezigns.

T-H-E E-N-D

Mr. Parkhill read the amazing document over again. His eyes, glazed
but a moment before, were haunted now. It was true: spelling, diction,
sentence structure, punctuation, capitalization, the use of the present
perfect for the present—all true.

"Is planty mistakes, I s'pose," suggested Mr. Kaplan modestly.

"Y-yes . . . yes, there are many mistakes."

"Dat's because I'm tryink to give *dip ideas,*" said Mr. Kaplan with the
sigh of those who storm heaven.

Mr. Parkhill girded his mental loins. "Mr. Kaplan—er—your composition doesn't really meet the assignment. You haven't described your
job, what you *do,* what your work *is.*"

"Vell, it's not soch a interastink jop," said Mr. Kaplan.

"Your composition is not a simple exposition. It's more of a—well, an
essay on your *attitude.*"

"Oh, fine!" cried Mr. Kaplan with enthusiasm.

"No, no," said Mr. Parkhill hastily. "The assignment was *meant* to be
a composition. You see, we must begin with simple exercises before we
try—er—more philosophical essays."

Mr. Kaplan nodded with resignation. "So naxt time should be no
ideas, like abot Shaksbeer? Should be only *fects?*"

"Y-yes. No ideas, only—er—facts."

You could see by Mr. Kaplan's martyred smile that his wings, like
those of an eagle's, were being clipped.

"And Mr. Kaplan—er—why do you use 'Kaplan' in the body of your composition? Why don't you say '*I* will make the foreman a cutter' instead of '*Kaplan* will make the foreman a cutter?' "

Mr. Kaplan's response was instantaneous. "I'm so glad you eskink me dis! Ha! I'm usink 'Keplen' in de composition for plain and tsimple rizzon: becawss I didn't vant de reader should tink I am *prajudiced* aganst de foreman, so I said it more like abot a strenger: '*Keplen* vill make de foreman a cotter!' "

In the face of this subtle passion for objectivity, Mr. Parkhill was silent. He called for corrections. A forest of hands went up. Miss Mitnick pointed out errors in spelling, the use of capital letters, punctuation; Mr. Norman Bloom corrected several more words, rearranged sentences, and said, "Woikers is exployted with an '*i*,' not 'y' as Kaplan makes"; Miss Caravello changed "fulls" to "fools," and declared herself uncertain as to the validity of the word "Justice" standing by itself in "da smalla da sentence"; Mr. Sam Pinsky said he was sure Mr. Kaplan meant "*opprassed* voikers of de voild, not *deprassed*, aldough dey are deprassed too," to which Mr. Kaplan replied, "So ve bote got right, no? Don' *chenge* 'deprassed,' only *add* 'opprassed.' "

Then Mr. Parkhill went ahead with his own corrections, changing tenses, substituting prepositions, adding the definite article. Through the whole barrage Mr. Kaplan kept shaking his head, murmuring "Mine gootness!" each time a correction was made. But he smiled all the while. He seemed to be proud of the very number of errors he had made; of the labor to which the class was being forced in his service; of the fact that his *ideas*, his creation, could survive so concerted an onslaught. And as the composition took more respectable form, Mr. Kaplan's smile grew more expansive.

"Now, class," said Mr. Parkhill, "I want to spend a few minutes explaining something about adjectives. Mr. Kaplan uses the phrase—er— 'most bad.' That's wrong. There is a word for 'most bad.' It is what we call the superlative form of 'bad.' " Mr. Parkhill explained the use of the positive, comparative, and superlative forms of the adjective. " 'Tall, taller, tallest.' 'Rich, richer, richest.' Is that clear? Well then, let us try a few others."

The class took up the game with enthusiasm. Miss Mitnick submitted "dark, darker, darkest"; Mr. Scymzak, "fat, fatter, fattest."

"But there are certain exceptions to this general form," Mr. Parkhill went on. The class, which had long ago learned to respect that gamin, The Exception to the Rule, nodded solemnly. "For instance, we don't say 'good, gooder, goodest,' do we?"

"No, sir!" cried Mr. Kaplan impetuously. " 'Good, gooder, *goodest*?' Ha! It's to leff!"

"We say that X, for example, is good. Y, however, is—?" Mr. Parkhill arched an eyebrow interrogatively.

"Batter!" said Mr. Kaplan.

"Right! And Z is—?"

"High-cless!"

Mr. Parkhill's eyebrow dropped. "No," he said sadly.

"Not high-cless?" asked Mr. Kaplan incredulously. For him there was no word more superlative.

"No, Mr. Kaplan, the word is 'best.' And the word 'bad,' of which you tried to use the superlative form . . . It isn't 'bad, badder, baddest.' It's 'bad' . . . and what's the comparative? Anyone?"

"Worse," volunteered Mr. Bloom.

"Correct! And the superlative? Z is the—?"

" 'Worse' also?" asked Mr. Bloom hesitantly. It was evident he had never distinguished the fine difference in sound between the comparative and superlative forms of "bad."

"No, Mr. Bloom. It's not the same word, although it—er—sounds a good deal like it. Anyone? Come, come. It isn't hard. X is bad, Y is worse, and Z is the—?"

An embarrassed silence fell upon the class, which, apparently, had been using "worse" for both the comparative and superlative all along. Miss Mitnick blushed and played with her pencil. Mr. Bloom shrugged, conscious that he had given his all. Mr. Kaplan stared at the board, his mouth open, a desperate concentration in his eye.

"Bad—worse. What is the word you use when you mean 'most bad'?"

"Aha!" cried Mr. Kaplan suddenly. When Mr. Kaplan cried "Aha!" it signified that a great light had fallen on him. "I know! De exect void! So easy! Ach! I should know dat ven I vas wridink! Bad—voise—"

"Yes, Mr. Kaplan!" Mr. Parkhill was definitely excited.

"Rotten!"

Mr. Parkhill's eyes glazed once more, unmistakably. He shook his head dolorously, as if he had suffered a personal hurt. And as he wrote "w-o-r-s-t" on the blackboard there ran through his head, like a sad refrain, this latest manifestation of Mr. Kaplan's peculiar genius: "bad—worse—rotten; bad—worse . . ."

Family of the Victim

From MONDAY NIGHT

By Kay Boyle

---

*Few passages in the fabric of Kay Boyle's closely woven work are
extricable from the context. This interval in Monday Night may be
a lapse from conventional technique but it is a highly successful one
and its isolation in point of view vividly defines it as the center of the
novel's motivation.*

*The rest of the movement—except incidental action—takes place
in the mind of one of the characters. Two men meet in Paris. One is
a young student of toxicology, the other a defeated writer. Both are
searching for a Dr. Sylvestre, an expert in poison whose testimony
in court has sent a number of suspected murderers to execution or life
imprisonment. The student admires the celebrated doctor; the writer
believes that the greatest story of his career will be the proof that his
testimony has been false, its victims innocent.*

*In the long night of wandering, the writer, exalted by liquor to a
level which ignores time and space, tells the story as it unfolds in his
mind—in bars, bistros, taxis, in the kitchen of Sylvestre's house
among his servants and in a dim railway station at dawn. Only once
is the curtain lifted on a wholly objective world in which two of
Sylvestre's victims—wife and son of a prisoner—are revealed in their
affliction. This is the passage: as tender yet as tragically incisive as
anything Kay Boyle has written.*

THE boy lay on his side, back turned against the light as well as
against the sound of the woman's voice reading aloud, and stared
through the bars of the long narrow crib at the wall-paper's red and
white design. The wall was so close that with a fingernail he could draw

what he liked on it, alter the women in the toile-de-Jouy until strips of
paper hung like saliva from their mouths as he distorted them, or scrape
their eyes until only circles of white plaster showed blank as horror
while they still sat, unable to rise and gather their skirts up and go,
fixed there, their little parasols open under the big round softly dipping
branches of the crimson trees.

It was warm and he had kicked the covers off and his legs, tapering,
slender, fretful, bare almost to the knee because the pajamas had been
bought new two years back, were drawn up double. In a little while the
long crib would be too small the way the pajamas were already too small,
and afterwards it might be the room and then the flat and then the street
outside that would have to be thrust aside or else exchanged for something bigger. Because of the hot black look in his heavy eyes and the
color in the sulky mouth things would have to keep on altering for him,
one thing be quickly, arrogantly discarded for the next, objects kicked
hard and impatiently enough eventually giving way to something
better or worse or merely to something different. Now he turned over
on his back and beat his bare feet in the bed.

"I'm thirsty. I want to get up," he said, and the woman's voice which
had been reading high, young and pretty in the room now stopped.
The boy gave a flap with his body like a fish tossed out on land, not in
desperation for life but in fury with the summer heat and the soreness
in his throat and the simple childish words she read. "I want a drink,"
he said again.

One lamp was lit in the room, one with a chromium base that stood
on the corner of the marble mantelpiece. The shade was imitation
parchment and the light it funnelled fell on the divan made up as a
bed where she had been lying reading the book about the donkey. The
sheet and pillowslip were green and now she sat up from them in a
thin green dress, half dressing-gown, half a housewife's overall in artificial silk, clean, trim and tailormade. She thrust her bare legs out from
the covers and they hung down towards the floor, the skin pure white,
the ankles and insteps veined blue, and with her toes, the nails on them
varnished crimson and opaque, she felt a moment for the high-heeled
gaping slippers that had fallen sideways as if just home from a dance
and dropped in weariness there by the bed.

"When you're all right we'll go to the zoo," she said and the boy saw
her head drop to stop the yawn or to seek the slippers too. "Next
Sunday if your throat's all right." Her hair was short and light and ar-
tificially curled and oiled; but the color at least was its own, a misty
yellow like the hair of little girls who later on will darken, with no
copper or even gold in it, almost as if it had succeeded in having no
describable color at all. Even growing up, even marrying and having a

child she hadn't darkened, or perhaps the white hair growing imperceptibly into the blond had kept it light. When she leaned over he could see the scalp where the part was, white and clean and the smooth curls twisted up from it. "But you'll have to begin sleeping the night through if you want to get well. If you don't sleep you won't get well nearly so quickly," she said.

She crossed the rug and the waxed parquet to the door into the hall and from his crib the boy watched her in the short green almost transparent dress and the high heels going out for the bottle of lemonade in the kitchen. When she came back carrying the little bottle and the glass, he beat his feet in the bed again.

"I want to go out now," he said.

"Yes," she said, pouring the lemonade out. "At one or two o'clock in the morning. It's a very good idea." He pushed himself up, half-sitting against the pillow, his face hot, his eyes black and, like objects glazed with varnish, singularly magnified and bright. "You drink this," she said, "and then try to go to sleep a little."

"If I want to go out I don't see why I can't go out," he said. He drank some of the warmish lemonade and the needles of it pricked behind his nose. Every time he took a swallow he looked up under his brows at her, hot, feverish, resentful. She looked very clean, the skin of her neck fresh and pale, and the arms naked almost to the shoulder thin and weak-looking and perfectly white. "If my father was here he'd make you let me do what I wanted," he said.

She took the empty glass out of his hand.

"Do you want to drink some more?" she said.

"No," he said, looking at his feet. "It's not cold enough and I don't like the taste. It's not good. It went bad because you left the top off."

"Now you try to go to sleep," she said. She stood by the crib holding the bottle and she might not have been talking to a child at all but talking to someone old enough to know, perhaps older than herself, but at least someone born cannier. "You know what happens tomorrow morning. You know the shops open."

"You said it's one o'clock," he said. He knocked one foot against the bars of the bed. "So if it's one o'clock then it isn't tomorrow morning, it's this morning. It's today the shops open."

"All right," she said. She put the glass and the bottle of lemonade on the mantelpiece and put the stopper back in it. "All right, this morning. In a little while now, in just a few hours, Camille will come and make the coffee and I'll have to get up and dress—"

"If it's today then get dressed now," the boy said. She came to the crib and leaned over it and moved the pillow slowly, inch by inch against his resistance, from behind him. "I don't want it smoothed out," he said, holding hard and furious to the bars, his head turned from the sight of her as she beat the pillow out and laid her hand beneath his head to slip it under him again. In the daytime, lying on his other side, he could see across the carpet and the furniture to the window and through it the chimneys of other houses standing against the colorless city sky, and one unpainted wooden dome—a theatre's or a church's —a little below the thick forest of jointed stove-pipes and tin crowns that turned fluctuating in search of the wind's or any air's direction. He could see all day this portion of the city's roofs, the faded sky, and these repairs, as individual as millinery, that had been made to chimneys so that clogged smoke could escape them; or he could see Camille in the room, sweeping, or see the doctor when he came, but the thin white breakable arms and the high heels and the black put on the lashes were as transient, as fragmentary, as alluring as a movie-actress' passage across the screen. All afternoon the air quivered with heat above the chimneys' heads, passive until the evening cooking began and the smoke stammered out across the sunset, and Camille walked in bedroom slippers in the hall or kitchen, slowly doing the room, slowly washing the dishes, slowly doing the dish-cloths out. About four he would begin asking Camille what time it was, although he knew, and would ask every twenty minutes what time it was by now until the door-bell rang three times and he would put the back of his hand to his mouth and scar it with his teeth to keep the sound of rapture in. "If it's already this morning you better get dressed now and have your breakfast and go get in the Metro," he said, holding tight to the bars so that she couldn't slip the pillow in.

"Maurice, let me fix you. Please be good," she said. She leaned over the cot, her pale thin body straining over him, only the rouge on her mouth and the black lashes left for color and the ten red blobs marking the ends of her hands. "Please let me make the bed cooler and then we'll both try to sleep a little—"

"I can't sleep," he said. "I don't want to. I'm not going to." She could feel the heat from his face as she raised him, the hot black curling hair, the golden burning throat and chin. "When you leave tomorrow morning I'm going to get up and get dressed and go away and you won't be able to find me."

"Maurice, be still," she said. "By Sunday you'll be well again and we'll go out. If it's nice weather we'll go to the zoo. If it rains we'll go see a cinema—" For an instant he saw it, the darkness and at the end of it the gleaming flickering square of light and the big shadowy figures moving, and even felt the suffocation of its promise, the wonder for what it would unfold like a top set spinning suddenly in him, and then he remembered tomorrow and the threshing in bed in a room without her that was tomorrow or today and he struck the wall with his fist. "We'll have an eskimo pie," she said, pulling the sheet straight, "and you'll forget you've been in bed ever like this, you'll forget—"

"I won't be here. I'm going to run away," he said. He had hurt his hand on the wall and now the tears rushed to his eyes, but still he did not move his head but kept it turned from her, the curls mussed, the cheek and ear and temple hot. She put her spread fingers in through his hair and said:

"You wouldn't leave me, would you, Maurice? If you ever left me I wouldn't have anyone."

He felt the fingers go but still he did not speak or move; he heard her cross the floor and heard the sighing of the divan when she sat down on it, and heard the slippers drop in fatigue to the floor; he lay with his face turned to the wall, staring bitterly at the mutilated women and the trees drawn red upon the paper's pattern, at the women's little shoes and the rings on their hands blurred now by the tears that he would swallow but not shed, at the shape of the leaves drawn delicately by hundreds on the branches and that he could begin destroying tomorrow, and suddenly she put out the lamp and he lay looking straight ahead into the chaotic dark.

For a long time he did not move but listened for the sound of her breathing as she fell asleep, but it did not come. He lay with his eyes dry now and wide open in the dark thinking of her as she would be alone, this room alone for her with his bed moved out of it and his books gone from the shelf and his photograph off the mantelpiece and the table Camille brought into the middle of the room at half-past six with just one place laid on it, and seeing it so he knew it would not be true. Even if he went there would never be just one place set: for her there would be two places no matter who came or went or died, and the thing that was fury or love in him softened and these other tears of pity for himself gushed from his open eyes and fell across his cheeks. In a moment he said in a low hard voice:

"It isn't true you wouldn't have anyone."

He held his crying back so that he could hear her speak; even his ears wet with his tears as he lay there, harking. She did not say anything for a little while and then she said the long way across the darkness:

"Listen, Maurice, everyone in the world belongs to his own age. You belong to people like André and Marcel and other children. When you go to school every morning you don't have the time to make life unsupportable for me like this." Once she had said that he did not hear the other words that came, and now the tears began flowing terribly, hotly, silently across his face. So that is it, so I make life unsupportable for her. So that is what I do. "Because you've been ten days ill now

you've become impossible. When you're at school every day you don't
have time to think about things like this," she was saying, "because
then you're with children the way you ought to be and I'm with
grown-up people—"

Suddenly his voice cried out, not like a child's any more but in
mature, hysterical anguish in the dark:

"Mama, mama, don't go to work tomorrow! I can't bear it if you go to
work tomorrow!" And her high girlish voice went quickly on over the
sound of his sobbing:

"Listen, Maurice, my dearest. I'm a woman and you are a child and
when you are away from your comrades and friends then I must suffer
from your boredom. Yes, it is boredom, simply boredom. And it is the
unnaturalness of a child being with someone a different age. I am a
woman, a grown woman alone in the world and I should not be alone.
So then when you are with me alone like this you have to suffer for
my loneliness too." She lay quite straight in the sheets, her eyes closed
but seeing like a picture her own body's slenderness lying between the
smooth green lengths of cloth, and seeing the passage of time as if it
were a thread slowly and steadily unravelling from her mind until there
would presently be nothing left of memory or indignation; only the
pitiless implacable knowledge that now what was once the future had
unravelled into the present, and in a little while more even the present
would have unravelled into the nothingness of the past. "I'm twenty
years older than you, Maurice, my dearest, but still I'm not old to other
people. I can't think of myself as being old yet. I'll be old soon enough
but before that I think I ought to try to make another kind of life for
you, and for me, for me too!" she said with sudden ferocity. "I want to
make a natural kind of life for both of us and so I have to begin with
myself, yes, with myself! If I had someone," she said in a small childish
voice which drifted into silence in the dark.

"Don't tell me," he thought, his two hands holding savagely to the
pillow. "Don't tell me. I don't want to know."

This was the first measure of the agitated dance, the eternal rehearsal
of that program for which the scenery was not quite completed, the
décor conceived, even prepared, but not yet executed; this the first
convolution of that spinning waltz of egos coupled and clasped heart
to heart, the stamping fretful minuet which child and mother practiced
tearfully, irreconcilably and tirelessly: the I, the You rent between wild
possession and escape but locked in one embrace and whirling faster
and faster towards passionate and incurable bewilderment. They had
come this far before, the brain swooning, all but the will effaced by
confusion, but now it seemed for the first time that the curtain was
about to rise.

"If I had someone else," she went on but she could not quite find the words to say it, "then I'd be with you more, I wouldn't have to get up and go out to work and I'd be here when you got home from school at night, and then on Thursdays—"

"Don't tell me," he said, holding the sound in. "Don't tell me."

"And then in the summer," her voice went musically on, clearly, effortlessly speaking like a bird's notes shaped in the dark. "Then next summer we'd be able to go away somewhere, you and I, perhaps to the seashore, instead of me having to stay here working in the city—"

"Don't say it," he thought fiercely to himself. "Don't say his name. I know it."

"When you grow up and when you meet a nice girl you like and you want to marry her," her voice went on, "then I'd do everything I could to make it easy for you. If you love a person you want them to be happy and I'd want you to find a girl your own age and I'd want you to marry her. I wouldn't be jealous of her or make trouble. I'd understand everybody belongs to people their own age, and I know you'll fall in love with a girl sometime and then you'll want to marry—"

He lay hard on his back, his hands clenched.

"No, I'll never want to," he said. "I'll never want to get married."

"Oh, yes, you'll want to get married some day," she went on quietly, "and I won't say a word. I'll do everything I can to make it easy for you because I'll understand. Even if I mind I won't show it so you won't know and you won't be unhappy. People aren't supposed to live alone, no one ought to be expected to live alone," she said, the ego's whimper as they whirled almost resorted to, almost heard.

He lay still, tense and straight and hot in the bed, his hands holding tight to the pillow under his spine and hair. And what about my father, he thought savagely. What about him? What are you going to do about my father if somebody—if anybody—if someone else—

He had never got the story consecutively from anyone, only in pieces over the period of years he had been alive, and told in different voices. One year she had sent him away for the summer; she had sent him to Trouville where a cousin of hers had taken an apartment for July and August, not near the beach or anywhere near the hotels but in a back street of the town. That was two years ago, when he was nearly six, but he had not forgotten. He remembered the look even of the liquid in their glasses at the café table, perhaps the first time he noticed that this wine poured out clear green and then, when the water was spilled into it, turned to milk. He remembered the cousin although he had not seen her since that July, and only the hat of the friend sitting at the café table with her, and the words not for an instant confused with the value of the bucket and shovel they had bought him but just as absolute, just as

enduring. She said "his father" as though talking of someone who had
passed by in the street, and she even looked towards something else until
for a little while he still believed she was not speaking about him at all.
The rain was falling beyond the café awning, a slanting broken down-
pour of seaside rain sliding drop by drop from the umbrellas and the
awning's fringe, and in the same voice that she might have said he
couldn't go down to the beach that day she said to the friend who didn't
know: "His father's in prison. I never believed a thing like that could
happen in our family; but then it's his side not hers. . . ." He was thinking about the new bucket and shovel and about his mother coming up
from Paris on Sunday when the stores were closed, because the thing
hadn't happened yet, it was just about to happen. The words had been
said but it was as if they had not yet been heard: the cousin and the
friend, the two women sat there drinking and talking together while he
looked out beyond the cornice of the awning at the rain and swung his
bare legs in his sandals underneath the table's edge.

"My father was killed in the war. He was killed in the war," he said,
as pleased and certain as if it was the conscious, not the subconscious
taking the defense up now. "My father was a general in the war," he
said louder so that they must stop and hear. "I never saw him because
he was killed before I was born in the war. That's why I never saw him."

The cousin turned away from her friend and looked across at him
and smiled. Her cheeks were full and high and hard and he could see
the grains of carelessly put-on powder lying on the skin, and in the
lenses of her glasses he watched the people under open umbrellas passing, no signal or gleam of sight behind the glass but the perfect, the
absorbing motion-picture of the wet shining street.

"Yes, of course he was, of course," she said. Her face was mottled
with color now from the drink or heat and she put one short hand forward in its white cotton glove and lifted the hair back off his forehead
where it clung to the skin. He was sitting up straight on the café's red
tin chair, not having started to be afraid yet or to know, still watching
in her glasses the movement of the people and the cars, and then the
friend leaned towards him. Under the brim of white braided straw there
was nothing, a small curiously bright cipher in which stood the edges
of her two gold teeth. In two years the words had not altered but
travelled intact through inconceivable time and space towards another
and profounder hearing.

"What war?" she had said, leaning over the table. "What war, my
little Maurice?"

He looked at the cousin's face again, and because it was not that
year but the year following that he began to count back to 1918 and see

the impossibility of it by ten years at least, he looked in surprise and mystification again at the woman friend.

"You tell her, you say what war it was," he said to the cousin. She sat silent, smiling at him, putting his curls back clumsily with her fingers. He could see the button of her glove forced into the buttonhole beneath the crushed pink oval of her palm's squeezed flesh as the hand moved just above his brows. "You tell her what war," he said, and then he stopped saying it abruptly and stopped looking at their faces, not out of bewilderment any longer but now because he knew. So it was my father she meant, so it was me. When the cousin spoke she did not give him any answer but said:

"I think her mistake was not to tell him. That's where she's made a lot of trouble for herself. Letting him have his father's picture beside his bed and this thing about being a general—"

The next time anything was said about it, it had another sound, clearer, simpler, more accurate than the truth. It was Sunday when his mother came and he asked her; she was going to stay until Monday morning but because he asked her they went away before. For a long time after she came he did not remember; they went to the beach and sat down in the sand, the three of them, eating raw tomatoes and drinking grape-fruit juice out of the bottles, and then he went in wading. But when he remembered he came running back, the pail and shovel left near the water in the damp sand, coming back to ask her to keep on telling the story to him or else make up another. Lie to me, he said with his lips against her bare smooth knee, lie to me, my love.

"Why didn't you say they didn't kill him in the war but put him in prison?" he said out loud.

She was sitting in her bathing-suit rubbing her arms with the oil and when he said this her hand stopped moving, the brown slender fingers motionless but clasping still the forearm's even flesh.

"Who?" she said, really in fright, as if the ghost had walked towards them and stretched out his hand.

"My father," the boy said. He rubbed one finger, with the sand like pepper on it, across her knee and watched the grains fall away. And suddenly she began moving, the legs drawing up to stand, the hand putting the cork back in the sunburn lotion, the head jerking to look at the cousin. When she stood up she stooped at once to pick up the towel and bag and then she let them drop again and started tying the ribbons of her bathing-shoes. But her hands moved so quickly that she could not make the laces hold around her ankles and she picked up the towel and flowered cretonne bag out of the sunlight again and tried to speak.

The cousin was sitting spread upon the sand, wearing a big straw hat and embroidering under the shade of it, working with silks, dark green and yellow, knot after silky fraying knot into the crumpled greyish linen on which the pattern was stamped in ink. She made no sign that she had heard them speaking and her hands did not falter. Only when his mother said in a quick low trembling voice: "You bitch, you dirty bitch," the cousin's face choked suddenly with color and she began quietly, embroidering still, to cry. He stood with his bare toes moving in and out of the sand watching the tears fall black and separate on the linen in her hands, and then his mother seized him by the shoulder and turned him savagely away and up the beach. She did not say anything until they got to the wooden walk and had gone along it until they stood opposite the street he and the cousin took twice or more often every day. There, facing the two rows of big-headed golden nails studding the way in the avenue for pedestrians to cross, she said:

"They had no right to put him in prison. That's why I didn't say it." Then he remembered the bucket and shovel left standing in the damp sand, but he could not go back. They packed their things before the cousin got to the apartment, and then they left for Paris, travelling at night, and on the train she told him a little more: she said, "I didn't tell you because it was a mistake. I always thought something would happen and the mistake would be corrected and I paid lawyers, I paid lawyers for three years and then it seemed nothing else could be done. Then I began telling you he was dead."

"When will he be dead?" he said, and he felt his heart rushing forward in bliss with the swift rushing of the train.

"What do you mean? What are you trying to say?" she said. She was looking out the window, her head turned from him so she would not have to look at him and know.

"When are they going to kill him? When will they guillotine him?" he said, and a fresh and inexplicable joy gushed from his heart; for the first time seeing prison as a pause, troubled and vague as purgatory and like it suspended between life and death, for the first time believing in the possible silencing of one man's voice in her ears, the perfect blotting out of one man's face.

Almost at once the girl began coming to the apartment that summer in Paris. At first she came back with his mother from work at night, and then she began coming earlier, perhaps an hour or less before his mother rang the bell. She would hang up her coat in the hall before coming into the sitting-room where the beds were, and on her way to the mantelpiece she'd say "Hello, kid" when he looked up from his lessons or the Mecano set at her. She wore low heels and fringed tongues slapped on the front of her shoes as she walked. She'd put her shell cigarette case down on the mantel by the lamp and take her plain hat off and throw her head back so that the short narrow nose looked smaller even, and stand there with her legs spread running the pocket-comb through her dark short-cropped hair. Or she might not wear a hat but come in and fling herself down on the divan where his mother had slept and stretch and yawn and lean up on one elbow to read the evening paper she had brought, carrying it rolled tight as a stick in her hand. She wore a square silver watch strapped on her wrist and she'd look at it from time to time until some time after seven the doorbell rang and Camille walked out of the kitchen to open it, or else he jumped up and went to open it first, or else the girl sat up abruptly and swung her feet off the bed and said, "I'm going! Wait," and crossed the room and pushed past them in the hall, stoop-shouldered, tall, and thin, and reached the door before them.

In the late afternoon or early evening the girl was this one thing: silent except for the sound of her yawning or humming, carelessly, casually insulting as she came in and flung herself, with her shoes on, down on his mother's bed. But at night she altered; with the darkness, like a miracle, the alteration came. She became so young, so reckless that Maurice sitting at the table with them and seeing the wine come and go and the things to eat getting better when she stayed watched with excitement first one bright wild face and then the other. After the month of July was over he began liking the way they shrieked their words with laughter at each other and the dances they did together to the radio music once the dishes had been taken out. If he woke late at night, he knew she was there still even before he quite heard the sound of their voices from the kitchen where they sat on the two stools smoking, or doing their nails, or merely talking after the light was out in the sitting-room and he was put to bed. All night it seemed he could hear their voices: the high delicate one and the lower, quieter, surer one, as if it was the first that always asked the questions and the second that answered, mingling like the drowsy voices of people mingling in sleep.

She was a Russian princess, or that is she had been a princess before the changes had come about in Russia, his mother told him. Once she had joined a roving White Russian company of cavalry and for two years she had passed for a man among them, and once she had walked up to the glass the body of Lenin lay under and cursed him in front of the guards before all the people and ended by spitting right on the glass.

"And then?" said Maurice, still too young to ask how she had got back to Russia or why she had been allowed to stay but listening to this story his mother might have invented for someone younger than he was or else more guileless.

"And then she came to France, she had to leave the country after that, and she became an automobile racer," his mother said. She was getting ready to go to work in the morning, standing in her black velvet dress in front of the bathroom mirror and putting the mascara on. "Sometimes she wears her cap like an automobile racer now, on the side of her head sort of. You notice when she comes in tonight if she doesn't make you think of an automobile racer."

Or another time, getting ready in the bathroom in the morning and looking at her own face in the sunlight that came in through the window from the court, she said quickly:

"Look, Maurice, I'm getting a little grey in my hair now and I haven't done anything with my life. I'm just the same age as Baya and she looks so young and she's been to nearly every country and ridden camels across the deserts and I never do anything but sell perfume and powder and sometimes go out dancing somewhere. That's all I'll ever be able to do and Baya—she's my age, she isn't any younger than I am—she's going to be an aviator."

"Are you and Baya twins?" Maurice said, sliding on the bathtub's edge, and his mother said:

"Yes, we're twins. We're twins, we're almost like sisters. Only she's braver than I am. She's more like a man."

It was on another Sunday that his mother and Baya had oysters and wine before lunch on a café terrace in the avenue de la Grande-Armée; it must have been March because his trotinette was new still and he went pedalling fast up and down the sidewalk while they sat at a table in the sun, Baya with no cap on, and her short hair brushed back, wearing a dark green jacket with a green leather flower in her buttonhole. The man, the implacable rival who had lived in photographs and in remembrance and legend with them since the beginning, was dead this spring; wiped out without the aid of war, without the guillotine by the two women's laughter as they rocked over the empty blue oyster shells in the first sun together. He had stopped fearing his possession, stopped needing him almost, since he knew he lay quiet now, the spring earth flung down upon his face, finally expired in his mother's memory. When they had finished, the two women took arms and walked slowly, their heads down, talking, not looking up or seeing the people coming back from church, but moving through them like two dreamers walking, while he pedalled his trotinette ahead, gliding and swerving fast, a single mounted herald laying a way for them through defamation and hostility.

Once back in the apartment they could not eat because of all the things they had to say. They sat at the table with their cigarettes while he ate steadily and rapidly, great sides of crust pushed into the gravy and carried dripping to his mouth, while his mother rose at the required moments and as if moving in a dream changed his plate and brought the cheese to him; dreamily, speechlessly moving around the table with her eyes on the girl who sat talking with the cigarette burning down short in her fingers, talking and talking in meaningless intensity and gravity of things that had happened in other places with other people, her head lowered so that only the thick black brows and the forehead and the dark uncombed pompadour showed. When his mother passed by her with the plate of fruit, Baya caught up his mother's hand and pressed the long slender fingers against her mouth as if in pain.

"Maurice, darling, have an apple, have a pear," his mother said quickly and she put the plate of fruit down on the table near him.

About four o'clock that day Baya came into the sitting-room with the clothes on. She had got them out of the trunk in the closet in the hall. She was dressed as a French army officer, the visored cap, black with gold braid on it, tipped on the side of her head, even the boots seeming to fit exactly, and the crop stuck under her armpit, and the face small, tough and reckless. It was something so palpable this time that all the rest he had been told or overheard or merely imagined about his father seemed as scant and as equivocal as fabrication. He followed her in wonder out onto the balcony in the sun where she leaned on the railing, and his mother followed in her silk dress, laughing.

"I'm going to let all the neighbors see me and make a scandal for you," Baya said. She lit a cigarette and dropped the dead match down onto the pavement five flights below where the Sunday afternoon families were wandering by, even the children dressed elegantly in black, the little boys as sailors in heavy mourning, the pale-faced girls in serge and patent-leather slippers walking two by two.

"What kind of a scandal? What do you mean by a scandal?" Maurice said, looking in wonder from a distance at her.

"They'll think your mother has a gentleman calling on her," Baya said.

"No, she wouldn't," he said. He stood with his hands behind him near the window, looking in stupefaction at the jacket, the breeches, the polished leather. "I wouldn't let her. I wouldn't let a man come here."

It seemed as if it were the first day of spring, even the earth that had been left in the flower-pots and forgotten all winter in the corners of the balcony asking for life now that the reviving of the world's life had begun; and his mother, weak with laughter at the sight of Baya, leaned against the sun-heated stone of the apartment house's wall and gasped out the high-pitched and partially broken sound he sometimes believed was singing beginning.

"My dear, the weather is truly remarkable today, truly remarkable," Baya said in a manly deep and artificial voice, in imitation of what might be an army officer's exact French or what she thought the neighbors expected of her, and his mother put her handkerchief to her lips and cried with laughter. She did not stop even when Maurice, standing motionless in the sunlight, said:

"When did my father wear that uniform?"

Baya shook the cigarette ashes down towards the street and smiled at two girls passing on the other side, and Maurice's mother touched the ends of her lashes with her finger and blew her nose.

"My mascara's running . . . he had it for his military service," she said. There was no strangeness or emotion in her voice and she went right on saying to Baya: "You know, his mother took it out of camphor when we were first married and she said, 'It's such superior cloth that I wake up at night and think of it lying wasted here in a trunk.'" She gave another burst of laughter. "She said, 'Let's hope they get on with their next war before the moths have a chance to get at it!'" Baya looked back over the epaulette on her shoulder for an instant and then went on smiling at the girls below. "And then when she was dying, poor thing, it all came out in the rest of them, the thing she'd taught them young," his mother said and she blew her nose again and laughed. "She was dying in the clinique in Rouen and when they found there wasn't any more hope for her, he sent me to the station to find out how much it was going to cost to have her sent from Rouen to Paris to be buried, and when he found out—of course, his sisters were in it too—it was more than the fare and so he said she'd have to come to Paris alive instead of coming dead by freight. His own mother, poor old Mrs. Coutet—"

Maurice stood watching the blue figure leaning on the rail, unable still to walk across the balcony's stone and impersonally touch the cloth or lay his hand against the belt.

"Where did my father wear it? How long did he wear it? Why didn't you ever show it to me before?" he said.

Baya turned back to them from the street below and crossed her legs facing them and leaned backwards on her elbows on the iron rail. She stood there looking at his mother's face, one smooth toe of the officer's boot tapping on the stone, her lip drawn up and softly whistling, before she began speaking.

"His uniform, his wife, his kid, the life he can't live handed me like a present," she said scarcely aloud, the casual, rakish smile neat as a boy's, the visored emblem of a nation's valor tipped carelessly over one ear.

The Trespasser

From THREE BAGS FULL
By Roger Burlingame

This novel is the saga of five generations of the Van Huyten family in a central New York village. By the will of Hendrik, the Dutch patroon who founded the village in 1795, his son was cut off and the family split. One branch continued in luxury, the other degenerated into poverty and degradation. Here the scions of the two branches come together in 1915 when Ruth's cousin Dick comes trespassing on her father's property and swims in the sacred Van Huyten lake.

RUTH VAN HUYTEN woke early in the morning on a hot July day in 1915. Her bedroom was toward the lake; the direct rays of the sun did not come in her window but the reflection from the water was a bright swirl on the ceiling. She could tell from looking at it that the lake was as calm as a stagnant pond. When there was air, the ceiling light would be quick and nervous. So, Ruth thought, it would be a forbidding day; she turned her small face into the pillow, trying to forget it, trying to ease back again into sleep. But she could not sleep and soon her mind was full of evil.

Ruth was fourteen. She thought constantly and fiercely; her mind reached mature heights and depths, yet her acts, to her surprise, were often childish. She would think something out into a superb pattern but when she came to follow it, her will jumped her impetuously out of the lines. Like a ouija board, she thought: the harder you tried to move it in a direction the harder it pulled you into the opposite. Ruth was concerned about herself, deeply and privately concerned, while she turned a hard face to the world. So no one called her a thoughtful child as they called her cousins, Jack Harlow and Ella Van Gogh, for a thoughtful child meant a good child, yet Ruth could think circles round them both. She did, in fact, most of their thinking for them. She had designed their Indian games and led them, being herself Lone Cat—led them often into trouble—with the other smaller cousins, Cornelius Van Gogh and Diana Harlow, trailing along behind until their parents had forbidden them to follow. And Ruth had penetrated the taboos and taught the others, slapping Jack in the face when her teaching offended him. But lately she studied herself.

She was disorderly in an ordered world. The neatness of the house, its smooth machinery, the soft-stepping servants, the quiet when Father was working or had a headache, the kisses, morning and night, stirred her to violence. So she had been driven (when she was younger) to smash the framed photograph of her great aunt Maria because she hated her "smug" face, to trip up the maid who was carrying Father's Postum, to remove the inside from Cousin Madison's birthday cake so that, at the height of the festivities the cake caved with its candles, to pinch the butler's behind and make him jump when he was pouring claret, to appear abruptly without her clothes in the midst of a dinner party and the later serious things of letting the cows out of the Miles pasture so that one of them was hit by an automobile, and setting fire to the boathouse on a day when she had been forbidden the boat.

The mere act of kneeling in church was enough to send a flood of sinful thought hurtling through her head. Even now, at the communion rail, she itched to pull the Reverend Snow's beard, to finish the sacred wine, to say a blasphemous word; when the plate was passed, she wanted to snatch the money off the red velvet: then she whispered, "God kill the devil in me, the black devil, he's inside me, here," and, at night, she prayed passionately for the devil to be killed.

He was in her diaphragm she thought, for it seemed to her she felt a swelling there when the mood came on her and once she had branded a little cross on it with a red hot hairpin. The brand was still there and she guessed it would always stay to shame her. No one had seen it—she had fought to hide it when the doctor had poked her for appendicitis and listened to her heart.

Many governesses had come and gone, saying, "Ruth is incorrigible," though Cousin Mary Bryce had said to the last one: "No one is incorrigible, Fräulein," after which there had been a talk between Cousin Mary and Mother with Ruth behind the curtains, listening. "Of course you and Nick can't be blamed for spoiling her a little, Hilda, but really—" "But what can I do, Mary, I can't—I can't think." "You must talk with her more—" "But, oh, dear Mary, wouldn't you—couldn't

you talk to her?" Ruth could never forgive Mother getting Cousin Mary
to talk to her. She hated Cousin Mary since.

With her face in the pillow, she concentrated on hating Cousin Mary,
thinking up bitter things to say to her, tortures for Cousin Mary until
she could feel the breathless tightness beneath her new breasts, but then
she raised herself to her knees in one quick motion, saying, "No. Not
today."

She got up, put on her bathing suit, went out of the room and down
the waxed stairs. It was cool and silent in the house; it was dark, for no
servant had yet waked and the shades were down. Ruth thought of all
the people above her in their stuffy beds, snoring: of Father with all the
paraphernalia of his imaginary sicknesses on the night table beside his
bed, of Mother with her mouth open. How nice it was, here in the cool
before they all got up and fussed around!

The parlor had been done over in the new "chaste" style and looked
to Ruth as sterile as a hospital with its painted walls. It must not be
called the parlor any more but the "living room." The dining room was
better with its ugly figured wall paper and its portraits: pompous grandfather, Hendrik Jr. and his first wife, Matilda, in their ridiculous cos-
tumes. Matilda had an arm round her daughter Maria—Aunt Maria
with the long nose and those funny pantalets.

But there was one portrait Ruth adored and when no one was looking
she made a little obeisance to it, a nod of recognition. It was of the
Countess Le Fevre, painted when she was Beatrix Van Huyten by the
man who invented the telegraph. Uncle Harry had left it to Father
when he died but there had been an awful fight over it with Aunt Eliza-
beth, the "Queen" as they called her. Ruth would like to look like that,
so cool and calm and sweet and wise and, if they had called her by a
beautiful name like Beatrix, maybe she would have. Be-a-trix, Be-atrix,
a quiet, sweet sound with a catch at the end of it. She must have had
Passion, too, for she had married a French count and all Frenchmen
have Passion. Dear Beatrix, look at me now at the beginning of this new
day and promise you will protect me. I love you.

The odd thing was that love began in the same place as the devil and
there was the same swelling there when she looked at Beatrix or threw
her arms round Norther's neck. Possibly the cross had done that; Ruth
could not remember love before the cross.

The red brick terrace was already warm under her feet but the grass
was still damp. Ruth had left off her stockings, knowing her mother
would not see her so early. The grass felt good. She ran over it to the
patch of woods that the Van Huytens had decided to keep "wild."
Three generations of children had played Indian there. Beatrix must
have played there, though she would not have been Lone Cat. Some

people said the woods were virgin, though this was ridiculous. A good deal of undergrowth had been let grow against the protests of Jones the gardener. The patch ran all the way into Queen Elizabeth's property: the line between was disputed—the place where it was supposed to run was the thickest part and there, once, a game had ended in wickedness. There Ruth had smoked her first cigarette and Valentine, the Queen's young second man, had seen her but had said nothing, being engaged at the moment with Madam Van Huyten's upstairs maid.

Ruth knew almost every tree. She could find her way anywhere without a sound. Lone Cat was proud of her silence in the woods. She could wriggle on her belly through places where it seemed no body could pass. Probably she still could, for she had not grown big and gawky like Ella with such enormous thighs, but she was slender and small and supple and always would be. I may be precocious, she thought, recalling an overheard conversation between Mary Bryce and her mother, but at least I've never had an awkward age.

She went down on her belly suddenly to try it and found her skill had not gone. So she wriggled along till she came by a secret way to her familiar hiding and diving place: a clearing right at the water's edge giving on a deep cove with a platform of moss to dive from. The whole place was carpeted with thick and squuddgy moss. She came here often for a certain purpose. No one but Jack Harlow knew this place; she had shown it to him lately for a reward. She and Jack had carved the hole in the tree together, making a bark door perfectly "camouflaged."

Ruth wriggled to the tree, opened the door and said, "Damn him, he's been here without me!" but he wouldn't have shown it to the others, ever. Jack was sweet on her since the last time they had rassled when Jack was thirteen and they had stopped suddenly in the middle of a rassle, both shy and red in the face for some reason. Ruth liked to remember that. She had a few warm memories like that that came and went like colored light.

She took the one remaining Sweet Cap from the package and put the package back in the tree to fool Jack. She scratched a match without noise—she could do that, too—lit the cigarette and poked the match into the moss. The smoke was delicious and her empty stomach made it dizzying. It made her feel seventh-heaven-drunk. Fairies might dance on the moss.

They did not, but something happened. Away back a twig snapped. An animal? Deer had been seen in the Wild Patch. But Ruth's deep-woods sense told her No. You couldn't take a chance. She filled her lungs with smoke, rose to the top of the world and crushed the last Sweet Cap into the moss. But it must be an animal, she thought as the trees swirled before her eyes. No person at this hour, no person. There, again, closer. But it must be a person; an animal would not be so quiet between the sounds. It was an Indian, as good at woods walking as she. She was afraid and drew back into the sheltering brush yet she could still see plainly. And suddenly she saw two brown hands close over two saplings and part them. A face looked through, looked round, and the person came out.

It was a man, no, a boy. He sniffed a moment, evidently smelling the smoke and his eyes showed an animal caution. But after a while he came full into the circle.

He was taller than Jack and older. He had a lot of unbrushed yellow hair. His fair skin was deeply tanned. He stood easily, yet Ruth knew that he was ready for quick action, that, if she made a sound, he would turn and vanish fast as a deer.

He wore a khaki shirt, half buttoned. The sleeves had been cut off high and were roughly hemmed. His khaki pants, too, were cut off above the knee. His legs were bare. On his bare feet were brown sneakers.

He was so close to Ruth that she could see the muscles moving in his legs and the little golden hairs. His hand was so close she could reach out and touch it. His hand was slender and strong.

Ruth could not see his face for he was looking away up the lake. But suddenly his head turned as if his eye had caught some flash from the south, so that she saw his high forehead and heavy straight eyebrows, his blue, moving eyes. His eyes were defiant, not afraid.

He walked away then to the moss-covered log that Ruth called the diving platform and kicked off his sneakers. Almost with a single motion his clothes dropped to his feet and he stepped to the edge.

He stood poised, facing the lake. His head and shoulders were in the full sunlight; the muscles played over his brown back as he raised his arms and moved his feet on the log, taking the perfect position.

Then, suddenly, he was gone and a long bright flash cut the water.

Ruth knew at once that it was the most beautiful thing she had ever seen. But she knew at the same time that she had had no right to see it. She did not try to explain this to herself. She simply knew it. She lay a moment shaking with a queer mixture of exultation, fear, and shame. It was in this moment that the devil possessed her.

What she did then she could never afterward understand though she twisted it this way and that to try to make it appear reasonable. Yet the impulse, when it came, was the familiar one of doing something terrible, something worse than what she had already done. Specifically, this impulse was to show herself to the boy and let him know she had seen him.

She plunged forward, scratching her face and arms until she was in the clearing. Then she stood up and the boy in the water saw her. It was a perfectly brazen, unconscionable act and she knew it while she did it, but the knowledge merely goaded her on.

The boy was well out now and swimming slowly back; he was looking at her quite unmoved.

"What are you doing?" she screamed and the foolish sound of her question made her angrier. "What are you doing on this property? It's my property! It's private! I'll have you arrested! I'll call the police!"

The boy did not answer, though he stopped swimming and began to tread water.

The moss gave way then under Ruth's feet; she stepped back, tripped and almost fell. She found her feet tangled in the boy's clothes. She saw the shapeless things through her blurred eyes and then, for no reason except that she was so mad, began trampling them into the soft moss. She stamped them down into the ooze and saw the green stain spread over them.

The boy called from the water:

"Git away from my clothes!"

His voice was steady. He even spoke in a drawl. It was then that Ruth realized what she had done. No doubt a murderer who, in some such blind madness has done in his man, might be recalled in the same way by a slow, calm voice and look down at the mangled corpse much as Ruth looked now at the poor, stained things beneath her feet. Then she turned and ran.

The house was still cool, still dark, still orderly and smelling of the morning. Ruth ran up the waxed stairs to her room and threw herself face down on the bed. For a long time, she dug her nails into the pillow and shuddered her sobs into its bitter softness. Her breath drew down at last into long sighing and, like a mocking echo, high in the trees, the hot locusts began their song.

The Handbag

From THE LOST WEEKEND

By Charles Jackson

Don, the hero of this story, is a pathological drunkard, with all the true addict's stealth and desperation. His brother and the girl Helen to whom he is engaged have tried to rescue him by taking him to the country for the weekend. But he has evaded them and started on one of the long debauches which, since his college days, have occupied most of his life.

Though Don is beyond redemption the reader is made to see the man who might have evolved from the careful culture of Don's background, with its emphasis on poetry and music. This sequence in the restaurant illustrates perhaps more clearly than any other in the book the author's power to lead the reader, step by step, from the rational objective scene into the fantasy of the alcoholic mind.

A COUPLE came in and sat down at the next table, on the bench beside him, another young man and a girl. He took them in, subtly, not staring, watching his chance to observe them unobserved, as if it were some kind of delightful game of skill. The girl took off her fur and put it on the bench with her handbag, between herself and him, not more than a foot-and-a-half from where he sat. He tried to place the kind of girl she was, mused on where she came from, what she did. It was a good enough fur—marten. He looked at the handbag. Brown alligator, with a large copper clasp, and a metal monogram in one corner: M. Mc. The young man wore a grey tweed suit, an expensive one, so rough and coarse that it looked as if small twigs were woven into it, chunks of rope and hemp, pieces of coal—he smiled with pleasure at

such an idea. Isn't that exactly the kind of suit he'd be wearing? he said
to himself—and then smiled again, for of course he wouldn't have said
it if the young man hadn't been wearing that kind of suit. He was delighted with this observation—it told him that his mind was working
keenly and at the top of its bent, with that hyper-consciousness that lay
just this side of intoxication. Well, he'd keep it this side, because he was
having a good time, enjoying his own aloofness to the scene around him.

He eyed the handbag again. What was in it? Lady-trifles, probably;
immoment toys; God what marvelous expressions, what felicity, who
else could have thought of them!—and suddenly, for an instant, he had
a craving to read Shakespeare, rush home and sit down with Antony and
Cleopatra and enjoy the feast of language that was, perhaps, the only
true pleasure in the world. But that was irrational, irresponsible: Shakespeare was there, would always be there, when he wanted him; the thing
to do was appoint a certain period, regularly, perhaps two hours every
day, every evening, why not, he had plenty of time, nothing but time—
his eye went back to the handbag.

M. Mc. Irish or Scotch? She was an attractive girl; black hair, beautiful fair complexion. Were they sleeping together? Was he nice to her?
They probably didn't begin to appreciate each other physically, they
were too young. The young man would be carried away in his own excitement, she in hers, with no thought of each other's sensations. Did
he know what his body did to her? Did she forget herself long enough
to prize his, did she lay her head on his stomach, feel his chest and
thighs, was he big? The questions suddenly seemed important, they
were all that mattered in the room—important, dangerous and exciting.
He felt reckless and elated, larger than life. If she were not there, if the
young man were alone, he would advance and find out a thing or two,
amused at his own daring, amused at the young man's shock. Or if the
young man should go, leaving the girl, if she should look over and see
him, let him speak to her, if he should move closer, if they should leave
together, go home—how he would teach her what it was to be with a
man! It was all one to him, for the moment he was like a god who could
serve either at will. The handbag caught his eye and he puzzled about
its contents.

He signaled for another gin-vermouth and turned his attention to the
room. Odd how he could sit there unobserved by others; he was the
only one alive in the place, the only one who saw. Their preoccupation
with each other, his own solidarity, completeness, self-sufficiency, aloofness, gave him a sense of elevation and excellence that was almost god-
like. He smiled with tolerance at the room, and felt so remote and apart
that he might have been unseen. He was unseen; for he had had to signal for minutes before he got the attention of the waiter, the bartender

had never glanced his way, no, not once since he had sat down, the baby-faced pianist had eyes only for the couples of men and girls, and they for each other. If he should melt into air, dissolve and leave not a rack behind (why had he never looked up what a rack was?), no one would notice. Some time later the waiter would come upon the empty glass at the empty table and wonder when he had gone.

Or if he should lift this handbag, pull it toward him, cover it with the skirt of his coat, who should see? What could be in it, how much money? What would it be like to steal a purse ('tis something, nothing, 'tis mine, 'tis his), how would you feel? Would it be fun, what kind of satisfaction would it give you? A dozen excitements possessed him: he was ridden with curiosity to know what was in the handbag, he could use the money (possibly a fair sum), he wanted to see for his own satisfaction if he could get away with it—commit the perfect crime. Absurd! But on a tiny, on a very small scale that's exactly what it would be. He would return the bag to the owner afterward, having removed and used the cash. Her address was bound to be inside and he would send the bag back in the mail, with a witty, charming anonymous note, signed, perhaps, "Mr. X—and sometimes W and Y." Oh, he could use the money (he wondered how much there was, he had to know), but mostly he wanted to see how it would feel to get away with it, he wanted to prove to himself that he could. It would be a new experience, unlike anything he had ever done; certainly that made the risk worthwhile, for how else was a man's life enriched if not by new experience, letting oneself in for all the million possibilities of various existence, trying everything, anything—"live dangerously"? He lost interest in these philosophies, however, as he now bent all his conscious will, all the keenness and alertness of his over-alert brain, to the attempt.

He had never been so sure of himself in his life, so much the master of his every smallest move, gesture, muscle; he was so calm, so thoroughly at ease and at home, that now he meant to prolong the moment as long as possible, savoring its every second to get the most out of it. He would take the bag and then stay—linger, not leave at all, not hurry, never move, possibly even order another drink in the assurance and security that no one knew what he was doing, that even if the bag were missed, it would be impossible to think that he had it. One look at him would show them it could never have been he. Preposterous that such a man, well-dressed, composed, a gentleman—he reached the bag with the tip of his fingers and pulled it a few inches his way.

Nobody saw, of course; he pulled it nearer, then signalled the waiter for another gin-vermouth. The waiter came and set it down before him. He watched the waiter's face. There was the bag, resting beside him, touching his coat, under the very eyes of the waiter, yet the man had seen nothing. He picked up the drink by the thin stem of the glass and slowly sipped; sweet and sharp and thick, a wonderful drink, why did he ever order anything else—but it was too slow, too subtle for his taste, he liked the immediate effect, the instant warmth, of liquor straight. Still, this was nice, it was all right for now, the stronger drink could wait, there were hours and days ahead, he twirled the stem slowly between his thumb and forefinger, and with the other hand he lifted the skirt of his coat and covered the bag.

It could go on forever, he could sit here all night, hiding the bag; he could even put it on the table in front of him and examine its contents then and there, for all that anyone would notice. How careless people were, and unobserving—how crafty, subtle, all-seeing himself. An idea struck him. It might be fun, after he got out in the street, say half an hour later—it would be fun to come back, ascend the stairs again, approach the surprised couple and address them, saying, "Here is your bag, see how easy it was, you didn't even know it was gone, did you?" The young man would half rise, the girl would look down at the bench beside her and exclaim, "Well of all—!" What would be the fun of getting away with it if you couldn't tell about it, show how clever you were, how easy it had been? Otherwise it would all be wasted. But he needed the money too, he wanted it now; and afterward his only concern would be to get rid of the bag, leave it in some impossible fabulous place where it would never turn up, never again, in his or anyone else's life.

The suspense was intoxicating, he was filled with admiration for his own shrewd, adroit and disarming performance, knowing that to an observer (but there were none) he gave only the impression of disinterest, thoughtful melancholy, ennui. He pulled the bag against his hip, adjusted the coat closer about him with a casual movement, and sipped the drink.

For some minutes after he emptied the glass, he sat there, his studied expression (wrinkled brow, faint pout, faint tilt of the head) showing that he played with the idea of ordering another drink. With an all but imperceptible shrug he made his decision—called the waiter, examined the check with care, paid with a bored air, tipped well. The waiter thanked him and left. He pulled the bag up under his arm, inside his topcoat, and sat a moment or two longer, stripping the cellophane from a pack of cigarettes, wadding it up, tossing it on the table, selecting a cigarette, tapping it down, lighting it. Reflectively he watched the match burn to his finger tips, then dropped it just in time. He reached for his hat and got up, pushing the table away with a scraping noise. He nodded goodnight to the bartender.

Near the stairs was a poster about some Village dance. He stopped to examine it, as if concerned to see who was the artist. Behind him, a wave of laughter swept the room. He turned and looked back with a philosophical smile at the men and girls convulsed with hilarity over some new double-meaning of the singer at the piano; then turned again and went down the stairs, his hat in his hand.

The bar below was crowded. He walked through the long room toward the street, slowly, regarding the huddled drinkers in a manner detached and aloof. He was the spectator still, unseen—truly he might have been invisible, the figure out of mythology, so unmarked was his passage through the crowded room, his very presence amid all the festivity. Near the end, he stopped and looked at himself in the mirror over the bar through a gap between two men on bar-stools. He smoothed back his hair, then put his hat on and adjusted it carefully. He gave the effect a last approving look and went on.

He saw the big doorman holding open the door for him. He reached into his pocket for a tip. He dropped a dime into the gloved hand, and someone behind him touched his shoulder. He turned. There was the bartender and waiter, the young man and girl from upstairs. His eyebrows went up, his mouth lifted in an enquiring smile. "Give us that bag," one of them said in slow, heavy, even tones—and he noticed that the entire room was quiet, every face at the bar turned toward the door and himself.

"Why certainly," he said, pleasantly, "here it is," and he produced the bag from under his coat and handed it directly to the girl herself with a faint bow.

He would never remember what was said then, who said it, or the order in which it was said. The young man was muttering in threat, the waiter said "Call a cop, Mike's on the corner," the girl said "Never mind, never mind, I've got my bag, that's all I wanted, please let him go," the bartender said "If you ever come back here again, if I ever see—" He stood there puzzled in the middle of it all, his polite patient half-smile trying to say for him, What's all the fuss, it's only a joke, I'm sure I didn't realize, truly I wasn't serious, I was only having a little— The doorman put big hands on his shoulders, turned him around, gave him a shove that made his neck snap, and he was in the street.

He recovered and adjusted his coat and hat and walked slowly, leisurely, away, trying not to hear what the doorman called after him, trying not to see the little group of cabbies staring at him in silent contempt. By the time he got to the corner and out of sight, moving as slowly and leisurely as he was able, his legs were shaking so violently he could hardly stand. He thought he would collapse, he wanted to collapse, wanted to give way, fall down, pretend to be very drunk, be picked up and taken care of by someone, a stranger. He thought of Helen in Bleecker Street and recoiled in terror. He stumbled into a cab in Sheridan Square, gave his address, and fell into the dark backseat as if it were his bed, his own bed at home. During the drive uptown, the blessed oblivion of time-out, he became so calm, so deathly relaxed and still, that he was barely able to respond with gratitude as he remembered the nearly-full pint at home. Was this what he had been seeking? He had reached the point where always there was only one thing: drink, and more drink, till amnesty came; and tomorrow, drink again.

Awakening

From BARREN GROUND
By Ellen Glasgow

The pattern of Dorinda Oakley's life in a section of starved Virginia farm land in the 1890's was as unvarying as the bleak countryside. She accepted it because she saw no hope of change. Her ten dollars a month as a grocery clerk went toward taxes and interest on the farm mortgage, her spare time toward helping her mother. But when Jason Greylock, the vacillating but charming son of the country doctor, came home to care for his seedy father and take over his practice, Dorinda's twenty-year-old heart awoke. The handsome girl, the young man with the New York air, fell in love and planned their marriage. In the blindness of her first happiness Dorinda assembled her trousseau and forgot Geneva Ellgood, daughter of the rich man of the county, who had known Jason in the city. In this scene comes her awakening and disillusion.

O N either side of the road the trees grew straight and tall, and overhead the grey arch of sky looked as if it were hewn out of rock. The pines were dark as night, but the oaks, the sweet gums, the beeches, and hickory trees were turning slowly, and here and there the boughs were brushed with wine-colour or crimson. Far away, she could hear the rumble of the storm, and it seemed to her that the noise and burden of living marched on there at an immeasurable distance. Within the woods there was the profound silence of sleep. Nothing but the occasional flutter of a bird or stir of a small animal in the underbrush disturbed the serenity. The oppressive air stifled her, and she felt that her breath, like the movement of the wind, was suspended.

"If I don't hurry, I shall never get out of the woods," she thought. "I ought not to have come."

Forgetting the attack of faintness, she quickened her steps into a run, and stumbled on over the wheelruts in the road, which was scarcely wider than a cart track. For a while this stillness was so intense that she felt as if it were palpitating in smothered throbs like her heart. The storm was gathering on another planet. So remote it was that the slow reverberations were echoed across an immensity of silence. The first mile was past. Then the second. With the ending of the third, she knew that she should come out into the pasture and the old cornfield at Five Oaks.

Presently a few withered leaves fluttered past her, flying through the narrow tunnel of the woods toward the clearer vista ahead. Immediately round her the atmosphere was still motionless. Like an alley in a dream the road stretched, brown, dim, monotonous, between the tall trees; and this alley seemed to her unutterably sad, strewn with dead leaves and haunted by an autumnal taint of decay. The fear in her own mind had fallen like a blight on her surroundings, as if the external world were merely a shadow thrown by the subjective processes within her soul.

Suddenly, without nearer warning, the storm broke. A streak of white fire split the sky, and the tattered clouds darkened to an angry purple. The wind, which had been chained at a distance, tore itself free with a hurtling noise and crashed in gusts through the tree-tops. Overhead she heard the snapping of branches, and when she glanced back, it seemed to her that the withered leaves had gathered violence in pursuit, and were whirling after her like a bevy of witches. As she came out of the shelter of the trees, the stream of wind and leaves swept her across the cornfield, with the patter of rain on her shoulders. Where the road turned, she saw the red barn and the brick dwelling of Five Oaks, and in obedience to the wind rather than by the exercise of her own will, she was driven over the field and the yard to the steps of the back porch. Her first impression was that the place was deserted; and running up the steps she sank into one of the broken chairs on the porch, and shook the water from her hat while she struggled for breath. On the roof of the house the rain was beating in drops as hard as pebbles. She heard it thundering on the shingles; she saw it scattering the chips and straws by the woodpile, and churning the puddles in the walk until they foamed with a yeasty scum. The sky was shrouded now in a crape-like pall, and where the lightning ripped open the blackness, the only colour was that jagged stain of dull purple. "I'm wet already," she thought. "In another minute I'd have been soaked through to the skin." Turning her head, she looked curiously at the home of her lover.

The thought in her mind was, "You could tell no woman lived here. When I get the chance, it won't take me long to make things look different." With the certainty that this "chance" would one day be hers, she forgot her anxiety and fatigue, and a thrill of joy eased her heart. Yes, things would be different when she and Jason lived here together and little children played under the great oaks in the grove. Her fingers "itched," as she said to herself, to clean up the place and make it tidy without and within. A rivulet of muddy water was pouring round the corner of the house, wearing a channel in the gravelled walk, which was littered with rubbish. Beside the porch there was a giant box-bush, beneath which several bedraggled white turkeys had taken shelter. She could see them through the damp twilight of the boughs, shaking drenched feathers or scratching industriously in the rank mould among the roots.

Leaning back, in her wet clothes, against the splits of the chair, which sagged on one rocker, she glanced about her at the refuse that overflowed from the hall. The porch looked as if it had not been swept for years. There was a pile of dusty bagging in one corner, and, scattered over the floor, she saw a medley of oil cans, empty cracker boxes and whiskey bottles, loose spokes of cart wheels, rolls of barbed wire and stray remnants of leather harness. "How can any one live in such confusion?" she thought. Glancing round through the doorway, she could distinguish merely a glimmer of light on the ceiling, from which the plaster was dropping, and the vague shape of a staircase, which climbed, steep and slender, to the upper story. It was a fairly good house of its period, the brick dwelling, with ivy-encrusted wings, which was preferred by the more prosperous class of Virginia farmers. The foundation of stone had been well laid; the brick walls were stout and solid, and though neglect and decay had overtaken it, the house still preserved, beneath its general air of deterioration, an underlying character of honesty and thrift. Turning away, she gazed through the silver mesh of rain, past the barn and the stable, to the drenched pasture, where a few trees rocked back and forth, and a flock of frightened sheep huddled together. Where were the farm labourers, she wondered? What had become of Jemima, who, Aunt Mehitable had said, was still working here? Two men living alone must keep at least one woman servant. Had the storm thrown a curse of stagnation over the place, and made it incapable of movement or sound? She could barely see the sky for the slanting rain, which drove faster every minute. Was she the only living thing left, except the cowering sheep in the pasture and the dripping white turkeys under the box-bush?

While she was still asking the question, she heard a shuffling step in the hall behind her and, looking hastily over her shoulder, saw the figure of the old man blocking the doorway. For an instant his squat outline, blurred between the dark hall and the sheets of rain, was all that she distinguished. Then he lurched toward her, peering out of the gloom. Yesterday she would have run from him in terror. Before her visit to Whistling Spring she would have faced the storm rather than the brooding horror at Five Oaks. But the great fear had absorbed the small fears as the night absorbs shadows. Nothing mattered to her if she could only reach Jason.

"Come in, come in," the old doctor was mumbling, with a dreary effort at hospitality.

He held out his palsied hand, and all the evil rumours she had heard since he had given up his practice and buried himself at Five Oaks rushed into her mind. It must be true that he had always been a secret drinker, and that the habit had taken possession now of his faculties. Though she had known him all her life, the change in him was so startling that she would scarcely have recognized him. His once robust figure was wasted and flabby, except for his bloated paunch, which hung down like a sack of flour; his scraggy throat protruding from the bristles of his beard reminded the girl of the neck of a buzzard; his little fiery eyes, above inflamed pouches of skin, flickered and shone, just as the smouldering embers had flickered and shone under Aunt Mehitable's pot. And from these small bloodshot eyes something sly and secretive and malignant looked out at her. Was this, she wondered, what whiskey and his own evil nature could do to a man?

"I am on my way back from Whistling Spring," she explained, while she struggled against the repulsion he aroused in her. "The storm caught me just as I reached here."

He smirked with his bloodless old lips, which cracked under the strain. "Eh? Eh?" he chuckled, cupping his ear in his hand. Then catching hold of her sleeve, he pulled her persuasively toward the door. "Come in, come in," he urged. "You're wet through. I've kindled a bit of fire to dry my boots, and it's still burning. Come in, and dry yourself before you take cold from the wetting."

Still clutching at her, he stumbled into the hall, glancing uneasily back, as if he feared that she might slip out of his grasp. On the right a door stood ajar, and a few knots of resinous pine blazed, with a thin blue light, in the cavernous fireplace. As he led her over the threshold, she noticed that the windows were all down, and that the only shutters left open were those at the back window, against which the giant box-bush had grown into the shape of a hunchback. There was a film of dust or wood ashes over the floor and the furniture, and cobwebs were spun in lacy patterns on the discoloured walls. A demijohn, still half full of whiskey, stood on the crippled mahogany desk, and a pitcher of water and several dirty glasses were on a tin tray beside it. Near the sparkling blaze a leather chair, from which the stuffing protruded, faced a shabby footstool upholstered in crewel work, and a pile of hickory logs, chips, and pine knots, over which spiders were crawling. While Dorinda sat down in the chair he pointed out, and glanced nervously over the dust and dirt that surrounded her, she thought that she had never seen a room from which the spirit of hope was so irrevocably banished. What a life Jason's mother must have led in this place! How had Jason, with his charm, his fastidiousness, his sensitive nerves, been able to stay here? Her gaze wandered to the one unshuttered window, where the sheets of rain were blown back and forth like a curtain. She saw the hunched shoulder of the box-bush, crouching under the torrent of water which poured down from the roof. Yet she longed to be out in the storm. Any weather was better than this close, dark place, so musty in spite of its fire, and this suffocating stench of whiskey and of things that were never aired.

"Just a thimbleful of toddy to ward off a chill?" the old man urged, with his doddering gestures.

She shook her head, trying to smile. A drop of the stuff in one of those fly-specked glasses would have sickened her.

Darkness swept over her with the ebb and flow of the sea. She felt a gnawing sensation within; there was a quivering in her elbows; and it seemed to her that she was dissolving into emptiness. The thin blue light wavered and vanished and wavered again. When she opened her eyes the room came out of the shadows in fragments, obscure, glimmering, remote. On the shingled roof the rain was pattering like a multitude of tiny feet, the restless bare feet of babies. Terror seized her. She longed with all her will to escape; but how could she go back into the storm without an excuse; and what excuse could she find? After all, repulsive as he appeared, he was still Jason's father.

"No, thank you," she answered, when he poured a measure of whiskey into a glass and pushed it toward her. "Aunt Mehitable gave me some blackberry cordial." After a silence she asked abruptly: "Where is Jemima?"

Lifting the glass she had refused, he added a stronger dash to the weak mixture, and sipped it slowly. "There's nothing better when you're wet than a little toddy," he muttered. "Jemima is off for the evening, but she'll be back in time to get supper. I heard her say she was going over to Plumtree."

A peal of thunder broke so near that she started to her feet, expecting to see the window-panes shattered.

"There, there, don't be afraid," he said, nodding at her over his glass. "The worst is over now. The rain will have held up before you're dry and ready to go home."

It was like a nightmare, the dark, glimmering room, with its dust and cobwebs, the sinister old man before the blue flames of the pine knots, the slanting rain over the box-bush, the pattering sound on the roof, and the thunderbolts which crashed near by and died away in the distance. Even her body felt numbed, as if she were asleep, and her feet, when she rose and took a step forward, seemed to be walking on nothing. It was just as if she knew it was not real, that it was all visionary and incredible, and as if she stood there waiting until she should awake. The dampness, too, was not a genuine dampness, but the sodden atmosphere of a nightmare.

"Why, it has stopped now!" she exclaimed suddenly. "The storm is over." Then, because she did not wish to show fear of him, she came nearer and held her wet dress to the flames. "You won't need a fire much longer," she said. "It is warmer out of doors than it is inside."

"That's why I keep the windows down." He looked so dry and brittle, in spite of the dampness about him, that she thought he would break in pieces if he moved too quickly. There was no life, no sap, left in his veins.

"I'm by myself now," he winked at her. "But it won't be for long. Jason comes back to-night."

"To-night!" Joy sang in her voice. But why hadn't he written? Was there anything wrong? Or was he merely trying to surprise her by his return?

"You hadn't heard? Well, that proves, I reckon, that I can keep a secret." He lurched to his feet, balanced himself unsteadily for an instant, and then stumbled to the window. Beyond him she saw the black shape of the box-bush, with a flutter of white turkeys among its boughs, and overhead a triangle of sky, where the grey was washed into a delicate blue. Yes, the storm was over.

"They ought to reach the station about now," he said. "When the windows are open and the wind is in the right direction, you can hear the whistle of the train." There was malignant pleasure in his tone. "You didn't know, I s'pose, that he'd gone off to get married?"

"Married?" She laughed feebly, imagining that he intended a joke. How dreadful old men were when they tried to be funny! His pointed beard jerked up and down when he talked, and his little red blinking eyes stared between his puffed eyelids like a rat's eyes out of a hole. Then something as black and cold as stale soot floated out from the chimney and enveloped her. She could scarcely get her breath. If only he would open the windows.

"Hasn't he told you that we are to be married next week?" she asked.

"No, he hasn't told me." He gloated over the words as if they were whiskey, and she wondered what he was like when he was not drinking, if that ever happened. He could be open-handed, she had heard, when the humour struck him. Once, she knew, he had helped Miss Texanna Snead raise the money for her taxes, and when Aunt Mehitable's cow died he had given her another. "I had a notion that you and he were sweethearts," he resumed presently, "and he'd have to look far, I reckon, before he could pick out a finer girl. He's a pleasant-tempered boy, is Jason, but he ain't dependable, even if he is my son, so I hope you haven't set too much store by him. I never heard of him mixing up with girls, except you and Geneva. That ain't his weakness. The trouble with him is that he was born white-livered. Even as a child he would go into fits if you showed him a snake or left him by himself in the dark—"

"But he loves me," she said stoutly, closing her ears and her mind to his words.

He nodded. "I don't doubt it, I don't doubt it. He loved you well enough, I reckon, to want to jilt Geneva; but he found out, when he tried, that she wasn't as easy to jilt as he thought. He'd courted her way back yonder last year, when they were in New York together. Later on he'd have been glad to wriggle out of it; but when Jim and Bob Ellgood came after him, he turned white-livered again. They took him off and married him while he was still shaking from fright. A good boy, a pleasant boy," continued the old man, smacking his dry lips, "but he ain't of my kidney."

When he had finished, she gazed at him in a dumbness which had attacked her like paralysis. She tried to cry out, to tell him that she knew he lied; but her lips would not move in obedience to her will and her throat felt as if it were petrified. Was this the way people felt when they had a stroke, she found herself thinking. On the surface she was inanimate; but beneath, in the buried jungle of her consciousness, there was the stirring of primitive impulses, and this stirring was agony. All individual differences, all the acquired attributes of civilization, had turned to wood or stone; yet the racial structure, the savage fibre of instinct, remained alive in her.

The room had grown darker. Only the hearth and the evil features of the old man were picked out by the wavering blue light. She saw his face, with its short wagging beard and its fiery points of eyes, as one sees objects under running water. Everything was swimming round her, and outside, where a cloud had drifted over the triangle of clear sky, the box-bush and the white turkeys were swimming too.

"You'll meet 'em on the road if you go by the fork," piped a voice beneath that shifting surface. "They will be well on the way by the time you have started."

Stung awake at last, she thrust out her arm, warding him off. The one thought in her mind now was to escape, to get out of the room before he could stop her, to put the house and its terrors behind her. It couldn't be true. He was drunk. He was lying. He was out of his head. She was foolish even to listen, foolish to let the lie worry her for an instant.

Turning quickly, she ran from him out of the room, out of the house, out of the stagnant air of the place.

At the beginning of the sandy road, where the water had hollowed a basin, she met the coloured woman, Idabella, who said "good-evening," after the custom of the country, as she went by. She was a handsome mulatto, tall, deep-bosomed, superb and unscrupulous, with the regal features that occasionally defy ethnology in the women of mixed blood. Her glossy black hair was worn in a coronet, and she moved with the slow and arrogant grace which springs from a profound immobility.

"The dreadful old man," thought Dorinda, as she hurried in the direction of Gooseneck Creek. "The dreadful, lying old man!"

The sun had riddled the clouds, and a watery light drenched the trees, the shrubs, and the bruised weeds. This light, which bathed the external world in a medium as fluid as rain, penetrated into her thoughts, and enveloped the images in her mind with a transparent brilliance.

"It isn't true," she repeated over and over, as she went down the sandy slope to Gooseneck Creek, and over the bridge of logs in the willows. When she reached the meadows, rain was still dripping from the goldenrod and life-everlasting. A rabbit popped up from the briars and scuttled ahead of her, with his little white tail bobbing jauntily.

"How funny it looks," she thought, "just as if it were beckoning me to come on and play. The rain is over, but I am soaked through. Even my skin is wet. I'll have to dry all my clothes by the kitchen fire, if it hasn't gone out. What a terrible old man!" Out of nowhere there flashed into her mind the recollection of a day when she had gone to a dentist at the County Courthouse to have an aching tooth drawn. All the way, sitting beside her father, behind Dan and Beersheba, she had kept repeating, "It won't hurt very much." Strange that she should have thought of that now! She could see the way Dan and Beersheba had turned, flopping their ears, and looked round, as if they were trying to show sympathy; and how the bunches of indigo, fastened on their heads to keep flies away, had danced fantastically like uprooted bushes. "It isn't true," she said now, seeking to fortify her courage as she had tried so passionately on the drive to the dentist. "When Jason comes back, we will laugh over it together. He will tell me that I was foolish to be worried, that it proved I did not trust him. When we are married, I will stand between him and the old man as much as I can. I am not afraid of him. No, I am not afraid," she said aloud, stopping suddenly in the road as if she had seen a snake in her path. "When Jason comes back everything will be right. Yes, everything will be right," she repeated. "Perhaps the old man suspected something, and was trying to frighten me. Doctors always know things sooner than other people. . . . What a dirty place it is! Ma would call it a pig sty. Well, I can clean it up, bit by bit. Even if the old man doesn't let anybody touch his den, I can clean the rest of the house. I'll begin with the porch, and some day, when he is out, I can make Jemima wash that dreadful floor and the window-panes. The outside is almost as bad too. The walk looks as if it had never been swept." In order to deaden this fear, which was gnawing her heart like a rat, she began to plan how she would begin cleaning the place and gradually bring system out of confusion. "A little at a time," she said aloud, as if she were reciting a phrase in a foreign language. "A little at a time will not upset him."

At the fork of the road, approaching the red gate, where the thick belt of woods began, her legs gave way under her, and she knew that she could go no farther. "I'll have to stop," she thought, "even if the ground is so wet, I'll have to sit down." Then the unconscious motive, which had guided her ever since she left Five Oaks, assumed a definite form. "If he came on that train, he ought to be here in a few minutes," she said. "The whistle blew a long time ago. Even if he waited for the mail, he ought to be here in a little while."

Stepping over the briars into the woods, she looked about for a place to sit down. An old stump, sodden with water, pushed its way up from the maze of creepers, and she dropped beside it, while she relapsed into the suspense that oozed out of the ground and the trees. As long as her reaction to this secret fear was merely physical, she was able to keep her thoughts fixed on empty mechanical movements; but the instant she admitted the obscure impulse into her mind, the power of determination seemed to go out of her. She felt weak, unstrung, incapable of rational effort.

A thicket of dogwood and redbud trees made a close screen in front of her, and through the dripping branches she could see the red gate, and beyond it the blasted oak and the burned cabin on the other side of the road. Farther on, within range of her vision, there were the abandoned acres of broomsedge, and opposite to them she imagined the Sneads' pasture, with the white and red splotches of cows and the blurred patches of huddled sheep.

While she sat there the trembling passed out of her limbs, and the strength that had forsaken her returned slowly. Removing her hat, she let the branches play over her face, like the delicate touch of cool, moist fingers. She felt drenched without and within. The very thoughts that came and went in her mind were as limp as wet leaves, and blown like leaves, in the capricious stir of the breeze. For a few minutes she sat there surrounded by a vacancy in which nothing moved but the leaves and the wind. Without knowing what she thought, without knowing even what she felt, she abandoned herself to the encompassing darkness. Then, suddenly, without warning from her mind, this vacancy was flooded with light and crowded with a multitude of impressions. Their first meeting in the road. The way he looked at her. His eyes when he smiled. The red of his hair. His hand when he touched her. The feeling of his arms, of his mouth on hers, of the rough surface of his coat brushing her face. The first time he had kissed her. The last time he had kissed her. No. It isn't true. It isn't true. Deep down in her being some isolated point of consciousness, slow rhythmic, monotonous, like a swinging pendulum, was ticking over and over: *It isn't true. It isn't true. True. True. It isn't true.* On the surface other thoughts came and went. That horrible old man. A fire in summer. The stench of drunkenness. Tobacco stains on his white beard. A rat watching her from a hole. How she hated rats! Did he suspect something, and was he trying to frighten her? Trying to frighten her. But she would let him see that she was too strong for him. She was not afraid. . . . The thoughts went on, coming and going like leaves blown in the wind, now rising, now fluttering down again. But far away, in a blacker vacancy, the pendulum still swung to and fro, and she heard the thin, faint ticking of the solitary point of consciousness: *True. True. It isn't true. It isn't true—true—true—*

No, he couldn't frighten her. She was too sure of her happiness. "Too sure of Jason," she repeated aloud.

The little sad, watery sun sputtered out like a lantern, and after a few minutes of wan greyness, shone more clearly, as if it had been relighted and hung up again in the sky. Colour flowed back into the landscape, trickling in shallow streams of blue and violet through the nearer fields and evaporating into dark fire where the broomsedge enkindled the horizon. She started up quickly, and fell back. When she put her hand on the slimy moss it felt like a toad.

Far down the road, somewhere in the vague blur of the distance, there was the approaching rumble of wheels. She heard the even rise and fall of the hoofs, the metallic clink of horseshoes striking together, the jolting over the rock by the Sneads' pasture, the splash of mud in the bad hole near the burned cabin, and the slip and scramble of the mare as she stumbled and then, recovering herself, broke into a trot.

It isn't true. It isn't true, tickled the pin point of consciousness. Her mind was still firm; but her limbs trembled so violently that she slipped from the stump to the carpet of moss and soaked creepers. Shutting her eyes, she held fast to the slimy branch of a tree. "When he turns at the fork, I will look. I will not look until he turns the fork."

The rumble was louder, was nearer. An instant of silence. The buggy was approaching the fork. She heard close at hand the familiar clink of the steel shoes and the sharper squeak of a loosened screw in the wheel. Rising on the sodden mould, she opened her eyes, pushed aside the curtain of branches, and looked out through the leaves. She saw Jason sitting erect, with the reins in his hands. She saw his burnished red hair, his pale profile, his slightly stooping shoulders, his mouth which was closed in a hard straight line. Clear and sharp, she saw him with the vividness of a flash of lightning, and beside him, she saw the prim, girlish figure and the flaxen head of Geneva Ellgood.

It isn't true. It isn't true. The pendulum was swinging more slowly; and suddenly the ticking stopped, and then went on in jerks like a clock that is running down. *It isn't true. It isn't true—true—true.*

She felt cold and wet. Though she had not lost the faculty of recollection, she was outside of time and space, suspended in ultimate darkness. There was an abyss around her, and through this abyss wind was blowing, black wind, which made no sound because it was sweeping through nothingness. She lay flat in this vacancy, yet she did not fall through it because she also was nothing. Only her hands, which clutched wood mould, were alive. There was mould under her finger nails, and the smell of wet earth filled her nostrils. Everything within her had stopped. The clock no longer ticked; it had run down. She could not think, or, if she thought, her thoughts were beyond her consciousness, skimming like shadows over a frozen lake. Only the surface of her could feel, only her skin, and this felt as if it would never be warm again.

"So it is true," she said aloud, and the words, spoken without a thought behind them, startled her. The instant afterward she began to come back to existence; she could feel life passing through her by degrees, first in her hands and feet, where needles were pricking, then in her limbs, and at last in her mind and heart. And while life fought its way into her, something else went out of her for ever—youth, hope, love —and the going was agony. Her pain became so intolerable that she sprang to her feet and started running through the woods, like a person who is running away from a forest fire. Only she knew, while she ran faster and faster, that the fire was within her breast, and she could not escape it. No matter how far she ran and how fast, she could not escape it.

Presently the running shook her senses awake, and her thoughts became conscious ones. In the silence the shuddering beats of her heart were like the unsteady blows of a hammer—one, two, one, one, two, two. Her breath came with a whistling sound, and for a minute she confused it with the wind in the tree-tops.

"So this is the end," she said aloud, and then very slowly, "I didn't know I could feel like this. I didn't know anybody could feel like this."

A phrase of her mother's, coloured with the barbaric imagery of a Hebrew prophet, was driven, as aimlessly as a wisp of straw, into her mind: "Your great-grandfather said he never came to Christ till he had thirsted for blood." Thirsted for blood! She had never known what that meant. It had seemed to her a strange way to come to Christ, but now she understood.

The wet briars tore her legs through her stockings. Branches whipped her face and bruised its delicate flesh. Once, when she came out of the woods, she slipped and fell on her hands and knees. The splinters of the fence pierced her skin when she climbed over the rails. But still she ran on, trying to escape from the fire within her breast.

Sidewalk Café

From *DODSWORTH*

By Sinclair Lewis

The search for greater horizons which was a reaction of Americans against their own world in the 1920's is one of the motives of Lewis' *Dodsworth*. Sam Dodsworth has been transplanted to Europe by his ambitious wife Fran from the midwestern city of Zenith where he has made his fortune manufacturing automobiles. After a bewildering time in London, they move to the continent. Sam, temporarily deserted by Fran, finds himself alone in Paris. Feeling the need to meditate on "what it was all about" Sam leaves his touring friends from Zenith and drifts into a café where he is exploited and deceived by his own countrymen. But the scene reaches beyond its people into the whole frustration of the transplanted American—transplanted not merely from home but from the entire set of values which form his character.

WHAT Tub and Matey and Sam did during their week together may be deduced by studying a newspaper list of "Where to Lunch, Dine, and Dance in Paris," the advertisements of dressmakers, jewelers, perfumers, furniture-dealers, and of revues; and by reprinting for each evening the more serious features of Tub's first night in Paris.

It was a fatiguing week, but rather comforting to Sam.

Through it, the pious admonitions of Matey, along with the thought of Minna von Escher and his own original virtue, prepared him to yield to temptation—only he saw no one who was tempting.

The Pearsons begged him to go on to Holland with them, but he said that he had business in Paris; he spoke vaguely of conferences with mo-

---

tor agents. Actually, he wanted a day or two for the luxury of sitting by himself, of walking where he would, of meditating in long undisturbed luxurious hours on what it was all about.

He had two hasty, stammering notes from Fran, in which she said that she missed him, which was all very pleasant and gratifying, but in which she babbled of dancing with Kurt von Obersdorf till three A.M. —of a day with Kurt in the country—of an invitation from Kurt's friends, the Von Arminals, to spend the next week-end at their place in the Harz Mountains. "And of course they'd be enchanted to have you also if you get back in time, asked me tell you how sorry they are you aren't here," her pen sputtered.

"Hm!" said Sam.

Suddenly he was testy. Oh, of course she had a "right" to be with Kurt as much as she liked. He wasn't a harem-keeper. And of course it would be puerile to rage, "If she has a right to be loose, then I have the same right." There was no question of "rights." It was a question of what he wanted, and whether he was willing to pay for it—whether he wanted new, strange loves, whether he could find them, and whether he was willing to pay in dignity, in the respect that Fran had for him despite her nervous jabbings.

When he had seen the Pearsons off for Amsterdam, with mighty vows to meet them in Zenith within six months, when he had for an hour sat outside the Café des Deux Magots, brooding on the Franocentric universe which had cataclysmically replaced the universe of business and creating motors and playing golf, then sharply, gripping the marble top of the little table with his huge hand, he admitted with no more reservations that he was hungry as a barren woman, hungry for a sweetheart who should have Fran's fastidiousness, Minna von Escher's sooty warmth, and Matey Pearson's shrewd earthiness.

He dined alone in a little Montparnasse restaurant filled with eager young couples: a Swedish painter with an Italian girl student, an American globe-trotter with his Polish mistress, pairs of white Russians and Italian anti-fascists. They all twittered like love-birds and frankly held hands over the vin ordinaire and horse-meat. And here, as it was very cheap, there were actually French people, all in couples except when they belonged to enormous noisy family parties, and the couples stroked each other's hands, unabashedly nuzzled each other's cheeks, looked into each other's eyes, the world well lost.

It was spring—spring and Paris—scent of chestnut blossoms, freshness of newly watered pavements, and Sam Dodsworth was almost as lonely as though he were at the Adlon with Kurt and Fran.

When he thought of Fran's cool, neat politeness to him, he was angry. When he looked about him at youth in love, he was angrier. This passion, ungrudging and unabashed, Fran had never given him. He had been robbed— Or robbed her? All wrong, either way. Had *enough*—

Oh, he was lonely, this big friendly man, Sam Dodsworth, and he wanted a man to whom he could talk and boast and lie, he wanted a woman with whom he could be childish and hurt and comforted, and so successful and rich was he that he had neither, and he sought them, helpless, his raw nerves exposed. So searching, he strolled after dinner to the Select, which was rivaling the Café du Dôme as the resort of the international yearners in Paris.

A man alone at a café table in the more intellectual portions of Paris, and not apparently expecting some one, is always a man suspect. At home he may be a prince, a successful pickpocket, or an explorer, but in this city of necessitous and over-friendly strollers, this city where any one above the rank of assassin or professional martyr can so easily find companions, the supposition is that he is alone because he ought to be alone.

But it is also a rule of this city of spiritual adventurers which lies enclosed within the simple and home-loving French city of Paris, this new Vanity Fair, of slimier secrets, gallanter Amelias and more friendly Captain Dobbinses than Thackeray ever conceived, that if such a solitary look prosperous, if he speak quietly to the waiters, not talk uninvited to the people at the next table, and drink his fine à l'eau slowly, he may be merely a well-heeled tourist, who would be gratified to be guided into the citadel of the arts by a really qualified, gently tourist-despising, altogether authentic initiate of the Parisian Hobohemia—a girl who has once had a book-review printed, or a North Dakota 'cellist who is convinced that every one believes him to be an Hungarian gipsy.

So it happened that when Samuel Dodsworth sat melancholy and detached at a table before the Select, four young people at another table commented upon him—psycho-analytically, biologically, economically; cleverly, penetratingly, devastatingly.

"See that big dumbbell there by himself?" remarked Clinton J. Gillespie, the Bangor miniaturist. "I'll bet he's an American lawyer. Been in politics. Fond of making speeches. He's out of office now, and sore about it."

"Oh, hell!" said the gentleman next. "In the first place he's obviously an Englishman, and look at his hands! I don't suppose you have room for mere hands in your rotten little miniatures! He's rich and of good family, and yet he has the hands of a man who works. Perfectly simple. He's the owner of a big country estate in England, crazy about farming, and prob'ly he's a baronet."

"Grand!" said the third, smaller, sharper-nosed man. "Perfect—except for the fact that he is obviously a soldier and— I'm not quite sure about this, but I think he's German!"

"You all," said the fourth, a bobbed-haired girl of twenty with a cherubic face, rose-bud mouth, demure chin, magazine-cover nose, and the eyes of a bitter and grasping woman of forty, "make me very sick! You know so much that isn't so! I don't know what he is, but he looks good for a bottle of champagne, and I'm going over and grab it."

"What the devil good, Elsa," complained Clinton J. Gillespie, "is it for you to come to Paris if you always go talking to Babbitts like that fellow? You never will become a novelist!"

"Won't that be fierce—when I think over some of the novelists that hang around this joint!" rasped Elsa, and she tripped to Sam's table, she stood beside him, warbling, "I beg your pardon, but aren't you Mr. Albert Jackson of Chicago?"

Sam looked up. She was so much like the edifying portrait of "Miss Innocence" on the calendar which the grocer sends you at New Year's that he was not irritated even by this most ancient of strategies. "No, but I wish I were. I am from Chicago, but my name is Pearson, Thomas J. Pearson. Loans and banking. Won't you sit down? I'm kind of lonely in Paris."

Elsa did not seat herself precipitately. It was impossible to say just when it was that she did sit down, so modestly did she slip into a chair, looking as though she had never had so unmaidenly an encounter, as though momently she would take fright and wing away. She murmured, "That was too silly of me! You must have thought I was a terribly bold little creature to speak to you, but you did look so much like Mr.—Mr. Jackson, who is a gentleman that I met once at my aunt's house in New Rochelle—my father is the Baptist minister there—and I guess I felt lonely, too, a wee bit—I don't know many people in Paris myself, though I've been here three months. I'm studying novel-writing here. But it was awfully kind of you not to mind."

"Mind? It was a privilege," Sam said gallantly . . . and within himself he was resolving, "Yes, you cute little bitch-kitty, you lovely little gold-digger, I'm going to let you work me as much as you want to, and I'm going to spend the night with you!"

And he was triumphant, after so much difficulty, at having been at last able to take the first step toward sin.

"And now, young lady, I hope you're going to let me buy you a little drink or something, just to show you think I'm as nice and respectable as if you'd met me in your aunt's house, too. What would you like?"

"Oh, I—I— I've scarcely ever tasted alcohol." Sam had seen her flip off two brandies at the other table. "What does one drink? What would be safe for a young girl?"

"Well— Of course you wouldn't touch brandy?"

"Oh no!"

"No, of course not. Well, what would you most like?"

"Well— Oh, you won't think it's awfully silly of me, Mr. Uh—"

"Mr. Thomas—Pearson J. Thomas."

"Of course—how silly of me! You wouldn't think it was awfully silly of me, Mr. Thomas, if I said I've often heard people speaking about champagne, and always wanted to taste some?"

"No, I wouldn't think that was a bit silly. I'm told it's a very nice innocent drink for young girls." ("I will! And tonight! She picked on me first!") "Is there any particular brand of champagne you'd like to try?"

She looked at him suspiciously, but she was reassured by his large and unfanciful face, and she prattled more artlessly than ever:

"Oh, you must think I'm a terrible little silly—just a regular little greenhorn—but I don't know the name of one single brand of any kind of wine! But I did hear a boy that I know here—he's such a hardworking boy, a student—but he told me that Pol Roger, Quinze, I mean 1915, was one of the nicest vintages."

"Yes, I'm told it's quite a nice little wine," said Sam, and as he ordered it, his seemingly unobservant glance noted that one of Elsa's young men shrugged in admiration of something and handed another of the three a five-franc note, as though he were paying a bet.

"Am I going to have collaboration in my first seduction?" he wondered. "I may need it! I'll never go through with it! I'd like to kiss this little imp half to death but— Oh, God, I can't pick on a kid younger than my daughter!"

While he talked ardently to Elsa for the next half hour—about Berlin and Naples, about Charles Lindbergh, who had just this week flown from New York to Paris, and, inevitably, about Prohibition and the novels that she hadn't yet quite started to write—his whole effort was to get rid of scruples, to regain his first flaunting resolve to forget the respectable Samuel Dodsworth and be a bandit.

He was helped by jealousy and champagne.

After half an hour, Elsa started, ever so prettily, and cried, "Why! There's some boys I know at the second table over. As you are alone in Paris— Perhaps they might be willing to take you around a little, and I'm sure they'd be delighted to meet you. They're such nice boys, and so talented! Do you mind if I call them over?"

"B' d'lighted—"

She summoned the three young men with whom she had been sitting and introduced them as Mr. Clinton Gillespie, late of Bangor, miniaturist, Mr. Charley Short, of South Bend, now in the advertising business but expecting shortly to start a radical weekly, and Mr. Jack Keipp, the illustrator—just what Mr. Keipp illustrated was forever vague. Unlike Elsa, they did not need to be coaxed to sit down. They sat quickly and tight, and looked thirsty, and exchanged droll sophisticated glances as Sam meekly ordered two more bottles of Pol Roger.

While taking his champagne, they took the conversation away from him. They discussed the most artistic of topics—the hatefulness of all other artists; and now and then condescendingly threw to that Philistine, Mr. Pearson J. Thomas, a bone of explanation about the people of whom they gossiped. After half a bottle each, they forgot that they thought of Elsa only as nice young men should think of a Baptist minister's daughter. They mauled her. They contradicted her. One of them —the sharp-nosed little man, Mr. Keipp—held her hand. And after an entire bottle, Elsa herself rather forgot. She laughed too loudly at a reference to a story which no Christmas-card cherub would ever have heard.

So jealousy and a very earnest dislike of these supercilious young men came to help kill Sam's reluctance.

"Hang it," he informed himself, "you can't tell me she hasn't been a little more than intimate with this Keipp rat! In any case, old Granddaddy Sambo would be better for her than this four-flusher. Give her a much better time. I *will!*"

His resolution held. Once he had accomplished the awful struggle of winning himself, once he turned from it to winning her, he began to see her (through a slightly champagne-colored haze) as wondrously desirable.

"Probably I'll kick myself tomorrow. I don't care! I'm glad I'm going to have her! Now to get rid of these young brats! Stop brooding, Sam, and speak your little piece! . . . I'll take her to the Continental, too, by thunder!"

Fran would have marveled to hear her taciturn Samuel chattering. Early he discovered a way of parrying these young geniuses—by admitting, before they hinted it, that he was a lowbrow, but that he ranked higher among the lowbrows than they among the highbrows.

This attack disorganized them, and enabled him to contradict them with cheerful casualness. He heard himself stating that Eddie Guest was the best American poet, and a number of other things which he had heard from Tub Pearson and which he did not believe. His crassness was so complete that they were staggered, being accustomed to having gentlemen as large and as rich as Mr. Pearson J. Thomas deprecate their own richness and largeness, and admire the sophistication of Mr. Gillespie, Mr. Short, and Mr. Keipp.

Elsa agreed with him in everything; made him ardent by taking his side against them; encouraged him till (with a mild astonishment at his own triumphs of asininity) he heard himself asserting that vacuum cleaners were more important than Homer, and that Mr. Mutt, of the comic strips, was a fuller-blooded character than Soames Forsyte.

And meantime, he was buying.

Mr. Gillespie, Mr. Short, and Mr. Keipp never refused another drink. After the champagne, Elsa suggested brandies (she had forgotten that it was a beverage of which she had scarcely heard) and there were many brandies, and the pile of saucers, serving as memoranda of drinks for which he would have to pay, rose and rose in front of Sam, while the innocent pioneer part of the table in front of Mr. Gillespie, Mr. Short, and Mr. Keipp was free of anything save their current brandies.

But Sam was craftily delighted. Could anything better show Elsa that he was a worthier lover than the sharp-nosed Mr. Keipp?

He was talking, now, exclusively to Elsa, ignoring the young men. He was almost beginning to be honest with her, in his desire to have sympathy from this rosy child. He decided that her eyes weren't hard, really, but intelligent.

He finally dared to grope under the table, and her hand flew to his, so warm, so young, so living, and answered his touch with a pressure which stirred him intolerably. He became very gay, joyous with the thought of the secret they were sharing. But a slight check occurred to the flow of his confidences.

Elsa cooed, "Oh, excuse me just a moment, dear. There's Van Nuys Rodney over there. Something I have to ask him. 'Scuse me a moment."

She flitted to a table at which sat a particularly hairy and blue-shirted man and he saw her drop all her preening in an absorbed conversation.

He sat neglected by his guests at his own table.

In three minutes, Mr. Jack Keipp lounged to his feet, muttered, "Pardon me a moment," and Sam saw him join Elsa and Van Nuys Rodney and plunge into talk. Then Mr. Gillespie yawned, "Well, I think I'll turn in," Mr. Short suggested, "Glad met you, Mr. Oh," and they were gone. Sam watched them stroll down the boulevard. He wished that he had been pleasanter to them—even Shorts and Gillespies would be worth having in this city of gaiety and loneliness.

When he looked back, he saw that Elsa, Mr. Keipp, and Mr. Rodney had vanished, complete.

He waited for Elsa to come back. He waited an hour, with the monstrous pile of saucers before him as his only companion. She did not come. He paid the waiter, he rose slowly, unsmilingly beckoned to a taxicab, and sat in it cold and alone.

The Bootlegger

From KIT BRANDON: A Portrait

By Sherwood Anderson

> On the opening page of this novel, its narrator explains that its
> fabric is woven from Kit Brandon's threads of memory. "Her story
> came to me in fragments. We were together for the purpose, that I
> might get her story as one of the multitude of curious, terrible, silly,
> absorbing or wonderful stories all people could tell if they knew how."
> Kit grew up among the isolated mountain folk who were forced by
> the poverty of their farms into the making and sale of moonshine
> whiskey. She married Gordon, son of Tom Halsey, who had become
> rich through bootlegging. The selected passage is a story told her by
> her father-in-law of his early days when Gordon's impending birth
> forced him to violence.

EVEN for the masters of the art of acquiring, for the men-handlers,
organization-handlers, money-getters, power-getters, there are bad
times. The hand slips. The brain doesn't work. A man becomes a captain of some great industry. He commands money, men, affairs. See how
cool, self-possessed and quiet he is. He is not an artist. He does not make
a fool of himself, say like a Vincent Van Gogh. He does not run across
fields, shout, try to catch the glory of the sun on a canvas, give the sun
to other men. He does not go God-seeking, wanting to give God to men.

He perhaps gets sick. He is in a hospital and there is a little blonde,
a nurse. Look out, man! She is holding his hand. "I can see you are a
man of feeling. How sensitive you are, so easily hurt."

"I am sure you are a man not understood. People think you are hard,
cruel, without feeling. What a mistake it is."

A sigh. A look of longing in a woman's eyes.

Or it is a show girl. The man, the grizzled old warrior of money, has gone to see a show. "Ah, there is one." Inner excitement in the old fellow. What hope, what longing. It is generally understood that blondes do it best.

As it happened, however, Tom Halsey was one of the lucky ones. A woman came to him when he was very young.

She was not a woman. She was a young girl but, in the mountains, young girls suddenly and mysteriously become women. Tom was working in a field, a sloping field, planted to corn in the spring, and the field went down to a mountain road. You went along the mountain road, perhaps a quarter of a mile, to the Halsey house, a large and rather comfortable log farmhouse. At the foot of the field, near the road, there was a spring and locust trees grew there, spreading their branches out over the spring. The locust puts out its leaves late in the spring. How delicate and feathery they are. The honey locust blooms riotously and the trees are covered with bees. They make a soft, sometimes loud, murmuring sound. Tom was hoeing corn, working it for the first time, and an odd caravan came along the road.

But the caravan wasn't so odd. It was a sight Tom had seen before. Some little mountain farmer had failed. He had been living on a mountainside farm somewhere back up in the hills, a man of fifty, with pale watery eyes and a little scrawny red beard, now turning gray. It looked dirty and the man was dirty. He had a wife and several children, some of them quite young.

Why, what a producer. It was, in the mountains, a common enough sight. Look. There are twelve, thirteen, perhaps fourteen kids. The man has two half-broken-down old horses and there is a wagon, the wheels tied in place by ropes, and on the wagon, pretty much covered with younger children clinging on, there are a few sticks of furniture, some dirty torn blankets and equally torn and dirty bed ticks. On one of the blankets, held in the arms of a girl child of eight, a sickly looking pale child, there is a babe and it cries lustily. The babe is not sickly. It will still be at the breast of the woman, the mother, who sits on the wagon beside the man. She is a huge fat woman who looks like an old Indian squaw. She may be that. She sits so placidly as the wagon crawls creaking along, Tom, in the field, near the fence and the spring, watching. She may be an Indian. There are still small fragments of Indian tribes in the hills.

Tom is standing and looking. He looks with impersonal eyes. The hill farmer on the wagon has had ill luck. He had a crop of corn planted and there came a great rain. The corn was planted on new ground in a sloping field and the man and the children had worked all winter clearing the land. It was a piece of cheap land, the timber having been taken off some years before.

And then the great rain came, the water washed down the hill and across the face of the field. There was nothing to be done. The man stood helpless. He was a man who had always had ill luck. His wife was slovenly, a bad housekeeper and a bad cook and as her children dropped from her . . . they came regularly, one after another, easily, falling from between her great thighs, they were all girl children. What is a man to do about that?

There was the great rain, all the good soil in the new ground washed away, the young corn gone, all washed away. There were three young calves and three cows and two sows, soon to farrow, in the field by the creek. It was a long narrow field and the grass was good. In the mountains when the great rains come, in country where the timber has been cut off, small mountain streams become suddenly torrents. It may happen without warning. The great rain may be above you, far up some mountain. It may be the rain comes at night, when a man is asleep. The calves, sows and cows were all drowned.

Last year the bean beetles took his beans. He had four fine hogs, fat, almost ready to kill. He had driven them down, out of an upper oak forest where they had grown fat on the fallen acorns. It was almost killing time but they all took the cholera and died.

What was the use? What was a man to do? The man had heard that in a distant town, far away, a hundred miles, there was work to be had for women and girls. Some of his girls were quite big now. There was a cotton mill in the town. It took such girls. It was no place for a man. They did not take a man of fifty, did not want such men, but a man must do something. Hungry children must be fed. The man sat sadly on the broken seat of his broken wagon beside his fat silent placid wife, driving his bony team. In the town to which he was going, a growing industrial town, the girls would find work. They would earn money. There were some five or six girls, now old enough to go to work. He himself would have to sit at home, with the fat wife, in a house in a mill village.

Or in the afternoon, he would wander about. There would be other men like himself, "mill daddies." His old woman was slovenly, a bad housekeeper. It might be that, in the end, he would begin working about the house, doing women's work, making beds, sweeping, helping with the cooking.

The wagon went its painful way along the road. There had been a dry time and there was dust. The wheels made crazy tracks in the road. Three or four older girls walked behind the wagon. The caravan passed, young Tom standing and staring, no word, no sign passed between him and the man, between him and the girls. It went down the sloping road, the crooked wheels catching on protruding rocks. Often the wagon came to a dead stop. "Why doesn't he make that fat old mother get out and walk?" There was a little creek to be forded and beyond a little rise just before you came to the Halsey house. The team struggled, the man slashing at them with a whip, Tom staring. "They'll never make it."

And how did the team manage to get up hills, up the sides of mountains? There were a hundred miles of such mountain road to be covered before the caravan reached the cotton-mill town.

Tom turned to go back to his work and then stopped. There was still another girl, belonging to the family, a slender pale woman child of fourteen or fifteen. She was coming along the road alone, stumbling along. She did not see Tom standing there.

She was bare-legged, bare-footed. She was ill. She stopped by the fence near the spring and struggled to get over, still not seeing Tom. Her cheeks were flushed, as with a fever, and she appeared as though drunken. Had the others forgotten her? She had become ill and had stopped beside the road to rest and was now trying to overtake the wagon, but she had noticed the spring just inside the field and was trying to get to it.

In such a family, one child would not be missed. She looked very ill. She might die. Something in Tom was touched.

Why, how pretty she was! Her illness had made her more pretty, even beautiful. She had got to the top of the rail fence, had one leg over— what a clear-cut lovely little face, now drawn with pain, lines of suffering showing on such a young face. She had yellow hair, a mass of it, fallen down over young shoulders. "She will fall," Tom thought. He sprang toward her.

It may have been his sudden appearance that startled her, threw her off balance. There was a little cry from her and she fell. She lay still on the grass under the fence.

And now something else happened. Tom had run to the girl under the fence, had picked her up, was holding her in his arms, and had faced about . . . she was unconscious, had perhaps struck her head in falling . . . he was facing the road and the Halsey house, and the wagon had struggled up the little slope and was before the house.

It broke down. There was a crash. One of the wheels had come off and the wagon with its contents, the few sticks of furniture, bedding, assortment of girl children of all ages, the fat old mother, the defeated mountain farmer, all were dumped in the road.

There were screams. There were cries. Tom, as he stood holding the unconscious girl child, saw his mother run out of the house to the road. At that time Tom was alone at home with his mother, a strong, rather mannish-looking woman. He laid the unconscious girl as tenderly as he could on the fence top, her arms and head hanging down on one side and her feet and bare slender legs on the other, and bolted over. With her in his arms he went, half running, along the road to the house.

It was Tom Halsey himself who afterwards told Kit Brandon of what happened to his young wife, the mother of his son Gordon who became Kit's husband.

He got her to the house that day, and afterwards for several weeks she was ill there. It was not thought she would live and several times Tom rode off to a distant town to bring a doctor, sometimes at night. As for her family, the wagon again patched, they went on their way, having spent the night and a part of the next day at the Halsey place. To the fat mother and perhaps to the father she was just another girl child. Such a woman could drop another. It was easy for her, and Tom's mother, although she looked mannish, had a woman's heart. She was glad enough to get the girl. "If she lives, she may be a comfort," she thought.

She did live and she became Tom's wife, but she was never strong. Tom told Kit the story of his short life with her and of her death.

He had got his own place and already he had got into the liquor business in a small way. He had got his neighbors, who were liquor makers . . . there were enough of them, all small makers, little groups of men going in together, buying a still . . . he had got them all to bring the stuff to him.

He told Kit how it was with him at that time. His son had been born and his wife was again ill. She had begun nursing her child but one of her breasts had caked and he had to take her off to a distant town to have it lanced. He had wanted to take her to a big town, perhaps to the very cotton-mill town that had swallowed up her family . . . she had never heard from them again after they disappeared down the road . . . there was a hospital at that place . . . he hadn't the money. He had got a mountain doctor who had done his job crudely. His wife's breast became infected and there was high fever.

Tom was in a fix. He was worried. He was frightened. The doctor who had lanced the breast told him that it would be dangerous to try to move her. He had come with his young wife into a new neighborhood, some thirty miles from his father's house and had bought a little farm there. He did not know his neighbors very well yet and already he was in debt to some of them. He had taken their liquor to handle, had begun to build up a trade in distant towns. He had taken several trips with his loaded wagon at night but some of the money that should have gone to the liquor makers had been spent.

He told Kit of calling his neighbors together. "This is how it is with me. My wife is dying and the doctor says she cannot be moved, but I intend to move her. I must have money."

Beside the cotton-mill town there was another industrial town, some thirty miles away, but there was no hospital in that place. Tom had been there several times. There was a man of the town.

A note of bitterness, of contempt, crept into Tom's voice when he spoke of that man.

It wasn't a pleasant picture. He was a man of fifty-five. There may be more such men among successful Americans than we other Americans care to realize. He had made money rapidly after a long early struggle . . . a big man, with a big head, big shoulders and body. Once he had been a laborer in a lumber camp. Often such men, when they succeed . . . they have done hard, heavy manual work during youth and early manhood . . . they are inclined to eat hugely, drink hugely.

Later they sit all day and every day at a desk. They go on with the heavy living and while they still appear strong there is a gradual breaking down of something inside. Tom said that this one had got hold of some invention. It was a tool, widely used and useful to farmers, not of the hills but of the Northern plains, and was built largely of wood. He had understood how to get money from banks, how to advertise. Perhaps he had come South, into a Southern industrial town, because wood was cheap there and labor cheap. He had been married but had no children and his wife had died.

He prided himself on being a sport, on living flashily. His mind had taken that turn. He drove a big sport motor car and wore heavy homespun clothes imported from England. He had got him a big house, at the edge of the town where he had set up his factory and had guests down from Northern cities. "You must come down to my place. It is in the mountains, in the Blue Ridge.

"If you want to bring a woman along . . ." Laughter. He poked the man in the ribs or slapped him on the back. "You know . . . make it a vacation," he said. This was before prohibition but there was local option in the county and he had built a bar in the basement of his house.

The Southern industrial town was a county seat and before and after the coming of prohibition, the jail there was constantly filled with violators of illicit liquor laws. They were all poor men or the sons of poor men, laborers in the factories in the town, sons of laborers, mountain farmers, caught at the still, sons of these men bringing moon whiskey in to serve the town. The rich and the well-to-do and the sons of these did not get into jail. The whole town knew of the bar in the rich man's house. He gave money to charity. He helped support the churches of the town.

Tom told Kit, speaking bitterly, stories of how the man lived. He loved getting the sons and daughters of the town people, sons and daughters of merchants, lawyers, successful doctors into his house and getting them drunk. He had become somewhat jaded about women but still loved touching them, the young ones. He wanted to put his hands on them, stand close, run his hands over young female bodies. There are such men. Once perhaps they had something to give a woman. It got lost, was petered away.

"I'd do anything for you, little girl. Do you want a fur coat?" . . . his hands on her. Hands creeping down over hips, over breasts. Men of the town, the respectable women of the town, older women, leaders in the churches, knew of these things. The town was filled with whispers. Nothing was done. The young people continued to go to the parties at his house. It was a little hard to refuse. "Be careful. Do not offend this man. He has power."

He wanted to be known as a sport, a dashing figure of a man, but he was also frugal. Men who grow rich are frugal and careful in small things. For his bar he brought in liquors from Northern cities . . . "You see," he said . . . he put on a white apron, became a bartender for his guests . . . "You see, it is good stuff. It is the real stuff."

But at the same time . . . you understand . . . when people have become a little drunk . . . how do they know? It is really foolish to waste good liquor. Mountain moon may be had at a low price. It may be colored with prune juice. A bottle of imported liquor costing, I assure you, enough, may be refilled.

Tom Halsey drove at night . . . it was a Saturday night . . . in at the man's driveway and on past the brightly lighted house to where there was a big brick garage. There was room in the garage for several cars. Tom drove his team—the wagon well loaded, and it made racket enough. It was no wonder that, later, when he became a successful illicit liquor man, making plenty of money, he insisted on big powerful, silent cars. The house of the successful manufacturer was surrounded by several acres of land and was outside the town limits.

It was a summer night and the house and yard were filled with young couples. Some of the young men, seen by Tom, as he drove in . . . they strolled along paths, past lighted windows . . . were in evening clothes. Young women were in light summer dresses. It is so nice, with your hands, to feel the body of a young woman, under a light summer dress.

Tom was in a hurry. There was a negro man, dressed in uniform, who came to him when he had stopped the team near the garage and Tom spoke to him. He didn't waste words. "Look here, nigger, I'm in a hurry. You tell your boss. Goddam your black soul, you get him out here, and quick."

He said no more. The man went and presently there was the big man, the rich man, the flashy one.

He was angry. He was upset. "Why, yes. I have bought stuff from you but for God's sake, man . . . haven't you any sense?" . . . he made a sign towards Tom's team . . . "bringing that in here. There are people here.

"I'll have nothing more to do with a man who is such a damned fool."

The two men were walking in a path near the garage. There was a light over the garage door and they went along the side of the building and stopped. Tom tried to explain. "But my wife is very ill. She may die. I must have money. I could unload it back here."

He even pleaded, but as the man did not at once respond his voice grew harsh. However he did not shout. He was sizing up his man. "He is pretty big." Tom was himself a small man. "He has led a certain kind of life for a long time now. He's probably soft." "That nigger of yours, in that uniform . . . there are 150 gallons . . . I want you to take it all . . . it is a hurry up matter with me . . . I tell you my wife is ill . . . I've got to have money and right now . . . It will be $300 . . . I know damned well you always have cash, plenty of it . . . you are the kind." His voice was growing more and more harsh. "You are the kind that likes to pull a big roll, flash it before people. Goddam you."

He was astonishing the man, throwing him off guard. "There are some bushes here." He pointed. They stood near the wall of the garage. "I'll unload it quickly enough. Your nigger can put it away. While I am unloading you will go into the house and get the money.

"If you haven't it on you. Have you?"

The man laughed. After all he had once been a lumberjack. If he had only taken care of his big body through the years. The man before him was after all small. "Why, you impertinent little runt!"

He got no further. Tom leaped and had him by the throat. He was like a wild cat fastened on to the throat of a horse. After all, the man would not shout. He would not dare. "Oh, these big bugs," Tom said, long afterwards, telling of the moment.

It didn't last long, a short struggle, the man's arms flailing about, hitting nothing, his breath going. Tom was close in where the big fists couldn't hurt him. His rather small hands were very powerful. "Will you or won't you? If you shout and they come I'll kill you and them." He let go the man's throat. He knew he had him. "If you go in there and don't come out with it, at once, I'll come in after you.

"I'm sorry," he said, "my wife's dying." The man went.

Tom drove home. He told Kit that he forgot about the liquor, did not remember to unload it. The way home was over very rough roads and the liquor was in glass fruit jars. They kept breaking, he said. There was a drip, drip, drip of mountain liquor in a mountain road. He lashed his team, nearly killing the horses. When he got to his house there were several men, mountain men, neighbors, loitering in the dark road before his house. Their women were inside. They were the men who had trusted him with the liquor but they were not there to collect. Their wives were trying to save Tom's wife, but it was too late. She died that night, just as he stopped his team before the house . . . steam arising in clouds from the half-dead animals . . . they breathed in gasps, nostrils vibrating . . . it was a pretty good team, young horses. His wife died but his son lived.

The Arrest of Helianos

From APARTMENT IN ATHENS
By Glenway Wescott

To the family of Mr. Helianos, a Greek publisher, war has brought progressive suffering. Their older son has died in battle and, with the German occupation of Greece, Mr. Helianos sees his small business rubbed out. Abandoning his country villa, he takes his family to a small apartment in Athens to begin a day-to-day struggle for survival. While he and his semi-invalid wife spend their days seeking food and fuel, Alex their younger son cares for Leda, his sister, whose mind has been stunted by the shock of German atrocities.

When Kalter, a German captain, is billeted with them and forces the family into cramped quarters, they become virtually his slaves, driving their undernourished bodies to supply his demands for service. With one mind, they rejoice when he goes home to Germany on furlough. But when he returns from Germany, bearing a major's insignia, he is an altered man. He asks little service, shows small considerations. The Helianos' are at first mystified because they cannot see, beneath this change, the deterioration of the man himself, the cracking up of the trained German soldier's morale. In the following passage Mr. Helianos, moved by a natural humanity and believing that he understands, at last, the real Major Kalter, seals his own fate.

THE last of those conversations of German and Greek was the strangest. It was not exactly a conversation, but rather a little drama and a revelation in the major's own person of that private weakness and defeat—in spite of which collective Germany was to triumph forever, with German after German forever taking up the burden whenever one

Copyright, 1944, 1945, by Glenway Wescott.

367

weakly put it down—of which he had spoken so eloquently on the previous evening.

It was in the afternoon, on the last day in May, a Monday; one of Kalter's free half-days. He had returned to the apartment just before midday. As it happened Helianos had procured somewhat more food than usual for the midday meal; and the weary officer had eaten less than usual; and the family had been able to make practically a normal meal. The children descended to the street to play. Mrs. Helianos, who was not feeling well, lay down to rest.

And then—it was about three o'clock—Helianos in a good mood ventured to the sitting room, thinking that the major might not be taking a nap and might like a talk. He had some political question or other to propound to him. To his amazement he found him at his desk with his head bent far forward over it, his face pressed in his hands, in tears.

At the sound of Helianos' coming in, he sprang to his feet, crying out, "In God's name, why must you come in here just now? There's a devil in you! When I am alone, when I need to be alone—"

The Greek apologized and started back out of the room but the tragic-faced German strode over to the door and shut it.

"It's too late now," he said, returning to his chair, pulling it around to face Helianos, grimacing to stop his tears, "it's too late to stand upon ceremony. I have talked too much already. Why, why did I have to take you, you damned Greek, into my confidence? What possessed me?"

Helianos in his astonishment, stammered, "I do not understand, sir, it must be a misunderstanding, a mistake." He apologized, nevertheless, for whatever it was; and begged to be allowed to go back to the kitchen if his presence made the major nervous; and offered to run and prepare a glass of hot wine; and wondered if perhaps the major had not fallen ill, and suggested calling a physician; and begged to be told something to do, if the major could think of anything agreeable or useful.

During which well-meaning discourse the unhappy officer, unhappier than ever or really ill, seemed not to pay attention.

Then when Helianos could think of nothing more to say, he said, "No, it makes no difference. You're a good fellow, Helianos, aren't you? Or perhaps you're not, I don't know . . ."

It was in a muttering voice with weakly impatient gestures of one hand. "That's the worst of it, God! I don't know, I can't judge. When a German officer loses confidence in his judgment of other men," he added, "it's the end, the end of everything, isn't it?"

Then he bared his teeth in a semblance of a smile, dried his eyes, blew his nose. "No, Helianos, sit down, I will tell you what the trouble is. I wish you to know that it is nothing dishonorable; I have done nothing. I assure you of that, for my self-respect.

"Also it is good to tell my trouble. It relieves my thinking about it, it passes the time, the deadly time."

Helianos sat down, with a more ambiguous feeling than any he could remember: embarrassment? inquisitiveness? sympathy? Added to which he half expected to feel, half hoped to feel, some sense of humor and slight rejoicing in the discomfiture of an enemy; except that one could scarcely think of a man in such disorder of mind as an enemy . . .

He himself was not a very self-centered man, and until the end of the conversation, too late, he did not realize that it could possibly concern him in any way. He was not thinking of himself at all, only of the German: almost his friend by that time anyway in spite of the war, and in spite of different political principles.

His friend Kalter, for all his pride of intellect and of nationality, Helianos had decided, was a poor violent emotional human being, one who doubtless needed, more than most men, to be sustained by that collected agreed organized humanity which he advocated, the state, even the world-state; one who at the moment, for some reason, needed a friend.

He was deathly pale, and now and then he drew an extremely deep breath with a slight shudder, as he controlled himself. It was a hot afternoon, and there was sweat on his upper lip as well as tears on his upper cheeks.

Then after a silence he began, with a bit of his violence, "You Greeks, and the other foreign nations, all of you—it's your damned conceit!— think that all the suffering of the war is on your side. It is not so! War is hard, I tell you, hard for everyone.

"Listen to me," he went on. "I told you that I had to make my will, a new will. Didn't it occur to you, stupid Greek, to wonder what had happened, why my old will was null and void? If you were my friend you would have wondered; but of course you aren't, how could you be?

"This is what happened:—Just before I returned home to Germany, my elder son, who was a fighter-pilot, crashed and was killed. Very well! almost every family has to give a son for the fatherland, sometimes more than one.

"Yes, very well, but while I was on my way home, my house in Königsberg was destroyed in an air-raid; a bomb set fire to it and my wife was burned, almost to death.

"And after I got there, while she lay unconscious, my younger son was killed in Russia.

"He was a young boy, a green soldier; he had never been at the front before. He wrote us shameful discouraged letters, the way green soldiers do, the poor youngster! He had not yet received any decoration or citation, he had done nothing to be proud of, he was killed like that.

"My wife lay at death's door for days and when she recovered consciousness, she was not in her right mind. They let me see her and she talked to me like a lunatic. Helianos, it was heartbreaking. It was indecent, Helianos, with all her hair burned away, half her face in bandages; and she talked nonsense; and the doctor did not know whether she would be insane the rest of her life or not.

"Then she got better and came to herself, and for two or three days she was wonderful. She comforted me for the death of our sons; she restored my faith in the future and in Germany, and my self-confidence.

"I can't tell you, Helianos, how it was. You wouldn't understand! With your Greek morality you couldn't. We were like a god and a goddess, there in the grim hospital, with her frightful bandages, in our grief and loss. Wonderful days! Then she died."

It was a good story, Helianos thought: a commonplace of today, an epitome of war; and as he listened to it he noted that Kalter's peculiar rough grudging voice was just right for it, softened by his fatigue, with the cadences of his grief. But bit by bit, word by word, he had a sense of unreality somehow, not the story itself, which was common and obvious truth, but the context—Kalter telling and himself listening; that was like fiction.

After all, it was the last thing he would have expected ever to see in reality on earth: a German officer grief-stricken, complaining of the commonplace of war. His mind ran back over all the past, the time when this weeping major was still the terrible captain, and wondered at it: the tyranny and insults and histrionics, then the metamorphosis, and his own curiosity and misinterpretation and forgiveness and relaxation, and appalling politics, and now this . . .

The rough voice choked on the words, "Then she died," and ceased; and Helianos did not know what to say, simply sitting there in a kind of false thoughtfulness. He found himself falsely thinking that one could scarcely begrudge these people the mastery of the world, if they wanted it enough to pay the same price they exacted of others; if they were willing to bring the common suffering and irreparable loss upon themselves as well as everyone else. Until that moment it had never seriously occurred to him that they were susceptible to the common suffering. His half-pity when he had stood peering at the major's bedside that night had not been very serious . . . Now it astonished him, and he realized that astonishment was in a way a tribute to the conquering race, and a measure of the depth of his own despair as one of the conquered: it had not occurred to him that conquerors could be unhappy!

Suddenly he felt that all this, acquiescence, rationalization, was idiotic nonsense. They were not willing to bring things upon themselves, no indeed; they told a plaintive story like other men, they shuddered and wept like other men, naturally; and each of them somehow blamed some-

one else for everything, and in fact someone must be to blame! Suddenly
Helianos' short stout weary person began to tremble with another of his
angers, shushing heart and sweating hand, lump in throat and knock in
knee; indignation against common misfortune and against fate, his in-
dividually, Greece's, and the rest of the world's for that matter, everyone's, even this German's as an individual.

Meanwhile this German said, "You have no idea, Helianos—you
don't know anything about it, you don't understand anything—but listen: I am so weary of the war! When we suffer too much, we get too
sensitive to the suffering of other people, even though we know that
their suffering is nothing like our own. I can't fight any more. All I want
in the world is to listen to music; to sit listening and remembering, remembering my martyred wife and my heroic boys; to pass the time, the
rest of my time. I know, of course, after the war everyone will feel like
this for a while. But I can't wait, I am in hell, hell on earth, I won't
wait."

He paused for a moment, covering his face with his hands, then un-
covering it and twisting it down like a tragic mask, clenching his hands
and giving little strokes in the air before him; striving either to control
his feeling or to enact it physically—Helianos could not tell which.

Then he said, "Seven weeks ago; two months will have passed in less
than a fortnight; it was on a Saturday. The hour coming round every
afternoon, and the day of the week, and the date of the month; and it
has been worse for me every minute. God, I've behaved well, I've been
good, going on at headquarters, letting everything else slide, treating you
so well, just trying to pass the time, talking, talking! I know the minute,
sixteen minutes before three, when it comes. Always an anniversary, every hour is a year long. Always in my mind, a huge horrible clock striking!"

Having said this, he sat in absolute immobility and in silence, and
shed tears again. It was a strange thing to watch; it was so imperturbable.
Suddenly his face all twisted into the ugliness of grief, and not one muscle in it moved after that; only the tear-ducts were alive and active, and
his tears were not drops but a little inundation down his cheeks, all the
way down to his chin. It was like seeing sculpture weep, not Greek
sculpture of course; Gothic sculpture . . .

He was facing the window, and the bright light caught the scar and
the scar-like mouth, emphasized the asymmetry of the nose, showed
up the deep lines and hollowed-out places in his cheeks, where the hand
of the sculptor had slipped.

Whereupon that sculpture was moved to say something more but for
a moment was unable to, with every muscle straining and straightening
it into shape; then said, "Helianos, listen, the reason I have been making

my will, the reason you see me in this shameful unmanly grief, like a damned Frenchman or damned Jew . . .

"Listen to me: I have decided to commit suicide. I cannot go on. It isn't that I will not, I cannot. I am good for nothing now, my nerves are broken. I can think all right, as a good German should think, I can talk as I should—I made it all clear to you, the great cause of the fatherland, didn't I?—but it's no good, the emotion is dead. I cannot bear to go on living, I loathe living. It is a psychopathic condition."

This speech was all in a half-whisper, soft and hurried like someone in love, and singsong like a sick infant; and when he fell silent his grimacing and tears began again. The spring sunshine made the tears shine down his cheeks, streaky, greasy. He began shaking his head back and forth, back and forth.

"One night," he murmured or mumbled softly, "one night I fell asleep without undressing, without getting into bed. That night you forgot to bring me my hot water—oh, Helianos, you're so forgetful!—and I did not wake up until the middle of the night. That night I knew that I couldn't go on, I stopped trying; and, Helianos, I can't tell you what a relief it was when I decided it. I could have done it then, only I had to wind up my affairs all in order, to hand over my responsibilities to von Roesch and the others, gradually, so they wouldn't notice it; and to re-make my will, for the musicians."

So, so, Helianos said to himself, so one did find out the causes of things sooner or later. He wondered if his wife was in the clothes closet; if this plaint had softened now to the point where she could not hear it. Unmanly grief indeed, although not really like that of any Frenchman or Jew he happened to know. While Kalter was silent he listened for Mrs. Helianos, and could not detect the least rustle or mousy stir or creak of the floor-board. He hoped she was not there. For, as she was a creature of heart rather than head, with her own bereavement, and her own thought of suicide, this would be worse for her poor failing spirit than any amount of clever hair-raising explanation of the German purpose, the Germanized world, Germany forever. Whether it moved her to compassion or to rancor and scorn, no matter, it would upset her.

He was glad, too, that the children were not indoors, especially young Alex possessed of the devil. To know that the German was in tears, heartbroken, would excite him so; and he might make some jubilant noise or impertinent remark or gleeful grimace which would irk poor Kalter unbearably.

It did not occur to Helianos that the threat of suicide was to be taken seriously; nevertheless the effect of it was to make the threatener more sympathetic to him. Perhaps any invocation of death or even mention of death does that. It is so universal and exalted a thing in itself . . .

But intermixed with his sympathy was also a certain uneasiness; as it were a slight revival of the way he used to feel in the old days, Kalter's unregenerate days. Now that the secret of his changed character was out, now that he had acknowledged and in fact dramatized his bereavement, might he not suddenly turn to some other aspect of himself, or turn back? The instant weakening of so powerful a creature, shameless avowal of a state of mind so shameful, and supererogation of death in the talk of killing himself—as if the deaths of a wife and two sons were not enough, to say nothing of the rest of the world delivered to death by German ambition!—it was all too strange for comfort; too sudden and incoherent for a Greek mind.

Still he could not think what to say. He thought himself stupid; the contemplation of grief always makes one stupid. And physical creature that he was, he still felt his rebellion against odious fate, everyone's fate, death, war; his tremor of knee and hindrance of speech. But at last he found his voice and said a very simple thing, "I am sorry, sir."

To which the major did not reply or respond even by a glance.

Then Helianos felt a stubbornness about it, and protested, determined to convince this self-absorbed sufferer that it really was so, he did pity him.

"May I tell you, Major Kalter," he went on, "I lost my son, two years ago on Mount Olympos. I can understand your unhappiness. My elder son; he was worth more than little Alex and little Leda. But I admit that it was not a great loss, compared with what you have lost."

It occurred to him with some bitter irony that he could scarcely say more than that! But in spite of bitterness his pity suddenly became quite real to him. It was as if he had tried not to feel it, not to mean it, but then did. Once more he was struck by the realization that Kalter was sincere, sincere at least in his suffering, sincere at last; therefore so was he.

Still, Kalter did not answer. Only his wet eyes seemed to dry up enough to focus on him; and they appeared to be ordinary humane grief-stricken eyes, like anyone else's, Helianos thought, not fierce or unfriendly; and he hung his head, he shook his hanging head as if in an effort to listen; and he began hunting in his uniform for a handkerchief. Helianos felt that his sympathy had been accepted.

"Oh, Major Kalter," he exclaimed, really meaning no harm, thinking out loud, "is it not intolerable? To think that two men, two men with too much power, fatal tragic men, should have brought all this tragedy upon us other men?"

Major Kalter's head jerked up to attention. "Two men? What do you mean?" he demanded. "What two men?"

"I mean the Fuehrer and the Duce," Helianos answered, without stopping to think.

That was his undoing. Major Kalter sprang to his feet and stumbled over to him, in a worse rage than ever before. Helianos too sprang to his feet and tried to get away but he was not quick enough.

"How dare you, you vile Greek," the major shouted, "how dare you say a word against the Fuehrer!" And he struck the vile Greek in the face, first one side, then the other side; resounding slaps.

"You stupid subnormal brute, filthy Slav! Defy the Fuehrer, will you? Sneer at the Italians, will you?"

And this time the look of shock and mortification, the Greek mouth gaping open, the Greek eyes puckered out of sight, did not satisfy him. This time he followed him, drove him stumbling back step by step across the room, and knocked him hard against the wall, and kicked him, with imprecations—damned coward, treacherous animal, cheating boot-licking old sick thing, sickening old fool—and all the while Helianos kept trying to apologize and he continued shouting, damning him, and accusing him of things.

"We'll pound it out of you, the nonsense! Damn you, damn you! You'll not speak of the Fuehrer again, we'll fix you," he threatened, with untranslatable curse-words, at the top of his voice; his voice breaking on the top-notes, in the worst insults and worst threats.

Away in the kitchen, meanwhile, Mrs. Helianos had heard the first shout and come scurrying to her post in the clothes closet; and there beneath the clothes and amid the shoes, when the slaps and kicks began, she began to weep, reaching up and drawing the hem of one of her dresses and the cuff of a pair of Helianos' trousers over her face, to muffle the sound of her weeping. Thus she heard all the major's insults, from which she gathered that Helianos had said something insulting about the German chief of state; the major alluded to it in every other shout.

"Whatever possessed Helianos, oh, whatever possessed him!" she cried, as softly as she could. "I warned him, what madness, whatever shall I do!" she lamented, stuffing the hem of a dress into her mouth to hush her cries, in order to hear more.

Then the major somewhat relaxed his angry effort, and the woman in the clothes closet heard her husband's softer voice apologizing, in unutterable regret and confusion; her husband sobbing softly and hiccoughing, stumbling away and sinking into a chair and still apologizing, which was heartbreaking for her to hear, shameful to hear.

And from what Helianos said—still, by way of apology, offering his vain condolences—she gathered that the major's wife and two sons were dead. It explained the German sadness and gentleness all month, which Helianos, poor accursed mortal, had so tormented himself to understand; it made the German violence of the moment more beastly. The major himself alluded to it in his diminishing shouts; his very natural sorrow for himself resuming at the end of his anger . . .

His shouts and his blows abated suddenly. His voice sounded normal, perhaps even quieter than usual, but still clear and with a little regular official martial rhythm, saying, "You poor rascally old Greek, I thought you were more intelligent than the others. I thought you knew better than this. You know what comes next, I presume. I now telephone the military police to come here and take you in custody."

He paused a while, to let that sink in, then said, quieter still, "I am sorry for you, you fool, but it cannot be helped. It is what has to be done in such a case."

Mrs. Helianos, in the clothes closet, hearing this, trembled so that it seemed impossible to get to her feet. She crawled out into the children's room on her hands and knees, and there quickly gathered strength, and hastened down the corridor, in despair but in hope; hope of preventing Helianos' arrest somehow, by protesting, arguing, imploring.

But when she reached the sitting-room door it opened, and there stood the major with his pistol drawn, pointed not at her but sideways at Helianos; and he snapped at her, "You unfortunate woman, your husband is under arrest. Go away!"

He slammed the door and locked it. There she stood a moment twisting the doorknob, pressing against the door, and through it she heard him repeat, still in the calm but percussive voice, the marching little rhythm, "Sorry, it must be, you're a fool, it's my duty . . ."

Then she hastened back to the clothes closet, knelt again and heard him quietly and concisely telephoning, and could not endure it. She stood up, and got her head entangled in the coats and skirts, which came down with a clatter of a couple of coat-hangers; and as she came through the children's room she caught a glimpse of herself in the mirror in that accidental, incongruous garb, like a madwoman, veiled with a petticoat, cloaked with trousers. She felt faint, and as fast as possible crept to her bed in the kitchen, shedding the old clothes behind her, and in her impatience, afraid of fainting away before she got there, tearing the bodice of her dress down off one shoulder as well.

She did not faint away; but her heart was so sick that she could only lie still, helpless, a long time—sweating and salivating, wringing her hands, biting her fingertips, listening to her blood ceasing, and starting again with a little thunder, and ceasing again—until after the soldiers had come and gone with Helianos, until Alex and Leda returned from wherever they had been all this time.

They came up the stairway from the street just as Helianos went down, between two soldiers—young, impassive, even good-natured fellows, for whom this was all in the day's work—followed half a flight up by Major Kalter, formal and portentous. The children saw their father before he saw them; instantly sensed what the escort of Germans meant; and turned and fled back down to the street.

Thus the last Helianos saw of them was their springing, skipping, fleeing away two steps at a time, as if they were afraid of him. He called after them, "Wait, your mother is ill! Alex, Leda, your mother has had a heart attack. Go and get the doctor for your mother!"